編著

楊凡

國際

IELTS

應考叢書

寫作篇

中華教育

國際 IELTS 應考叢書

寫作篇

□
編著
楊 凡

□
出版
中華書局（香港）有限公司
香港北角英皇道 499 號北角工業大廈一樓 B
電話：(852) 2137 2338　傳真：(852) 2713 8202
電子郵件：info@chunghwabook.com.hk
網址：http://www.chunghwabook.com.hk

□
發行
香港聯合書刊物流有限公司
香港新界荃灣德士古道 220-248 號
荃灣工業中心 16 樓
電話：(852) 2150 2100　傳真：(852) 2407 3062
電子郵件：info@suplogistics.com.hk

□
印刷
美雅印刷製本有限公司
香港觀塘榮業街 6 號海濱工業大廈 4 字樓 A 室

□
版次
2002 年 2 月初版
2023 年 5 月第 12 次印刷
© 2002 2023 中華書局（香港）有限公司

□
ISBN：978-962-231-267-8

本書導讀

　　英文寫作是英文程度的綜合反映，它在考試中的重要性是不容忽視的。如何在短期內達到 IELTS 考試的要求，在短短六十分鐘內完成兩篇文章，並得到令人滿意的成績？本書作者憑藉對 IELTS 寫作的深刻理解和認識，以及多年的 IELTS 教學經驗，為廣大考生編寫了這本書，具有以下特點：

　　1.作者收集歸納了大量模板式句型，並介紹了一種"模板式作文法"，使得考生在考試前就能寫好相當數量的字數（對於 250 字的議論文，可事先寫好 100 字）。

　　2.作者按照 IELTS 考試作文的命題內容，分類整理了多種寫作素材和佳詞妙句，考生將其牢記在心，可以保證在寫作時有充分的思路和寫作內容。

　　3.從審題到尋找理由，從構思到最後定稿，作者全方位地講述了寫作的整個過程，為考生構築起一個高分作文的框架結構。

　　4.詳盡介紹各種文體，尤其是議論文的寫作方法，並列出各寫法的優缺點，使不同層次的考生均能根據自身情況揚長避短，找到最適合自己的寫作捷徑。

　　5.寫作範文與常見文法錯誤分析將理論形象化，歸納分析得分點與失分點。

　　總之，有關 IELTS 寫作的任何問題都可在本書中找到答案。這是一本極有見地的寫作參考書，不僅能用它來準備 IELTS 考試，而且對平日的英文寫作也大有裨益。

目錄

contents

前　言

　　一篇250字的IELTS作文,在你未上考場之前就已經寫好了100字以上,你相信嗎?這就是事實。

　　本書作者結合三年多的IELTS寫作教學經驗,在歸納IELTS命題規律的基礎上,首創了"模板式作文法",它既簡單又實用,無數考生最初連一句話也寫不完整,經過一個月的學習,採用這種方法,最終在考試中取得6分以上的成績,這就是"模板式作文法"成功的最好證明。模板式作文法的魅力在於將寫作考試巧妙地轉化成了"完形填空",有利於考生集中記憶,在考前做足準備工作,節省臨場思考時間。

　　當你看到這本書時,如果不幸距離考試時間只剩一星期,甚至只有一天了,請直接看本書的第二章第六節"常用的模板式句型",從中找出一些句型,拼成自己的模板,儘管放心去考試吧。如果你有一定的基礎,得6分甚至7分,並非難事。

　　不管你的基礎如何,只要花一個月左右的時間,仔細閱讀本書,作者保你作文得6分以上。IELTS作文三大題型(議論文、信、圖表作文)和四大評分標準(審題、結構、思路、語言)在本書中都有詳盡的講解,讀者只要細細消化本書內容,不僅能輕鬆攻克IELTS作文,而且會切實提高自己的英文寫作水平。

　　有的同學會問,大家都使用模板句型,文章會不會寫得都一樣呢? 請放心,本書並不只給大家一個模板,讓所有的人都使用它,而是按照開頭段、理由段、讓步段和結尾段分別給出了上百個模板句型供大家選擇使用。根據排列組合原理,它們可以組合成數量幾乎是天文數字的文章模板。所以,重複的可能性幾乎是不存在的。

本書作者通過三年的積累,在本書中歸納了大量模板句型和點睛詞句,並按照 IELTS 命題內容分類收集了數量可觀的素材,這一切都能直接運用於考試當中,不僅豐富考生的作文內容,而且切實提高作文的質量。各個層次的考生可以根據自己的語言水平和思維方式選擇最合適的主題句、支持句、結束句等,組織成獨具風格的作文。此外,大量的範文和文法錯誤分析爲考生樹立起一面鏡子,使大家從中認清自身尚需完善的不足之處和亟需改正的錯誤,找到差距,迎頭趕上。這種極有目標的學習指導在考前是最有效的,本書作者深諳中國學生作文的薄弱環節,並熟悉 IELTS 作文判分規律,因此,選擇本書無疑會幫助你攻克寫作這道難關。通過閱讀本書,你會發現,原來被認爲最難的寫作部分其實是四項考試中最容易準備、最有把握的。

祝廣大考生 IELTS 寫作贏取高分!

國際IELTS應考叢書
寫 作

CHAPTER I

IELTS 寫作
概 述

WRITING

寫作概述

對絕大多數同學來說,寫作是 IELTS 四項測驗(聽力、閱讀、寫作、口試)中最難的一項。很多同學從來就沒有用英文寫過文章。但寫作反映一個人的綜合英文程度,因此它又是四項測驗中最重要的,尤其對於留學類的同學,決定是否錄取你的教授會特別關注你的寫作成績。如果你的 IELTS 其他幾項考得不太好,造成總分較低,不夠學校的錄取要求,但你的作文成績考了個 7 分,那麼學校很可能會考慮錄取你。反之,即使你的平均分數達到了要求,但如果作文分數較低,例如只有 5 分,那麼學校很可能不會錄取你。

IELTS 寫作部分測試要求寫兩篇文章。測試時間是 60 分鐘。

General training 寫作的第一篇是要求寫一封英文信,字數不少於 150 個字。題目給定一個問題,要求寫信諮詢、抱怨、感謝、邀請、道歉、給出建議,或提出申請等等。

General training 寫作的第二篇是要求寫一篇議論文,字數不少於 250 個字。

Academic 寫作的第一篇要求對圖表數據進行描述、解釋和說明,字數不少於 150 個字。

Academic 寫作的第二篇也要求寫一篇議論文,字數不少於 250 個字。

作文評分實行 9 分制,沒有半分,即你的作文得分不可能是 5.5、6.5 等。兩篇文章分別評分,互不影響。最後的得分中第一篇佔 40% ,第二篇佔 60% 。計算出來的分數如果不是整數,就四捨五入,6.4 就是 6 分,6.5 就是 7 分。

作文考試時,會發給你一張試題紙和一張答案紙。在試題紙上用英文寫着試題(只有英文,沒有中文),你需要將你的文章寫在答案紙上。

　　兩篇文章的時間一共是 60 分鐘。具體分配沒有硬性要求。根據不同的字數要求、寫作難度、佔分比例,我們建議大家寫第一篇文章(信或圖表作文)用時 20 分鐘,寫議論文用時 40 分鐘。大家在最開始練習的時候,可以不受時間的限制,但應不斷提高速度,在考試前達到時間的要求。

　　IELTS 考試要求用鉛筆答題。2B 鉛筆比較黑,比較粗,適合畫圈,不適合寫作文;HB 鉛筆比較軟,比較淺,也不合適。比較適合的是自動鉛筆或 B 型鉛筆。大家在平常練習寫作時,就應該使用鉛筆,以達到熟悉的目的。

ACCESS TO IELTS

國際IELTS應考叢書
寫 作

CHAPTER II

議 論 文

WRITING

❖ 一、概 述 ❖

1. 字數和時間要求

字數要求在 250 字以上。

字數太少肯定會被扣分,所以我建議一定要寫 250 字以上。不管寫得怎麼樣,先要滿足字數的要求。

那麼需不需要寫太長呢? 只要你寫得對,寫得好,寫的字數越多越好,越能得高分。但由於時間的限制,寫 300 字就已經算寫得很多了。

但另一方面,如果只是爲了湊字數,把一些不相關的內容扯進文章裏,而且文法錯誤很多,反而會被扣分,因此不如集中精力把要求的 250 字寫好。

在考試中,也沒有必要一個一個地數字數。一般每行大約 10 個字。所以數一下行數,就可以知道大致的字數了。實際上,評卷官也不會一個一個地數字數,只是根據他自己的感覺。

兩篇文章的時間一共是 60 分鐘。根據不同的字數要求、寫作難度、佔分比例,我們建議大家寫議論文用 40 分鐘。大家在最開始練習的時候,可以不受時間的限制,兩三個小時寫完一篇也可以。但應不斷提高速度,在考試前達到時間的要求。

2. 命題內容

議論文的考試題目很多,但就內容而言,主要可分爲以下四類:

(1) 學生生活

例1 How should a student choose the future career, whose opinions and what kind of information he/she considers in making the decision? Give the reasons.
學生該如何選擇職業? 在做決定時,應考慮誰的意見和哪些方面? 請提出你的看法(注意:實際考試中,在試題紙上的試題只有英文,沒有中文,這裏的中文是作者附加的)。

例2 In the last 20 years, the assessment of students has undergone major transformation.
Many educational institutions no longer use formal examinations as a means of assessment as

they believe formal examination results are an unfair indication of a student's ability. To what extent do you agree or disagree with this statement?

在過去 20 年裏，評價學生能力的方法經歷了較大的變化。許多教育部門已不再把正式考試作爲一種評價方式。因爲他們認爲正式考試的結果並不能眞正反映學生的程度和能力。你多大程度上同意或不同意此觀點？

例 3　Some people think young children can have a better education in a boarding school far from home, while others claim that a day school or the home is a better one. What's your opinion? Give your reasons.

有些人認爲青少年就讀寄宿學校能接受較好的教育，而另外一些人認爲讀日校或在家更好些。提出你的觀點和理由。

例 4　Should uniform be introduced into schools and should students be required to wear uniforms?

學校該不該實行穿校服的制度？該不該要求學生穿校服？

例 5　In recent years, many young people decide to further their study abroad. What are the benefits and drawbacks of studying abroad?

近幾年來，許多年輕人打算到國外繼續深造。請談談出國留學的利與弊。

（2）家庭生活

例 1　Families are not as close as before. Give reasons for this change, and suggest some ways to bring families closer.

家庭關係沒有以前那麼親密了。請解釋原因並提出能夠使家庭更密切的方法。

例 2　Nowadays, nurseries and kindergartens take care of children from an early age, so women can return to their work and children can get used to the society early. Is this a good thing? What's your opinion?

現在，越來越多的小孩很早就被送到托兒所和幼稚園。這樣一來，婦女就可以重返工作崗位，而小孩則能夠儘早適應社會。請問這是否是個好現象？說出你的觀點。

例 3　Some people believe that children should engage in educational pursuits in their spare time, otherwise they are wasting their time. Do you agree or disagree?

有些人認爲孩子們的課餘時間應該是有教育意義的，否則他們就是在浪費時間。你同意還是不同意？

(3) 科技與媒體

例 1 What are the advantages and disadvantages of the internet?

互聯網的利和弊是什麼?

例 2 Advertisements are getting their way into people's lives. Discuss the effects of advertisements on people. Should all ads be banned?

廣告充斥人們的日常生活。討論廣告對人們的影響。廣告該不該被禁止?

例 3 With the wide application of computers in all aspects of life, more and more children indulge too much in computer games. Discuss the effects of computer games on children. What's your opinion about it?

隨着電腦在日常生活各個方面的廣泛應用,越來越多的兒童沉迷於電腦遊戲而不能自拔。討論電腦遊戲對兒童的影響。你是怎麼看這個現象的?

例 4 There have been many technological developments in the 20th century, for example, computers and electric power. Choose either of them, describe the changes it has brought about and discuss whether all the changes are positive.

在二十世紀有很多技術進步,比如電腦和電力。選擇其中的一個,描述它所帶來的變化並討論所有這些變化是否是正面的。

(4) 社會生活及社會問題

例 1 Many pop and sports stars earn millions of dollars a year. On the other hand, most people in "ordinary" professions like nurses, doctors and teachers earn only a small fraction of the income of these "stars". What do you think about this phenomenon? Is it fair?

許多明星如歌星和體育明星每年能賺數百萬美金。而另一方面,許多平凡的職業如護士、醫生和老師每年的收入僅僅是明星收入的很小一部分。你怎麼看待這種現象? 公平嗎?

例 2 Traffic is developing rapidly all round the world at present. What are the traffic problems in your country? What causes these problems? Make some recommendations.

目前世界上交通發展很快。你們國家的交通問題是什麼? 什麼引起了這些問題? 提出一些建議。

3. 作文命題形式

命題形式分為三大類:

(1) 對立觀點式

兩個事物或兩個觀點讓你任選其一。這類試題在考試中佔30%。

例 1　Some people think young children can have a better education in a boarding school far from home, while others claim that a day school or the home is a better one. What's your opinion? Give your reasons.

有些人認為青少年就讀寄宿學校能接受較好的教育,而另外一些人認為讀日校或在家更好些。提出你的觀點和理由。

(一種觀點是青少年應該就讀寄宿學校,另一種觀點是青少年應該就讀日校或在家。)

例 2　Who should be responsible for children's education, the school or the parents? Give your opinion and tell the reasons.

誰應負責孩子的教育,學校還是父母? 說出你的觀點和理由。

(2) 單一觀點式

一個事物或一個觀點讓你支持或反對。試題中常有 Do you agree or disagree 的字樣,這類試題在考試中佔50%。

例 1　Many pop and sports stars earn millions of dollars a year. On the other hand, most people in "ordinary" professions like nurses, doctors and teachers earn only a small fraction of the income of these "stars". What do you think about this phenomenon? Is it fair?

許多明星如歌星和體育明星每年能賺數百萬美金。而另一方面,許多平凡的職業如護士、醫生和老師每年的收入僅僅是明星收入的很小一部分。你怎麼看待這種現象? 公平嗎?

(實際上是問你:明星是否應該獲得高額收入。)

例 2　Some people believe that children should engage in educational pursuits in their spare time, otherwise they are wasting their time. Do you agree or disagree?

有些人認為孩子們的課餘時間應該是有教育意義的,否則他們就是在浪費時間。你同意還是不同意?

（實際上是問你：你是否同意"孩子們的課餘時間應該是有教育意義的"這一觀點。）

（3）論説式

描述一個現象，讓你說明原因或提出解決方法等。這類試題在考試中佔20%。

例 1 How should a student choose the future career, whose opinions and what kind of information he/she considers in making the decision? Give the reasons.
學生該如何選擇職業？在做決定時，應考慮誰的意見和哪些方面？說出原因。

例 2 Traffic is developing rapidly all round the world at present. What are the traffic problems in your country? What causes these problems? Make some recommendations.
目前世界上交通發展很快。你們國家的交通問題是什麼？什麼引起了這些問題？提出一些建議。

也可以將這三類題目分為兩大類，即將對立觀點式和單一觀點式統稱為辯論式（argument），這兩類的寫法基本上是相同的。辯論式的題目，我們介紹三種寫法：五段論式、對稱式、反證法，分別在本章的第二節、第三節、第四節中介紹。論說式題目的寫法在本章的第五節中介紹。

4. 寫作格式

IELTS 作文考試不要求寫標題（如：記我的老師，我最難忘的一件事等），所以在考試時，直接從第一段開始寫，不要寫標題，以免耽誤時間，如果有錯誤，豈不壞了大局？

寫作時，要注意分段，不要只寫成一段。分成幾段才合適呢？不同的結構有不同的段數，請詳見本章的第二節到第五節。

分段時有兩種格式：

（1）傳統式（或稱經典式）

這種格式，每段的第一行向右縮進去一點，與寫中文文章類似。這時，段與段之間可以空一行，也可以不空。如：

（現在，大家在看範文的時候，不要看範文的內容，只看它的格式。）

Now, most of the jobs in society that are high-paying, powerful, and demand a lot of responsibility are held by men. I think the government should reserve a percentage of these jobs for females.

Firstly, the problem of unfair employment distribution comes from social convention. At a young age most girls are not encouraged to pursue political office, business success, or professional prestige. On the other hand, boys are told to do these things. As a result, men hold the high level jobs but this does not mean they are very good at what they do. If the government set a quota for hiring women to do high level work, such as working in the government itself, then perhaps women would be more inspired to be ambitious in their life plans.

Furthermore, to legislate a percentage of high level jobs for women would work to fight the unwritten sexist rules of the workplace. For instance, if a man and a woman both competed for a managerial position of a company, and both were equally qualified and had the same experience and background, there is little doubt who would get the job. Even more, if the man was less qualified and less experienced than the woman, the man would still probably get the job because of his sex. Therefore, the government should reserve a certain percentage of high level jobs to ensure that some highly trained women could be hired.

On the other hand, there are many arguments against the use of a quota system for women. It is true that the injustice and discrimination could be reversed. This is to say that some qualified men might be denied a job while some unqualified women would be given one. Nevertheless, a quota system would break down some barriers between the men and the women. With the help of this practice, the sexism in the workplace will disappear gradually.

To sum up, from what I have mentioned above, it is not difficult to get the conclusion that the government should reserve a percentage of these jobs for females.

　　上面這篇文章的寫作格式就是傳統式,由於每段的第一行向右縮進去一點,也可以依外觀稱為縮進式。這種格式,段與段之間也可以加空一行。如:

Now, most of the jobs in society that are high-paying, powerful, and demand a lot of responsibility are held by men. I think the government should reserve a percentage of these jobs for females.

Firstly, the problem of unfair employment distribution comes from social convention. At a young age most girls are not encouraged to pursue political office, business success, or professional prestige. On the other hand, boys are told to do these things. As a result, men hold the high level jobs but this does not mean they are very good at what they do. If the government set a quota for hiring women to do high level work, such as working in the government itself, then perhaps women would be more inspired to be ambitious in their life plans.

Furthermore, to legislate a percentage of high level jobs for women would work to fight the unwritten sexist rules of the workplace. For instance, if a man and a woman both competed for a managerial position of a company, and both were equally qualified and had the same experience and background, there is little doubt who would get the job. Even more, if the man was less qualified and less experienced than the woman, the man would still probably get the job because of his sex. Therefore, the government should reserve a certain percentage of high level jobs to ensure that some highly trained women could be hired.

On the other hand, there are many arguments against the use of a quota system for women. It is true that the injustice and discrimination could be reversed. This is to say that some qualified men might be denied a job while some unqualified women would be given one. Nevertheless, a quota system would break down some barriers between the men and the women. With the help of this practice, the sexism in the workplace will disappear gradually.

To sum up, from what I have mentioned above, it is not difficult to get the conclusion that the government should reserve a percentage of these jobs for females.

（2）現代式（或稱流行式）

這種格式，每段的第一行不向右縮進，但段與段之間空一行分開。如：

Now, most of the jobs in society that are high-paying, powerful, and demand a lot of responsibility are held by men. I think the government should reserve a percentage of these jobs for females.

Firstly, the problem of unfair employment distribution comes from social convention. At a young age most girls are not encouraged to pursue political office, business success, or professional prestige. On the other hand, boys are told to do these things. As a result, men hold the high level jobs but this does not mean they are very good at what they do. If the government set a quota for hiring women to do high level work, such as working in the government itself, then perhaps women would be more inspired to be ambitious in their life plans.

Furthermore, to legislate a percentage of high level jobs for women would work to fight the unwritten sexist rules of the workplace. For instance, if a man and a woman both competed for a managerial position of a company, and both were equally qualified and had the same experience and background, there is little doubt who would get the job. Even more, if the man was less qualified and less experienced than the woman, the man would still probably get the job because of his sex. Therefore, the government should reserve a certain percentage of high level jobs to ensure that some highly trained women could be hired.

On the other hand, there are many arguments against the use of a quota system for women. It is true that the injustice and discrimination could be reversed. This is to say that some qualified men might be denied a job while some unqualified women would be given one. Nevertheless, a quota system would break down some barriers between the men and the women. With the help of this practice, the sexism in the workplace will disappear gradually.

To sum up, from what I have mentioned above, it is not difficult to get the conclusion that the government should reserve a percentage of these jobs for females.

　　上面這篇文章的寫作格式就是現代式,由於每段的第一行不向右縮進,從左邊看是齊頭的,也可以依外觀稱為齊頭式。
　　從寫作格式上看,只有傳統式和現代式兩種,雖然簡單,但應引起同學們的重視。根據作者主講的培訓班上同學的情況,在交作業及模擬考試時,總有一些同學把格式寫錯。如用現代式,段與段之間卻不加空一行,這是不對的,它看起來特別像一大段。下面的寫作格式是不對的。

Now, most of the jobs in society that are high-paying, powerful, and demand a lot of responsibility are held by men. I think the government should reserve a percentage of these jobs for females.
Firstly, the problem of unfair employment distribution comes from social convention. At a young age most girls are not encouraged to pursue political office, business success, or pro-

fessional prestige. On the other hand, boys are told to do these things. As a result, men hold the high level jobs but this does not mean they are very good at what they do. If the government set a quota for hiring women to do high level work, such as working in the government itself, then perhaps women would be more inspired to be ambitious in their life plans.

Furthermore, to legislate a percentage of high level jobs for women would work to fight the unwritten sexist rules of the workplace. For instance, if a man and a woman both competed for a managerial position of a company, and both were equally qualified and had the same experience and background, there is little doubt who would get the job. Even more, if the man was less qualified and less experienced than the woman, the man would still probably get the job because of his sex. Therefore, the government should reserve a certain percentage of high level jobs to ensure that some highly trained women could be hired.

On the other hand, there are many arguments against the use of a quota system for women. It is true that the injustice and discrimination could be reversed. This is to say that some qualified men might be denied a job while some unqualified women would be given one. Nevertheless, a quota system would break down some barriers between the men and the women. With the help of this practice, the sexism in the workplace will disappear gradually.

To sum up, from what I have mentioned above, it is not difficult to get the conclusion that the government should reserve a percentage of these jobs for females.

有的同學在一篇文章中,兩種格式混着用,比如第一段的第一行向右縮進去一點,從第二段開始,又用上了現代式,這也是不對的。下面的格式是錯誤的。

Now, most of the jobs in society that are high-paying, powerful, and demand a lot of responsibility are held by men. I think the government should reserve a percentage of these jobs for females.

Firstly, the problem of unfair employment distribution comes from social convention. At a young age most girls are not encouraged to pursue political office, business success, or professional prestige. On the other hand, boys are told to do these things. As a result, men hold the high level jobs but this does not mean they are very good at what they do. If the government set a quota for hiring women to do high level work, such as working in the government itself, then perhaps women would be more inspired to be ambitious in their life plans.

Furthermore, to legislate a percentage of high level jobs for women would work to fight the unwritten sexist rules of the workplace. For instance, if a man and a woman both competed for a managerial position of a company, and both were equally qualified and had the same experience and background, there is little doubt who would get the job. Even more, if the man was less qualified and less experienced than the woman, the man would still probably get the job because of his sex. Therefore, the government should reserve a certain percentage of high level jobs to ensure that some highly trained women could be hired.

On the other hand, there are many arguments against the use of a quota system for women. It is true that the injustice and discrimination could be reversed. This is to say that some qualified men might be denied a job while some unqualified women would be given one. Nevertheless, a quota system would break down some barriers between the men and the women. With the help of this practice, the sexism in the workplace will disappear gradually.

To sum up, from what I have mentioned above, it is not difficult to get the conclusion that the government should reserve a percentage of these jobs for females.

考試中,格式錯誤會扣 0.5 分或 1 分,這是十分可惜的。同學們在平時練習時,就要按照正確的格式寫,這是保證在考試時格式正確的最好方法。

5. 評分標準

評卷官主要從以下四點評定你的作文分數:

(1) 審 題

文章是否切題,是否回答了題目所要求的問題。如前所述,IELTS 的作文題目都是和大家的日常生活相關的,所以題目並不艱深,測驗單位也並不想在審題上給同學們設置很多的障礙。但也有一些需要注意的地方,如題目中遇到生字怎麼辦? 兩個或多個問號怎麼辦? 在本章的第七節中會對這些問題作詳細的介紹。

(2) 結 構

文章的結構也是一個很重要的問題。分幾段合適? 先寫什麼,後寫什麼? 本章的第二節到第五節將詳細介紹各種寫法的文章結構。

(3) 內 容

要說出一些理由支持自己的觀點,這在很多同學眼中也是一個難關。主要是沒有思路。如何想出合適的理由呢? 在本章的第八節會給大家一些建議。

同學們在平時也應注意多讀多背,尤其是與 IELTS 作文考試內容相關的文章,多積累素材。這樣在考試時就不怕沒有話說了。本章第十二節寫作素材中將一些好的句子分門別類,大家要將它們背熟,並要注意仿寫和改寫。本章第十三節提供了一些範文,這些都能為大家提供一些寫作素材。

(4) 語 言

有的同學中文底子很好,用中文作文,他們就會文思泉湧,下筆千言,但是一用英文作文就好像被縛住了手腳,不知如何下手。有的同學不怕沒有思路,但如果寫英文一寫就錯。確實,很多同學以前從來就沒有寫過英文文章。所以語言這一項應該是絕大多數同學的難題。

語言首先要正確,即沒有文法錯誤。其次要儘可能的優美,這樣才能在語言這一項上獲得高分。

語言包括用字和句子兩個方面。用字一方面是要多樣化,如在文章中三個地方出現"重要"這個意思,三個地方最好用不同的字。英文中表示"重要"這個意思的字很多,如:important, significant, vital, crucial 等,如果三個地方都用 important 就不太好。另一方面,要注意用一些複雜(sophisticated)的好字,比如我們想描述戶外活動有助於身體健康,可以有以下的三個句子:

Outdoor activities are good to people's health.

Outdoor activities are helpful to people's health.

Outdoor activities are beneficial to people's health.

很顯然,第三個句子最好,第一個句子最差。因為 beneficial 是一個 sophisticated 的字,而 good 則太普通了。關於用字方面的問題,請詳見本章的第九節。

句子實際上是文章的最基本單位。大家在寫作時,一要注意多寫複雜的句子,即多寫長句,長句應佔到全文的60%。另外還要注意句式多變,使用儘可能多的句式,如主詞子句、受詞子句、形容詞子句、副詞子句等,而不是只使用其中的一種。另外還可以根據情況,使用諸如倒裝句式、插入語句式等特殊句式。關於句子這一部分問題,請詳見本章的第十節。

語言是大家面臨的難題,本章第十一節詳細分析了同學們經常犯的一些文法錯誤,大家應該仔細閱讀,這樣就可以避免在寫作時再犯同樣的錯誤。

在審題、結構、內容、語言這四項中,最重要的是結構和語言。

❖ 二、五段論式寫法的結構 ❖

辯論式的題目(argument),我們共介紹三種寫法:五段論式、對稱式、反證法,分別在本章的第二節、第三節、第四節中介紹。本節介紹五段論式的寫法。

1. 結 構

一篇結構好的文章,應該分為開頭、中間和結尾三大部分。在開頭段說明自己的觀點,在中間部分說出支持自己觀點的理由,最後得出結論。

那麼在中間部分說出幾個理由好呢? 一個理由太少,四個理由太多,一般說出兩個或三個理由比較合適。另外,在結尾段之前最好再寫一段讓步段。所以,五段論式寫法的結構共分五段或六段。

第一段:提出觀點

第二段:理由段 1

第三段:理由段 2

第四段:理由段 3

第五段:讓步段

第六段:結尾段,得出結論

如果寫三個理由段,就是六段,如果寫兩個理由段,就是五段。

五段論式結構並不是 IELTS 考試要求必須遵守的寫法,而是約定俗成的。它的寫法符合論述有力、結構清楚的考試要求。評卷官決不會以文章結構新奇為美,所以我們沒有必要冒險去另闢蹊徑。下面我們將詳細介紹各段的寫法。

2. 開頭段

開頭段一般包括以下三方面內容:

(1) 引題

(2) 旗幟鮮明地表明自己的觀點

（3）引起下文

2.1 引　題

　　這三方面內容中，最重要的是旗幟鮮明地表明自己的觀點。但是在說出自己的觀點之前，應該用幾句話引題，將題目說一下。不能一上來就說出自己的觀點，這樣顯得有些突兀，缺乏必要的交代和過渡。

　　引題主要有以下幾種方法：

（1）介紹當前形勢

例1　Topic：Some people are of the opinion that keeping pets such as cats and dogs is beneficial to city dwellers. What do you think?

一些人持有這個觀點：飼養寵物比如貓和狗對城市居民是有好處的。你怎麼認爲？

Nowadays raising pets such as dogs and cats is becoming more and more popular in big cities.

近來，飼養寵物如貓和狗在大城市裏越來越流行。

例2　Topic：How to solve the problem of traffic jams in big cities in Taiwan? To develop public transportation or to develop private cars?

怎樣解決台灣大城市裏的交通擁擠問題？ 是發展公共交通還是發展私人汽車？

The problem of traffic jams in big cities is very common in developing countries and Taiwan is of no exception.

大城市中的交通擁擠問題在發展中國家非常普遍，台灣也不例外。

（2）提出問題

例1　Topic：How to solve the problem of traffic jams in big cities? To develop public transportation or to develop private cars?

怎樣解決大城市裏的交通擁擠問題？ 是發展公共交通還是發展私人汽車？

How can we solve the problem of traffic jams in big cities?

我們怎樣解決大城市中的交通擁擠問題呢？

（3）介紹不同的觀點

例1　Topic：Which one do you like：a small family or a large family?

你喜歡哪一個：小家庭還是大家庭？

Some people hold the opinion that the large family is superior to the small family in many ways. Others, however, contradict the large family.

有些人認爲大家庭在很多方面優於小家庭。然而另外一些人反對大家庭。

例 2　Topic：How to solve the problem of traffic jams in big cities? To develop public transportation or to develop private cars?

怎樣解決大城市裏的交通擁擠問題？是發展公共交通還是發展私人汽車？

Some suggest that we should give priority to the development of private cars, but others argue that public transportation should be put in the first place.

有些人認爲我們應該優先發展私人汽車，但是另外一些人認爲應把公共交通擺在優先位置。

（4）連續發問式

例 1　Topic：Some students like to have outdoor activities. Others like indoor activities. Which do you prefer? Give specific reasons and examples to illustrate your answer.

有些學生喜歡戶外活動。另外一些學生喜歡戶內活動。你喜歡哪一個？提出原因和例子說明你的觀點。

Have you ever gone swimming in a hot stuffy summer day? Have you ever been to the seashore to see the splendid waves? Have you ever stood on the peak of a mountain with cloud around you? Have you ever walked in the quiet silver moonlight? If you have no experience like these, your life is an inadequate one.

你曾經在炎熱鬱悶的夏天去游泳嗎？你曾經到海邊去看絢麗的波浪嗎？你曾經站在山頂上，讓白雲圍繞着你嗎？你曾經走在安靜的銀色月光下嗎？如果你沒有這樣的經驗，你的生活是不充實的。

　　這種開頭方法比較新穎，語言也比較優美，但並不是每個題目都適合。而且需要有較好的語言水準。

（5）個人經歷式

　　可以用與題目相關的個人經歷來作爲引題。

例 1　Topic：Some people believe formal examination has more disadvantages so we should not use it as a means of assessment. Do you agree or disagree with this statement?

一些人認爲正式考試有更多的缺點,所以我們不應把它作爲評價學生的方法。你是否同意這個觀點?

　　在引題時,你可以說,你在中學時,考試成績很優秀。但上了大學以後,發現創造力和想像力以及自己的學習能力很差,所以你認爲考試確實是弊大於利,它不能真實反映學生的程度和能力。

　　用這種方法引題,一定要注意不要介紹自己的經歷太多,一般三句話左右就可以了,要儘快入題。

(6) 名人名言及諺語式

　　如果有與題目特別合適的名人名言或諺語,將它用作開頭,會給人耳目一新的感覺。

例1 Topic:Many pop and sports stars earn millions of dollars a year. On the other hand, most people in "ordinary" professions like nurses, doctors and teachers earn only a small fraction of the income of these "stars". What do you think about this phenomenon? Is it fair?

許多明星如歌星和體育明星每年能賺數百萬美金。而另一方面,許多平凡的職業如護士、醫生和老師每年的收入僅僅是明星收入的很小一部分。你怎麼看待這種現象? 公平嗎?

你的觀點是這些明星應該獲得高額收入,可以這樣開頭:

Just as the saying goes:"no pains, no gains", the super stars have undergone painstaking training and practice and they sacrifice a lot for what they have gained. So I think they should get high salary.

正如常言所說,"沒有汗水,就沒有收穫",明星們經歷了艱苦的訓練,而且他們爲所獲得的犧牲了很多。所以我認爲他們應該獲得高額收入。

　　有些諺語通用性很強,特別適合辯論型的題目,如:

No garden is without weeds.

任何花園都有雜草。

Every coin has two sides.

每枚硬幣都有兩面。

可以將這樣的諺語用在開頭段,如:

Just as the saying goes:"no garden is without weeds", television has both advantages and disadvantages.

正如常言所說,"任何花園都有雜草",電視有利也有弊。

名人名言和諺語也可以用在文章的其他部分,如理由段、讓步段、結尾段。我們在本章的第九節"用字的注意事項及常用字"中,提供了一些寫作中常用的名人名言和諺語,供大家參考。

這六種引題的方法中,前三種比較好掌握,是常用的方法。這幾種方法還可以合併使用,比如前三種方法就經常一起使用。

例 Topic:How to solve the problem of traffic jams in big cities in China? To develop public transportation or to develop private cars?

怎樣解決中國大城市裏的交通擁擠問題? 是發展公共交通還是發展私人汽車?

The problem of traffic jams in big cities is very common in developing countries and China is of no exception. As how to solve this problem, people hold different opinions. Some suggest that in China, we should give priority to the development of private cars, but others argue that public transportation should be put in the first place.

大城市中的交通擁擠問題在發展中國家非常普遍,中國也不例外。至於怎樣解決這個問題,人們有不同的意見。一些人認為,在中國,我們應該優先發展私人汽車,但是另外一些人認為,應把公共交通放在首要位置。

引題時,要注意以下兩點:

(1) 不能照抄題目

不能將題目原封不動地重寫一遍作為引題,這樣會讓評卷官覺得你的語言能力不強,直接影響你的成績。應該用自己的話將題目改寫一下,作為引題。

(2) 引題部分不宜過多、過長

在說出自己的觀點之前,必要的交代一定要有。但要注意引題不要過長。尤其是採用連續發問式、個人經歷式、名人名言式引題時,一定要儘快入題。

2.2 旗幟鮮明地表明自己的觀點

這三方面內容中,最重要的是旗幟鮮明地表明自己的觀點。這種寫法,一定要在開頭段就說出自己的觀點。旗幟鮮明的意思是必須贊成一方,不能腳踏兩條船。

例 1 Some people think young children can have a better education in a boarding school far from home, while others claim that a day school or the home is a better one. What's your opinion? Give your reasons.

有些人認為青少年就讀寄宿學校能接受較好的教育,而另外一些人認為讀日校或在家更好些。提出你的觀點和理由。

這個題目,你的觀點或者是青少年就讀寄宿學校能接受較好的教育,或者是青少年讀日校或在家更好些,不能認為就讀寄宿學校和讀日校或在家都好。

例 2 Should uniform be introduced into schools and should students be required to wear uniforms?

學校該不該實行穿校服的制度? 該不該要求學生穿校服?

這個題目,你的觀點或者是學生應該穿校服,或者是學生不應該穿校服,不能認為穿不穿校服都可以。

同意哪一個觀點都可以,對評分不會有任何影響,不用考慮是否和評卷官的觀點一致。主要應該考慮同意哪種觀點會有更多的理由,會有更多的話可說。

說出自己的觀點,可以有以下幾種方法:

(1) 直接說出自己的觀點。

例 Topic: Should uniform be introduced into schools and should students be required to wear uniforms?

學校該不該實行穿校服的制度? 該不該要求學生穿校服?

In my opinion, students should wear uniforms in school.

我的意見是,學生在學校應該穿校服。

(2) 先說出對方觀點,然後說自己不同意這種觀點。

例 Topic: Should uniform be introduced into schools and should students be required to wear uniforms?

學校該不該實行穿校服的制度? 該不該要求學生穿校服?

學校該不該實行穿校服的制度？該不該要求學生穿校服？

Despite the fact that the majority may hold the opinion that students should wear uniforms in school, I doubt whether the argument can bear much analysis.

雖然大多數人可能會認為學生在學校應該穿校服，我懷疑這個觀點是否能經得起分析（即不同意這種觀點，也就是認為學生在學校不應該穿校服）。

（3）用一個讓步副詞子句，先說對方的觀點，再說自己的觀點。

例 Topic：Which one do you like：a small family or a large family？

你喜歡哪一個：小家庭還是大家庭？

While the majority may like to live in a large family, I prefer to the small one.

雖然大多數人可能會喜歡居住在大家庭裏，我更喜歡小家庭。

（4）先說出雙方觀點，然後說自己同意哪一個。

例 Some people think students should go abroad to study. Others, however, believe they should finish their university education in their home country. From my point of view, I vote for the latter one.

有些人認為學生應該去國外上大學，然而另外一些人認為他們應該在本國完成大學學業，我同意後一個觀點（即學生應該在本國完成大學學業）。

也可以說同意前一個觀點（**the former one, the previous one, the first one** 等）。但人的閱讀習慣一般是從前到後，對後一個觀點印象較深，所以一般都說同意後一個觀點（**the latter one**），將所支持的觀點放在後面就可以了。

（5）在說雙方觀點時，順便說出自己的觀點。

Topic：Which one do you like：a small family or a large family？

你喜歡哪一個：小家庭還是大家庭？

When faced with the decision of a small family or a large family, quite a few would claim that we should live in a large family, but others, in contrast, deem the small family as the premier choice and that is also my point.

當面對小家庭和大家庭的選擇時，相當一部分人說我們應該居住在大家庭裏，但是另外一些人把小家庭作為他們的選擇，這也是我的觀點。

在說雙方觀點時,順便說出自己的觀點是喜歡小家庭。

以上是五種常用的說出自己觀點的方法。說出自己的觀點,有一些常用的句型可以套用,請詳見本章第六節。

2.3 引起下文

在開頭段中,引題和說出自己的觀點是必須的。在開頭段的最後,也可以再用一句話引起下文。這句話的中文意思是:我持有這樣的觀點,原因如下。這句話用英文可以有多種表述方法。如:

There are numerous reasons why I hold this opinion, and I would explore a few of the most important ones here.
我持這個觀點有很多原因,我在這裏願意說出其中最重要的幾個。
Among countless factors which influence my decision, there are two/three conspicuous aspects.
在影響我的決定的數不清的因素中,有兩個/三個顯而易見的方面。
My arguments for this point are listed as follows.
這個觀點的論據列舉如下。
The reasons are presented below.
原因列舉如下。

與引題和說出自己的觀點相比,引起下文不太重要,可有可無。如果你下面的理由段有很多的內容可寫,在開頭段中也可以不寫這一句引起下文。

寫引起下文句的好處在於這是一句與題目無關的話。也就是說,可以在考試之前就準備好這樣一句話,不管出什麼題目,都可以用這樣一句話。所以比較適合一般程度的同學。

引起下文的另一個好處是,它使開頭段和理由段的連接非常自然。

實際上,開頭段中的三個部分:引題、說出自己的觀點、引起下文都有一些固定的句式,大家應融會貫通。這些固定的句式應該在考試之前就寫好。我們將這些固定的句式稱爲模板式句型。在下面要講的理由段、讓步段、結尾段中也有一些模板式句型。我們在本章的第六節爲大家歸納了大量的模板式句型。同學們應該參考它們,總結提煉出適合自己的模板式句型。這個工作一定要在考試之前完成,這樣考試時,寫作的任務就變成了**填空**,這對於寫作取得高分關係重大。

3. 理由段

　　在開頭段之後,要寫兩個或三個理由段來支持自己提出的觀點。也就是說,要回答一個"爲什麼"的問題:爲什麼你這麼認爲,爲什麼你認爲中學生應該穿校服,爲什麼你認爲學生應該去國外上大學,等等。

　　理由段是文章的最主要的組成部分,應該是大家的寫作重點。

　　每個理由段(paragraph)由表達單一中心思想(controlling idea or central idea)的一組句子構成,包括一個主題句(topic sentence)和若干個支持句(supporting sentences)。每個理由段的寫法基本上是一樣的,我們下面以一個理由段爲例介紹理由段的寫法,最後再稍微說明三個理由段之間的關係。

3.1 主題句

　　主題句(topic sentence)是表達理由段主題的句子,用以概括段落大意(announce the main idea of the whole paragraph),要求全段其他文字都圍繞它展開。寫好主題句對寫好整個理由段非常重要。請看下面的例子:

例 1 Television presents a vivid world in front of us. It tells us what is happening right now in the world. Television not only gives us the news in which we are interested but also shows it in pictures more powerful than words. In particular, important events are often broadcast live so that the audiences feel as if they are participating.

電視在我們面前展現了一個生動活潑的世界。它告訴我們世界上正發生什麼事。電視不僅告訴我們感興趣的新聞,而且還用比文字更有力的圖像來顯示它。而且,重要的事件經常在電視上現場直播,以至於觀眾就好像身臨其境一樣。

Television also plays an educational role in our daily life. We are often attracted by the programs about life in foreign countries which we want to know about. We can also learn about history by watching related programs. English programs are popular among the people who are studying this language. What is more, university TV has been recognized as the most effective method of part-time education.

電視在我們的日常生活中還起到教育的作用。我們經常被反映我們想要了解的外國生活的節目所吸引。我們通過觀看相關的節目能學到歷史知識。英語節目在正在學習這種語言的人們當中很受歡迎。而且,電視大學已經被公認是最有效的業餘教育的方法。

這兩個理由段是說電視的好處。第一段的主題句是 Television presents a vivid world in front of us,意思是電視在我們面前展現了一個生動活潑的世界,整個段落都是圍繞電視如何使形象生動來展開的。第二段的主題句是 Television also plays an educational role in our daily life, 意思是電視在我們的日常生活中還起到教育的作用,整個段落都是圍繞電視如何起到教育的作用來展開的。

在寫主題句的時候,要注意以下幾點:

(1) 每個理由段必須要有一個主題句。

這是必須要求的,評卷官肯定要找理由段中的主題句。沒有主題句,整個理由段顯得很散,沒有中心。

中國學生在寫文章時,不注意寫主題句,或者認為段落中的每句話都是主題句,這都是不對的。每個理由段必須要有主題句,而且就是一句話,由它來說出整個段落的主要意思。

(2) 將主題句放在理由段的段首。

主題句放在理由段的哪裡合適呢? 我們強烈建議大家:將主題句放在理由段的段首。絕大多數應放在第一句。

為什麼要把主題句放在理由段的段首,甚至是第一句呢? 這是有理論依據的。英文的段落展開方法比較簡單,主要有兩種:演繹法(Deductive Method)及歸納法(Inductive Method)。演繹法指的是由觀點到例子及論據,所以主題句在該段話的第一句。但有時,第一句是個過渡性或描述性的句子,這時主題句有可能放在該段話的第二句。總之,主題句在第一句或第二句,都是演繹法。歸納法是指由例子及論據到觀點,所以主題句在該段話的最後一句。據統計,英文段落中有 70% 左右是用演繹法寫的,而且其中絕大部分主題句在第一句。有 20% 左右是用歸納法寫的。極少數的段落主題句在中間的某一句或者沒有主題句。

主題句通常放在理由段的段首,開門見山。其作用是使文章的結構更清晰,更具說服力,便於讀者迅速地把握主題和想像全段的內容。主題句也可以放在段中,起到承上啟下的作用,或放在段尾,起概括全段的作用。但初學者比較難於掌握,因而在 IELTS 考試中,考生應儘量採用將主題句放在理由段段首的寫作手法。

我們將主題句放在理由段的第一句,不僅直截了當、開門見山,便於整個理由段的寫作,而且符合 IELTS 作文考試及評卷的實際情況。IELTS 作文考試的時間很緊迫,同學們要審題、想思路、想好字、寫好的句子,沒有必要花很多時間琢磨將主題句放在哪裏。評卷時,評卷官看你的文章的時間很短,他不會很仔細地找你的理由段的主題句。他很可能就看一下第一句,如果他覺得不是主題句,他就會認爲你的這個理由段沒有主題句,你的成績就會受到影響。

主題句有時也可以放在第二句,這時第一句常常是一個表示層次關係的句子,這也是可以的,詳見下面的第四點。

(3) 主題句不宜過長、過於複雜。

主題句應該很醒目、很簡單,讓人一看就能明白它的意思。主題句最好用簡單句,比如:

Television presents a vivid world in front of us.
電視在我們面前展現了一個生動活潑的世界。
Television also plays an educational role in our daily life.
電視在我們的日常生活中還起到教育的作用。
Outdoor activities can improve our physical health greatly.
戶外活動能大大促進我們的身體健康。
They can build my mind greatly.
它們能鍛煉我的思想。

也可以用結構簡單的複合句,比如:
Television is important because it plays an educational role in our daily life.
電視是重要的,因爲它在我們的日常生活中起到教育的作用。

這雖然是一個複合句,但是結構很簡單,很容易明白它的意思。
主題句一定不要用複雜的句子和很長的句子。下面的句子就不適合做主題句:
As a convenient communicational tool, movies, especially TV programs, help the people in the areas of social work, education, advertisements and so on.
作爲方便的交流工具,電影,尤其是電視,幫助了社會生活、教育、廣告等領域的人們。

這句話比較長,不適合做主題句。它的中心意思是說電影和電視能夠幫助在很多領域工作的人。所以下面的句子更合適:

They help the people in many kinds of areas.
它們幫助在很多領域工作的人。

　　總之，主題句越簡單越好，越明瞭越好，讓人一看就知道它的意思，而不需要想半天才明白你要說什麼。

（4）主題句前面最好要有表示層次關係的連接詞。

　　我們要寫兩到三個理由段，在每個理由段的主題句前面最好要有表示層次關係的連接詞，這樣顯得層次很清楚，也便於評卷官的閱讀。

　　最常見的一組連接詞是：First，Second，Third，或者 Firstly，Secondly，Thirdly，意思是"第一、第二、第三"。由於沒有"第四"（最多寫三個理由），所以，Third 或 Thirdly 常改爲 Finally。比如我們說電視的好處，可以用下面三個主題句：

First, television presents a vivid world in front of us.
第一，電視在我們面前展現了一個生動活潑的世界。
Second ,television also plays an educational role in our daily life.
第二，電視在我們的日常生活中還起到教育的作用。
Finally, television is very entertaining.
最後，電視是非常有娛樂性的。

　　類似的簡單的連接詞還有：
第一個理由段主題句前的連接詞：
First of all, To begin with, The first reason is that, ...
第二個理由段主題句前的連接詞：
Next, Another factor is that, ...
第三個理由段主題句前的連接詞：
Furthermore, What is more, Last but not least, ...

　　也可以用稍微複雜一點的連接詞，尤其是第一個和第二個理由段主題句前的連接詞，比如，第一個理由段主題句前的連接詞：
The main reason that can be seen by everyone is that _____.
每個人都能看到的主要原因是_____。
加上主題句後，該理由段的第一句爲：

The main reason that can be seen by everyone is that television presents a vivid world in front of us.
每個人都能看到的主要原因是電視在我們面前展現了一個生動活潑的世界。

第二個理由段主題句前的連接詞：
Another factor we must consider is that _____.
我們必須考慮的另一個因素是_____。
加上主題句後，該理由段的第一句為：
Another factor we must consider is that television also plays an educational role in our daily life.
我們必須考慮的另一個因素是電視還在我們的日常生活中起到教育的作用。

在主題句之前也可以用一個句子起連接的作用。比如：
The main reason can be seen by everyone. Television presents a vivid world in front of us.
主要的原因每個人都能看到，電視在我們面前展現了一個生動活潑的世界。

這時主題句是該理由段的第二句，這也是可以的。

(5) 主題句不能太抽象，要有具體的內容。

特別抽象的詞，如：important（重要的）、necessary（必需的）、helpful（有幫助的）、useful（有用的）等都不能單獨做主題句。如：

Television is very useful.

Television is very important.

上面兩句話都不適合做主題句，因為它們都太抽象，沒有說出具體的內容。你的觀點是：電視是好的，電視的好處多。你要說出兩三個理由論述它為什麼很重要、很有用。

避免主題句過於抽象的一個方法是看主題句中是否有關鍵詞，如果有，則說明不抽象。段落的主題句對主題的限定主要是透過句中的關鍵詞來表現的。關鍵詞要儘量寫得具體些。準確地把握關鍵詞是清楚地表達段落主題、寫好段落主題句的重要前提之一。請看下面兩句：

Television presents a vivid world in front of us.

電視在我們面前展現了一個生動活潑的世界。
Television also plays an educational role in our daily life.
電視在我們的日常生活中還起到教育的作用。

　　這兩句話中的關鍵詞分別是 vivid（生動活潑的）和 educational（教育的）。這兩句話都是比較好的主題句。

　　important、necessary、helpful、useful 這些詞不能單獨做主題句，不是說它們不能出現在主題句中，你可以接着往下寫。比如：

Television is important because it plays an educational role in our daily life.
電視是重要的，因爲它在我們的日常生活中起到教育的作用。
Advertisements are helpful to the consumers.
廣告對消費者來說是有幫助的。

　　上面兩句話也是很好的主題句。

（6）主題句也不能太具體，應是一定程度上的抽象和概括。

　　主題句是表達理由段主題的句子，它概括段落大意，說出整段的主要意思，要求全段其他文字都圍繞它展開。所以主題句應是一定程度上的抽象和概括，而不能是具體的事實和細節。比如下面兩句話都不適合做主題句：

Important events are often broadcast live on television.
重要的事件經常在電視上現場直播。
Television shows news in pictures more powerful than words.
電視用比文字更有力的圖像來顯示新聞。

　　這兩句話雖然都是說電視的好處，但都太具體了。顯然，一句更抽象的 Television presents a vivid world in front of us 更適合做該理由段的主題句。

　　再看下面兩句話：

University TV has been recognized as the most effective method of part-time education.
電視大學已經被公認是最有效的業餘教育的方法。
We can learn English by watching television.

我們可以藉由看電視來學習英語。

這兩句話也都太具體了，不如 **Television also plays an educational role in our daily life** 更適合做該理由段的主題句。

(7) 主題句不餽用集合句，也不餽含有不同意思的並列成分。

一個理由段只能有一個中心意思（one paragraph, one main idea）。而集合句是用對等連接詞（如 and）把兩個獨立的句子連接成為一個句子，這兩個句子是並列的關係，沒有主次之分，這就造成了兩個中心意思。所以集合句不能做主題句。

例 Television presents a vivid world in front of us and it also plays an educational role in our daily life.
電視在我們面前展現了一個生動活潑的世界，而且在我們的日常生活中還起教育作用。

那麼你這個理由段是說它生動活潑呢，還是說它能起到教育的作用呢？可見這就造成了這個理由段有兩個中心意思，所以這個集合句不適合做主題句。

同樣地即使是簡單句，如果含有不同意思的並列成分，也不能做主題句。

例 Topic：Travelling is more important than reading books in order to understand the people and the world. Do you agree or disagree with the statement?
為了了解人和世界，旅行比讀書更重要。你是否同意這個觀點？

你的觀點是不同意，即你認為讀書更重要。你的一個理由段的主題句是：Reading is the most romantic and the safest kind of travelling.（讀書是最浪漫和最安全的旅行。）the most romantic and the safest 是句子中的兩個並列成分，它們的意思是不同的，這也造成了這個理由段有兩個中心意思：讀書是最浪漫的（很有趣）和最安全的。所以它也不適合做主題句。

句子中的兩個並列成分如果意思相同，則不受這一條的限制，可以做主題句。使用意思相同的詞的作用是強調。比如題目是：你認為中學生是否應該穿校服？你認為應該，你的一個理由段的主題句是：It encourages thrift and frugality.（它鼓勵節儉。）thrift 和 frugality 都是節儉的意思，所以上面這句話做主題句是可以的。

(8) 構思主題句可以有兩種思路。

第一種思路是圍繞事物或觀點本身的優點或缺點來寫,要想出該事物或觀點的兩個或三個優點或缺點。

例 1 題目:電視的利與弊。你的觀點:電視利大於弊。你的三個理由段的主題句是:

First, television presents a vivid world in front of us.

Second, television also plays an educational role in our daily life.

Finally, television is very entertaining.

這就是圍繞電視本身的優點來寫。

例 2 題目:飼養寵物到底好不好。你的觀點:飼養寵物不好。你的三個理由段的主題句是:

First, it is harmful to people's health.

第一, 它對人的身體健康不好。

Second ,it can disturb us so that we can not have rest.

第二,它能干擾我們休息。

Finally, it has a negative influence on the relationships between the neighbours.

最後,它對鄰里關係有不好的影響。

這是圍繞飼養寵物本身的缺點來寫。

圍繞事物或觀點本身的優點或缺點,這種寫法的優點是對大多數題目都比較貼切,而且說服力強。缺點是有些題目不太容易想出理由,會有思路上的障礙。

第二種思路是圍繞該事物對不同的對象都有利或都有弊來寫。這種思路對某些題目來說特別合適。比如一個題目是問廣告的利與弊,你的觀點是廣告利大於弊,你的三個理由段的主題句是:

It is important to the manufacturers.

它對製造商很重要。

It is necessary to the media.

它對媒體來說很必須。

It is helpful to the consumers.

它對消費者很有幫助。

這幾個句子說明廣告對不同的對象（製造商、媒體、消費者）都有利，所以它很重要。對這個題目來說，很貼切也很巧妙。這種思路的優點是比較好構思，大家通常都能想出來。但缺點是它只對少數題目比較貼切，對大多數題目來說，這種思路有些勉強，不比第一種思路（圍繞事物或觀點本身的優點或缺點來寫）的說服力更強。如前面的關於電視的利與弊的題目，如果用下面三個主題句（使用第二種思路）：

Television is important to old people.

電視對老年人來說是重要的。

Television is important to students.

電視對學生來說是重要的。

Television is important to children.

電視對孩子來說是重要的。

這樣寫也可以，但可以看出，它們沒有我們前面的那三個主題句合適。

大家在構思主題句時，可以按照這樣的過程：先按照第二種思路，看是否與題目特別貼切，如果很貼切，就照這種思路寫。如果不是很貼切，再按照第一種思路想，儘可能想出兩三個理由來。如果實在想不出來，也可以按照第二種思路來寫。畢竟，不貼切也比不寫強很多。

3.2 支持句

在主題句之後，要寫若干句支持句來支持主題句。我們看下面的例子：

Television presents a vivid world in front of us. It tells us what is happening right now in the world. Television not only gives us the news in which we are interested but also shows it in pictures more powerful than words. In particular, important events are often broadcast live so that the audiences feel as if they were participating.

電視在我們面前展現了一個生動活潑的世界。它告訴我們世界上正發生什麼事。電視不僅告訴我們感興趣的新聞，而且還用比文字更有力的圖像來顯示它。而且，重要的事件經常在電視上現場直播，以至於觀眾就好像身臨其境一樣。

以上這段由四句話組成。第一句是主題句，直截了當指出電視在我們面前展現了一個生動活潑的世界。接着列舉三個支持句對其補充和支持，指出它告訴我們世界上正發生什麼事。不僅告訴我們感興趣的新聞,而且還用比文字更有力的圖像來顯示它。重要的事件經常在電視上現場直播,以至於觀眾就好像身臨其境一樣。句子銜接自然,步步緊扣主題。

主題句確定後,開始選擇和主題有關的訊息和素材。常用的方法就是句子展開前加以設問,然後解答,即設問 — 解答(why-because)的方法。下面我們透過舉例來看一看這種方法是如何完成的。

假設(suppose):Television presents a vivid world in front of us.

設問(why):Why can we say television presents a vivid world in front of us?

解答(because):

Because:It tells us what is happening right now in the world.

Because:Television not only gives us the news in which we are interested but also shows it in pictures more powerful than words.

Because:In particular,important events are often broadcast live so that the audiences feel as if they were participating.

當然,在寫成段落時,沒有必要在每個句子開頭寫上 because,但是在動筆展開句子時,頭腦裏要想着這個字,這種方法能幫助你把注意力集中在主題句,圍繞主題思想層層展開。

寫支持句時,要注意以下幾點:

(1) 如果寫三個理由段,支持句應該寫三句左右;如果寫兩個理由段,支持句應該寫五句左右。

寫三個理由段比寫兩個理由段好。一個原因是理由更加充分,另一個原因就是每個理由段可以少寫幾句。寫支持句也是大家的弱點,主要是沒有思路,寫不了那麼多,造成同一句話一直重複。每個理由段若少寫幾句,能避免這個現象。

支持句應該寫幾句,還與寫的句子的長短有關。總之,既要保證論述清楚,又要滿足字數的要求。

(2) 支持句大部分應該是複雜的句子。

主題句應該是簡單句,支持句大部分應該是複雜的句子。如果支持句大部分也是簡單句,那麼你的文章在語言這一項就不能獲得高分。一般而言,一篇文章如果很切題,文章結構也很好,語言沒有文法錯誤,但句子都很簡單,沒有複雜的句子,這樣的文章最多能得 5 分或 6 分。實際上,難免會有一些文法錯誤,這樣就不能保證 5 分或 6 分了。

什麼是複雜的句子,怎樣才能寫出複雜的句子呢? 請詳見本章的第十一節。

(3) 支持句可以是說理的句子,也可以舉例。

支持句可分爲兩類:說理的句子和舉例。說理的句子經由擺事實、講道理來解釋說明主題句。比如,前面我們舉的例子中: It tells us what is happening right now in the world. Television not only gives us the news in which we are interested but also shows it in pictures more powerful than words. In particular, important events are often broadcast live so that the audiences feel as if they were participating。這些都屬於說理的句子,它們用來解釋說明 Television presents a vivid world in front of us。

支持句中大部分應該是說理的句子,但也可以舉例。舉例也是解釋說明主題句的一種方法,叫做"例證法"。舉例不僅說服力強,而且一般類似記敘文,比較好寫。

例 **1** The second reason for my propensity for outdoor activities is that they can build my mind greatly. In sports, one must learn to fight with no matter what is left in his body. I will never forget the feeling when I raced to the final line first in a 3000-metre running. I could hardly breathe in the last 100 metres. I gave all my strength to move one foot ahead of the other. I won at last and I learned much from the race.
我傾向於戶外活動的第二個原因是它們能大大地鍛煉我的思想。在運動中,一個人必須學會不管身體中還剩下什麼都要奮鬥。我永遠也不會忘記我第一次參加 3000 米長跑的感覺。在最後 100 米我幾乎不能呼吸。我使盡全身力氣向前移動身體。最後我贏了,而且我從中學到了很多。

這個理由段的主題句是 they(outdoor activities) can build my mind greatly,支持句的第一句是個說理的句子:In sports, one must learn to fight with no matter what is left in his body。下面就是一個例子,說自己如何在一次運動中學會了堅持。
這是用自己的例子來說明主題句,整個理由段寫得還是不錯的。

例 **2** Family does play a significant role in shaping children's inclination and character. Because the family is children's most direct source of knowledge and other experience, those who are brought up in good family tend to possess many pleasant characters. Several centuries ago, there in Europe was a famous family: Bernoullis. This family is distinguished by its scientific contributions to the world. It brought up more than 20 great scientists and mathematicians so that there are so many formulas titled with the name：Bernoullis. It is a force-ful example to demonstrate the importance of the family.

家庭在塑造孩子的傾向和性格方面起到重要的作用。因為家庭是孩子的知識和其他經驗的最直接的來源，那些在好的家庭中長大的孩子傾向於擁有好的性格。幾個世紀以前，在歐洲，有一個著名的家庭：貝努里。這個家庭以它對世界的科學貢獻而著名。它培養了超過 20 個大科學家和數學家，以至於有很多以貝努里命名的公式。這是一個說明家庭重要性的強有力的例子。

這個理由段的主題句是 Family does play a significant role in shaping children's incli-nation and character，支持句的第一句是個說理的句子：Because the family is children's most direct source of knowledge and other experience，those who are brought up in good family tend to possess many pleasant characters。下面就是一個例子，說明家庭的重要性。這是用歷史人物做例子，一般比舉自己的例子更客觀，更有說服力。

舉例子時，要注意不要太多。一篇文章中，只在一個理由段中舉一個例子就可以了，千萬不能在每個理由段都用例子來做支持句。這主要是因為，寫例子的句子一般都比較簡單，類似於記敘文，不容易寫出特別複雜的句子。所以在語言這一項上會拉低文章的層次，不容易得高分。舉例時，還要注意不要太長。因為例子比較容易寫，所以有的同學就將例子寫得很長、很詳細，造成該理由段特別長，這樣也不好。舉例的理由段一般會長一些，但要注意將例子概括一下，用三四句話就可以了。

實際上，說理的句子中也包括羅列事實，有時候，羅列事實和舉例的區分不很明顯。

(4) 支持句之間應根據相互關係使用適當的連接詞。

寫支持句時，要注意連接詞的運用。支持句之間一般會有關係，如因果、遞進、轉折等。這時要使用連接詞，使句子之間連貫。有關各種關係的連接詞請詳見本章的第九節。

(5) 支持句必須圍繞主題句來寫。

支持句是通過支持主題句來支持文章的觀點的，必須圍繞理由段的主題句來寫。能支持文章的觀點，但與主題句無關的句子，不能出現在該理由段之中。

理由段由一個主題句和若干個支持句組成。有的參考書介紹段落的寫作方法時，提到段落最後要寫一個結尾句。實際上，IELTS 考試中的議論文屬於比較短的文章，在理由段中，根本沒有必要寫結尾句。

3.3 三個理由段之間的關係

以上我們以一個理由段為例,介紹了理由段的寫法。每個理由段的寫法是一樣的。

兩個或三個理由段可以均衡分佈,但有所側重更好,這樣顯得重點突出。這時,應該把寫得多的、寫的好的理由段作為第一個理由段。三個理由段既可以都寫五行,又可以分別寫六行、四行、四行,後者可能會更好。

但要注意,三個理由段都要論述充分,不能相差太懸殊。三個理由段分別寫六行、四行、四行,這很好,但不能寫成八行、兩行、兩行。

4. 讓步段

4.1 寫讓步段的目的

對於辯論式(argument)的題目,我們強烈建議大家寫讓步段。

辯論式的題目涉及兩個事物(或兩個觀點)或者一個事物(或一個觀點)的兩個方面,兩個方面都不是完全正確,也不是完全錯誤。所以在你的文章中最好把問題的兩個方面都考慮進去,這樣顯得文章很完整,也說明文章的作者是個看問題很全面的人。

寫讓步段的另一個好處是可以增加一些字數,尤其當考生不能想出足夠理由,滿足不了字數要求的時候。

4.2 讓步段的內容

讓步段寫什麼內容呢?

如果題目是一個事物(或一個觀點)的兩個方面,那麼讓步段只能寫你的觀點的另一方面。比如:題目是問電視的利與弊。你的觀點是電視的利大於弊。用兩個或三個理由段論述電視的好處後,在讓步段中應該說電視的不好。

如果題目是兩個事物(或兩個觀點),那麼在讓步段中,你既可以說自己觀點的不好,也可以說對方觀點的好處。這兩種思路選擇其一,不要都寫。一般來講,最好說對方觀點的好處。因為這樣把兩個事物(或兩個觀點)在你的文章中都提到了。比如:題目是大家庭好還是小家庭好。你的觀點是大家庭好。用兩個或三個理由段論述大家庭的好處後,在讓步段中你既可以說大家庭的不好,也可以說小家庭的好處,但最好說小家庭的好處。否則,如果讓步段寫大家庭的不好,那麼在你的文章中,只提到了大家庭,沒有提及小家庭,相當於把題目變成討論大家庭好不好了。

例 1 Topic:*Most high level jobs are done by men. Should the government encourage a certain percentage of these jobs to be reserved for women?*
大多數高層次的工作由男性來做。政府是否應該鼓勵保留一定比例的這種工作給女性?

你的觀點是:I think the government should reserve a percentage of these jobs for females.
讓步段應該寫這種做法(保留一定比例的這種工作給女性)的弊端。一個合適的讓步段如下:

On the other hand, there are many arguments against the use of a quota system for women. It is true that the injustice and discrimination could be reversed. This is to say that some qualified men might be denied a job while some unqualified women would be given one. Nevertheless, a quota system would break down some barriers between the men and the women. With the help of this practice, the sexism in the workplace will disappear gradually.
另一方面,也有一些反對這種做法的意見。確實,不公和歧視可能會反過來。這就是說,一些合格的男性可能會被一個工作所拒絕,而一些不具備資格的女性會得到這個工作。然而,保留一定比例這種工作給女性的做法會打破男性和女性之間的一些障礙。在這種做法的幫助下,工作領域的性別歧視將會逐漸消失。

例 2 Topic:*Some people like to travel alone, others like to travel together with several friends. Which do you like better?*
有些人喜歡獨自旅行,另外一些人喜歡和朋友一起去旅行。你喜歡哪一種?

你的觀點是喜歡和朋友一起去旅行。
讓步段可以寫和朋友一起旅行的弊端,也可以寫獨自旅行的好處。但最好寫獨自旅行的好處。一個合適的讓步段如下:

Of course, travelling alone has its own merits. You can change your destination at any time; you can stay in one place as long as you like; you can learn to be independent and make new friends; you can learn to deal with problems by yourself. But I still like to travel with friends, because I think that the most important thing during travel is to get pleasure and relaxation. With friends, you can get all these things easily.

當然了,獨自旅行也有它的優點。你可以在任何時候改變你的目的地,只要你喜歡,你就可以停留在一個地方,你可以學會獨立,結交新的朋友,你可以學會自己處理問題。但是我還是喜歡和朋友一起旅行,因為我認為在旅行中,最重要的事情就是得到快樂和休息。和朋友在一起,你可以很容易地得到這些。

4.3 讓步段段首應有連接詞

在讓步段段首,應有表示這是讓步段的連接詞。最常用的表示讓步段的連接詞包括:However(然而)、On the other hand(另一方面)、Of course(當然了)。

也可以寫得更複雜一點,比如:

However, it can not be denied that _____.

然而,不可否認的是_____。

On the other hand, we must admit that _____.

另一方面,我們必須承認_____。

例

On the other hand, there are many arguments against the use of a quota system for women.

另一方面,也有一些反對這種做法(保留一定比例的這種工作給女性)的意見。

Of course, travelling alone has its own merits.

當然了,獨自旅行也有它的優點。

On the other hand, we must admit that examination also has some disadvantages.

另一方面,我們必須承認考試也有一些弊端。

However, it can not be denied that there are some negative influences brought about by raising pets.

然而,不可否認的是,飼養寵物帶來了一些反面的影響。

有這些表示讓步段的連接詞,使得文章的結構很清楚。我們為大家準備了一些這樣的連接詞,請詳見本章第六節。

4.4 選材要避重就輕

寫讓步段的目的是爲了使文章更完整,同時有助於達到字數的要求,而不是爲了推翻自己的觀點。所以,在讓步段的選材上要注意避重就輕。如果寫自己觀點的不好,應該選擇小小的不好。如果寫對方觀點的好,應該選擇小小的好。否則會對自己的觀點產生不利的影響。

例 題目是電視的利與弊。你的觀點是電視的利大於弊。用兩個或三個理由段論述電視的好處後,在讓步段中應該說電視的不好。

On the other hand, television can also be harmful, especially to children who don't have enough experience to make a clear distinction between fantasy and reality. They want to imitate what they see, which sometimes is dangerous. They believe the violence they see is normal and acceptable. This may be the reason why "television generations" are more violent than their parents. But it is not the television's fault. We should tell our children how to handle these problems properly.

另一方面,電視也是有害的,尤其是對孩子來說,他們沒有足夠的經驗在幻想和現實之間做一個明確的區分。他們想要模仿他們看到的東西,這在有時是危險的。他們相信他們看到的暴力是正常的和可接受的。這大概是爲什麼"電視的一代"比他們的父母更充滿暴力的原因。但這不是電視的錯。我們應該告訴我們的孩子如何正確地處理這些問題。

這個讓步段從語言上看非常好,這就是在語言上 8 分的標準。它用了很多好字,比如:distinction、fantasy、reality、imitate、violence、normal、acceptable、violent。從句子上看,它用了很多形容詞子句和受詞子句。雖然語言很好,但在內容上,有些選材過重:電視能夠毒害下一代。這勢必對文章的觀點:電視的利大於弊有所影響,讀文章的人不禁要問,電視還是利大於弊嗎? 如果不想浪費這些好詞,可以選擇電視的弊大於利這個觀點,那麼上述內容可作爲第一個理由,很有說服力。如果非要認爲電視的利大於弊,那麼在讓步段中,應選擇電視的一個微小的不好,也可以寫出好的句子。比如,下面的讓步段不僅語言不錯,而且在內容上也比較合適:

On the other hand, there are some complaints about the television. For example, some children spend hours before the little screen, ignoring their study, outdoor activities and even their family. Parents say that these kids are indifferent to nearly everything and premature somehow.

另一方面,關於電視也有一些抱怨。比如,一些孩子在這個小小的螢幕前面花費了很多時間,忽略了他們的學習、戶外活動,甚至他們的家庭。家長們說這些孩子幾乎對任何事情都漠不關心,而且從某種程度上說有些早熟。

4.5 點到為止,不要過多過長

讓步段不要寫很多、很長,一般相當於一個理由段的長度就可以了。由於在讓步段的最後還要寫些別的內容(詳見下一點4.6),所以一般寫三句話左右就可以了。同時要注意,要嘛說自己觀點的不好,要嘛說對方觀點的好處。這兩種思路選擇其一,不要都寫。

4.6 在讓步段的最後,最好再回到自己的觀點上來

這也是我們強烈建議大家做的。在讓步段,說完自己觀點的不好或者對方觀點的好處之後,再回到自己的觀點上來,強調對方觀點的好處還是不能和自己觀點的好處相比,我還是贊成我自己的觀點。這樣,不僅能達到使文章很完整的目的,而且還能強化自己的觀點。

例1 *Topic*:*Some people like to travel alone*, *others like to travel together with several friends. Which do you like better?*

有些人喜歡獨自旅行,另外一些人喜歡和朋友一起去旅行。你喜歡哪一種?

你的觀點是喜歡和朋友一起去旅行。讓步段應寫獨自旅行的好處。

Of course, travelling alone has its own merits. You can change your destination at any time; you can stay in one place as long as you like; you can learn to be independent and make new friends; you can learn to deal with problems by yourself. But I still like to travel with friends, because I think that the most important thing during travel is to get pleasure and re-laxation. With friends, you can get all these things easily.

當然了,獨自旅行也有它的優點。你可以在任何時候改變你的目的地,只要你喜歡,你就可以停留在一個地方,你可以學會獨立,結交新的朋友,你可以學會自己處理問題。但是我還是喜歡和朋友一起旅行,因為我認為在旅行中,最重要的事情就是得到快樂和休息。

和朋友在一起,你可以很容易地得到這些。

在寫了幾句獨自旅行的好處之後,又回到自己的觀點上來(注意轉折詞 but),說明還是喜歡和朋友一起旅行。

例2 *Topic*:*Some people believe that growing up in a large family*,*with several sisters and brothers*,*offers more advantages than disadvantages*. *Other people think that having the only child is more advantageous*. *What is your opinion*?
有些人認為在一個大家庭長大,有幾個兄弟姊妹的好處更多。另外一些人認為獨生子女好處更多。你的意見是什麼?

你的觀點是在一個大家庭長大,有幾個兄弟姊妹的好處更多。讓步段應寫獨生子女的好處。

Admittedly, the only one child may possess a larger space and more attention from his parents than the children in a large family. They can also have opportunities to learn to be independent and solve problems by themselves. But things seem to have both positive and negative sides. Good conditions sometimes lead to bad results. I know some children who come from the one-child family. They appear more or less overbearing, selfish and lacking in cooperation with other people.
必須承認,獨生子女會比大家庭中的孩子擁有更大的空間和父母更多的關注。他們還有機會學會獨立並獨自處理問題。但事情都有正面和負面。好的條件有時會導致壞的結果。我認識一些來自獨生子女家庭的孩子,他們或多或少都表現出傲慢、自私,並缺乏與其他人合作的精神。

在寫了兩句獨生子女的好處之後,又回到自己的觀點上來(注意轉折詞 but),說明獨生子女還是不好(即有兄弟姊妹較好)。
從上面的例子可以看出,讓步段實際上是兩重轉折,有兩個轉折詞。先用一個轉折詞(如:However 或 On the other hand)轉到對方的觀點上去,再用一個轉折詞(如:But 或 Nevertheless)轉回到自己的觀點上來。

5. 結尾段

通常有兩種寫法：

（1）重申觀點

（2）總結主題句

第一種方法是將第一段中說出自己觀點的句子再說一遍，第二種方法是將各理由段的主題句再說一遍。兩種方法都需要將原來的句子改寫（paraphrase）一下，不能原封不動地把原句再寫一遍。

文章不能沒有結尾段。否則文章結構就不完整。沒有結尾段的文章，在其餘幾個部分寫得都很好的情況下，最多只能得 6 分。所以在考試時，如果還剩下兩分鐘還沒寫結尾段的話，應該趕緊寫結尾段。

但與文章的其餘幾個部分（開頭段、理由段、讓步段）相比，結尾段不是很重要。評卷官不會特別看你的結尾段，所以沒有必要在結尾段花費太多的時間，應把主要精力用在開頭段、理由段和讓步段上。

因此，我們建議大家採用第一種寫法，即重申觀點，因爲這種寫法更簡單。這種寫法是用一句話結尾。

這句話可分爲兩部分，第一部分是一個連接詞，如：

In a word（一句話）、In short（簡而言之）、Generally（一般地）、On the whole（總之）、In brief（簡而言之）、In conclusion（總之）。

第二部分是重申觀點，最簡單的方式是：

I think/believe/hold/suggest that _____.

我認爲_____。

也可以寫得稍微複雜一點，如：

It is sagacious to support the statement that _____.

支持這個觀點_____是明智的。

It is safely to draw the conclusion that _____.

得出這個結論_____準沒錯。

It is not difficult to get the conclusion that _____.

不難得出這個結論_____。

在第一部分和第二部分之間,也可以加一句套話,如:

for the reasons presented above,

根據上面所列的原因,

given the factors I have just outlined,

根據我剛才列出的因素,

if we take a careful consideration,

如果我們仔細考慮,

在三部分中各任選一個,就可以拼成一個相當不錯的結尾,如:

On the whole, if we take a careful consideration, it is not difficult to get the conclusion that

_____.

總之,如果我們仔細考慮,不難得出這個結論_____。

In conclusion, for the reasons presented above, it is sagacious to support the statement that

_____.

總之,根據上面所列的原因,支持這個觀點_____是明智的。

In short, given the factors I have just outlined, it is safely to draw the conclusion that

_____.

簡而言之,根據我剛才列出的因素,得出這個結論_____準沒錯。

下面我們以"中學生是否應該穿校服"這個題目為例,提供幾個比較合適的結尾。

On the whole, if we take a careful consideration, it is not difficult to get the conclusion that students should wear uniforms.

總之,如果我們仔細考慮,不難得出這個結論,中學生應該穿校服。

In conclusion, for the reasons presented above, it is sagacious to support the statement that students should wear uniforms.

總之,根據上面所列的原因,支持中學生應該穿校服的觀點是很明智的。

In short, given the factors I have just outlined, it is safely to draw the conclusion that students should wear uniforms.

簡而言之,根據我剛才列出的因素,得出中學生應該穿校服的結論準沒錯。

關於結尾段常用的句式,可參考本章的第六節。

五段論式結構清楚,易學易用,是寫 IELTS 議論文常用的一種寫法,大家應該熟練掌握。下面我們完整地看一篇用五段論式寫的文章。

Topic：*Some people believe television has more disadvantages. Others think it is more advantageous. What do you think?*

Everything in the world has its own two sides. Without exception, there are both advantages and disadvantages brought about by television. In my opinion, everyone should admit that its advantages outweigh its disadvantages.

The main reason that can be seen by everyone is that television presents a vivid world in front of us. It tells us what is happening right now in the world. Television not only gives us the news in which we are interested but also shows it in pictures more powerful than words. In particular, important events are often broadcast live so that the audiences feel as if they were participating.

Another factor we must consider is that television also plays an educational role in our daily life. We are often attracted by the programs about life in foreign countries which we want to know about. We can also learn about history by watching related programs. English programs are popular among the people who are studying this language. What is more, university TV has been recognized as the most effective method of part-time education.

On the other hand, there are some complaints about the television. For example, some children spend hours before the little screen, ignoring their study, outdoor activities and even their family. Parents say that these kids are indifferent to nearly everything and premature somehow. Nevertheless, it is not the television's fault. We should tell our children how to handle these problems properly.

In short, given the factors I have just outlined, it is safely to draw the conclusion that television is more advantageous.

世界上任何事物都有兩面。沒有例外，電視給我們帶來了好處，也帶來了弊端。我的意見是它利大於弊。

每個人都能看到的主要原因是電視在我們面前展現了一個生動活潑的世界。它告訴我們世界上正發生什麼事。電視不僅告訴我們感興趣的新聞,而且還用比文字更有力的圖像來顯示它。而且,重要的事件經常在電視上現場直播,以至於觀眾就好像身臨其境一樣。

我們必須考慮的另一個因素是電視在我們的日常生活中還起到教育的作用。我們經常被反映我們想要了解的外國生活的節目所吸引。我們透過觀看相關的節目能學到歷史知識。英語節目在正在學習這門語言的人們當中很受歡迎。而且,電視大學已經被公認是最有效的業餘教育的方法。

另一方面,關於電視也有一些抱怨。比如,一些孩子在這個小小的螢幕前面花費了很多時間,忽略了他們的學習、戶外活動,甚至他們的家庭。家長們說這些孩子幾乎對任何事情都漠不關心,而且從某種程度上說有些早熟。但這並不是電視的錯,我們應該做的是告訴我們的孩子如何正確地處理這些問題。

簡而言之,根據我剛才列出的因素,完全可以得出這個結論,電視是利大於弊的。

❖ 三、對稱式寫法的結構 ❖

1. 結 構

可分為四段或五段。我們先看一下四段的寫法。

第一段:非常簡單,說一下爭議的問題,不要提出自己的觀點。

這和五段論式的寫法完全不同。五段論式的寫法,在開頭段一定要旗幟鮮明地說出自己的觀點。而對稱式寫法,只說一下這是一個有意思的問題、有爭議的問題即可,相當於五段論式寫法的開頭段的引題部分。

例 1 Topic:The idea of having a single career is becoming an old fashioned one. The new fashion will be to have several careers or ways of earning money. Do you think whether having several careers throughout life is a new fashion?

只有一個職業正成為一個過時的觀點。新的時尚是有很多職業來謀生。你認為一生有多個職業是不是一個新的時尚?

一個合適的開頭爲：

With the development of society, nowadays more and more people change their jobs frequently. Whether having several careers throughout life is the new fashion is an interesting question.

隨着社會的發展，現在越來越多的人經常更換他們的職業。在一生中有好幾個職業是否是一個新的時尚，這是一個有意思的問題。

例 2 Topic：Some people think children should be taken care of at home by their mothers. Others argue that it would be good for them if they are sent to kindergartens? What is your opinion？

有些人認爲孩子應該在家由母親照顧。另外一些人認爲，如果孩子們被送到幼稚園去，將會對他們有好處。你的意見是什麼？

一個合適的開頭爲：

Everything in the world has its own two sides. Without exception, the discussion about whether or not children should be taken care of at home by their mothers is a very controversial one. There are people on both sides of the argument who have very strong feeling.

世界上的任何事物都有兩面。沒有例外，關於孩子是否應該在家由母親照顧是一個非常有爭議的問題。在這個問題的兩面都有一些人深有感觸。

第二段、第三段：雙方觀點各佔一段。分別論述雙方觀點的優點，或者贊成該觀點的原因。

如果題目是關於一個事物的利與弊，那麼應該一段寫該事物的好處，一段寫該事物的不好。比如，題目是問電視的利與弊，那麼一段應寫電視的好處，一段應寫電視的不好。

如果題目是關於一個觀點，問你支持或反對。那麼應該一段寫贊成該觀點的原因，一段寫反對該觀點的原因。比如，題目是問中學生是否應該穿校服？那麼一段應寫中學生爲什麼應該穿校服（或者說穿校服的好處），一段應寫中學生爲什麼不應該穿校服（或者說穿校服的不好）。

如果題目是關於兩個事物或兩個觀點的，如：大家庭好，還是小家庭好。那麼應該一段寫大家庭的好處，一段寫小家庭的好處。又比如題目是：中學生是應該出國上大學，還是應該在本國上大學。那麼應該一段寫爲什麼應該出國上大學（或者說出國上大學的好處），一段寫為什麼應該在本國上大學（或者說在本國上大學的好處）。

第二段和第三段是文章的主要部分，雙方觀點各佔一段。看起來是平衡的、對稱的。所以這種寫法叫作對稱式。

第四段：提出自己的觀點。

這種寫法也不能沒有自己的觀點，應在第四段中提出。

我們看一個完整的例子：

例 Topic：*Some people think children should be taken care of at home by their mothers. Others argue that it would be good for them if they are sent to kindergartens? What is your opinion?*

有些人認為孩子應該在家由母親照顧。另外一些人認為如果孩子們被送到幼稚園去，將會對他們有好處。你的意見是什麼？

Everything in the world has its own two sides. Without exception, the discussion about whether or not children should be taken care of at home by their mothers is a very controversial one. There are people on both sides of the argument who have very strong feeling.

Looking after children at home does seem to have a number of advantages. Firstly, mothers may be able to provide a more practical education for their children than kindergartens can. Secondly, a child's home is likely to provide a more relaxed atmosphere than what a kindergarten can offer. Mothers can also keep their children away from negative influences. The last advantage is that mothers are often said to know what is best for their children.

Many people, however, argue that children should be sent to the kindergarten. Firstly, children are isolated at home, while in the kindergarten, they are given opportunities to develop in the social context and become accustomed to communicating with peers independently. Next, kindergartens can provide professionally trained teachers and all kinds of educational facilities from which children can benefit. Finally, mothers can concentrate on their work and develop their career, which is also helpful to the social development.

In my opinion, I believe that children should be taken care of in kindergarten instead of being educated at home by their mothers. In this way, both children and their mothers can get benefits. Mothers are able to advance their careers and the family need not live on one income. At the same time, children can get better education. They can learn to be independent and to solve problems by themselves.

全文共四段：

第一段：引題，孩子應該在家由母親照顧，還是應該被送到幼稚園去，這是一個有爭議的問題。

第二段：孩子在家由母親照顧的好處。

第三段：孩子被送到幼稚園去的好處。

第四段：說出自己的觀點：孩子應該被送到幼稚園去。

2. 段落展開的方法

在對稱式寫法中，第二段和第三段是文章的主要部分。這兩段的第一句話一般是一句總述，比如：

There are several reasons which suggest that _____.

有幾個原因說明_____。

There are several reasons why _____.

至於爲什麼_____有幾個原因。

Many people argue that _____.

很多人認爲_____。

這句話常用的句式，請詳見本章的第六節。

下面的話展開有三種方法：

第一種方法是，如果能想出多個理由，每個理由可以只寫一到兩句話，這一到兩句話應該都是比較複雜的句子。比如：

Topic：Some people think children should be taken care of at home by their mothers. Others argue that it would be good for them if they are sent to kindergartens? What is your opinion?

有些人認爲孩子應該在家由母親照顧。另外一些人認爲如果他們被送到幼稚園去，將會對他們有好處。你的意見是什麼？

　　文章的第二段和第三段,可以按以下方式展開:

Looking after children at home seems to have a number of advantages. Firstly, mothers may be able to provide a more practical education for their children than kindergartens can. Secondly, a child's home is likely to provide a more relaxed atmosphere than what a kindergarten can offer. Mothers can also keep their children away from negative influences. The last advantage is that mothers are often said to know what is best for their children.

Many people, however, argue that children should be sent to the kindergarten. Firstly, children are isolated at home, while in the kindergarten, they are given opportunities to develop in the social context and become accustomed to communicating with peers independently. Next, kindergartens can provide professionally trained teachers and all kinds of educational facilities from which children can benefit. Finally, mothers can concentrate on their work and develop their career, which is also helpful to the social development.

　　第二段寫孩子在家被照顧的好處,第三段寫把孩子送到幼稚園去的好處。第二段和第三段分別寫了三個理由,每個理由都只寫了一句話或兩句話,但這一句話或兩句話都是比較複雜的句子。

　　又比如:

Topic: *The idea of having a single career is becoming an old fashioned one. The new fashion will be to have several careers or ways of earning money. Do you think whether having several careers throughout life is a new fashion?*

只有一個職業正成為一個過時的觀點。新的時尚是有很多職業來謀生。你認為一生有多個職業是不是一個新的時尚?

There are several reasons which suggest it may be the new fashion. Firstly, in today's economy, job security is lowering and many companies are dismissing highly trained people who are therefore often forced to seek other careers. Secondly, many people often do not like their jobs, perhaps because they initially choose the wrong field of work and these people are likely to have many careers in their lives as they seek what they want. Finally, technology is changing quickly. Old jobs are becoming obsolete, thus making workers redundant and new opportunities are emerging. The result is many careers change.

However, there are several reasons why having multiple careers may not be the new fashion. Firstly, most people marry and have children, and so they need a steady reliable income because of their family responsibilities, even if they are dissatisfied with their jobs. Secondly, people are generally afraid of change, and like the security of doing what they know. Finally, most people are ambitious and want to advance their careers as quickly as possible, and usually the best way to do this is to stay at the same job.

　　第二段寫多個職業會成為新的時尚的原因,第三段寫多個職業不會成為新的時尚的原因。第二段和第三段分別寫了三個理由,每個理由都只寫了一句話或兩句話,但這一句話或兩句話都是比較複雜的句子。

　　第二種方法是,如果只能想出一個理由,那麼與五段論式理由段的寫法類似,應先寫一句主題句,再寫若干支持句。比如:

Topic: Some people would like to live in the city. Others prefer to live in the country. What is your choice?

　　文章的第二段和第三段,可以按以下方式展開:

Many people argue that living in the city has more advantages. Many people appreciate the convenience of the city. Living in large cities, people can participate in political activities and they have easier access to news. The cultural lives in the city are colorful. For example, people can often visit exhibitions and see the latest films. In the city, there are good schools and universities for the children where they can get a better education, there are good hospitals for the patients where they can get better medical treatment and there are big department stores for the housewives where they can buy a great variety of goods made in every part of the world.

While many people in the countryside are trying to come to the cities, the city dwellers have recognized the attractions of the country. The country is free from contaminated environment. In the countryside, the air is clean, the food is fresh and the houses are usually spacious with large yards around them. If one enjoys fishing and gardening, the countryside is where he should live. Medical studies have proved that rural residents can live longer than urban residents.

　　第二段寫居住在城市的好處,只寫了一個好處:方便。第三段寫居住在鄉村的好處,只寫了一個好處:沒有污染。在第一句總述的句子之後,寫了一個主題句,然後分別寫了若干支持句。

在這種段落展開的方式中,有的時候如果不易歸納出主題句,也可以不寫。在第一句總述的句子之後,直接寫支持句,實際上把總述的句子當作主題句。比如:

Topic: *Who should be responsible for children's education, the school or the parents? Give your opinion and tell the reasons.*
誰應負責孩子的教育,學校還是父母? 說出你的觀點和理由。

Who is responsible for the education of the students? Some people claim that it is the school's duty to educate children. Other people argue that parents should play a more important role. On such a controversial issue, people seldom reach an absolute consensus.

Some hold the opinion that school should take the main responsibility. In the school, there are many professionally trained teachers and therefore children can be taught knowledge and skills more systematically. There are also a lot of well-equipped educational facilities from which children can benefit. More importantly, children are given opportunities to communicate with peers. These people maintain that the original purpose of the establishment of schools is to release parents from educating their children.

On the other hand, other people hold the opinion that parents should be more responsible for children's education. Parents are the first teachers of their children. What they say and what they do will have deep influence on their children who usually imitate them. Because the family is children's most direct source of knowledge and other experience, those who are brought up by good parents tend to possess many pleasant characters. What is more, in school, there are so many children and relatively much fewer teachers so each child gets inadequate individual attention. At the same time, parents know their children more than teachers and they know what is the most effective way suitable for their children.

From my point of view, both teachers and parents should be responsible for the students' education. The school is a place where children can not only master knowledge and skills they need in their future but also learn how to adapt themselves to the society. Family education is also very important in addition to school education. They should cooperate with each other to achieve our common goal, which is to raise our children to be useful people in society.

第二段寫學校應負責孩子的教育。這一段沒有明顯的主題句,在第一句總述的句子

Some hold the opinion that school should take the main responsibility 之後,直接寫了若干支持句。實際上這句總述的句子就是這一段的主題句。

第三段寫家長應負責孩子的教育。這一段也沒有明顯的主題句,在第一句總述的句子 On the other hand, other people hold the opinion that parents should be more responsible for children's education 之後,直接寫了若干支持句。實際上這句總述的句子就是這一段的主題句。

3. 對稱式寫法的優點

對稱式寫法具有以下幾個優點:

(1) 這種寫法是少部分題目所要求的

有些題目中含有 discuss(討論)、compare(比較)、contrast(對比)、to what extent(在什麼程度上)、to what degree(在什麼程度上)等字樣,這要求考生討論問題的兩方面或者將這兩方面做比較。這時最好用對稱式寫法。如果用五段論式的寫法,則必須寫讓步段。但即使這樣,也不如用對稱式寫法好。

(2) 這種寫法比較新穎

有的參考書根本沒有談到對稱式這種寫法。在大多數的補習班中,老師也不介紹這種寫法。但是,雖然具體的寫法不同,一般都會提到五段論式的寫法。這就使得考試中用五段論式寫法的人特別多。所以如果你使用對稱式的寫法,會比較新穎。這在一定程度上會佔一些便宜。尤其是一些寫作基礎較好的同學,如果有志作文拿 8 分,應該嘗試這種寫法。

(3) 適合思路少的同學

五段論式的寫法實際上是一邊倒。要求在其中的一方上花很多的筆墨。要想出兩個或三個理由,每個理由還要寫三到五句支持句。有的同學思路比較少,對作文題目,或者想不出兩個以上的理由(只想出一個理由,是不能用五段論式的寫法的),或者寫不了很多的支持句。這時可以考慮用對稱式。對稱式的特點是雙方觀點都說一說,想出多個理由也行,想出一個理由也行。因此它適合思路少的同學。

(4) 適合比較難想出理由的題目

IELTS 考試的作文題目雖然大部分和我們的日常生活相關,但有相當一部分題目要想出兩個或三個理由來還是比較困難的。對有些題目，連老師也很難在很短的時間內想出很合適的兩個或三個理由來。這時可以考慮用對稱式。如前所述，只想出一個理由，就可以用對稱式的寫法寫。

4. 對稱式寫法的缺點

對稱式的寫法雖然有上述四大優點，但它也有一個很大的缺點，那就是：容易論述不清。比如：

題目是：孩子在家由母親照顧好，還是應該送到幼稚園去？

第一段：引出題目。

第二段：寫孩子在家由母親照顧的好處。

第三段：寫孩子送到幼稚園去的好處。

第四段：我的觀點是孩子應該送到幼稚園去。

這時讀你文章的人就會產生疑問，為什麼孩子應該送到幼稚園去呢？孩子在家由母親照顧有很多好處，把孩子送到幼稚園去也有很多好處，為什麼孩子應該送到幼稚園去呢？這就是對稱式寫法的缺點：容易論述不清。這是一個非常嚴重的缺點，那還能用這種寫法嗎？能，只是我們要借助一些方式來彌補這一缺陷。

5. 彌補方式

對稱式寫法雖然有容易論述不清的缺陷，但我們可以借助以下的方法加以彌補。

（1）最後一段說出自己的觀點，不能太短。

不能像五段論式的寫法那樣把最後一段寫得很短。在說出自己的觀點之後，應該再說幾句自己觀點的好處，這樣可以強化自己的觀點，避免給人論述不清的感覺。

例1 題目是：孩子在家由母親照顧好，還是應該送到幼稚園去？

最後一段是：

In my opinion, I believe that children should be taken care of in kindergarten instead of being educated at home by their mothers. In this way, both children and their mothers can get benefits. Mothers are able to advance their careers and the family need not live on one income. At the same time, children can get better education. They can learn to be independent and to solve problems by themselves.

在說出自己的觀點(孩子應該送到幼稚園去)之後,又說了幾句把孩子送到幼稚園去的好處。

例 2 Topic：*The idea of having a single career is becoming an old fashioned one. The new fashion will be to have several careers or ways of earning money. Do you think whether having several careers throughout life is a new fashion?*
只有一個職業正成爲一個過時的觀點。新的時尙是有很多職業來謀生。你認爲一生有多個職業是不是一個新的時尙?
最後一段是:

In my opinion, I do not think having several careers is the new fashion. Almost everyone marries and needs reliable income to support his family. Everyone likes job security. Everyone has ambition to develop his career. If people leave their jobs, they usually have to start again at a much lower rank, and they usually do not like to do this. For these reasons, I believe having multiple careers throughout life will never be popular.

在說出自己的觀點(有多個職業不是一個新的時尙)之後,又說了幾句話,解釋爲什麼有多個職業不是一個新的時尙。

在最後一段,在指出自己的觀點之後,再說幾句自己觀點的好處。這時,可以說新的好處(即在前面第二段或第三段說自己觀點好處的時候,沒有提到的好處)。也可以說前面提到過的好處,但這時,應該用不同的字句改寫一下(paraphrase),而不要將原來的字句再原封不動地重寫一遍。

(2) 在寫自己不贊成的觀點時,用一些不確定性的字。

這樣會給評卷官一個印象,即作者不贊成這個觀點。這就造成一個好的結果,評卷官還沒有看到你的最後一段(即還沒有看到你的觀點),就已經知道你是贊成哪個觀點了。這當然說明你論述得還是很清楚的,從而彌補了對稱式寫法論述不淸的問題。在寫自己贊成的觀點的時候,就不要用任何不確定的字。

常用的不確定性的字包括:
may(可能),seem(似乎),be likely to do(可能),perhaps(也許),maybe(可能),probably(可能),be said to do(據說),might(可能),it is said that(據說)。

例 Looking after children at home seems to have a number of advantages. Firstly, mothers may be able to provide a more practical education for their children than kindergartens can. Secondly, A child's home is likely to provide a more relaxed atmosphere than what a kindergarten can offer. Mothers can also keep their children away from negative influences. The last advantage is that mothers are often said to know what is best for their children.

在這段中,用了很多不確定性的字。如:seem, may, be likely to do, be said to do 等,說明作者不贊成這個觀點。

(3) 先寫不贊成的觀點,後寫贊成的觀點。

即在第二段中說自己不贊成的觀點,在第三段中說自己贊成的觀點。人的閱讀習慣是從前往後閱讀,因此對後面的觀點印象較深。而且人是很容易受到暗示,很容易被說服的。因此,先說不贊成的觀點,後說贊成的觀點,然後說出自己的觀點是後一種觀點,就會給人以順理成章的感覺。反之,如果先說自己贊成的觀點,評卷官被說服了,再說自己不贊成的觀點,評卷官又被說服了。這時,你在最後一段再說自己的觀點是前一種觀點,就會給人論述不清的印象。

比如:

題目是:孩子在家由母親照顧好,還是應該送到幼稚園去?

如果你的觀點是:孩子應該送到幼稚園去。

那麼,第二段應該寫孩子在家由母親照顧的好處,第三段應該寫孩子送到幼稚園去的好處。

又比如:

題目是:只有一個職業正成為一個過時的觀點。新的時尚是有很多職業來謀生。你認為一生有多個職業是不是一個新的時尚?

如果你的觀點是:一生有多個職業不是一個新的時尚。

那麼,第二段應該寫為什麼一生有多個職業是一個新的時尚,第三段應該寫為什麼一生有多個職業不是一個新的時尚。

(4) 對自己贊成的觀點可適當增加篇幅。

雙方觀點各佔一段,可以平均分配字數,也可以對自己贊成的觀點適當增加篇幅,略微多寫一兩句。這樣在篇幅上稍微強化自己的觀點。

(5) 上述四種方法,最好綜合使用。

對稱式寫法雖有論述不清的危險,卻也有所需思路少等好處。有志使用這種寫作方法的同學,應該注意將上述四種方法在一篇文章中都使用上。即:第二段寫自己不贊成的觀點,用一些不確定性的字;第三段寫自己贊成的觀點,適當增加篇幅;最後一段指出自己的觀點之後,再寫幾句自己觀點的好處(或贊成自己觀點的原因),這樣基本上就可以避免論述不清的問題了。

下面我們看一個完整的例子:

Topic:*The idea of having a single career is becoming an old fashioned one. The new fashion will be to have several careers or ways of earning money. Do you think whether having several careers throughout life is a new fashion?*
只有一個職業正成為一個過時的觀點。新的時尚是有很多職業來謀生。你認為一生有多個職業是不是一個新的時尚?

With the development of society, nowadays more and more people change their jobs frequently. Whether having several careers throughout life is the new fashion is an interesting question.

There are several reasons which suggest it may be the new fashion. Firstly, in today's economy, job security is lowering and many companies are dismissing highly trained people who are therefore often forced to seek other careers. Secondly, many people often do not like their jobs, perhaps because they initially choose the wrong field of work and these people are likely to have many careers in their lives as they seek what they want. Finally, technology is changing quickly. Old jobs are becoming obsolete, thus making workers redundant and new opportunities are emerging. The result is many careers change.

However, there are several reasons why having multiple careers may not be the new fashion. Firstly, most people marry and have children, and so they need a steady reliable income because of their family responsibilities, even if they are dissatisfied with their jobs. Secondly, people are generally afraid of change, and like the security of doing what they know. Finally, most people are ambitious and want to advance their careers as quickly as possible, and usually the best way to do this is to stay at the same job.

In my opinion, I do not think having several careers is the new fashion. Almost everyone marries and needs reliable income to support his family. Everyone likes job security. Everyone has ambition to develop his career. If people leave their jobs, they usually have to start again at a much lower rank, and they usually do not like to do this. For these reasons, I believe having multiple careers throughout life will never be popular.

全文共四段。

第一段:引題,一生有多個職業是不是一個新的時尚,這是一個有意思的問題。

第二段:一生有多個職業是一個新的時尚的原因。其中用了一些不確定性的字:may、perhaps、be likely to 等。

第三段:一生有多個職業不是一個新的時尚的原因。

第四段:說出自己的觀點:一生有多個職業不是一個新的時尚。在說出自己的觀點之後,又強調了幾句為什麼一生有多個職業不是一個新的時尚。

6. 寫五段的情況

對稱式可以寫成四段,也可以寫成五段。寫五段的結構是:

第一段:非常簡單,說一下爭議的問題,不要提出自己的觀點。

第二段和第三段:雙方觀點各佔一段,分別論述雙方觀點的優點。

第四段:寫雙方觀點各自的缺點。

第五段:提出自己的觀點。

由上我們可以看出,寫五段與寫四段的唯一區別是,前者多一個寫雙方觀點各自的缺點之第四段。這種寫法也是不錯的,同時可以增加一些字數。

我們看一個完整的例子:

Some people would like to live in the city. Others prefer to live in the country. What is your choice?

Many people argue that living in the city has more advantages. Many people appreciate the conveniences of the city.

Living in large cities, people can participate in political activities and they have easier access to news. The cultural lives in the city are colorful. For example, people can often visit exhibitions and see the latest films. In the city, there are good schools and universities for the children where they can get a better education, there are good hospitals for the patients where they can get better medical treatment and there are big department stores for the housewives where they can buy a great variety of goods made in every part of the world.

While many people in the countryside are trying to come to the cities, the city dwellers have recognized the attractions of the country. The country is free from contaminated environment. In the countryside, the air is clean, the food is fresh and the houses are usually spacious with large yards around them. Air pollution, noise and overcrowding which are the biggest problems confronting townspeople seem strange for rural residents. If one enjoys fishing and gardening, the countryside is where he should live. Medical studies have proved that rural residents can live longer than urban residents.

However, living either in the city or in the country has its disadvantages. The city is always noisy and overcrowded, and its air is heavily polluted. But in the countryside, far away from numerous exciting activities, one may feel isolated and uninformed.

In my opinion, I prefer to live in the countryside, relaxing and appreciating the quiet and peaceful natural beauty. Besides the benefits I mentioned above, the crime rate is much lower in the countryside than in the city. So the safe, quiet and cheap life in the country appeals to me deeply.

全文共五段。
第一段：引題，居住在城市，還是居住在鄉村，這是一個有爭議的問題。
第二段：居住在城市的好處。
第三段：居住在鄉村的好處。
第四段：居住在城市和居住在鄉村的缺點。
第五段：說出自己的觀點：居住在鄉村。在說出自己的觀點之後，又說了幾句居住在鄉村的好處。

7. 最後觀點可以折衷

　　五段論式的寫法，在第一段指出自己的觀點，必須要旗幟鮮明，一定要贊成其中的一個觀點。

　　對稱式的寫法，在最後一段說出自己的觀點，既可贊成其中的一個觀點，也可以採取折衷的方案，認爲雙方觀點都有優點，同時也都存在不足之處，應該取長補短，優勢互補。我們看一個完整的例子：

Topic：*Who should be responsible for children's education, the school or the parents? Give your opinion and tell the reasons.*
誰應負責孩子的教育，學校還是父母？ 說出你的觀點和理由。

Who is responsible for the education of the children? Some people claim that it is the school's duty to educate children. Other people argue that parents should play a more important role. On such a controversial issue, people seldom reach an absolute consensus.

Some hold the opinion that school should take the main responsibility. In the school, there are many professionally trained teachers and therefore children can be taught knowledge and skills more systematically. There are also a lot of well-equipped educational facilities from which children can benefit. More importantly, children are given opportunities to communicate with peers. These people maintain that the original purpose of the establishment of schools is to release parents from educating their children.

On the other hand, other people hold the opinion that parents should be more responsible for children's education. Parents are the first teachers of their children. What they say and what they do will have deep influence on their children who usually imitate them. Because the family is children's most direct source of knowledge and other experience, those who are brought up by good parents tend to possess many pleasant characters. What is more, in school, there are so many children and relatively much fewer teachers so each child gets inadequate individual attention. At the same time, parents know their children more than teachers and they know what is the most effective way suitable for their children.

From my point of view, both teachers and parents should be responsible for the children's education. The school is a place where children can not only master knowledge and skills they need in their future but also learn how to adapt themselves to the society. Family education is also very important in addition to school education. They should cooperate with each other to achieve our common goal, which is to raise our children to be useful people in society.

全文共四段。

第一段：引題，誰應負責孩子的教育，家長還是學校，這是一個有爭議的問題。

第二段：為什麼學校應負責孩子的教育。

第三段：為什麼家長應負責孩子的教育。

第四段：說出自己的觀點：學校和家長都應負責孩子的教育。

❖ 四、反證法寫法的結構 ❖

五段論式和對稱式是寫 IELTS 議論文最常用的兩種方法，大家應該確實掌握。

下面，我們再介紹一種反證法，這種方法不太常用，主要是為了開闊一下大家的思路，起一個參考的作用。

反證法一般寫五段。

第一段：引題，旗幟鮮明地說出自己的觀點，引出下文。

第二段：不贊成的觀點的一個缺點。

第三段：不贊成的觀點的另一個缺點。

第四段：贊成的觀點的一個優點。

第五段：結尾段，重申觀點。

可以看出，第一段和第五段的寫法與五段論式是一樣的，只是中間三段的寫法不同。實際上，五段論式是從正面論述，而反證法式是從反面論述，透過論述對方觀點的不好來論述自己的觀點。

這種寫法只能用於對立觀點式的題目，即題目中有兩個事物或兩個觀點，讓你任選其一。如：

Topic：Some people think young children can have a better education in a boarding school far from home, while others claim that a day school or the home is a better one. What's your

opinion? Give your reasons.
有些人認爲靑少年就讀寄宿學校能接受較好的敎育，而另外一些人認爲讀日校或在家更
好些。提出你的觀點和理由。

　　對於單一觀點式題目，即題目中只提出一個觀點或事物，讓你支持或反對，使用這種
寫法是不合適的。如：

Topic：Many pop and sports stars earn millions of dollars a year. On the other hand, most
people in "ordinary" professions like nurses, doctors and teachers earn only a small fraction
of the income of these "stars". What do you think about this phenomenon? Is it fair?

許多明星如歌星和體育明星每年能賺數百萬美金。而另一方面，許多平凡的職業如護
士、醫生和老師每年的收入僅僅是明星收入的很小一部分。你怎麼看待這種現象？ 公平
嗎？

　　下面我們看一個完整的例子。

Topic：*Some people think young children can have a better education in a boarding school far
from home, while others claim that a day school or the home is a better one. What's your
opinion? Give your reasons.*

有些人認爲靑少年就讀寄宿學校能接受較好的敎育，而另外一些人認爲讀日校或在家更
好些。提出你的觀點和理由。

There has been much disagreement over children's education in recent years. Some people
think they should go to a boarding school. Others believe studying in day schools is more advantageous. Which you prefer depends on your own experience, life style and emotional
concern. As for as I am concerned, I am for the latter one.

One of the disadvantages of studying in boarding schools is that such schools are usually
much more costly than day schools. Most families can not afford it easily, not to mention
there are many families living below the poverty line. Even for children from rich families,
they will gradually develop a sense of superiority. Moreover, students in boarding schools
tend to spend more time in some useless things such as primping and they will be definitely
diverted from study.

Another drawback we could not neglect is that children can not get better education in boarding schools. In school, although the teachers are highly trained and the educational facilities

are well-equipped, there are so many children and relatively much fewer teachers so each child gets inadequate individual attention. What is more, far away from their parents' supervision, they tend to be distracted from learning by other things because they are not old enough to restrain themselves.

One strong benefit of learning in day schools is that children will have more opportunities to communicate with their parents. This will not only prevent the creation of generation gap between them but also be helpful to children's education. Family education, which is an important supplement of school education, plays an indispensable role in shaping children's characters.

In conclusion, I strongly commit to the statement that children should study in boarding schools.

　　談到這裏,IELTS 議論文中考得最多的辯論式題目(argument)的寫法就講完了。我們講了三種寫法:五段論式、對稱式、反證法式,其中五段論式易學易用,簡單明瞭,結構清晰,是大家應該重點掌握的方法。對稱式對思路的要求不高,而且也考慮到了問題的兩個方面,如果能掌握好寫作技巧,也能彌補論述不清的缺點。反證法只是給大家一個新的思路,並不要求大家掌握。

　　有的同學可能會問,千千萬萬的考生都用這兩三種結構,不覺得重複嗎? 我們認為,結構就是一種模式化的東西。在中學階段,用中文寫作的中學生會運用一些寫作技巧,以求文章新穎、別緻,但若將此觀念引用到 IELTS 議論文的寫作中來,效果可能相反。因為:

1) 中英兩種語言的差異很大,中文屬分析性語言,注重意合,強調語言的含蓄性;英語屬綜合性語言,注重型合,強調語言的直接性。因而結構簡單清晰更符合英語習慣。

2) IELTS 作文是一個淺顯的學術性寫作,它只要求考生具有初步的寫作能力。在結構方面只要求合理,新穎別緻的結構還不是 IELTS 作文考察的重點。

3) 若追求構思新穎、佈局巧妙,卻沒有較強的英語語言駕馭能力,很容易偏離主題,或者思想表達不清,實在是得不償失。

　　因此,在 IELTS 作文考試中,只使用這兩三種模式化的結構是沒有問題的,這也是經過實踐驗證的。大家應該把注意力放在思路和語言上,多累積寫作素材,多累積好的句子。這種認識一定先要在觀念上確立起來。

五、論說式題目的寫法

1. 分 類

論說式題目在 IELTS 議論文考試中佔 20% – 30%,論說式題目主要分為以下五類:

(1) 說明原因

這是論說式題目中考得最多的一類,佔論說式題目的一半以上。

例 Topic:Traffic is developing rapidly all round the world at present. And the problem of traffic jams is becoming more and more serious. What causes the problem? Make some recommendations to solve it.

目前,世界上交通發展很快。交通擁擠問題正變得越來越嚴重。是什麼引起了這個問題? 提出一些解決這個問題的建議。

(2) 涉及因素

例 Topic:When you are seeking for a job, what factors do you consider?

當你找工作時,你考慮哪些因素?

(3) 解決措施

例 Topic:Traffic is developing rapidly all round the world at present. And the problem of traffic jams is becoming more and more serious. How can we solve this problem?

目前,世界上交通發展很快。交通擁擠問題正變得越來越嚴重。我們如何解決這個問題?

(4) 混合型

題目中有兩個論說式的要求,通常是"原因 + 解決措施"以及"涉及因素 + 解決措施"。

例 1 Topic:Traffic is developing rapidly all round the world at present. And the problem of traffic jams is becoming more and more serious. What causes the problem? Make some recommendations to solve it.

目前,世界上交通發展很快。交通擁擠問題正變得越來越嚴重。是什麼引起了這個問題? 提出一些解決這個問題的建議。

這是"原因+解決措施"。

例 2 Topic：Families are not as close as before. Give reasons for this change, and suggest some ways to bring families closer.

家庭關係沒有以前那麼密切了。請解釋原因並提出能夠使家庭更密切的方法。

這也是"原因+解決措施"。

例 3 Topic：There are lots of difficulties for the newly-arrived students in the first several days of school. What are the difficulties they will face on the first period? How can they overcome them? Give some suggestions.

新生在開學頭幾天會遇到一些困難。他們會遇到什麼困難? 他們應該怎樣解決? 提出一些建議。

這是涉及"因素+解決措施"。

(5) 其他

數量極少,幾乎可以不予考慮。

2. 寫 法

論說式題目的寫法比較簡單,基本上與五段論式相同。一般寫成五段:

第一段:引題

這種題目一般不在第一段說出自己的觀點。這是因為觀點都比較長,我們在下面要介紹,一般要說出三個原因、解決措施或涉及因素。所以在第一段中沒有必要將這些原因先說一遍。因為在下面的幾段中還要詳細說明。

第二段、第三段、第四段:根據題目的要求,分別說出三個原因、解決措施及涉及因素,一個問題佔一段。

具體寫法與五段論式的理由段相同,先要寫一句主題句,然後寫若干句支持句。關於主題句和支持句,請詳見五段論式寫法中的講解。

第五段：結尾段，重申自己的觀點。

　　這時應將自己的觀點再說一遍，由於第一段中沒有說出自己的觀點，所以要在最後一段中將中間三段的主題句再說一遍。要注意改寫（paraphrase），而不要原封不動地重寫一遍。

　　與五段論式寫法不同的是這種寫法一般不適合寫讓步段，因為這不是一個有爭議性的題目。

例1　題目是：如何解決交通擁擠的問題？

你的三個解決措施是：多修路，發展公共交通，加強交通法規。

然後，你寫一個讓步段，說另一方面，這些措施也不太管用。

這當然令人啼笑皆非了。所以說大部分的論說式題目是不適宜寫讓步段的。但並不是任何論說式題目都不能寫讓步段。

例2　題目是：你認為什麼是二十世紀最偉大的發明？

這個題目實際上是屬於原因類的論說式題目，雖然題目中沒有明說，但實際上是讓你說出原因。

第一段：引題，然後說電視是二十世紀最偉大的發明。

第二段、第三段、第四段：說出三個理由，即電視的三個好處。

讓步段：說出電視的一到兩個缺點，然後說這些缺點都是微不足道的，或是有彌補措施的。

最後一段：重申觀點，電視是二十世紀最偉大的發明。

這種方法也是可以的，電視有一兩個缺點也不影響它成為二十世紀最偉大的發明，但這種可以寫讓步段的論說式題目比較少。

3. 說出原因的例文

Topic：Why do people attend university?

Nowadays many people go to university after graduation from high school. Why do they attend university? Different people have different purposes. In my mind, the following factors need to be taken into consideration.

The most important reason is that students can learn new knowledge from the study in the university. There are many teachers, professors with abundant teaching experience who teach students lots of new knowledge and help them to solve the problems in their study. With their help, students can learn a lot of useful basic and professional knowledge which is very helpful for their future work. Without the necessary knowledge, students can not contribute to the society after they finish their study in the university.

Secondly, students are given opportunities to enrich their experience. Usually, people often have uncomfortable feeling to live with a stranger, because they do not know each other and perhaps their habit and personality are different. But for the long run, it is good for them. They have to cooperate with each other and solve a lot of problems they will face together. Gradually, they can learn how to care and understand other people. It is a preparation for students, who will definitely cooperate with other people after they enter the society.

Finally, studying in university is helpful to students' psychological development. Before their studying in college, their life was often arranged by their parents and their study was often arranged by their teachers. It is very different for them to live and study in college, because students studying in college have to arrange their life and study by themselves. They have to learn to be independent and solve the problems by themselves. Therefore, the experience of studying in the university does play an important role in shaping students' characters.

In conclusion, by studying in the university, students can learn lots of new knowledge, learn how to adapt themselves when they enter the society and learn to be a strong man in spirit.

4. 涉及因素的例文

Topic: *When you are seeking for a job, what factors do you consider?*
當你找工作時,你考慮哪些因素?

How can we choose a satisfactory job? In my experience, I think you will make the decision according to the following factors.

Firstly, salary is the most important factor. Most people marry and have children. Some people even need to provide financial support for their parents. So they need a steady reliable income because of their family responsibilities. To live more comfortably is a part of human nature. Everyone wants to live in a big house, often travel abroad and have his own car. All these things need enough money which you should consider at first when you choose your job.

Secondly, I must like the job. Most people are ambitious and want to advance their careers, and usually the best way to do this is that they like their jobs. Only if they are interested in what they do, can they put all of their energy into it, and therefore, they are likely to gain great achievements in their field of work.

Finally, the job should be promising as a stable career. In today's economy, technology is developing quickly. Some old jobs and skills are becoming out-dated, and many highly trained people doing these jobs are dismissed and therefore are forced to seek other careers. Some new emerging jobs are full of development potential. The skills and training gained from working in these jobs are in demand. Therefore, these jobs are often well-paid and have good future prospects. I will undoubtedly choose these jobs.

To sum up, when I choose my job, I consider if it is well-paid, if I like it and if it has a good future prospect.

5. 出現多個問號的情況

　　在考試中,論說式的題目經常出現多個問號,即提出多個問題。有時題目沒有問號,但也是提出多個要求。通常是要求"原因＋解決措施"以及"涉及因素＋解決措施"。

例1 Topic: Families are not as close as before. Give reasons for this change, and suggest some ways to bring families closer.
家庭關係沒有以前那麼密切了。請解釋原因並提出能夠使家庭更密切的方法。
　　這是要求"原因＋解決措施"。

例2 Topic: There are lots of difficulties for the newly-arrived students in the first several days of school. What are the difficulties they will face on the first period? How can they overcome them? Give some suggestions.

新生在開學頭幾天會遇到一些困難。他們會遇到什麼困難？他們應該怎樣解決？提出一些建議。

這是要求"涉及因素＋解決措施"。

這時怎麼寫呢？應保持文章的整體結構不變,即兩頭小,中間大。開頭和結尾的寫法大體上與一個問號的題目的寫法一致,只是略作變化。中間部分應先寫原因或涉及因素,再寫解決措施。可以寫成兩大段,一段寫原因或涉及因素,一段寫解決措施。也可以寫成三大段,其中兩段寫原因或涉及因素,一段寫解決措施。或者一段寫原因或涉及因素,兩段寫解決措施。

用一段寫時,最好寫出兩個或三個原因和涉及因素及解決措施。每個原因和涉及因素及解決措施只寫一到兩句,這與對稱式的寫法差不多。用兩段寫時,應每段只寫一個原因和涉及因素及解決措施。先寫一個主題句,再寫若干句支持句(這與五段論式的寫法差不多)。

注意,多個問號時不同的問題應在不同的段落中回答。不能混在一起。

下面的寫法是正確的:

正確的寫法 1

　　第一段:開頭,引題
　　第二段:原因 1
　　第三段:原因 2
　　第四段:解決措施(多個)
　　第五段:結尾

正確的寫法 2

　　第一段:開頭,引題
　　第二段:原因(多個)
　　第三段:解決措施 1
　　第四段:解決措施 2
　　第五段:結尾

正確的寫法 3

　　第一段:開頭,引題

第二段:原因(多個)
第三段:解決措施(多個)
第四段:結尾

下面的寫法是錯誤的:

錯誤的寫法

第一段:開頭,引題
第二段:原因1,解決措施1
第三段:原因2,解決措施2
第四段:原因3,解決措施3
第五段:結尾

也就是說,原因(或涉及因素)與解決措施要分開寫,不能混在一起寫。混在一起寫容易論述不清楚。同時,原因和解決措施在大多數情況下並不是一一對應的。

題目有多個問號時,結尾段有時也可以省略不寫,尤其在用一段寫解決措施的時候。這時再寫一個結尾段顯得有些囉嗦。

下面我們看一個例子。

Topic: *Families are not as close as before. Give reasons for this change, and suggest some ways to bring families closer.*
家庭關係沒有以前那麼密切了。請解釋原因並提出能夠使家庭更密切的方法。

Nowadays the relationship between family members is not as close as before. But as what factors contribute to this problem, different people have diverse opinions. As for as I am concerned, it results from the following reasons.

The first reason is that people spend much time on their study and work. Compared with the past, social competition is becoming more and more fierce and people have to face greater work pressure. Therefore, people have to devote almost themselves to their careers. What is more, many jobs require people to work in other cities and many children have to leave their parents at an early age to study or work elsewhere. As time passes, these people become emotionally estranged from their families.

Another reason is that people enjoy more forms of entertainment and amusement. Nowadays there are various kinds of recreational facilities such as watching TV, surfing the Internet or playing video games which occupy people's spare time. As a result, they would be diverted from enjoying chats with their family members.

To bring families closer, urgent steps must be taken into effect. Firstly, people should keep frequent touch with family members, especially those who live away from one another. A regular phone call can bring them the care they need. Secondly, never bring your work home and leave it in your office. It is a good idea to spend more time with family members. And most importantly, we should often convey the concept of family to our children.

In the final analysis, a close family relationship can surely be maintained as long as we realize the significant role it plays in our lives.

本文採用的是正確寫法 1：
第一段：開頭,引題。
第二段：原因 1：花費更多時間在工作和學習上。
第三段：原因 2：人們享有更豐富的娛樂形式。
第四段：解決措施(兩個)：保持經常的聯絡和不要把工作帶回家中。
第五段：結尾。

❖ 六、常用的模板式句型 ❖

實際上,開頭段中的三個部分：引題、說出自己的觀點、引起下文,以及各理由段主題句前的連接詞、讓步段段首的連接詞、結尾段都有一些固定的句式,大家應熟練。我們將這些固定的句式稱為模板式句型。我們為大家歸納了大量這樣的模板式句型,同學們也要學會演繹出適合自己的模板式句型。這個工作一定要完成於考試之前,這樣考試時寫作的任務就變成了填空,這對於大家的寫作取得高分至關重要。一篇文章完整的模板句字數加起來會在 100 字左右,也就是說,這 100 字要完成於考試之前,在考場上只專心寫其餘的 150 字。這 150 字是與題目有關係的,不能事先寫好。

下面就是一篇文章完整的模板。

（開頭段）

Everything in the world has its own two sides. Without exception, _____ （這裏填上題目中所要求論述利弊的事物,如:電視、電腦或廣告等）has both advantages and disadvantages. As far as I am concerned, its advantages outweigh its disadvantages. There are numerous reasons why I hold this opinion, and I would explore a few of the most important ones here.

（第一個理由段）

The main reason that can be seen by everyone is that _____.（這裏寫 第一個理由段的主題句）（這裏寫第一個理由段的支持句）

（第二個理由段）

Another factor we must consider is that _____.（這裏寫第二個理由段的 主題句）（這裏寫第二個理由段的支持句）

（第三個理由段）

The argument I support in the first paragraph is also in a position of advantage because _____.（這裏寫第三個理由段的主題句）（這裏寫第三個理由段的支持 句）

（讓步段）

On the other hand, it cannot be denied that _____（這裏填上題目中所要 求論述利弊的事物,如:電視、電腦或廣告等）also has some advantages/disadvantages.（寫 自己觀點的不好或對方觀點的好處）Nevertheless,（回到自己的觀點）

（結尾段）

On the whole, if we take a careful consideration, it is not difficult to get the conclusion that _____（這裏填上題目中所要求論述利弊的事物,如:電視、電腦或廣告 等）has more advantages/disadvantages.

　　下面是用上述模板寫的一篇文章,文章中斜線處為模板內容。

Everything in the world has its own two sides. Without exception, television *has both advantages and disadvantages. As far as I am concerned, its advantages outweigh its disadvantages. There are numerous reasons why I hold this opinion, and I would explore a few of the most important ones here.*

The main reason that can be seen by everyone is that television presents a vivid world in front of us. It tells us what is happening right now in the world. Television not only gives us the news in which we are interested but also shows it in pictures more powerful than words. In particular, important events are often broadcast live so that the audiences feel as if they were participating.

Another factor we must consider is that television also plays an educational role in our daily life. We are often attracted by the programs about life in foreign countries which we want to know about. We can also learn about history by watching related programs. English programs are popular among the people who are studying this language. What is more, university TV has been recognized as the most effective method of part-time education.

On the other hand, *it cannot be denied that* televison *also has some disadvantages*. Some children spend hours before the little screen, ignoring their study, outdoor activities and even their family. Parents say that these kids are indifferent to nearly everything and premature somehow. *Nevertheless*, it is not the television's fault. We should tell our children how to handle these problems properly.

On the whole, *if we take a careful consideration*, *it is not difficult to get the conclusion that* television *has more advantages*.

　　有的同學會問,大家都這樣寫,不都寫得一樣了嗎? 上面的模板只是我們給大家舉的一個例子。用來告訴大家模板是什麼東西,怎麼使用。它是從下面很多模板句中總結出來的。大家應該仔細閱讀下面的模板句型,從各部分中找出自己滿意的句子,拼成一篇完整的文章模板。這樣,每個同學的模板就會和別人的不同了。

　　大家在準備文章模板時,要注意以下幾點:

(1) 應該準備多個模板以適應不同的題型,任何一個模板都不是任何題目都能套進去的。我建議大家,五段論式寫法準備三個,對稱式寫法準備一個,論說式題目模板準備一個。

(2) 不要僵化,要注意靈活使用,尤其是寫作基礎較好的同學,要注意結合具體的題目而加以變化。

(3) 將模板盡善盡美是很重要的,但同時也要注意不斷提高自己的寫作水準。如果模板部分語言很漂亮,而其餘的部分(即另外 150 字)錯誤百出,讓人不知所云,作文分數也不會高。

　　因此我們建議大家寫議論文的步驟是：

（1）審題

一般用時 2～3 分鐘，至少將題目看兩遍，尤其是有些特殊要求的題目，請詳見下面第七節"審題的注意事項"。

（2）列寫作綱要

在試題卷上（不是在答案紙上）列出寫作要點，可以用中文，也可以用英文。沒有時間打草稿，只能列一些要點（如：主題句）。一般用時 3～5 分鐘。

（3）選擇模板

根據題目的類型（辯論式還是論說式）及確定的寫法（五段論式還是對稱式），選擇適合題目的模板。一般用時 1 分鐘。

（4）進行寫作

將自己熟記的模板直接寫到作文中，根據具體的題目將不能事先準備的部分填上。一般用時 25 分鐘。

（5）修改文章

寫作時難免會有些錯誤，在文章寫完之後應進行檢查、修改。一般用時 3～5 分鐘。

　　下面就分別列出各種模板句型：

1. 五段論式寫法－開頭段－引題

　　實際上，下面的模板句適合各種寫法（五段論式寫法、對稱式寫法、論說式寫法）開頭段的引題部分。

As one of the most important inventions of the twentieth century , _____ has a wide application in all aspects of our lives.

作爲 20 世紀最重要的發明之一，_____在我們生活的所有方面都有廣泛的應用。

As the proverb goes："So many people, so many minds.", it is quite understandable that people from different backgrounds put different interpretations on the same issue.

就像俗語所說，"有多少人，就有多少觀點"。來自不同背景的人對同樣的問題有不同的看法是可以理解的。

And a new problem has arisen: _____.
一個新的問題產生了: _____。

Admittedly, there are merits to both arguments.
必須承認,雙方觀點都有優點。

Along with the development of society more and more problems are brought to our attention, one of which is that _____.
隨着社會的發展,越來越多的問題引起我們的注意,其中一個是_____。

All these opinions make sense, and consequently it is hard to decide which one is more reasonable.
所有這些觀點都有道理,因此很難決定哪一個更有道理。

Admittedly, there are merits to both sides of the argument.
必須承認,這個問題的兩面都有優點。

As to whether it is a blessing or a curse, however, people take different attitudes.
然而,關於它是一個好事還是一個壞事,人們有不同的態度。

As the proverb goes: "Every coin has its two sides", _____ is no exception.
正如俗語所說,"每枚硬幣都有兩面",_____也不例外。

As we know, _____ bring many benefits and conveniences to people.
正如我們知道的,_____給人們帶來了很多好處和方便。

As society develops, people are attaching much importance to _____.
隨着社會的發展,人們意識到_____的重要性。

Along with the rapid development of the society, remarkable changes have taken place in _____.
隨着社會的快速發展,在_____上已經發生了顯著的變化。

Admittedly, both sides are reasonable. But they are one-sided.
必須承認,雙方意見都有道理,但它們都是片面的。

As a result, some people even suggest that _____.
因此,一些人甚至提出_____。

Advocates of _____ proclaim that _____.
贊成_____的人聲稱_____。

As to whether it is worthwhile _____, there is a long-running controversial debate. It is quite natural that people from different backgrounds may have divergent attitudes towards it.
關於_____是不是值得,有長期的爭議。不同背景的人對它自然有不同的態度。

At present, some people think _____, while others claim _____. Both sides have their merits.
目前,一些人認為_____,然而其餘人聲稱_____。雙方都有道理。

As social advances amazingly, people's demands have become increasing diversified.
隨着社會的發展,人們的需求變得多樣化。

But others hold the view that _____.
但是其他的人認為_____。

But on the other hand, there are also many people who strongly advocate the _____.
但是另一方面,還有很多人強烈贊成_____。

Both sides of the argument have very strong feelings and sound reasons.
問題的兩面都很有道理。

But people who are _____, in the other hand, maintain that _____.
但是另一方面,_____的人堅持認為_____。

Both sides of the question are well supported by sound reasons.
問題的兩面都有很好的理由支持。

But people who _____ assert that _____.
但是_____的人聲稱_____。

Before giving my opinion, I think it is important to look at the argument on both sides.
在提出我的觀點之前,我認為看一看問題的兩面是很重要的。

But there are also people who are strongly opposed to _____.
但也有一些人強烈反對_____。

But the people who are against _____ also have sound reasons.
但是,反對_____的人也有很好的理由。

But others, on the other hand, contend that _____.
但是另一方面,另外一些人主張_____。

Before rendering my opinion, I think it is important to take a glance at the arguments on both sides.
在說出我的觀點之前,我認為先看一下雙方的觀點是重要的。

But people who advocate _____, on the other hand, argue that _____.
但是另一方面,贊成_____的人認為_____。

Despite the advantages _____ has, some people claim, we shall not lose sight of its adverse effects on _____.
雖然_____有一些好處,一些人認為我們不應該不看它對_____的負面影響。

Everything has a good side and a bad side, and _____ is no exception.
任何事情都有好的和壞的方面,_____也不例外。

For years, _____ has been seen as _____. But things are quite different now.

一直以來，_____被認爲是_____。但是現在情況大不相同。

However, there are a large number of people who hold a different view concerning this case.
然而，關於這件事，有很多人持有一個不同的觀點。

However, some others argue that _____.
然而，一些人辯論說_____。

However, as to whether it is a blessing or curse, there arises a heated debate among people with different backgrounds.
然而，它是一件好事還是一件壞事，在不同背景的人中引起了激烈的爭論。

However, views on this issue vary from person to person.
然而，不同的人對這個問題有不同的觀點。

However, recently this phenomenon has triggered a heated discussion as to whether _____.
然而，近來這個現象引起了關於是否_____的熱烈討論。

However, there are also some others who contend that _____.
然而，也有一些人主張_____。

However, like anything else, _____ has more than one face.
然而，像其它事物一樣，_____也有多面性。

However, with the advance of the human civilization, there is an increasing number of people who have raised doubts about whether _____.
然而，隨着人類文明的進步，懷疑是不是_____的人越來越多。

However, there is a good side and a bad side to everything. _____ is no exception.
然而，任何事物都有兩面。_____也不例外。

It is so crucial that we can not afford to make a single mistake. However, it is not always

easy to make a prudent and satisfying choice. Sometimes we find ourselves involved in dilemmas.
它是那麼的重要，我們不能出一點差錯。然而，做出一個謹慎和滿意的選擇是不容易的。有時我們發現自己處於進退兩難的局面。

It would inevitably evoke a strong repercussion among people from different walks of life.
它不可避免會引起不同生活背景的人的強烈反響。

It has caused a heated public debate among us Chinese.
它在我們中國人中已經引起了一個熱烈的公眾討論。

It becomes so widespread that people can't help asking：＿＿＿＿＿.
它變得那麼普遍，人們不禁要問：＿＿＿＿＿。

In the process of modern urban development，we often find ourselves in a dilemma.
在現代城市化的發展中，我們經常發現我們處於進退兩難的境地。

In recent years，an increasing number of people have begun to challenge against the existing practice of ＿＿＿＿＿. They argue that ＿＿＿＿＿.
最近，越來越多的人開始懷疑現在的＿＿＿＿＿的做法。他們認為＿＿＿＿＿。

It is quite natural that people seldom reach a total agreement on such a long-running contro-versy.
人們對這樣一個長期有爭議的問題不能達成一致，這是很自然的。

Recently the phenomenon has aroused wide concern. Some people are in alarm that ＿＿＿＿＿.
最近，這個現象引起了廣泛的關注。一些人警覺＿＿＿＿＿。

The human race has entered a completely new stage in its history. With the increasingly rapid economic globalization and urbanization，more problems are brought to our attention.
人類已經進入了歷史上一個全新的時代。隨着經濟全球化和城市化的進程，更多的問題引起了我們的關注。

People rarely reach an absolute consensus on such a controversial issue.
人們很少會在這樣一個有爭議的問題上達成絕對的一致。

People from different background would put different interpretations on the same case.
不同背景的人們會對同一件事提出不同的理解。

While the rhythm of people's life is speeding up, a lot of changes have taken place in people's daily habit. _____ is mushrooming everywhere.
隨着人們生活節奏的加快，人們的日常習慣發生了很多變化。_____在各處快速增長。

With the development of society, _____.
隨着社會的發展，_____。

We have just crossed the threshold of the 21st century and the curtain of the new millennium is slowly rising. With the steady growth in the country's economy as well as the people's living standard, the rhythm of people's living is speeding up and a lot of changes have taken place in their daily life.
我們剛來到21世紀，新世紀的序幕緩緩升起。隨着國家經濟和人們生活水準的提高，人們的生活節奏加快，日常生活發生了很多變化。

_____ is rapidly gaining its popularity all over the country.
_____在全國很快地流行開來。

_____ plays such an important role that it undeniably becomes the biggest concern of the present-day world. There arouses a question: is it a blessing or a curse?
_____起到這樣重要的作用，它不可避免地受到當今世界最大的關注。一個問題出現了：它是一件好事還是一件壞事呢？

The discussion as to whether the _____ is a blessing or a curse arouses most people's interests.
關於_____是一件好事還是一件壞事的討論引起了大多數人的興趣。

_____ undoubtedly plays increasingly significant role in modern life.
_____毫無疑問在現代生活中起到日益重要的作用。

That is a very important thing for people nowadays.
這對現在的人是一個非常重要的事情。

The phenomenon has aroused wide concern among the people.
這個現象已經引起人們的廣泛關注。

Some people welcome it with applause. They claim it is a good idea.
一些人極力贊成這個觀點。他們認為這是一個好的想法。

Now we are entering a new era, full of new knowledge and innovative ideas.
現在我們正在進入一個充滿了新的知識和思想的全新時代。

Some people suggest that _____.
一些人說_____。

There is no denying that everything has more than one face and _____ is no exception.
不可否認任何事物都有多面性,_____也不例外。

Some people deem it is a dangerous signal and call for public awareness of the negative effects it has brought about. Some even put forward a proposal that _____.
一些人說它是一個危險的信號,要大眾警覺它所帶來的負面影響。一些人甚至提出一個建議_____。

With the steady growth in the country's economy as well as people's living standards, _____.
隨着國家經濟和人民生活水準的穩定增長, _____。

There arouses a very controversial issue as to whether we should _____.
我們是否應該_____是一個有爭議的問題。

Some people are of the opinion that _____.
一些人認爲 _____。

Many people claim that _____.
很多人聲稱_____。

On the other hand, some other people strongly despise the above attitude.
另一方面，一些人強烈反對上面的觀點。

There aroused a heated debate as to whether we should _____.
我們是否應該_____引起了熱烈的討論。

Some people contend that _____ has proved to bring many advantages.
一些人主張_____已經被證明帶來很多好處。

Those who argue for _____ say that _____.
那些贊成_____的人說_____。

People have different ideas about it.
人們對它有不同的看法。

Recently, the issue of _____ has been brought into public focus.
最近，_____這個問題引起了大家的關注。

There is a heated debate over _____.
關於_____有激烈的爭論。

There is no denying that there is some truth in the above point of view.
不可否認，上述觀點有一些道理。

With the development of the society, _____ is increasingly important.
隨着社會的發展，_____ 越來越重要。

This issue should be well taken into consideration.
這個問題應該仔細考慮。

To my mind, this is one of the side-effects brought about by this modern world.
在我看來，這是現代社會帶來的一個副作用。

_____, just like anything else in the world, have their bright side and dark side.
像世界上其他事物一樣，_____有積極的一面也有消極的一面。

_____ has caused significant changes in family life and education.
在家庭生活和教育上，_____ 已經引起了重大的變化。

Yet when it comes to _____, people from different backgrounds hold different attitudes.
然而，當說到_____，來自不同背景的人持有不同的觀點。

The opponents argue that _____.
反對者認為_____。

Undeniable, there are points in both sides of the argument.
不可否認，問題的雙方都有道理。

Some people advocate that _____.
一些人贊成_____。

They hold that _____.
他們認為_____。

The discussion about whether or not _____ is a very controversial one.
關於是否_____的討論是非常有爭議的。

People's views, however, are divergent on the matter in question. Some people are of the opinion that _____.

然而人們關於這個問題的觀點是不同的。一些人認爲_____。

It is often the case that _____.
通常情況是_____。

There is a long-running controversy as to whether _____, of which people have quite different opinions.
關於_____是一個長期的爭議，人們持有不同的觀點。

Now we are entering a brand new era full of opportunities and innovations, and great changes have taken place in people's attitude towards some traditional practices.
現在我們正在進入一個充滿機會和革新的新時代，人們對一些傳統做法的態度發生了很大的變化。

This issue is so controversial that people can hardly reach an absolute consensus.
這個問題是那麼有爭議，人們很難達成絕對的一致。

Recently there arises a heated debate over whether it is wise to _____. People's views, however, are divergent on the matter in question.
最近，關於_____是否是明智的引起了激烈的爭論。人們在這個問題上的觀點是不同的。

People, who advocate that _____, have their sound reasons.
贊成_____的人有他們的道理。

This has aroused a heated debate among the citizens. Some people welcome the program with applause; others strongly oppose it.
這在市民中引起了激烈的爭論。一些人熱烈贊成這個項目，另外一些人強烈反對它。

Recently, there is a heated debate on the issue of _____.
最近，關於_____有一場激烈的爭論。

Those who criticize it argue that _____.

批評它的人認為＿＿＿＿＿＿＿。

Of course, ＿＿＿＿＿＿＿ also have some negative effects.
當然,＿＿＿＿＿＿＿也有一些負面的影響。

Nothing in the world is perfect, so is the ＿＿＿＿＿＿＿.
世界上沒有完美的事物,＿＿＿＿＿＿＿也一樣。

The controversial issue is often brought into public focus. People from different backgrounds hold different attitudes towards the issue.
這個有爭議的問題經常引起大眾的關注。來自不同背景的人對這個問題有不同的態度。

Other people's opinion is just the opposite. They strongly believe that ＿＿＿＿＿＿＿.
其他人的觀點正好相反,他們認為＿＿＿＿＿＿＿。

This is a very controversial issue and people hold quite different opinions of it.
這是一個有爭議的問題,人們持有不同的觀點。

With the remarkable development of human civilization, people enjoy better living standards and the qualification of citizens has improved greatly.
隨着人類文明的發展,人們生活水準提高了,市民的素質也大大提高了。

Those people who approve of the practice of ＿＿＿＿＿＿＿ hold that ＿＿＿＿＿＿＿.
贊成＿＿＿＿＿＿＿的做法的人認為＿＿＿＿＿＿＿。

Towards the same issue, many others advocate that ＿＿＿＿＿＿＿.
對同樣問題,很多人認為＿＿＿＿＿＿＿。

When asked ＿＿＿＿＿＿＿, some people think ＿＿＿＿＿＿＿ is more desirable while some prefer
＿＿＿＿＿＿＿.
當被問到＿＿＿＿＿＿＿,一些人認為＿＿＿＿＿＿＿更好,然而一些人喜歡＿＿＿＿＿＿＿。

With the rapid development of science and technology, ＿＿＿＿＿＿＿.

隨着科學和技術的快速發展,＿＿＿＿。

Recently the issue of whether or not ＿＿＿＿ has been in the limelight and has aroused wide concern in the public.
最近,是否＿＿＿＿的問題已經成爲人們關注的中心並引起了大眾的廣泛關注。

Those who oppose it argue that ＿＿＿＿.
反對它的人認爲＿＿＿＿。

There is probably a little bit of truth in both arguments and the opinions stated by the both sides make sense and consequently, it is hard to choose the best of them.
兩個觀點都有正確性,都有道理,因此很難從中選出最好的。

It has long been regarded as a beneficial practice to ＿＿＿＿. However, in recent years, some people have been raising doubts about this practice.
＿＿＿＿一直被認爲是一個好做法。然而近年來,一些人一直在懷疑這種做法。

This question is a very controversial one.
這是一個很有爭議的問題。

We can't deny that we have benefited a lot from ＿＿＿＿.
我們不能否認我們已經從＿＿＿＿中受益很多。

Recently, this phenomenon has aroused wide concern.
最近,這個現象引起了廣泛的關注。

＿＿＿＿ have been very popular and hot in recent years.
近年來＿＿＿＿非常流行。

Just as the saying goes: "No garden is without weeds." ＿＿＿＿ has both advantages and disadvantages.
正如俗語所說,"沒有無雜草的花園。"＿＿＿＿有優點也有缺點。

Nowadays, _____.
近來,_____。

In recent years, there is a growing number of people who _____.
近年來,越來越多的人_____。

In these days, the issue of whether _____ has aroused people's discussion.
近來,關於是否_____的問題引起了人們的討論。

There are people on both sides of the argument who have very strong feelings.
爭論的雙方都有一些人深有感觸。

Just as the saying goes: "So many people, so many minds." It is quite understandable that views on this issue vary from person to person.
正如俗語所說,"有多少人,就有多少個觀點。"人們對這個問題的觀點是不同的,這是可以理解的。

Some people like _____.
一些人喜歡_____。

With the steady growth in the country's economy as well as the people's living standard, people attach more importance to _____.
隨着國家經濟和人民生活水準的提高,人們意識到_____的重要性。

Recently, this phenomenon has aroused wide concern and heated public debate has arisen.
最近,這個現象引起了廣泛的關注並激起了熱烈的討論。

There is a good side and a bad side to everything. It goes without saying that _____.
任何事物都有好的方面和壞的方面。不用說_____。

Inevitably, on the other side, there are others who strongly advocate the practice of
_____.

另一方面,不可避免的,其餘一些人強烈贊成_____的做法。

Recently, there is a heated debate as to whether _____.

最近,關於_____有一個熱烈的爭論。

On such a controversial issue, people seldom reach an absolute consensus.

在這樣一個有爭議的問題上,人們很少達成絕對的一致。

Those people who are strongly against the practice assert that _____.

那些強烈反對這個做法的人認爲_____。

On the contrary, the advocates also advance cogent arguments in defense of the system.

相對地,贊成者提出了有利的證據維護這個做法。

With the development of society, people's ideas about _____ have changed dramatically.

隨着社會的發展,人們關於_____的觀念發生了很大的變化。

This phenomenon also poses us a prominent social problem:_____.

這個現象給我們提出了一個嚴重的社會問題:_____。

To this issue, different people come up with various solutions.

關於這個問題,不同的人提出了不同的解決方案。

Recently, this phenomenon has been brought to public attention with people standing on both sides.

近來,這個現象引起了大眾的關注,人們持兩種對立觀點。

The issue whether it is good or not to _____ has aroused a heated discussion all over the

country.
關於_____是好是壞的問題在全國引起了熱烈的討論。

Those who have already benefited from practicing it sing high praise of it.
從這個做法中受益的人們強烈贊成它。

This is a controversial issue, which often arouses heated discussions among people.
這是一個有爭議的問題,經常引起人們的熱烈討論。

Of course, _____ also has advantages to some extent.
當然,_____在某種程度上也有優點。

They often fall into two big groups, one for it and the other against it.
他們通常分為兩組,一組贊成它,一組反對它。

Those people who strongly approve of _____ have cogent reasons for it.
強烈贊成_____的人有強而有力的理由。

Nowadays, more and more people agree that _____.
現在,越來越多的人同意_____。

Some people even put forward the idea that _____.
一些人甚至提出_____。

Nevertheless, people seldom reach an absolute consensus on such a controversial issue.
然而,在這樣一個有爭議的問題上,人們很少達成絕對的一致。

It is not easy to render the reasons for this complicated phenomenon which involves several factors.
替這個牽涉到幾個因素的複雜的現象做出解釋不是一件容易的事情。

There are some people who voice serious doubts about _____.
有一些人強烈懷疑_____。

When it comes to _____, most people believe that _____, but other people regard _____ as _____.

當涉及到_____，大多數人認爲_____，但其餘的人把_____當作_____。

When asked about _____, the vast majority of people say that _____, but other people view _____ as _____.

當被問到_____，大多數人認爲_____，但其餘的人把_____當作_____。

When faced with _____, quite a few people claim that _____, but other people think of _____ as _____.

當面臨_____，相當多的人認爲_____，但另一些人把_____當作_____。

When it comes to _____, the majority of people think that _____, but other people conceive _____ differently.

當涉及到_____，大多數的人認爲_____，但另一些人意見不同地認爲_____。

There is a general discussion today on the issue of _____. Those who criticize _____ argue that _____. They believe that _____.

關於_____有着廣泛的討論。批評_____的人認爲_____。他們認爲_____。

There is a public debate today about the problem of _____. Those who object to _____ argue that _____. They believe that _____.

今天，關於_____有公開的爭論。反對_____的人認爲_____。他們認爲_____。

There is a public controversy nowadays over the issue of _____. Those who criticize _____ argue that _____. They believe that _____, but people who favor _____, on the other hand, argue that _____.

今天，關於_____有着普遍的爭議。批評_____的人認爲_____。他們認爲_____。但是另一方面，贊成_____的人認爲_____。

There is much discussion nowadays as to the problem of _____. Those who object

_____ argue that _____. They believe that _____, but people who advocate _____, on the other hand, argue that _____.

今天, 關於_____有着很多的討論。反對_____的人認爲_____。他們認爲_____。但是另一方面, 贊成_____的人認爲_____。

Nowhere in the world has the issue of _____ been more popular than _____.

世界上沒有地方關於_____的爭論比_____更普遍。

The story is not rare. It has now drawn public attention to the problem of _____.

這個故事不罕見。它現在引起了大眾對_____問題的關注。

The incident is not isolated. It has now drawn much attention to the issue of _____.

這個事件不是孤立的。它現在引起了大眾對_____問題的關注。

The case is not rare. It has now drawn increasing attention to the plight of _____.

這個故事不罕見。它現在引起了大眾對_____的困境的注意。

Until recently, _____ was viewed as _____. But it is changing now.

直到最近, _____被認爲是_____。但是現在改變了。

Until recently, _____ was regarded as _____. But people are taking a fresh look at it.

直到最近, _____被認爲是_____。但是人們正在用新的眼光看待它。

Some people hold the opinion that _____ is superior to _____ in many ways. Others, however, think quite differently on the question of _____.

一些人認爲_____在很多方面都優於_____。然而, 其他人在_____的問題上的看法相當不同。

There will often spring up a heated discussion as to _____. A sizable percentage of the people like to _____.

關於_____通常激起激烈的討論。相當比例的人喜歡_____。

Some people say that _____, other people suggest that _____.

一些人認為_____,另外一些人認為_____。

Some say _____ , but others take a negative attitude.
一些人認為_____, 但其餘的人持相反的態度。

Many people have the idea that _____. However, many others disagree that _____.
Both sides of the question of whether _____ are supported by good reasons.
很多人認為_____。然而,其他人不同意_____。關於是否_____這個問題的兩
方面都被很好的理由所支持。

Many people would claim that _____.
很多人聲稱_____。

The dilemma is whether it is better to _____.
是不是_____更好是一個進退兩難的問題。

We always face the circumstances：_____ or _____. There are advantages and disadvantages on both sides.
我們總是面臨這樣的境況:_____或_____。兩方面都有優點和缺點。

To choose _____ or choose _____ is something of a dilemma to the public.
選擇_____還是_____對大眾來說是一個進退兩難的事。

Upon to the question that which is better, _____ or _____, people have different
opinions about it. _____ has its advantages, but at the mean time, it has many disadvantages, too.
關於_____或_____哪一個更好的問題,人們有不同的觀點。_____有它的好
處,但同時它也有很多不好之處。

In a modern society, people have the freedom to choose _____ or _____. Although
they normally coexist peacefully, they deserve some close examination.
在現代社會,人們有選擇_____或_____的自由。雖然它們一般會和平共存,但是
它們值得仔細的思考。

It is often difficult for people to decide whether to choose _____ or choose _____.
選擇_____還是選擇_____對人們來說通常是困難的。

One of the difficult questions that many people are today facing across the world is whether to choose _____ or choose _____. More and more, _____ is seen as the main method in _____ (doing something). Yet there are some people who cast serious doubts on _____.
今天很多人正面臨的一個難題,是選擇_____還是選擇_____。_____越來越被看作是_____的一個主要方法。但是也有一些人懷疑_____。

_____ and _____ are two totally different ideas that have caused heated debate over a long period of time.
_____和_____是兩個完全不同的觀點,在很長一段時間裏,引起了激烈的爭論。

Some people believe _____ because _____. These people point out the fact that _____. They also argue that _____. However, other people stand on a very different ground. They believe that _____. They firmly point out that _____.
一些人認爲_____因爲_____。這些人指出_____。他們還認爲_____。然而,另外一些人站在不同的立場上。他們認爲_____。他們堅定地指出_____。

Some people believe that _____. Other people take the view that _____.
一些人認爲_____。另外一些人認爲_____。

_____ has done many good things.
_____已經做了很多好事。

This problem is a much debated one in that it affects everybody in their daily lives.
這個問題是很有爭議的,在於它影響了每個人的日常生活。

People may prefer one to another, although some have no opinion about it.
雖然一些人沒有什麼觀點,人們可能會喜歡一個,不喜歡另一個。

The title statement is the focus in these days and any speech about it would surely strike the top lines of most newspapers.

這個問題是近來的焦點,任何關於它的說法都會引起大部分報紙頭版頭條的關注。

To agree or disagree with it is a matter of balancing between its pros and cons.

同意還是反對它,是一個在它的優點和缺點之間取得平衡的問題。

This controversy describes the dilemma faced by many people.

這個爭論反映了很多人面臨的難題。

When it comes to _____, most people tend to believe A. But others consider B.

當說起_____,大多數人相信 A,但是另一些人會考慮 B。

Some people hold the opinion that A is superior to B in many ways. Others, however, contradict A.

一些人認為 A 在很多方面比 B 有優勢,然而,另一些人反對 A。

Some people think A. Others, however, believe B. Which you prefer depends on your own experience, life style and emotional concern.

一些人認為 A,然而,另一些人相信 B。你更喜歡哪一個取決於你的經驗,生活方式和情感因素。

Everything in the world has its own two sides. Without exception, A has both advantages and disadvantages.

世界上每件事情都有兩個方面。毫無例外,A 既有優點也有缺點。

Whether A is a very controversial question. There are people on both sides of the argument who have very strong feelings.

是否選擇 A 是一個有爭議的問題。雙方的態度都很強硬。

There are different views concerning this topic.

關於這個話題,有不同的看法。

Both patterns of _____ present advantages and disadvantages.
_____ 兩種模式都有優點和缺點。

Nowhere in the world has the issue of A been so much debated like in our society.
一些地方擁護的觀點 A 在我們的社會則引起爭議。

Nowadays, some may hold the opinion that A. But others have a negative attitude.
現在,一些人持有 A 的觀點。但是另一些人則持有相反的態度。

2. 五段論式寫法－開頭段－說出自己的觀點

Personally, I would prefer _____ because I think _____ has more advantages.
我個人更喜歡_____,因為我認為_____有更多的優點。

According to my personality and fondness, I would prefer _____ rather than _____.
根據我的個性和喜好,我傾向於_____而不是_____。

In my point of view, I like _____ much more than _____.
在我看來,我喜歡_____比_____要多得多。

Considering the social atmosphere today, it is not a time to choose _____. It is high time
to choose _____.
考慮到今天的社會環境,選擇_____不是時候。是選擇_____的大好時機。

The advantages of _____ always outweigh the disadvantages.
_____的好處總是超過它的不好。

Although at first glance these arguments sound reasonable and appealing, they are not borne
out by a careful consideration.
雖然初看一眼,這些論據看起來是合理的和吸引人的,它們都經不起仔細的考慮。

But I would have to say that, if I were faced with the decision, I would probably follow the

contemporary trend and choose _____.
但是我要說，如果我面臨這個決定，我願意跟隨當代的潮流選擇_____。

Anyway, I agree with the idea of _____.
不管怎麼說，我同意_____。

In my opinion, the advantages of _____ are more than those of _____.
我認為，_____的好處比_____的多。

I do strongly support the idea that _____.
我強烈支持這個觀點_____。

But if I am concerned, I can only disagree with the title statement and the reasons are given below.
但是就我而言，我不同意上述觀點，原因如下。

Again, I would state my objection to this issue after analyzing the following three reasons.
在分析下面三個原因後，我願意提出對此觀點的反對。

But if one has considered the following perspectives, he could only agree with the title statement as I do.
但是如果一個人考慮到下面的論據，他只能像我一樣同意這個觀點。

I totally agree with this statement, and I will explain why this is the case.
我完全同意上述觀點，我願意解釋為什麼。

I completely disagree with this statement that choosing _____ has more advantages than choosing _____.
我完全不同意選擇_____比選擇_____有更多好處的觀點。

Personally, I side with the latter opinion.
我個人同意後一個觀點。

I side with the former view that _____.
我同意前一個觀點_____。

However, along with the positive effects, they have resulted in new social problems to solve.
但是,伴隨着積極的影響,它們還導致了新的需要解決的社會問題。

While _____ has many merits to our lives, their drawbacks should not be ignored.
_____在我們的生活中有許多優點,但是它的缺點也不容忽視。

The other side of the coin has voiced strong opinion saying that _____.
另一方面是_____。

Obviously, _____ is good in many aspects. However, the other side of the coin voices its strong opposition.
很明顯,_____在很多方面有優點,但另一方面也有很大的缺點。

Though _____(事物或觀點 A)has some advantages and it is popular to some extent, _____(事物或觀點 B)will continue to play a more important role and will not fade out in people's life.
雖然 A 有許多優點,並且在一定程度上很普遍,但 B 將繼續佔有更重要的地位,而不會從人們的生活中消失。

While it is indispensable to mankind, it also brings us serious problems to solve.
雖然它對於人類是不可或缺的,它也為我們帶來很多問題。

Personally, I am in favor of the former point of view.
我個人更喜歡前者的觀點。

Despite its merits, it also brings some problems to solve.
儘管它有很多優點,它也帶來一些問題要解決。

To my mind, the advantages far outweigh the drawbacks.

我認為,優點遠遠多於缺點。

As far as I am concerned, this proposal seems a bit absurd and ridiculous.
在我看來,這個提議有點荒謬可笑。

I can hardly share the proposal that _____.
我很難同意這個提議_____。

At first thought, the idea seems to be a sound and attractive one, but carefully weighing in the mind, I can hardly consent to this proposal because it is so inconceivable and impractical.
猛然一看,這個主意是合理和吸引人的,但仔細考慮之後,我不能同意這個提議,因為它難以實現也不切實際。

At first thought, this opinion seems to be sensible and sound. But at the second thought, I find that it is not often the case.
猛然一看,這個主意很合理,但再一想,我發現並不總是這樣。

For my part, I stand on the latter opinion that _____.
站在我的立場,我支持後一種意見_____。

Despite its good intentions, I think _____ doesn't make sense.
雖然有很好的意圖,我想_____沒有道理。

However, despite of the popularity of _____, its impacts on people are often negative.
但不管_____多麼流行,它對人的影響是負面的。

But after careful consideration of the above reasons, I, personally, stand on the side of the advocates.
經過仔細地考慮上面的原因之後,我個人站在擁護這個觀點的立場上。

Personally, I stand on the side of the latter.
我個人支持後一種觀點。

But I can hardly share this point of view.
但我很難支持這個觀點。

On the surface of it, this suggestion seems to be attractive, but thinking again, we would find it may lead to a set of problems.
表面上看，這個建議很吸引人，但是反覆想，我們發現它會帶來很多問題。

Superficially, all the above sounds reasonable and constructive. However, I strongly disagree with it.
表面上看，以上觀點很合理，很有建設性。但是，我反對它。

Though the opinion stated above seems to have some merits, it overlooks some deeper and more basic factors.
雖然以上的意見有一些優點，但它沒有注意到較深一層的和較基本的因素。

However, just as a coin has its own two sides, _____ has its demerits.
但是，正如每枚硬幣都有兩面，_____也有它的缺點。

From the reasons presented above, I think the pros outweigh the cons.
從上面列出的原因，我認為正面超過了反面。

As far as I am concerned, I am inclined to be on the side of the latter view.
我的觀點更傾向於後者。

Personally, I side with the latter opinion.
我個人意見更傾向於後一種意見。

Superficially, the above sounds reasonable and interest-earning. But when carefully weighing in the mind, we find that it goes against the fact.
表面上看，上述觀點很合理，但經過仔細考慮之後，我們發現它違背事實。

In spite of the disadvantages of the system, we can not pay no heed to the fact that it brings

us more advantages.
不管這個系統多麼不好，我們不能忽略這樣的事實，它為我們帶來很多好處。

After a thorough consideration, for my part, I am in favor of the latter view that _____.
經過徹底的考慮，我贊成後一種觀點_____。

Despite the advantages advocated by some people, I am totally against this view.
儘管這些優勢被許多人擁護，我完全反對這個觀點。

If asked to make a decision, I would prefer _____.
如果被要求做出決定，我更喜歡_____。

However, in my opinion, I prefer the idea that _____.
但是，我的觀點是_____。

But its bright side should not keep us from following closely its dark side.
但它的好處不能掩蓋它如下的缺點。

Taking into consideration both sides of the issue, I tend to favor the latter view.
考慮到雙方面的論點，我傾向於後者。

Despite the advantages _____ has, it has its disadvantages.
儘管_____有優點，也存在許多不足。

From my part, I completely agree with the latter.
從我這方面，我完全同意後者。

Some people think _____. My opinion is identical with theirs.
一些人認為_____，我的觀點和他們的觀點一樣。

However, if I have to choose one of these two, I am in favor of the latter opinion that _____.
但是，如果我必須從兩者中選擇其一，我傾向於後者_____。

As far as I am concerned, it is advisable _____.
我認爲更明智的是_____。

But I think it is unadvisable to _____.
但我認爲_____是不明智的。

Personally, I hold that _____.
我個人認爲_____。

With views of both sides considered, I think that _____.
兩方面都考慮過之後, 我認爲_____。

When considering opinions of both sides, I am inclined to take sides with the latter.
考慮過兩方面的觀點後, 我傾向於後一種觀點。

But when we consider these two sides more carefully, we can see that the harm outweighs the merits.
但當我們仔細考慮過兩方面的因素之後, 我們能夠看到弊大於利。

Sound and attractive as their arguments may seem, they can't bear closer analysis.
儘管他們的論點是如此的合理和吸引人, 但卻禁不起進一步的分析。

Carefully weighing in the mind, we easily find how fallacious they are.
仔細考慮之後, 我們極易發現它們是不合理的。

At the first thought, it may seem to be an attractive idea, but it doesn't bear closer analysis.
一開始好像是一個有吸引力的主意, 但它禁不起更深入的分析。

A close scrutiny of these arguments would reveal how fallacious it is.
對這些爭論的詳細的研究揭示出它是多麼的荒謬。

There is some element of truth in these arguments, but they overlook a deeper and most basic

factor that _____.
這些爭論有一些正確之處,但它們卻忽略了更深一層和更基本的因素_____。

However, logical and valid the arguments may be, they only skim the surface of the issue.
不管這些爭論顯得多麼有理和有效,它們只是看到了問題的表面。

If it is up to me to make a choice between _____ and _____, I would rather choose _____ over _____.
若要我在_____和_____之間做出選擇,我寧願選擇_____。

Generally, I prefer to _____.
通常,我更喜歡_____。

Yet I am, and probably always will be, a deep lover of _____.
我是_____的深愛者。

If I were forced to agree with one of the two methods, my choice would be for _____.
如果硬要我選擇兩種方式之一,我的選擇是_____。

Yet I am one of many people who feel that _____.
我是支持_____的人之一。

I support the second system.
我支持第二種觀點。

In spite of all the claims of _____, I doubt the value of _____.
不管_____的所有聲明,我懷疑_____的價值。

However, although many people _____, I feel that it is better to _____.
但是,雖然很多人_____,我感覺_____更好。

I would have to say that, if I were faced with the decision, I would probably follow _____.

我不得不說,如果我面對這個決定,我將按照_____來做。

I believe that the title statement is valid.
我認為上面的觀點是正確的。

I find the statement of _____ to be too narrow.
我發現對_____的論述範圍太窄了。

Deep down, I disagree with the above statement, and support the superiority of _____.
深入地說,我不同意上面的觀點,而支持_____。

Although I appreciate that _____, I cannot agree with the title agreement.
雖然我欣賞_____,我不同意這個協議。

At the risk of sounding too direct, I prefer to _____.
恕我直言,我更傾向於_____。

Now, it is commonly believed that _____, such people think _____, but I wonder whether _____.
現在,大多數人相信_____,這些人認為_____,但我懷疑是否_____。

Now, it is widely held that _____, such people think _____, but I wonder whether _____.
現在,大多數人相信_____,這些人認為_____,但我懷疑是否_____。

Now, it is generally accepted that _____, such people believe _____. But I wonder _____.
現在,被廣泛接受的觀點是_____,這些人認為_____,但我懷疑_____。

Now, it is increasingly acknowledged that _____, such people think _____, but I doubt whether _____.
現在,被廣泛接受的觀點是_____,這些人認為_____,但我懷疑_____。

No idea is more untrue now than the one that _____.
沒有一個觀點比這個觀點更不可信_____。

No opinion is so foolish now as the one that _____.
沒有一個觀點比這個觀點更愚蠢_____。

No view is more dangerous now than the one that _____.
沒有一個觀點比這個觀點更危險_____。

No belief is so undesirable as the one that _____.
沒有一個觀點比這個觀點更令人不快_____。

No issue is more important now than the one that _____.
沒有一個觀點比這個觀點更重要_____。

I feel such an attitude is negative, and that it can bring only further misfortune.
我感覺這個態度是消極的,只會帶來更大的不幸。

My opinion is identical with theirs.
我的意見和他們的一樣。

I fully agree with the statement that _____.
我完全同意這個論點_____。

In my opinion, it is more advisable to _____ than to _____.
我的意見是,_____比_____更明智。

To be frank, I cannot agree with their opinion for the reasons below.
坦率地說,我不能同意這個意見,原因如下。

Personally, I prefer _____, I think _____ has more advantages.
我個人更傾向於_____,我認為_____有更多的優點。

Personally, I am standing on the side of _____.
我個人站在_____一邊。

Despite the fact that most people like _____, I would like to choose to _____.
儘管許多人都喜歡_____，我個人卻選擇_____。

Although many people believe that _____, I doubt whether the argument bears much analysis.
雖然許多人相信_____，我懷疑這個論點是否經得起分析。

In the discussion, many people suggest that _____, but I argue that _____.
在討論中，許多人建議_____，但我認為_____。

But whatever the advantages of A, I like B.
但不論 A 有多少優點，我喜歡 B。

After pondering this question on many occasions, I have finally reached the conclusion that _____ is something I truly want to do and is worthwhile.
反覆考慮這個問題之後，我最後得出一個結論，_____，那是我真正想做的，而且它是值得做的。

But I cannot share this point of view for several reasons.
但因為很多原因我不同意這個觀點。

In my opinion, I argue that _____.
就我的意見，我認為_____。

Nonetheless, pound for pound, I reckon that _____ is more advantageous.
然而，權衡再權衡，我認為_____有更多優點。

My view is that _____.
我的看法是_____。

When faced with _____ , we find comfort in the idea that _____ .
當面對_____ ,我擁護_____的觀點。

There is no evidence to suggest that _____ .
沒有論據支持_____。

From my point of view, it is more advisable to choose A than to choose B.
依我的看法,選擇 A 而不是選擇 B。

Despite the fact that most people prefer A, I would like to choose B because the following reasons.
儘管許多人更喜歡 A,我還是選擇 B,因爲_____。

Many people advocate that _____ . They claim that _____ . My opinion is the same as theirs in the following reasons.
許多人提議_____。他們主張_____。我的看法和這些人一樣,是因爲以下的原因。

Thinking logically, I can only say that the title statement is valid.
從邏輯上考慮,我只能說這個觀點是正確的。

I fully support the statement above.
我完全支持以上觀點。

In my opinion, A is as important as, if not more than, B.
我的觀點是 A 比 B 更重要。

From my point of view, I vote for the latter one.
從我的觀點看,我選擇後者。

As far as I am concerned, its advantages outweigh its disadvantages.
我的觀點是,它的優點多於缺點。

From my point of view, it is more advisable/sagacious to choose A rather than B.

從我的觀點出發,選擇 A 比選擇 B 更有遠見。

In my part, I prefer A rather than B as my inclination.
我的觀點是,我更傾向於 A 而不是 B。

At the risk of addressing the issue too directly, the advantage of A always outweighs that of B.
坦率地說,A 的優點比 B 多。

When faced with the decision of A or B, quite a few would claim that _____, but others, in contrast, deem A/B as the premier choice and that is also my point.
當面對 A 或 B 的決定,大多數人認爲_____,但另一些人卻相反,把 A/B 作爲首選,這也是我的觀點。

When it comes to _____, the majority would support A. Others, however, like me, regard B as the propensity.
當有_____原因時,大多數人支持 A。但是另一些人,像我,更傾向於 B。

While the majority may stick to the idea of A, I would like to prefer B.
當大多數人堅持觀點 A 時,我更傾向於 B。

In my part, I would like to vote for A/B.
以我的觀點,我選擇 A/B。

As far as I am concerned, I have a preference for A over B.
就我來說,我更偏愛 A 而不是 B。

Certainly, I am aware of that both methods have potential pitfalls, nevertheless, from my point of view, I vote for A.
確實,我意識到兩種方式都有潛在的缺陷,不過,從我的觀點出發,我選擇 A。

Despite the fact that A has a unique advantage over B, it cannot compete with B in many cases.

儘管 A 比 B 多一個優點,但在很多方面卻不能和 B 相比。

As for me, A is preferable in many ways.
對我來說,A 在很多方面有優勢。

Despite the fact that A enjoys considerable advantage of _____, it cannot be compared with B in several main aspects.
儘管 A 在_____方面有相當大的優勢,但在很多主要的方面卻不能和 B 相比。

Although A possesses substantial advantage over B, it cannot be compared with B in more concrete advantages.
雖然 A 擁有的潛在優勢超過 B,但在很多具體的優勢上卻無法和 B 相比。

The advantages claimed for A over B are now being debated. Nonetheless, measure for measure, I confess that A/B is more advantageous.
A 比 B 優點更多的結論是有爭議的。但是,衡量再衡量,我確信,A/B 有更多的優勢。

The advantages of A carry more weight than those of B.
A 的優點比 B 多。

No doubt, I prefer A, since there are too many benefits that outnumber its disadvantages. But B, on the other hand, has advantages no more than its disadvantages.
毫無疑問,我選擇 A,因為它的優點超過它的不足。而 B 則弊大於利。

To choose A or choose B is something of a dilemma to the public because they sometimes are confused by the seemingly good qualities of A, and neglect the genuinely good aspects of B.
大眾有時候在 A 或 B 的選擇上感到困難,因為他們有時被 A 表面上的優點所蒙蔽,而忽視了 B 的真實優點。

After pondering this question on many occasions, I finally reached the opinion that A is something worthy to do and I cannot skip it.
反覆考慮這個問題後,我最後得到這樣的結論,A 值得去做,我不會放棄它。

As far as I am concerned, I agree that _____.
就我來說,我同意_____。

Despite the fact that the majority hold the opinion that A, I doubt whether the argument can bear much analysis.
儘管許多人擁護 A,我懷疑這個論點是否經得起分析。

Although it is an admirable idea, A is not always a realistic option.
雖然這是一個好主意,A 卻不是一個實際的選擇。

Contrary to generally accepted ideas, I would like to prove that _____.
與被普遍接受的觀點相反,我將證明_____。

However, I do not think that this view can hold water.
但是,我不認為這個觀點有價值。

Some people argue as if it is a general truth that A. But to be frank, I cannot agree with them for the following reasons.
一些人議論 A,好像它是一個普遍的事實。但坦率地說,以下原因使我不能同意它。

On the surface of it, this may seem to be a good solution, but if thinking again, we would point out some drawbacks.
表面上看,這是一個好的解決方案,但再一想,我們能指出一些缺點。

When it comes to, we find comfort in the idea that _____.
當這個觀點出現時,我們發現它有一些讓人欣慰的地方_____。

Until recently, _____ was viewed as the prime argument. But people are taking a fresh look at it.
直到最近,_____作為最初的看法,但人們有了全新的認識。

At first thought, it may seem to be an attractive idea, but it does not bear closer analysis when we find _____.

表面上看，這是一個很吸引人的觀點，但它經不起仔細分析，當我們發現＿＿＿＿＿＿＿。

Superficially, it seems to be a sound solution, but when carefully weighing in the mind, we find that ＿＿＿＿＿＿.
表面上看，它似乎是一個徹底的解決方案，但當仔細考慮之後，我們發現＿＿＿＿＿＿＿。

A scrutiny of these arguments would reveal how fallacious they are.
詳細審查這些論點可以揭開它們的不足。

To suggest that ＿＿＿＿＿＿ is the most obvious kind of nonsense.
＿＿＿＿＿＿的建議顯而易見是胡說。

A close inspection of these arguments would reveal how flimsy they are.
仔細審查這些觀點將會看出它們是多麼脆弱。

3. 五段論式寫法 – 開頭段 – 引起下文

There are many instances supporting my view.
有很多實例支持我的觀點。

There are no less than three advantages in ＿＿＿＿＿＿ as rendered below.
＿＿＿＿＿＿有不少於三個優點，如下所述。

There are many instances in our daily life that can verify this.
在我們的日常生活中，有很多實例可以證明它。

I support this with the following reasons.
我支持它的原因如下。

And I would like to present two explanations to confirm you that I am right.
我願意說出兩個原因來證明我是對的。

There are three advantages of _____ as follows.
_____有三個好處如下。

A number of causes account for my point.
大量的原因說明了我的觀點。

The following reasons should be taken into consideration.
下列原因必須被考慮。

The reasons are chiefly as follows.
原因主要有以下方面。

I can see that many of the advantages of _____ seem obvious.
我能看到許多似乎顯而易見的優點_____。

I believe that I have found some solid advantages.
我相信我已經找到了一些可靠的優點。

There are numerous reasons why I advocate the argument of _____, and I would explore a few of the most important ones here.
為什麼我擁護_____的觀點有很多原因，我將提出幾個最重要的。

Among countless factors which influence my decision, there are two/three conspicuous aspects.
在無數個影響我的決定的因素中，有兩三個顯而易見的因素。

My arguments for this point are listed as follows.
關於這個觀點，我的論述如下。

The reasons are presented below.
原因如下。

This view is based on the propensity of following points.

這個看法基於以下幾點傾向。

There are three premier causes as follows.
三個主要原因如下。

This quite different view is based on the propensity of following points.
不同的看法基於以下幾點原因。

To assume that _____ is destined to miss the following points.
假設_____注定會忽略以下幾點原因。

But the problems I have with the above statement are as follows.
上面觀點的問題如下。

4. 五段論式寫法－理由段－第一個理由段主題句前的連接詞

　　請注意，有些也能當作第二個及第三個理由段主題句前的連接詞。
The main reason is that _____.
主要原因是_____。

One very strong argument for _____ is that _____.
_____的一個非常有力的理由是_____。

The reasons are quite clear. Above all, _____.
原因非常清楚。首先，_____。

The most important benefit of _____ is that _____.
_____的最重要的好處是_____。

The main reason why I prefer _____ is that _____.
我傾向_____的主要原因是_____。

The first reason can be seen by every person.
第一個原因每個人都能看到。

Those who object to this idea forget a universal truth.
反對這個觀點的人忘記了一個普遍的事實。

First, we can observe easily that _____.
首先，我們能容易地看到_____。

I disagree with the title statement because I consider _____.
我不同意這個觀點因為我認為_____。

One of the notorious disadvantages of _____ is that _____.
_____的一個惡名昭彰的缺點是_____。

The reason why I disagree _____ is that _____.
我不同意_____的原因是_____。

The first and most important reason is that _____.
第一個也是最重要的原因是_____。

It is an obvious fact that _____.
_____是一個顯然的事實。

It is very clear that _____.
_____是很清楚的。

I agree with the above statement because I believe that _____.
我同意上面的論述，因為我相信_____。

On a substantive level, they are preferable because _____.
實質上它們更可取，因為_____。

_____ is preferable to _____ because _____.
_____比_____更好,因為_____。

I can see that one of the advantages of _____ seems obvious.
我能看到_____的一個優勢顯而易見。

One of the reasons that are given for _____ is that _____.
_____的一個原因是_____。

Perhaps this is because of the simple fact that _____.
也許這是因為簡單的事實_____。

One of the strengths of _____ is that _____.
_____的一個優點是_____。

We should not lose sight of the fact that _____.
我們不能忽視這樣的事實_____。

The problem I have with the above statement is that _____.
上述觀點的問題是_____。

One of the most important things about _____ is that _____.
關於_____的一個重點是_____。

_____ has the benefit/advantage that _____.
_____有這樣的優點_____。

Perhaps most telling is _____.
也許很明顯的是_____。

One of the primary causes is that _____.
一個主要的原因是_____。

I agree with the statement without reservation since _____.
我毫無保留地同意這個觀點，因為_____。

Beyond enormous obvious reasons, there lies a more in-depth cause.
除了許多顯而易見的原因，還有一個深層的原因。

No one could neglect/deny the fact that _____.
沒有人能忽視這個事實_____。

The above point is certainly true if _____ is considered.
如果_____被考慮進去，上述觀點一定正確。

At the risk of sounding too simplistic, it seems to me that the main propositions can be summarized in one saying.
也許聽起來太簡單，對我來說，主要原因可以被歸結為一句話。

One of the most attractive points is that _____.
最吸引人的一個觀點是_____。

Certainly no other reason in my decision is more crucial than the one as follow.
我的決定中沒有其他原因比這一個更關鍵。

In term of substantive level, the reason mentioned below seems to be advisable and deserve
more consideration.
實質上，下面的原因是明智的，值得仔細考慮。

The main reason for my propensity is that _____.
我這種傾向的主要原因是_____。

A particularly notable case of this matter is _____.
特別值得注意的是_____。

The undeniable deficiency in this remark is that it is negligent of the bare fact that _____.

這個論述中有很多不能否認的事實就是它忽視了＿＿＿＿＿的事實。

The main problem with this argument is that it is ignorant of the basic fact that ＿＿＿＿＿.
這個論點的主要問題是它忽視了＿＿＿＿＿的基本事實。

There is some element of truth in the consideration of ＿＿＿＿＿, but a deeper and more basic fact that ＿＿＿＿＿ is ignored in this statement.
考慮＿＿＿＿＿有很多事實因素,但是,一個較深層的和較基本的事實＿＿＿＿＿在論述中被忽略了。

We may look into every possible reason, however, foremost reason for ＿＿＿＿＿ is ＿＿＿＿＿.
我們也許能看到每一個可能的原因,然而,＿＿＿＿＿的首要原因是＿＿＿＿＿。

The reasons for ＿＿＿＿＿ varied, nevertheless, they lie in the fact that ＿＿＿＿＿.
＿＿＿＿＿的原因是各式各樣的,不過,它們基於這樣的事實＿＿＿＿＿。

5. 五段論式寫法－理由段－第二個理由段主題句前的連接詞

It might also be noted that ＿＿＿＿＿.
也可以注意到＿＿＿＿＿。

But there is a further more subtle point we must consider ＿＿＿＿＿.
但是有一個非常微妙的觀點我們必須考慮＿＿＿＿＿。

Another reason why I agree with the above statement is that I believe ＿＿＿＿＿.
另一個為什麼我同意上面觀點的原因是＿＿＿＿＿。

What is also worth noticing is that ＿＿＿＿＿.
另一個值得注意的是＿＿＿＿＿。

Another reason why I prefer the argument is that ＿＿＿＿＿.

我擁護這個觀點的另一個原因是＿＿＿＿＿。

There is another factor that deserves some words here.
另一個原因值得說一說。

A more essential factor why I advocate the argument is that ＿＿＿＿＿.
我為什麼同意這個觀點的一個更根本原因是＿＿＿＿＿。

Also, it is arbitrary to judge ＿＿＿＿＿ according only to the excuse I mentioned in the above paragraph.
僅憑我上面闡述的理由就判斷＿＿＿＿＿非常武斷。

To make a moral sense, I think that another reason why I prefer the argument of ＿＿＿＿＿ is that ＿＿＿＿＿.
出自道義心，我認為另一個原因為什麼我擁護＿＿＿＿＿是＿＿＿＿＿。

Another reason why I advocate the attitude of ＿＿＿＿＿ is that ＿＿＿＿＿.
我贊成＿＿＿＿＿的另一個原因是＿＿＿＿＿。

Another reason for me to choose ＿＿＿＿＿ is that ＿＿＿＿＿.
我選擇＿＿＿＿＿的另一個原因是＿＿＿＿＿。

A further reason why I prefer ＿＿＿＿＿ is that ＿＿＿＿＿.
我傾向＿＿＿＿＿的一個更進一步的原因是＿＿＿＿＿。

Another benefit of ＿＿＿＿＿, which ＿＿＿＿＿ almost cannot achieve, is that ＿＿＿＿＿.
＿＿＿＿＿的另一個好處，也是＿＿＿＿＿幾乎不能達到的是＿＿＿＿＿。

A more personal reason why I like ＿＿＿＿＿ is that ＿＿＿＿＿.
我喜歡＿＿＿＿＿的另一個個人的原因是＿＿＿＿＿。

＿＿＿＿＿ is superior in another way, that is ＿＿＿＿＿.
＿＿＿＿＿在另一方面佔優勢，那就是＿＿＿＿＿。

The second reason for my propensity for _____ is that _____.
我傾向於_____的第二個原因是_____。

There is another obvious advantage for _____, that is _____.
_____有另一個顯著的優點,是_____。

In addition, _____.
而且,_____。

_____ has also had a bad effect on _____.
_____在_____上也有一個不好的影響。

Another innate characteristic of _____ is _____.
_____的另一個本質特徵是_____。

It even might be said that _____.
甚至可以說_____。

Another factor shows that _____.
另一個因素說明_____。

Moving on to wider themes, _____.
讓我們轉移到更寬的主題,_____。

The second thing that must be taken into consideration is that _____.
必須考慮的第二個因素是_____。

Perhaps another reason why _____ is superior to _____ lies in the fact that _____.
也許為什麼_____優於_____是基於_____的事實。

Another factor that should be taken into consideration is _____.
另一個應該考慮的因素是_____。

Likewise, common sense tells us that _____.
同樣地,常識告訴我們_____。

From a _____(如:personal and psychological) perspective, I also prefer to _____
because_____.
從一個_____(例如:個人的和心理上的)角度,我更傾向於_____因為_____。

Another reason why I would usually prefer to _____ is that _____.
我更傾向於_____的另一個原因是_____。

I have found a solid advantage.
我發現了一個具體的好處。

There is also a further more subtle point to consider.
需要考慮一個更敏感的要點。

What is interesting is that _____.
有趣的是_____。

If we turn our attention to _____, we see that _____.
如果把我們的注意力轉到_____,我們可以看到_____。

_____ also deserve a mention here.
_____也值得在這裏提到。

A more personal reason why I feel that _____ is that _____.
一個個人原因為什麼我認為_____是因為_____。

At an individual level, I feel that _____.
站在個人立場,我認為_____。

Another reason why I dispute the above statement is that I believe that _____.

我懷疑上面的觀點的另一個原因是,我相信_____。

6. 五段論式寫法－理由段－第三個理由段主題句前的連接詞

One very strong argument for _____ is that _____.
_____的一個非常有力的理由是_____。

The third and very important reason is that _____.
第三個也是非常重要的原因是_____。

Those who object to this idea forget a universal truth.
反對這個觀點的人忘記了一個普遍事實。

Finally, the incomparable advantage of _____ is that _____.
最後,_____的不能比擬的好處是_____。

The third, not the last is that _____.
第三,但不是最後,是_____。

In addition, _____.
而且,_____。

The last factor to be taken seriously is _____.
最後一個需要認眞考慮的因素是_____。

Similarly, these reasons are also usable when we consider that _____.
同樣地,當我們考慮_____時,這些原因同樣有用。

The argument I support in the first paragraph is also in a position of advantage because _____.
在第一段中我支持的觀點有許多優點,因爲_____。

What is more, _____.
而且_____。

Moreover, _____.
而且_____。

In addition, _____.
此外, _____。

Last but not least, _____.
最後但不是不重要, _____。

Furthermore, _____.
此外, _____。

7. 五段論式寫法－理由段－舉例子：

For example, _____.
例如, _____。

For instance, _____.
例如, _____。

It can be given a concrete example.
可以給一個具體事例。

Take _____ for an example, it is a very obvious case.
以_____為例, 這是一個非常明顯的例子。

There is one impressive example I want to mention here.
我想給大家一個印象深刻的例子。

Let's see an example.
讓我們看一個例子。

To give some concrete examples, _____.
給一些具體事例,_____。

It is best illustrated if given the following example.
如果提出以下事例可以更好的闡明。

We could take _____ as an example, _____.
我們可以把_____作為一個例子,_____。

_____ is an outstanding example.
_____是一個顯著的例子。

Let me provide an example.
讓我提供一個事例。

An example of this fact is _____.
這個論據的一個事例是_____。

Perhaps the most important example of _____ is that _____.
也許_____最重要的例子是_____。

As I remember, /I now still remember that / I will never forget _____.
根據我的記憶,/我現在仍然記得/我永遠也不會忘記_____。

To illustrate this, there is an example that is very persuasive.
為說明這個觀點,有一個例子非常具有說服力。

An instance that accompanies this reason is that _____.
一個伴隨這個原因的例子是_____。

An example can give the details of this argument, _____.
一個例子能提供這個論點的詳細資料, _____。

It is a forceful example to demonstrate the importance of _____.
一個有力的例子能說明_____的重要性。

History presented many examples of _____.
歷史呈現許多_____方面的事例。

The modern example of this is _____.
現代事例是_____。

In order to see this point clearly, let us see an example: _____.
為把這點看得更清楚, 讓我們看一個事例: _____。

I can give you another illustration about it, _____.
我可以提供你另一個關於它的事例, _____。

In fact, a good example of this is that _____.
事實上, 關於它的一個好的事例是_____。

Let me give you an example, _____.
讓我舉一個例子, _____。

An example to show this can be found in the story that _____.
一個例子可以從_____的故事中找到。

I can quote a common example, _____.
引用一個一般事例, _____。

I have a bad experience with it.
關於它我有一段不好的經歷。

8. 五段論式寫法－讓步段

As a matter of fact, there are also some disadvantages in _____.
事實上,_____也有一些缺點。

However, we also cannot deny that _____.
然而,我們也不能否認_____。

It cannot denied that there still exist some disadvantages of _____.
不能否認,_____存在着許多的不足。

Of course, this will produce some negative effects on _____.
當然,這會產生許多在_____方面的負面影響。

Of course, I am not denying the merits of _____.
當然,我不否認_____的優點。

_____, by contrast, is blessed with advantages.
對比之下,_____有優勢。

On the other hand, it cannot be denied that _____.
另一方面,不能否認_____。

However, we must say _____.
但是,我們必須說_____。

Of course, it is true that the argument I disagree hold a little bit of water.
當然,我不同意的觀點也有一些優點。

However, we must admit that _____.
但是,我們必須承認_____。

9. 五段論式寫法 - 結尾段：

But if all these factors are contemplated, the advantages of _____ carry more weight than those of _____.
但是如果仔細考慮所有這些因素，_____的好處超過_____的好處。

From what has been discussed above, we may finally draw the conclusion that _____.
從上面所討論的，我們會最後得到結論_____。

So, as I see it, _____.
所以，正像我所看到的，_____。

So from what has been discussed, one can reach only this conclusion：_____.
所以，從上面所討論的，一個人只能得到這個結論：_____ 。

After understanding the reasoning above, it's quite safe now to say：to choose _____ is a wise action.
在了解上面的原因後，現在可以很安全地說：選擇_____是明智的。

Now, after close examination, it is not difficult to draw the conclusion that only choosing _____ is sensible.
現在，在仔細考慮後，不難得到這個結論：只有選擇_____是明智的。

So, in comparison with _____, _____ is surely a clever choice.
所以，和_____相比，_____確實是一個明智的選擇。

So if we take a careful consideration, it is not difficult to get the conclusion：_____.
所以，如果我們認真地考慮一下，不難得到結論：_____。

It is obvious for us to conclude that _____.
對我們來說，得到_____是顯然的。

If considered seriously, _____.
如果認眞考慮,_____。

So, based on the above discussion, I agree with the opinion that _____.
所以,基於上述討論,我同意_____。

Once you have known all of these, you must agree with me that _____ is right.
如果你知道所有這些,你一定會同意_____是對的。

There is no question in my mind that _____.
_____在我看來是沒有問題的。

In general / On the whole / Generally, _____.
總而言之,_____。

All in all, _____.
總而言之,_____。

In brief / In summary / In sum / In conclusion / In short / In a word , _____.
總而言之/綜上所述,_____。

To sum up / To conclude / To summarize, _____.
總而言之/綜上所述,_____。

But all in all, I would say the advantages outweigh the disadvantages. With the advance of society, if we encourage the merits and eliminate the drawbacks, all people will enjoy a better life.
但總而言之,優點多於缺點。隨着社會的進步,如果我們發揚優點,排除缺點,所有人都會過更好的生活。

There is probably a little bit of truth in both arguments. For my part, I completely agree with the latter.
兩種觀點都有一點道理。站在我的立場,我完全同意後者。

Based on the above discussion and analysis, we can see that _____.
基於上述討論和分析,我們可以看到_____。

What we must do is to encourage the strength and diminish the weaknesses to the least extent.
我們必須做的是發揚長處,最大限度地排除不足。

In conclusion, although _____ has its negative effects, it can to a great extent bring us more advantages.
總之,雖然_____有它的負面影響,但它會在最大限度內為我們帶來很多好處。

From what has been discussed above, I think the correct attitude is that _____.
透過上面的討論,我想正確的態度是_____。

In a word, I can hardly share the proposal that _____.
一句話,我不能同意_____的提議。

From what has been stated above, I suppose that _____.
透過上面的陳述,我支持_____。

I firmly commit to the notion that _____.
我的觀點很鮮明,是_____。

To sum up, I feel that, overall, there are strong positive effects of _____.
總之,我認為_____有很大的正面影響。

All the above suggest that we can come to the simple conclusion that _____.
所有上面的建議使我們得到一個簡單的結論_____。

We may discover that _____.
我們可以發現_____。

128

Taking into all these factors, we may reasonably come to the conclusion that _____.
考慮到所有的因素,我們可以合理地得到結論_____。

From what has been discussed above, we may safely arrive at the conclusion that _____.
從上面的討論中,我們很自然地得到結論_____。

Therefore, it is not difficult for us to come to the conclusion that _____.
因此,我們不難得到結論_____。

All in all, the advantages of _____ outweigh the disadvantages.
總之,_____的優點多於它的缺點。

From what has been mentioned above, we can clearly see that _____.
從上面我們所談到的,我們能很清楚地看到_____。

Consequently, I strongly commit to the notion that _____.
因此,我的主張是_____。

All in all, I should say that _____.
總之,我必須說_____。

From what has been discussed above, we can see _____ does more harm than good to us. Therefore, I strongly approve of the motion that _____.
從上面我們所討論的,我們可以看出_____弊大於利。因此,我的主張是_____。

From the above comparison and contrast, anyone can safely conclude that _____.
從以上的比較,任何人都可以得到這樣的結論_____。

When the advantages and disadvantages are carefully compared, the most striking conclusion is self-evident.
當仔細比較了長處和短處之後,最有力的結論就不言而喻了。

Judging from all evidence offered, we may reasonably come to /draw the conclusion that

_____.
從所提供的證據來看,我們可以得到以下結論_____。

For the reasons presented above, I strongly commit to the notion that _____.
根據以上所述的理由,我堅決同意這個觀點_____。

All the evidence justifies an unshakable view that _____.
所有的證據證明了一個不可動搖的觀點_____。

All the evidence supports an unmistakable conclusion that _____.
所有的證據證明了一個千眞萬確的結論_____。

In a word, _____.
換句話說,_____。

In short, _____.
簡言之,_____。

Generally, _____.
通常,_____。

On the whole, _____.
總體上,_____。

In brief, _____.
總之,_____。

In conclusion, _____.
結論是,_____。

Taking into account of all these factors, we may reach the conclusion that _____.
考慮到所有這些因素,我們能得到這樣的結論_____。

All reliable evidences point to one saying, that is _____.
所有可靠的論點用一句話說出,那就是_____。

For the reasons presented above, I strongly commit to the notion that _____.
由於上面的原因,我認為_____。

Given the factors I have just outlined, I can only say that _____.
透過我提出的因素,我只能說_____。

It is sagacious to support the statement that _____.
支持這個觀點_____是明智的。

It is safely to draw the conclusion that _____.
很自然地得出結論_____。

It is not difficult to get the conclusion that _____.
不難得出結論_____。

Recognizing the fact that _____ should drive us to conclude that _____.
意識到_____這樣的事實,可以讓我們得到一個結論_____。

To put all into a nutshell, I _____.
簡而言之,我_____。

10. 對稱式寫法 – 開頭段

請注意,五段論式開頭段引題中的一部分句子也可以用在這裏。

People rarely reach an absolute consensus on such a controversial issue.
人們很少能在這個有爭議的問題上取得完全一致的意見。

Many people have the idea that _____. However, many others disagree that _____.

Both sides of the question of whether _____ are supported by good reasons.
一些人持有這樣的觀點_____ ,但是另一些人不同意_____。這個問題的雙方都有好的理由來支持_____。

Before giving my opinion, I think it is important to look at the argument on both sides.
在提出我的觀點之前,我認為看看辯論雙方的論點是非常必要的。

On such a controversial issue, people seldom reach an absolute consensus.
在這樣一個有爭議的觀點上,人們很少能達成絕對的一致。

_____ has caused significant changes in family life and education. Some of these changes have been beneficial while others have been adverse.
_____導致家庭生活和教育的重要改變。一些改變非常有益,然而另一些改變卻相反。

The discussion about whether or not _____ is a very controversial one.
對是否_____的論述是有爭議的。

This issue is so controversial that people can hardly reach an absolute consensus.
這個論點很有爭議,人們很難達成共識。

This is a very controversial issue and people hold quite different opinions of it.
這是一個很有爭議的論點,人們所持的觀點大相逕庭。

It is quite natural that people seldom reach a total agreement on such a long-running controversy.
很自然地,人們很少在長期爭論中達成一致意見。

Both sides of the question are well supported by sound reasons.
雙方的觀點都有充足的證據。

There is probably a little bit of truth in both arguments and the opinions stated by the both sides make sense and consequently, it is hard to choose the best of them.

兩種觀點都有些道理,因此很難從中選擇最好的。

11. 對稱式寫法 – 中間兩段開頭句

People who support _____ give some or all of the following reasons.
支持_____的人提出以下原因。

But other people set forth a totally different argument about this case.
但其他人對此提出了一個完全不同的論點。

Some people examine this issue from another angle.
一些人從另一個角度檢視這個觀點。

On the other hand, there are also many opponents who strongly _____.
另一方面,有許多反對者強調_____。

On the other hand, _____ also have some negative effects.
另一方面,_____也有負面影響。

There are several reasons which suggest that _____.
有幾個原因說明_____。

There are several reasons why _____.
有幾個原因說明為什麼_____。

Many people argue that _____.
很多人認為_____。

12. 對稱式寫法 – 最後一段提出自己的觀點

With views of both sides considered, I think that _____.
考慮雙方的觀點後,我認為_____。

All the above opinions make sense. Therefore it is really hard for me to draw a definite conclusion. Here I would like to take a more balanced position that _____.
上面所有的觀點都很有意義。而且我很難得到一個明確的結論。我希望站在一個更平衡的立場上_____。

All the opinions above make sense, and consequently it is hard to come an absolute conclusion. In my opinion, _____.
上面所有的觀點都很有意義,因此很難得到絕對的結論。我的意見是,_____。

Admittedly, both sides are reasonable. But they are one-sided. In my opinion, _____。
無可否認的,雙方都有道理,但都很片面。我的意見是,_____。

Taking into account both sides of argument, I think _____.
考慮到雙方的論點,我認為_____。

As far as I am concerned, I think there is truth in the argument of these two parties. I would like to have a balanced view.
至於我,我認為兩方面的論述都有其正確性。我將提出一個平衡的看法。

To sum up, we cannot deny that both sides are well-grounded. In my opinion, _____.
總之,雙方都有充分的根據,我的觀點是_____。

There is probably a little bit of truth in both arguments and the opinions stated by the both sides make sense and consequently, it is hard to choose the best of them.
兩種觀點都有些道理,因此很難從中選擇最好的。

All these opinions make sense, and consequently it is hard to decide which one is more reasonable.
所有這些意見都很有意義,因此很難決定哪個論點更有道理。

From what has been mentioned above, we may see that there is some truth in both arguments. Personally, I side with the latter opinion.

從以上論述中,我們可以看到雙方的論述都有些道理。我個人更支持後一種觀點。

Admittedly, there are merits to both arguments. As far as I am concerned, I would like to take a more balanced position. That is to say, _____。
無可否認的,兩種論點都有自己的優點,就我來說,我將站在一個更平衡的位置上,也就是說,_____。

13. 論說式 - 開頭段

　　請注意,五段論式開頭段引題中一部分的句子也可以用在這裏。

In my mind, the following factors need to be taken into consideration.
我認爲,下列因素必須被考慮。

There are several reasons for this phenomenon.
這種現象的出現有許多原因。

As to how to _____, people put forward various suggestions.
關於怎樣_____, 人們提出不同的建議。

There are a number of reasons for this phenomenon.
這種現象的出現有許多原因。

Regarding these reasons, I think there are some ways to _____.
考慮到這些原因,我認爲有許多方式去_____。

In order to minimize the negative effects described above, people set forth different solutions and here I would explore only two key ways.
爲了減小上面所描述的負面影響,人們提出不同的解決方法,在這裏我將提出兩種主要的方式。

I strongly suggest that effective steps be taken as soon as possible to protect the community

from the adverse impacts of _____.
我強烈建議儘快採取有效步驟去保護社會不受_____的負面影響。

There are several reasons for this problem.
這個問題有幾方面的原因。

The causes may be inner and outer influence.
原因可能是內部的和外部的影響。

The following suggestions should be taken into consideration when we are seeking solutions to _____.
當我們尋找_____的解決方案時,下列建議必須被考慮。

❖ 七、審題的注意事項 ❖

　　IELTS 議論文的題目雖然是用英文命題,但涉及的詞語和句式比較簡單,遠低於 IELTS 閱讀的難度。所以一般不會造成大家理解上的障礙。

　　大家在開始寫作之前,一定要用 2～3 分鐘將題目仔細看幾遍,至少應該看兩遍。若匆忙下筆,最後才發現文不對題,或者忽略了題目中的一個特殊要求,這時要想改正,也沒有時間了。

大家在審題時,要特別注意以下幾點。

1. 遇到生字怎麼辦

　　作文題目中的字大部分都是比較淺顯的單字,應該都在大學英語單字的範圍之內。這比 IELTS 閱讀的要求低很多。所以作文題目中一般不會出現特別生僻的字。

　　如果作文題目中出現了一些難字,出題者一般會提供一些線索,幫助你猜出它的意思。你不認識的字與它前後的詞會有一種反義或同義的關係。

　　在辯論式的題目中,題目提到兩個觀點,它們一定是對立的,即意思相反。所以你若知道一個觀點的意思,就可猜出另一個觀點的意思,即使其中有你不認識的生字。

比如：

Topic：Some people think children should be taken care of at home by their mothers. Others argue that it would be good for them if they are sent to kindergartens? What is your opinion? 有些人認爲孩子應該在家由母親照顧。另外一些人認爲如果他們被送到幼稚園去，將會對他們有好處。你的意見是什麼？

　　kindergarten 這個字不是人人都認識。但幾乎每個人都能猜出它是"幼稚園"的意思。的確，一個觀點是孩子應該在家由母親照顧，另一個觀點是孩子應該送到一個地方去，那能把孩子送到哪裏去呢？ 根據它們的反義關係，不難猜出這個字的意思。

　　題目中的生字，更多的是與前後的單字構成同義的關係。出題者如果認爲題目中有一個字大多數的考生會不認識，他會用一些方法對這個字進行解釋。大家要熟悉這些解釋的方法。通常使用的方法包括：

> （1）破折號後面的字句是對其前面的字的解釋。
> （2）用同位語結構，用同位語或同位語子句，對前面的字進行解釋。
> （3）用形容詞子句，常用的連接詞是 in which。
> （4）舉例子，常用的字是 for example 或 such as。

　　比如，題目中有一個字是 coeducation。它的中文意思是"男女同校"，題目中可能會用下面的方式進行解釋：

coeducation —— boys and girls study in the same school.

coeducation, a practice that boys and girls study in the same school.

coeducation, in which boys and girls study in the same school.

　　又比如題目中有一個字是 pet，它的中文意思是"寵物"，題目中可能會用舉例子的方式對它進行解釋：Pets such as dogs and cats。

　　所以大家在讀題目的時候，遇到不認識的生字時不要緊張。只要你有一定的字彙量，如果題目中出現你不認識的字，一般會有解釋的。你要注意看這個字前後的字句，用反義或同義關係爭取猜出它的意思。

　　如果題目中有一個字，你不認識，又因爲各種原因，不能猜出它的意思。這時，可以在文章中儘量避開它，說得模糊一些。

比如：

Topic：Some people think children should be taken care of at home by their mothers. Others argue that it would be good for them if they are sent to kindergartens? What is your opinion?

有些人認爲孩子應該在家由母親照顧。另外一些人認爲如果他們被送到幼稚園去,將會對他們有好處。你的意見是什麼?

假如你不能猜出 kindergarten 的中文意思,那麼可以避開它。這時,應該選擇贊成第一個觀點,即孩子應在家由母親照顧,在讓步段時,也可以不說送到幼稚園去的好處(因爲你不知道 kindergarten 的意思,所以沒法說),而說孩子在家由母親照顧也有不足之處。這相當於把題目改成了"孩子是否應該在家由母親照顧"了。雖然不是特別好,但也比一字不寫強多了。

2. 多個問號怎麼辦

大多數的題目中只有一個問號或者一個要求,這比較好辦,按照題目的要求去做就可以了。

有一部分題目中有兩個或多個問號,或者是兩個或多個要求。大多數情況下,兩個都是論說式的問號或要求,這部分題目的做法,在本章論說式題目的寫法這一節中已經作了詳細的介紹。下面介紹另外幾種情況。

(1) 一個問號是論說式的,一個問號是辯論式的。

選定一主一次去論述,一般都應該選擇辯論式的問號爲主,這種情況,在考試中出現過多次,大家應特別留意。

例 1 How to solve the problem of traffic jams in big cities in China? To develop public transportation or to develop private cars?
怎樣解決中國大城市裏的交通擁擠問題? 是發展公共交通還是發展私人汽車?

這是一個有兩個問號的題目,第一個問號是論說式的,第二個問號是辯論式的,應該以第二問號爲主。第一個問號可以在開頭段作爲引題。比如:

例 2 In 1995, an Englishman killed a burglar who broke into his house. He was sentenced. Do you think he should be sentenced? How can we protect our properties?
在 1995 年,一個英國人殺死了一個闖進他家的竊賊。他被判刑了。你認爲他該被判刑嗎? 我們應如何保護自己的財產呢?

這也是一個有兩個問號的題目,第一個問號是辯論式的,第二個問號是論說式的,應該以第一個問號爲主。

（2）兩個問號都是辯論式的。

　　選定一主一次去論述，一般是選擇後一個問號，或者選擇有 argue 的那個問號。

　　一般說來，兩個問號都是辯論式的，這種情況出現得很少。在考試中，只出現過下面這一次。

例 Is it possible for a woman to be a good mother and a successful career woman at the same time? Some people argue that the government should pay some money to women so that they can stay at home to look after the children. Do you agree or disagree?

一個女人能同時成為一個好母親和一個成功的職業女性嗎？一些人認為，政府應該給婦女一些錢，這樣她們能待在家裏照顧孩子。你同意還是不同意？

　　這個題目有兩個問號，都是 argument 型的。應該以後一個問號為主去討論。而且後一個問號有 argue 這個字。

　　這兩種情況的處理原則是：一主一次，以一個問號為主去討論。但另一個次要的問號一定要處理，不能漏掉，否則會扣分。

處理次要問號，有以下三種方法：

（1）放在開頭段，作為引題。

　　這是最簡單的方法，適用於大多數的題目。

例 How to solve the problem of traffic jams in big cities? To develop public transportation or to develop private cars?

怎樣解決大城市裏的交通擁擠問題？是發展公共交通還是發展私人汽車？

　　這是一個有兩個問號的題目，第一個問號是論說式的，第二個問號是辯論式的，應該以第二個問號為主。第一個問號可以放在開頭段，作為引題。比如：

How can we solve the problem of traffic jams in big cities? Some suggest that we should give priority to the development of private cars, but others argue that public transportation should be put in the first place. In my opinion, I am for the latter one.

（2）放在結尾段，提建議。

這時可以多說幾句，達到與一個理由段一樣的篇幅。如果文章前面部分寫得比較少，可以用這種方法增加一些字數。

例 In 1995, an Englishman killed a burglar who broke into his house. He was sentenced. Do you think he should be sentenced? How can we protect our properties?
在 1995 年，一個英國人殺死了一個闖進他家的竊賊。他被判刑了。你認爲他該被判刑嗎？我們應如何保護自己的財產呢？

這是一個有兩個問號的題目，第一個問號是辯論式的，第二個問號是論說式的，應該以第一個問號爲主。第二個問號可以放在開頭段作爲引題。但也可以放在結尾段，提建議。這樣更適合這個題目。比如：

How do we protect our house in a proper way? Firstly, we must increase our awareness and know the extent of danger. Nowadays the public crime is high and safety is minimising. There are many serious crimes such as kidnapping, rape and robbery, which threaten our safety. Secondly, we must take some efficient measures. For example, we can install a special kind of door with which without opening the door, we can see who is visiting. And it is necessary to learn the telephone number of the police station by heart so that we can dial it in case of an emergency as quickly as possible.

（3）可作爲一個理由。

有時也可以把次要的問號作爲一個理由來處理。比如：

例 Is it possible for a woman to be a good mother and a successful career woman at the same time? Some people argue that the government should pay some money to women so that they can stay at home to look after the children. Do you agree or disagree?

兩個問號，以第二個問號爲主去討論，第一個問號可作爲一個理由。比如你的觀點是：政府應該給婦女一些錢，讓她們能待在家裏照顧孩子。其中一個理由可以是：一個女人不能同時成爲一個好母親和一個成功的職業女性。又比如你的觀點是：政府不應該給婦女一些錢,讓她們能待在家裏照顧孩子。其中一個理由可以是:一個女人能同時成為一個好母親和一個成功的職業女性。

3. 要求提到正反面

有些題目中含有 discuss(討論)、compare(比較)、contrast(對比)、to what extent(在什麼程度上)、to what degree(在什麼程度上)等字樣,這要求在文章中討論問題的兩方面或者將這兩方面做比較。這時,最好用對稱式寫法。如果用五段論式的寫法寫,則必須寫讓步段。但即使這樣,也不比對稱式寫法好。

例1 Some people believe that in order to improve the quality of education, high school students should be encouraged to criticize and evaluate the teachers. Others feel that this way result in the loss of respect and discipline in the classrooms. Discuss both views. Use your own knowledge and experience to support your idea.

一些人認為,為了提高教育品質,應該鼓勵高中生批評和評價老師。另外一些人認為,這會造成對老師的不尊重和課堂上沒有紀律。討論這兩種觀點,用你的知識和經歷來支持你的觀點。

題目中含有 discuss,必須要在文章中提到問題的兩個方面。不是用對稱式寫法,就是必須寫讓步段,用對稱式寫法較好。

例2 Nowadays it is believed that one cannot obtain the necessary qualifications for success through studies at universities or similar academic institutions. To what extent do you agree or disagree with this opinion? Use your own experience and knowledge to support your arguments.

現在人們認為一個人不能通過在大學或類似的學術機構獲得成功所必需的資格。你在多大程度上同意或者反對這個觀點? 用你的經歷和知識來支持你的觀點。

題目中含有 to what extent,必須要在文章中提到問題的兩個方面。不是用對稱式寫法,就是必須寫讓步段,用對稱式寫法較好。

4. 題目中有 For example, such as

For example 和 such as 是舉例子。這時要注意題目中是否有 choose either of them 或

choose one of them 的字樣。如果有,應從中選一個來寫。如果沒有,應以 For example 或 such as 前面的字為主來寫,而不要太常提到 For example 或 such as 的例子。

例 1 There have been many technological developments in the 20th century, for example, computers and electric power. Choose either of them, describe the changes it has brought about and discuss whether all the changes are positive.
在二十世紀有很多科技進步,比如說電腦和電力。選擇它們之中的一個,描述它所帶來的變化並討論這些變化是否都是正面的。

　　題目中有 choose either of them,所以必須寫電腦或電力中的一個,不能寫別的科技進步,如農藥。另外這個題目有兩個要求,描述它所帶來的變化並討論這些變化是否都是正面的。應該以後一個要求(討論這些變化是否都是正面的)為主,因為它是 argument 型的,另一個要求(描述它所帶來的變化)可以放在開頭段作為引題來處理。

例 2 Some people are of the opinion that keeping pets such as cats and dogs is beneficial to city dwellers. What do you think?
一些人持有這個觀點:飼養寵物比如貓和狗對城市居民是有好處的。你怎麼認為?

　　應以 such as 前面的字 pets(寵物)為主來寫,可以在文章中提到貓和狗,但不能過多。也就是說,文章中要寫飼養寵物好不好,而不是養貓養狗好不好。

5. 並列成分統一處理

　　有一少部分題目中包含並列成分,這時要注意它們是綁在一起的,要同意就全部同意,要反對就全都反對。不能同意一個,反對另一個。

例 Some people argue that the nutrition and quality of fast food decreased and that traditional cooking methods are forgotten. Do you agree or disagree?
有些人認為快餐的營養和品質降低而且傳統的烹飪方法被遺忘了。你同意或不同意?

　　快餐的營養和品質降低和傳統的烹飪方法被遺忘是題目中的並列成分。要同意就全都同意,要反對就全都反對。也就是說,你的觀點只能是快餐的營養和品質降低而且傳統的烹飪方法被遺忘,或者是快餐的營養和品質沒降低而且傳統的烹飪方法沒有被遺忘。而不能同意一個,反對另一個。

6. 區分特別類似的題目

有時在考試中遇到的題目與以前見過的題目特別類似,這當然是件好事。但也不要欣喜若狂,不要急於下筆。很多考試題目是重複使用的,但也有些題目會稍作變化,這時要注意這些變化,否則容易文不對題。

比如,以前見過的題目是電視對人的影響,你考試的題目是電視對年輕人的影響。這兩個題目是有區別的,你在文章中不能說電視對老年人或兒童如何好或如何不好。

再比如,以前見過的題目是應不應該在超級市場安裝監視器,你考試的題目是應不應該在住宅區安裝監視器。如果你不注意看清題目的區別,大寫在超級市場安裝監視器如何如何地不好,顯然是文不對題了。

7. 注意特殊要求

有些題目中有一些特殊要求,一定要在你的文章中反映出來。最常見的特殊要求是Use your own knowledge and experience to support your idea(用你的知識和經歷來支持你的觀點)。這時,應在你的文章中用例證法,舉你本身的例子來支持你的觀點。

例 1 Some people believe that in order to improve the quality of education, high school students should be encouraged to criticize and evaluate the teachers. Others feel that this way result in the loss of respect and discipline in the classrooms. Discuss both views. Use your own knowledge and experience to support your idea.
有些人認為為了提高教育品質,應該鼓勵高中生批評和評價老師。另外一些人認為這會造成對老師的不尊重和課堂上沒有紀律。討論這兩種觀點,用你的知識和經歷來支持你的觀點。

例 2 Nowadays it is believed that one cannot obtain the necessary qualifications for success through studies at universities or similar academic institutions. To what extent do you agree or disagree with this opinion? Use your own experience and knowledge to support your arguments.
現在人們認為一個人不能通過在大學或類似的學術機構獲得成功所需的資格。你在多大程度上同意或者反對這個觀點? 用你的經歷和知識來支持你的觀點。

注意,這時要保證五段論式或對稱式的整體結構不變,只是在寫支持句的時候考慮用例證法,舉你自己的例子來支持你的觀點。舉例子時,注意不要太多。一篇文章中,只在一個理由段中舉一個例子就可以了,千萬不能每個理由段都用例子來做支持句。這主要是因為,寫例子的句子一般都比較簡單,類似於記敍文,不容易寫出特別複雜的句子。所以在語言這一項上會拉低你的文章的層次,不容易得高分。舉例時,還要注意不要太長。因為例子比較容易寫,所以有的同學就將例子寫得很長,很詳細,造成該理由段特別長,這樣也不好。舉例的理由段一般會長一些,但要注意將例子概括一下,用三四句話就可以了,總長度不應該超過理由段應有的長度太多。

注意上面兩個題目中含有 discuss 和 to what extent,必須要在文章中提到問題的兩個方面。不是用對稱式寫法,就是必須寫讓步段,用對稱式寫法較好。

總而言之,IELTS 作文考試並不想在審題上給大家設置很多障礙,所以絕大多數題目還是很好理解和把握的。只要大家注意上面所說的幾點,審題這一方面應該是沒有問題的。

❖ 八、如何找到理由及思路 ❖

IELTS 議論文的題目千變萬化,但是從內容上看,主要分為學生生活、家庭生活、科技與媒體、社會生活四大部分。對於大多數題目,大家還是有話可說的。

有的同學為什麼會沒有思路呢? 有的是因為書讀得太少,平時遇到問題也不善於思考。還有的同學是受到中文寫作的影響,以為必須要想出特別新穎、立意特別高的理由。實際上這些並不是 IELTS 議論文的要求,IELTS 寫作在理論上屬於淺顯的學術寫作(beginner of academic writing)。從理由這一項上講,它只有一個要求:具有相關性(relevant),也就是說,所寫的理由只要和題目要求相關就可以了。在滿足這個前提下,理由越簡單、越貼近生活越好。因為這樣,大家越會寫,越能寫出來。

同學們在準備理由及思路的時候,要注意多讀、多背,同時還要注意分類。多讀、多背是指多讀、多背一些好的句子,注意分類是指將這些句子按照主題分門別類地記憶,這樣在考試時便於聯想起來。分類不僅要按照學生生活、家庭生活、科技與媒體、社會生活分為四大部分,還要分得更詳細一些,如電視、廣告、環境污染、交通擁擠等。作者根據多年的 IELTS 寫作教學經驗,並結合近年來 IELTS 寫作考試題目,為大家分類歸納了很多好的句子,大家應該讀熟、背熟這些句子。它們可以作爲寫作素材,也可以用於學習語言(寫出正確的、優美的句子)。有些可以直接用於考試之中,更重要的是能夠拓展大家的思路。這些句子,請詳見本章第十二節。

下面我們從正反兩方面,爲大家總結一下十大常用的理由和六大不能寫的理由。

1. 十大常用的理由

這十大常用的理由的通用性較強,適合的題目較多。但通用的東西,有時與具體的題目結合得不是特別緊密。所以大家在審題時,應該先不要想這些通用的理由,而應該圍繞題目,想一想有哪些理由特別適合這個題目呢?如果實在想不出來,再從下面的十個理由中看一看有沒有合適的。作者不希望這十個理由成爲"萬金油",而希望它們成爲"救命仙丹"。

(1) 方便

相應字:convenient(方便的)、convenience(方便)
例題:電腦、出外吃飯、Internet、電話、城市生活

(2) 效率

相應字:efficient(方便的)、efficiently(方便地)、efficiency(方便)
例題:電腦、電話、Internet、汽車

(3) 節省和浪費

節省:save time(節省時間)、save money(節省金錢)、save space(節省空間)、economical(經濟的)、thrift(節儉)、thrifty(節儉的)、frugal(節儉的)、frugality(節儉)
浪費:waste time(浪費時間)、waste money(浪費金錢)、waste space(浪費空間)、costly(花費很大的)、time-consuming(耗時的)、lavish(浪費的)

(4) 人的心理健康(人的性格)

好的性格:independent(獨立的)、independence(獨立)、independently(獨立地)、cooperate(合作)、cooperative(合作的)、cooperation(合作)、compete(競爭)、competitive(競爭的)、

competition（競爭）、team spirit（團隊精神）、considerate（體貼的）、confident（自信的）、confidence（自信）、confidently（自信地）、ambition（雄心）、ambitious（有雄心的）、individuality（個性）、creativity（創造力）、creative（有創造力的）、tolerate（容忍）、tolerant（容忍別人的）、tolerance（容忍）、mental health（心理健康）、spiritual health（心理健康）、psychological health（心理健康）、sociable（好與人交流的）、perseverance（堅定不移）、deal with problems by themselves（獨立解決問題）、solve problems by themselves（獨立解決問題）

不好的性格：overbearing（傲慢的）、selfish（自私的）、conservative（保守的）、isolated（孤立的）

培養人的性格常用的字：cultivate（培養）、foster（培養）、develop（培養、開發、發展）、encourage（鼓勵）、enrich（豐富）、improve（提高、促進）、enhance（增強）

(5) 娛樂

相應字：colorful（豐富多彩的）、pleasure（快樂）、joy（快樂）、recreation（娛樂）、entertain（娛樂）、entertaining（有娛樂性的）、entertainment（娛樂）、leisure time（休閒時光）、interesting（有趣的）、relax（休息）、relaxed（寬鬆的）、relaxation（休息）、dull（無趣的）、monotonous（單調的）、tired（疲倦的）、bored（厭煩的）、tiredness（疲倦）、boring（令人厭煩的）、tiring（令人疲倦的）、fatigue（疲勞）、lonely（孤獨的）、loneliness（孤獨）、weary（疲倦的）、weariness（疲倦）

注意 tired（疲倦的）、bored（厭煩的）、boring（令人厭煩的）、tiring（令人疲倦的）的用法：
I am bored very much. 我很厭煩（無聊）。
Reading is boring. 閱讀令人厭煩。

(6) 環境

相應字：environment（環境）、environmental（環境的）、pollute（污染）、polluted（污染的）、pollutant（污染物）、pollution（污染）、poisonous（有毒的）、contaminate（污染）、contamination（污染）、contaminated（污染的）、contaminant（污染物）、dirty（髒）、hygiene（衛生）

(7) 身體健康

相應字：health（健康）、physical health（身體健康）、healthy（健康的）、disease（疾病）、strong（強壯的）、strength（力量）、energetic（精力充沛的）、energetically（精力充沛地）

(8) 安全和危險

相應字：safe（安全的）、safety（安全）、safely（安全地）、in safe（安全地）、danger（危險）、

dangerous（危險的）、in danger（處於危險之中）、risk（冒險）、hazard（危險）、hazardous（危險的）

（9）經驗

相應字：experience（經驗）、social experience（社會經驗）、enter the society（進入社會）

（10）人道

相應字：humane（人道的）、humanity（人性）、fair（公平的）、unfair（不公平的）、help（幫助）、assist（協助）、free（自由的）、freedom（自由）、freely（自由地）、privacy（隱私）

同學們在考試的前一天可以將這些理由再看一遍。在考試時，如果真的想不出與題目特別速配的理由，可以從上面的十個理由中，看一看有沒有合適的。一般能找出一到兩個，可能有時不是特別恰當，但總比什麼也不寫好得多。

2. 六大不能寫的理由

（1）文不對題的理由不能寫

不能寫與題目毫不相關的理由，尤其是對於那些能輕鬆找到理由的題目。IELTS 考試中，有些題目比較偏，確實不太容易想出特別切題的理由，這時可以選擇那些與題目有些關係，但並不是特別合適的理由。但更好的辦法是用對稱式寫法，因爲這種寫法對思路的要求不高，只想出一個理由即可（有時甚至可以不必歸納出主題句，請詳見對稱式寫法部分的講述）。總之，最好不要寫文不對題的理由，尤其是離題很遠的理由。

（2）限制考題的理由不能寫

所寫理由不能使題目限制在一個前提條件。

例 Topic：學校得到一筆錢，有人認爲應建一座圖書館，有人認爲應建一座體育館。你的觀點是什麼？

觀點是：應建一座圖書館。

一個理由是：學校已經有兩座體育館了，但一座圖書館也沒有。

這個理由就屬於限制考題的理由，是不能寫的。

(3) 重複的理由不能寫

兩個或三個理由應該各異其趣,互為補充,不能是意思一樣的。

例 Topic:電腦的利與弊

觀點是:電腦的利大於弊。

理由一:效率高

理由二:速度快

理由三:省時間

應該看出,這三個理由實際上是一樣的,這是不可以的。

(4) 不好寫、不會寫的理由不能寫

新穎、高深的理由固然好,但一般需要較好的語言程度。如果一個理由特別合適,但涉及的英文字句你都不熟悉,我看也只好忍痛割愛了。對一般程度的同學來說,越簡單的理由、越生活化的理由越好。對於大多數同學,不要把太多的精力放在想高深理由上,應把重點放在語言上。尤其在考試中,不要在想理由上花費太多的時間,想出兩三個切題的理由,就可以開始寫了。

(5) 道德水準過高或過低的理由不能寫

例 Topic:用筆寫信好,還是用電腦寫信好。

觀點是:用電腦寫信好。

理由一:用電腦寫信,看不出是誰寫的。

試想,如果評卷官受過匿名信的陷害,你會得多少分呢?

(6) 有關政治的理由不能寫

政治題材歷來是敏感的,在寫作及口語考試中都應儘量避免。

3. 寫理由時的句式

寫理由時,也就是寫主題句時,儘可能用簡單句。句子通常用所要論述的事物做主詞,也可以用代名詞來代替該事物(因為在開頭段已經提及了該事物)。在寫理由的時候,可以考慮使用下面的"萬能句式"。

It is helpful to_____.
It is beneficial to_____.
It is favorable to_____.
It does favor to_____.
以上四句話的意思是:它有利於_____。

It is harmful to_____.
It is detrimental to_____.
It does harm to_____.
It is unfavorable to_____.
以上四句話的意思是:它對_____有害。

如:Outdoor activities do favor to people's physical health.
戶外活動對人的身體健康有好處。
Playing games is beneficial to children's psychological development.
玩遊戲有利於孩子們的心理發展。
Raising pets is harmful to people's health.
飼養寵物對人的健康有害。

但是同樣應該注意,越是萬能的,用的人越多。所以大家在使用時,應儘量先用別的句式。如果實在用別的句式有困難,或者在考試時,一時想不起來,再考慮用上面的句式。

4. 一些題目的理由

　　下面，我們結合一些題目，從正反兩方面提出一些理由，供大家參考，希望帶給大家一些啟發，開展大家的思路。對其中一些理由，補充了一些支持句來解釋說明。

例 1　Topic：In some countries the average worker is obliged to retire at the age of 50, while in others people can work until they are 65 or 70. Meanwhile, we see some politicians enjoying power well into their eighties. Clearly, there is little agreement on an appropriate retirement age. Until what age do you think people should be encouraged to remain in paid employment? Give your reasons.

在一些國家，一般勞動者被要求在 50 歲退休，而在別的一些國家，人們可以工作到 65 歲或 70 歲。同時，我們可以看到一些政治家從政一直到 80 多歲。很明顯，對於什麼是較合適的退休年齡，人們很難達成一致意見。你個人認為應該鼓勵人們工作到什麼年齡？請說明觀點及理由。

For(贊成)：

(1) It is helpful to old people's physical health.
　　有利於老年人的身體健康。

(2) It is beneficial to the social development.
　　有利於社會發展。
　　Old people are more likely to be conservative. They are reluctant to accept new ideas.
　　老年人更可能保守。他們不願意接受新的觀點。
　　Forcing old people to retire from their positions help promote young people so that the young can bring their talent into full play.
　　強迫老年人退休有助於提升年輕人，這樣年輕人能充分發揮他們的才能。

(3) It can offer more job opportunities to release the unemployment pressure.
　　能提供更多的就業機會來減輕失業壓力。

Against(反對)：

(1) There are many jobs suitable for old people.
　　有很多適合老年人的工作。

(2) It violates the working rights of old people.

它侵犯了老年人工作的權利。

(3) It is harmful to old people's mental health.

對老年人的心理健康有害。

If they are forced to retire from work, they will feel they are abandoned by the society.

如果他們被迫退休,他們會感到被社會拋棄了。

(4) It can bring economic problems.

會帶來經濟問題。

Some old people still work because of their family responsibilities even if they want to retire.

因為他們的家庭責任,一些老年人仍然工作,即使他們想退休。

(5) It is a waste of employers' money.

這是浪費僱主的錢。

To hire new hands, the employers have to spend more money training them.

為了僱用新手,僱主們不得不花費更多的錢訓練他們。

(6) Age is not a predictor of people's ability.

年齡並不表示人的能力。

例2 Topic: Some people think young children can have a better education in a boarding school far from home, while others claim that a day school or the home is a better one. What's your opinion? Give your reasons.

有些人認為青少年就讀寄宿學校能接受較好的教育,而另外一些人認為讀日校或在家更好些。提出你的觀點和理由。

Boarding school(寄宿學校):

(1) It is helpful to students' psychological development.

有助於學生們的心理健康發展。

Students are given opportunities to learn to be independent. Studying in boarding school is also beneficial to cultivate their sense of team spirit and cooperation. They will become accustomed to competing with others gradually.

學生們有機會學習獨立。在寄宿學校學習還有助於培養他們的團隊精神和合作的意識。他們會逐漸變得習慣於和別人競爭。

（2）Students can have more time to study.
　　學生們有更多的時間學習。

（3）Parents can concentrate on their work and advance their careers.
　　父母們可以專心於他們的工作，發展他們的事業。

（4）Students are less likely to be spoiled by their parents.
　　學生們不容易被他們的父母們寵壞。

Day school（日校）：

（1）Students have more opportunities to communicate with their parents.
　　學生們有更多和父母溝通的機會。

（2）Students' home can provide them a better living and studying condition.
　　學生們的家能提供一個更好的生活和學習的環境。

（3）Parents can save some money.
　　父母們能節省一些錢。

（4）Parents can keep their children away from negative influence.
　　父母們能使他們的孩子遠離負面的影響。

（5）Family education also plays an important role in shaping children's inclination and character.
　　家庭教育在塑造孩子的性向和性格上起到重要的作用。

例 3 Topic：With the wide application of computers in all aspects of life, more and more children indulge too much in computer games. Discuss the effects of computer games on children. What's your opinion about it?

隨着電腦在日常生活各個方面中的廣泛應用，越來越多的兒童沉迷於電腦遊戲而不能自拔。討論電腦遊戲對兒童的影響。你是怎樣看這個現象的？

For（贊成）：

（1）Computer games can improve children's intellectual ability.
　　電腦遊戲能提高孩子們的智力。

（2）They are helpful to the development of children's mental health.
　　它們有助於孩子們的心理健康發展。

They train children to respond quickly. Children can learn to solve problems by themselves.

它們訓練兒童迅速反應。孩子們能夠學會自己解決難題。

（3）They can arouse children's interests in computer science.

它們會激起兒童對電腦科學的興趣。

（4）They can bring children great pleasure and amusement.

它們會帶給孩子們很大的快樂和娛樂。

Against（反對）:

（1）They waste much of time of children.

它們浪費了兒童的很多時間。

They tear children away from learning, their main task. They distract children's attention from their studies.

它們將孩子們從學習,他們的主要任務中分開。它們分散了孩子們對學習的注意力。

（2）They are harmful to children's physical health. 它們對孩子們的身體健康有害。

（3）They are harmful to children's psychological development. 它們對孩子們的心理發展有害。

Spending too much time in front of the little screen, children tend to be isolated, unsociable and self-centered somehow. What is more, many computer games contain violence and pornography.

在小小的螢幕前面花費了太多的時間,孩子們在某種程度上傾向於孤立、不愛與人交流和以自我為中心。而且,很多電腦遊戲包含暴力和色情的內容。

例 4 Topic: What are the advantages and disadvantages of the internet?

互聯網的利和弊是什麼?

Advantages（利）:

（1）It is convenient.

它是方便的。

（2）It saves us much time. / It makes us work more efficiently.

它節省了我們很多時間。/它使我們工作更有效率。

（3）It saves us much money.

它節省了我們很多錢。

（4）It also plays an important role in education.

它還在教育上起到重要的作用。

（5）We can make a lot of friends from different backgrounds.

我們能認識來自不同背景的朋友。

（6）It stimulates our interest and curiosity in computer science.

它會激起我們對電腦科學的興趣和好奇。

Disadvantages（弊）：

（1）It wastes much time of children.

它浪費了兒童的很多時間。

It tears children away from learning, their main task. They distract children's attention from their studies.

它將孩子們從學習，他們的主要任務中分開。它們分散了孩子們對學習的注意力。

（2）It is harmful to children's physical health. 它對孩子的身體健康有害。

（3）It is harmful to children's psychological development. 它對孩子的心理發展有害。

Spending too much time in front of the little screen, children tend to be isolated, unsociable and self-centered somehow. What is more, internet contains violence and pornography.

在小小的螢幕前面花費了太多的時間，孩子們在某種程度上傾向於孤立、不愛與人交流和以自我為中心。而且，網際網路上包含暴力和色情的內容。

（4）It makes copyright laws easier to be violated. 它使得版權法更容易被侵犯。

例5 Topic：Traffic is developing rapidly all round the world at present. What are the traffic problems in your country? What causes these problems? Make some recommendations.

現在交通在世界上發展很快。你們國家的交通問題是什麼？是什麼引起了這些問題？提出一些解決建議。

Reasons（原因）：

（1）The number of vehicles increases much more than the building of roads.

車輛的增長比道路的建設快得多。

(2) There are too many private cars and not enough public buses.
有太多的私人汽車，沒有足夠的公共汽車。

(3) Many people do not obey the traffic rules.
很多人不遵守交通規則。

Recommendations(解決措施):

(1) The government should invest more money in the building of new roads.
政府應投資更多的錢在公路的建設上。

(2) The development of public transportation should be put in the first place.
公共交通的發展應該放在首位。

(3) We should teach people to comply with the traffic rules strictly.
我們應該教育人們嚴格遵守交通規則。

例 6 Topic: Families are not as close as before. Give reasons for this change, and suggest some ways to bring families closer.
家庭關係沒有以前那麼密切了。請解釋原因並提出能夠使家庭關係更密切的方法。

Reasons(原因):

(1) Competition is becoming more and more fierce and people suffer from serious work pressure.
競爭正變得越來越激烈，人們承受很大的工作壓力。

(2) People now enjoy more forms of entertainment.
人們現在享有更多形式的娛樂。

(3) People have changed their attitude towards family life.
人們已經改變了他們對家庭生活的態度。

(4) Many workers have to work in other cities and children leave their parents to study at an early age.
很多工人不得不在其他城市工作，孩子們很小就離開父母去學習。

Recommendations(解決措施):

(1) We should keep frequent touch with our family members.
我們應該和家庭成員經常保持聯絡。

（2）We should try to spend more time with families.
我們應該儘量多花些時間與家人在一起。

（3）Never bring your work home, leave it in your office.
永遠不要把你的工作帶回家，把它留在你的辦公室。

（4）We should teach our children the concept of family when they are young.
我們應該在孩子還很小的時候就教導他們樹立家庭的觀念。

例 7 Topic：Some people say that it is not right for the government to spend so much money on artistic projects, such as galleries and sculptures. Do you agree with them? Please explain your reasons.
有人認為政府不應該在藝術項目上花那麼多資金，比如說美術館和雕塑。你是否同意？
請解釋理由。

For（贊成）：

（1）They provide a better living environment for citizens.
提供市民一個更好的生活環境。

（2）They make city life colorful.
使城市生活豐富多彩。

（3）They enrich people's cultural life.
豐富了人們的文化生活。

（4）They are helpful to the local tourism.
有利於當地的旅遊業。

（5）They can provide more employment opportunities.
提供更多的就業機會。

（6）They can improve the investment environment.
改善投資環境。

Against（反對）：

（1）They benefit only a small percentage of people.
只有利於一小部分人。

（2）They destruct the natural environment.
破壞了自然環境。

（3）They waste the taxpayer's money.

浪費了納稅人的錢。

例 8　Topic：Today，it is not allowed to raise pets in many cities，especially in modern cities．Do you agree or disagree with this?

現在，許多城市禁止市民養寵物，尤其是在一些現代化大都市。你是否同意這種做法?

For(贊成)：

（1）It is helpful to people's physical health.

對人的身體健康有好處。

（2）Walking the pets is beneficial to the owner's health too，especially to old people.

遛寵物也有助於主人的身體健康，尤其是對老年人。

（3）It is beneficial to people's mental health.

有助於人們的心理健康。

They can bring spiritual consolation to old people．With the help of pets，they can dispel the feeling of loneliness.

它們給老年人帶來了精神安慰。在寵物的幫助下，他們會消除孤獨感。

（4）Pets have some practical uses.

寵物有一些實際的用處。

（5）Raising pets does favor to children's psychological development.

養寵物有助於孩子的心理發展。

They can learn to be considerate and tolerant.

他們可以學會關心別人和容忍別人。

（6）Pets bring entertainment and amusement to us.

寵物能給我們帶來娛樂。

Against(反對)：

（1）Raising pets wastes us much time.

飼養寵物浪費我們很多時間。

（2）Pets cost us much money.

寵物花費我們很多錢。

(3) They are harmful to our physical health.

對我們的身體健康有害。

They are dirty and can spread some diseases.

它們很髒而且能傳染一些疾病。

(4) Raising pets has a negative influence on the relationship between neighbours.

飼養寵物對鄰里關係有不好的影響。

例 9 Topic：Soap opera affects family and community relationship. Do you agree or not?

What are the merits and demerits of soap operas?

有人認為，如果整天沉迷於肥皂劇會導致個人和鄰里及社區關係的疏遠。你同意嗎？

For(贊成)：

(1) It tears people away from communicating with neighbours and local community.

使人們不能和鄰里及社區交流。

(2) It makes people too romantic.

使人們過於浪漫。

(3) It is harmful to people's physical health.

對人的身體健康有害。

(4) It occupies the time so that people cannot concentrate on their work and study.

浪費時間，使人們不能專心於工作和學習。

(5) It is harmful to the development of people's intellectual ability.

對人的智力發展有害。

Against(反對)：

(1) It enriches people's cultural life.

豐富了人們的文化生活。

(2) It brings us much pleasure and amusement.

給人們帶來了很多快樂。

(3) It sometimes plays an educational role.

有時能起到教育的作用。

(4) It helps release work pressure.

有助於紓解工作壓力。

(5) It is important to the TV station.

對電視台來說是重要的。

例 10　Topic：Corporal punishment has been practiced in many schools for quite a long time. In recent years, people's attitudes towards this practice have undergone drastic changes. Nowadays, many people strongly oppose it. Should corporal punishment be abolished?

體罰在許多學校存在多年。近年來,人們對體罰的看法發生了很大變化。現在許多人強烈反對體罰,我們該不該廢除體罰呢?

For(贊成)：

(1) It helps reinforce the discipline which is the basis of all achievements.

有助於加強紀律,這是一切成就的基礎。

(2) It is helpful to the management of teachers and parents.

有助於教師和家長(對孩子)的管理。

Against(反對)：

(1) It is harmful to children's physical health.

對孩子的身體健康有害。

(2) It is harmful to children's mental health.

對孩子的心理健康有害。

According to the studies, children who have ever suffered from corporal punishment tend to be violent when they grow up.

根據研究,受過體罰的孩子在長大後有暴力傾向。

(3) It violates children's human rights.

侵犯了孩子的人權。

例 11　Topic：Many pop and sports stars earn millions of dollars a year. On the other hand, most people in "ordinary" professions like nurses, doctors and teachers earn only a small fraction of the income of these "stars". What do you think about this phenomenon? Is it fair?

許多明星如歌星和體育明星每年能賺數百萬美元。而另一方面,許多平凡的職業如護士、醫生和老師每年的收入僅僅是明星們收入的很小一部分。你怎麼看待這種現象? 公平嗎?

For(贊成):
(1) They enrich our cultural life.
　　他們豐富了我們的文化生活。
(2) They have suffered from painstaking training.
　　他們承受了艱苦的訓練。
(3) They sacrifice a lot for what they have gained.
　　他們為所獲得的付出了很多。
(4) It is the outcome of the market economy.
　　這是市場經濟的產物。

Against(反對):
(1) It discourages the enthusiasm of people in other working fields.
　　打擊了其他工作領域的人的熱情。
(2) It will have a negative influence on the development of young people.
　　將對年輕人的發展起到負面的影響。
(3) What they gain is much more than what they pay.
　　他們獲得的比他們付出的多得多。
(4) They are not indispensable.
　　他們並不是不可或缺的。

例 12　Topic: Should uniform be introduced into schools and should students be required to wear uniforms?
學校該不該實行穿校服的制度? 該不該要求學生穿校服?

For(贊成):
(1) Wearing uniforms helps cultivate children the sense of thrift.
　　有助於培養孩子一種節儉的意識。
(2) Students can concentrate on their studies.
　　學生們會專心於學習。

(3) It helps foster a sense of team spirit and cooperation.

有助於培養一種團隊精神和合作的意識。

(4) Parents can save some money.

父母會省一些錢。

(5) Parents can spend less time on children's clothing.

父母會在孩子的穿衣上花更少的時間。

(6) It is helpful to the management of the schools.

有助於學校的管理。

(7) Wearing uniforms can enhance discipline.

穿校服會加強紀律性。

Against(反對):

(1) It is harmful to students' psychological health development.

對學生的心理健康發展有害。

(2) It increases parents' economic burdens.

增加了家長的經濟負擔。

(3) It does harm to students' individuality and creativity.

損害學生的個性和創造力。

(4) The school life would be dull and monotonous.

學校生活將會單調。

(5) It violates the students' legal rights.

它侵犯了學生們的合法權利。

❖ 九、用字的注意事項及常用字 ❖

1. 用字的注意事項

單字是構成文章的最小單位。豐富的字彙是寫作的基本材料,好的文章需要豐富的字彙作爲基礎。同學們在用字時,要注意以下兩點:

(1) 用字多樣化

用字要多樣化,如在文章中三個地方出現"重要"這個意思,三個地方最好用不同的字。英語中表示"重要"這個意思的字很多,如:important、significant、vital、crucial 等,如果三個地方都用 important 就不太好。

又如,表示"不能"的單字及片語有:can not do、fail to do、be unable to do;表示"不同的"的單字及片語有:distinct、distinctive、different、not the same。

(2) 儘量用複雜(**sophisticated**)的字彙

比如我們想描述戶外活動有助於身體健康,可以用以下的三個句子:

Outdoor activities are good to people's health.

Outdoor activities are helpful to people's health.

Outdoor activities are beneficial to people's health.

很顯然地,第三個句子最好,第一個句子最差。因為 beneficial 是一個 sophisticated 的字,而 good 則太普遍了。

我們看下面一段話,這段話在語言上特別好。除了句式複雜多變外,它的完美表現要歸功於使用了很多準確的 sophisticated 的字彙。

On the other hand, television can also be *harmful*, *especially* to children who don't have enough *experience* to make a clear *distinction* between *fantasy* and *reality*. They want to *imitate* what they see, which sometimes is dangerous. They believe the *violence* they see is *normal* and *acceptable*. This may be the reason why "television generations" are more *violent* than their parents. But it is not the television's fault. We should tell our children how to *handle* these problems *properly*.

字彙量少是大家的共同弱點。實際上,寫作對字彙量的要求沒有閱讀大,只要具備大學英語單字即可。但與閱讀相比,寫作對使用這些字彙的要求高。閱讀要求的是認知能力,即看見英文,知道中文的大概意思即可。而寫作則要求能夠正確地使用並拼寫正確。

要滿足寫作對字彙的要求,一方面一定要達到大學英語單字的字彙量,另一方面應重點掌握寫作中出現頻率極高的核心字彙,並結合句子,在句子中記憶這些字。下面我們分動詞、形容詞、名詞分別表列了寫作中出現頻率極高的核心字彙，大家一定要背熟這些字彙。由於篇幅有限，沒有列出例句。在下一節講解句子結構時，很多例句中都包含這些字彙，請大家對照學習。

2. 常用的動詞

abide by/obey/	遵守	charge	收費
observe		cherish	珍視
abolish	廢除	claim	宣稱
abuse	虐待；濫用	coexist	共存
accommodate	供給；調節	coincide with	與……相符
acquire	獲取	collect	收集
adore	崇拜；愛慕	commute	來回往返於
allocate	分配	condemn	譴責
alter	改變	consult	諮詢
appeal to /attract	吸引	contaminate	污染
approach	對待；處理	contribute to	貢獻
approve of	贊成	crack down on	打擊
arise	出現	cultivate	培養
arouse	激發	defy	不服從；藐視
assume	承擔（責任）	degenerate	退化
attach	賦予；貼上	degrade	使降級
attain/ obtain/	獲得；取得	depreciate	貶值
acquire		deprive(of)	剝奪
attend	參加；就讀	desert	拋棄
ban	禁止	detect	偵查
blossom	興旺發達	deter	阻止
boom	繁榮	deteriorate	惡化
bring sb. /sth. into	充分調動……	determine	決定
full play	的積極性	disclose	揭露
censor	審查	discourage	使氣餒
characterize	以……爲特色	diversify	使多樣化

divert	使分心	install/ set up/	安裝
dominate	佔優勢	erect/ fix/ mount	
drop out	退學;放棄	lavish	浪費
eliminate	消除	maltreat	虐待
endanger	危害	maximize	使最大化
enlighten	啓發	minimize	使最小化
enrich	豐富	mould /build	塑造
entertain	招待;娛樂	neglect	忽視
evaluate	評價	oblige	強迫
evolve	演變	observe/follow	遵從
exaggerate	誇張	overcome	克服(困難)
exert	施加(壓力)	participate	參與
expel	排除;開除	perform	履行;表演
explore	探究	please	取悅
expose	揭露	preserve	保留;保護
give full play to	充分發揮	prohibit	禁止
guarantee	保證;擔保	publicize	宣傳
hamper	妨礙;牽制	pursue	追求
hinder/ impede/	阻礙	quit	放棄
block/ hamper		quote	引用
idealize	理想化	refine	精煉
identify	辨認	reflect	反映
ignore	無視;不理睬	reform	改革
imitate	模仿	refresh	使恢復
impair	危害;傷害	regulate	管制;調控
impose/confine/	限制	rehabilitate	改造
place restrictions		reject	剔除
on/ restrict/ limit		relax	休養
incur	招致;引發	release	釋放
inflict	使⋯⋯承受	render	給予
inherit	繼承	represent	代表
innovate	改革創新	resort to	訴諸於;採取
invest money in	投資	restore	重建;恢復

restrain	約束	supervise	監督
retain	保留	control	控制
roam	閒逛	surpass	超過
sacrifice	犧牲	survive	生存
shirk	迴避	threaten	威脅
shun	迴避	tolerate	忍受
signify	表示;意味	treasure	珍視
spoil/ indulge	寵壞;溺愛	trigger	引發
spread	傳播	underestimate	低估
steer	駛向;掌舵	undermine	危害
stick to	堅持	unload	擺脫負擔
stimulate	刺激	vanish	消失
stipulate /set	規定	wither	退化;萎縮
substitute	代替	wreck	摧毀

3. 常用的形容詞、副詞

absurd	荒唐的	complicated	複雜的
addictive	上癮的	confident	自信的
affectionate	有感情的	contemptible	可鄙的
aggressive	有上進心的	contributive	有貢獻的
alert	敏銳的;警惕的	corrupt	腐敗的
arduous	費勁的	delicious	美味可口的
artistic	藝術的	demanding	要求高的
authoritative	權威性的	desirable	值得要的
awkward	尷尬的	detrimental	有害的
balanced	平衡的	devious	偏離正道的
cogent	使人信服的	dishonorable	不光彩的
cold-blooded	冷血的	disturbed	受到干擾的
cold-hearted	無情的	eccentric	古怪的
compassionate	富於同情心的	economical	經濟的
compatible	兼容的	enlightened	開明的;文明的

evil	邪惡的	instructive	有教育意義的
exotic	異國的	intellectual	智力的
fallacious	荒謬的	interim	中間的;過渡的
fashionable	時髦的	interpersonal	人際關係的
feasible	可行的	intimate	密切的
fictitious	虛假的	inviolable	不可侵犯的
flexible	靈活多樣的	inward	內在的
fruitful	有成效的	irreparable	不可挽回的
glamorous	富有魅力的	irresistible	不可抵抗的
gorgeous	輝煌的	irreversible	不可挽回的
humane	人道的	irritating	惱人的
ignorant(of)	無視的;無知的	isolated(from)	隔絕的
impressive	令人印象深刻的	laudable	可讚譽的
		lavishly	大方地
inborn	天生的	legitimate	合法的
incompatible	不調和的	loyal	忠誠的
incompatible	不合時宜的	luxurious	奢侈的
inconceivable	不可思議的	magnanimous	寬宏大量的
indecent	不妥的;不檢點的	mature	成熟的
		misleading	誤導的
indifferent	冷漠的	misrepresented	不如實敍述的
indispensable	不可或缺的	money-oriented	向錢看的
inexhaustible	取之不盡的	multilateral	多方面的
infectious	傳染性的	nourishing	有營養的
inferior	低人一等的	obscure	晦澀的
infirm	(身體)弱的	out of date/	過時的
influential	有影響力的	old-fashioned	
ingrain	根深蒂固的	palatable	美味的
inhumane	不人道的	perilous	危險的
initially	首先	permissive	寬容的;許可的
innocent	無辜的	pernicious	有害無益的
inquisitive	多管閒事的	poisonous	有毒的
insalubrious	有害無益的	pornographic	色情的

potential	潛在的	superficial	表面現象的
practical	實際的;務實的	tempting	吸引人的
preferential	優惠的	time-honored	久享盛名的
pressing	緊迫的	traditional	傳統的
prevailing	佔主導地位的; 流行的	typical	典型的
		unadvised	輕率的
professional	專業的	uncompromising	不妥協的
prosperous	繁榮昌盛的	unconcerned	冷漠的
prudent	明智的	uneasy	不自在的
psychological	心理的	unethical	不道德的
rational	理性的	unfeeling	冷漠的
resentful	憤怒的	unhealthy	不健康的
reverse	相反的	unified	同一標準的
rewarding	值得的	unique	獨特的
ridiculous	荒謬的	unjust	不公平的
rigid	嚴格的	unscrupulous	肆無忌憚的
rough	粗略的	unsociable	不善於社交的
self-contemptuous	自卑的	untimely	不合時宜的
shabby	破舊不堪的	unwholesome	不健康的
sheltered	受保護的	utterly	完全;絕對地
sociable	好交際的	vexing	令人煩惱的
sole	唯一的	vivid	形象的
stern／strict	嚴格的	voluntary	自願的
stressful	有壓力的	vulnerable	易受傷害的
stringent	嚴厲的	well-grounded	有充足理由的
stylish	時髦的	wholesome	健康的

4. 常用的名詞

abolishment	廢除	budget	預算
absurdity	荒唐;謬論	burden	負擔
abuse	濫用	campaign	運動
achievement	成績	candidate	候選人
acquaintance	熟人	capacity	能力
adaptation	改寫;適應	celebrity	名人
admiration	崇拜	character	性格
adventurer/	探險者	characteristic	特點
explorer		charm	魅力
adverse impact	負面影響	clerk	職員
adversity	逆境	cohesion	凝聚力
affection	友情/感情	colleague	同事
alienation	疏遠	collectivism	集體主義
ambition	志向	comfort	舒適
amusement	娛樂	commercial	商業廣告
anecdote	軼事	commercialization	商品化
apathy	冷漠無情	commodity	商品
applause	鼓掌	companion/ partner	同伴
approach	方法	conformity	一致
architecture	建築	consensus	同意
art	藝術	consultation	諮詢
assault	攻擊	consumption	消費
assessment	評估	content	內容
association	聯想;聯繫	contentment	滿意;滿足
athlete	運動員	contribution	貢獻
availability	可得到的東西	correlation	相關性
barrier	障礙	costume	服裝
behavior	行為	creativity	創造性
beneficiary	受益人	criteria	條件

cruelty	殘忍	evaluation	評價
customer	顧客	exception	例外
cybercrime	網路犯罪	exhibition	展覽
depression	沮喪;低沉	exploration	探險
deprivation	剝奪	export	出口
descendant	後代	favor	喜好
deterioration	惡化	feature	特點
detour	繞道	fidelity	忠實
developed countries	發達國家	flexibility	靈活性
developing countries	發展中國家	forefather/ancestor	祖先
digestion	消化吸收	freedom	自由
dignity	尊嚴	frustration	挫折
discipline	紀律	gallery	美術館
discomfort	不舒服	garment	服裝
discontent	不滿足	goodwill	善意
discrimination	歧視;區別	grace	雅緻
disgust	反感	graduate	畢業生
disorder	無序狀態	guardian	監護人
disorientation	迷失方向感	halt	停止;終止
disposition	性格	hardship	艱難險阻
distraction	干擾	heritage	遺產
diversity	多樣化;多樣性	horizon	地平線
domain	領域	hostility	敵對
duplication	重複(建設)	humanity	人性
durability	耐用	idol	偶像
duration	持續時間	immunity	免疫力
economy	經濟	import	進口
employee	僱員	indication	跡象
employer	僱主	indictment	控告
endeavor	努力做	indifference	不關心
enjoyment	享受	individuality	個性化
enthusiasm	熱情;狂熱	industry	工業;行業
equality	平等	inequality	不平等

infrastructure	基礎設施	morality	道德
ingenuity	獨創性	motion	提議
initiative	主動性	muscle	肌肉
instruction	教導	myopia	近視
instructor	教師	nationality	民族;國籍
integrity	誠實	norm	準則
intellectual	知識分子	notion	觀念;想法
intelligence	智能	obligation	義務
interaction	交際	obstacle	障礙物
interference	干涉	occupation	職業
interpretation	解釋	opponent	對手
intolerance	不寬容	originality	獨創性
intrusiveness	干涉	outcome	產物
involvement	參與	outlook	觀點;景色
jealousy	妒嫉	participation	參與
jogging	慢跑	pastime	消遣
joint effort	共同努力	peer	同齡人
journalist/	記者	penalty	刑罰;處罰
correspondent		perseverance	堅定不移
joy/ delight	快樂	personality	性格
lack	缺乏	perspective	看法
landmark	標誌性建築;里	popularity	普及;流行
	程碑	popularization	普及
license	執照	practice	做法
life expectancy/	壽命	precaution	防範
life span		prerogative	特權
literacy	讀寫能力	principle	原則
manufacturer	製造商	profession/	職業
match	匹配	occupation	
measure	測量;評估	proficiency	精通
millennium	千年	promotion	提升
minority	少數人	prospect	前景
misconduct	行為不正	prosperity	繁榮

protocol	協議	strength	實力
prudence	慎重	stress	壓力
public opinion	輿論	substance	物質
punishment	懲罰	supplement	補充
purity	純潔性	sympathy	同情
rebellion	反叛	symptom	症狀
recovery	恢復	talent	人才
regression	衰退	teenager	青少年
regulator	監控者	temper	性情;煩躁
reliability	可信度	temptation	誘惑
remedy/ therapy	療法	threshold	開端
remote education	遠程教育	tip	提示;技巧
revelation	揭示/表現	tolerance	寬容
revenue	總收入	tragedy	悲劇
reward	獎賞;報酬	trait	特點
rumor/gossip	謠言;傳聞	trap	陷阱
satisfaction	滿足	triviality	瑣事
self-discipline	自律	troublemaker	搗亂者
self-respect /	自尊心	tutor	導師
self-esteem		uniformity	一致
shortcoming	缺點	vanity	虛榮心
side-effect	副作用	variety	多樣性;種類
signal	信號	verdict	判決
skyscraper	摩天大樓	vexation	煩惱
sociologist	社會學家	victim	受害者
soul	靈魂	vitality/ vigor/	活力,精力
specialty	專業	energy/ vim	
spelling	拼寫	void	空虛
status	地位	warmth	溫暖
stereotype	成見	weakness	缺點
straightforwardness	直率	withdrawal	退出;撤退
strain	壓力;過度疲勞	zeal	熱情
strategy	策略		

5. 常用的連接詞

文章中句子之間應該連貫，這需要在句子之間使用連接詞。常用的連接詞如下：

(1) 表層次：

first，firstly	to begin with	further	in the first place
second，secondly	to start with	still	furthermore
third，thirdly	what's more	last	last but not the least
also	and then	next	besides
and	equally important	too	moreover
besides	in addition	finally	

(2) 表轉折：

by contrast	although	though	yet
at the same time	but	despite the fact that	even so
in contrast	nevertheless	even though	for all that
notwithstanding	on the contrary	however	in spite of
on the other hand	otherwise	instead	still
regardless			

(3) 表因果：

　　掌握好表示因果的連接詞是十分重要的，幾乎所有的寫作試題都要求寫原因或可以寫原因。議論文的基本模式是擺事實、講道理，講道理就是說明原因。寫作測試的文體決定了表達原因的連接詞的重要性。

therefore	consequently	because of	for this reason
thus	hence	due to	owing to
so	accordingly	thanks to	on this account
since	as	on that account	in this way
for	as a result	as a consequence	

(4) 表讓步：

still	nevertheless	concession granted	naturally
in spite of	all the same	of course	despite
even so	after all		

(5) 表遞進：

furthermore	moreover	likewise	what is more
besides	also	not only... but also...	
too	in addition		

(6) 表舉例：

for example	for instance	for one thing	that is
to illustrate	as an illustration	a case in point	

(7) 表解釋：

as a matter of fact、frankly speaking、in this case、namely、in other words

(8) 表總結：

in summary	in a word	thus	as has been said
in brief	in conclusion	altogether	in other words
to conclude	in fact	finally	in simpler terms
indeed	in short	in particular	that is
in other words	of course	on the whole	to put it differently
namely	in all	therefore	to summarize

(9) 表強調：

of course	indeed	surely	as a matter of fact
above all	most important	in particular	that is to say
certainly	in fact	anyway	in this case
naturally	obviously	no doubt	actually
clearly			

(10) 表比較：

in comparison	likewise	however	like
similarly	equally	in the same way	unlike

(11) 表時間：

after a while	afterward	next	now
again	and then	presently	second
as long as	at last	shortly	simultaneously
at length	at that time	since	so far
before	earlier	soon	still
eventually	finally	subsequently	then
formerly	further	thereafter	until
in the first place	in the past	until now	when
last	meanwhile	lately	

6. 常用的名言和諺語

Virtue and a trade are the best portion for children.

德行和一門技能是給孩子最好的遺產。

Better early than late.

寧早勿遲。

A man can do no more than he can.

量力而為。

Honesty and diligence should be your eternal mates.

誠實和勤奮應成為你永遠的伴侶。

Early birds catch worms.

早起的鳥兒有蟲吃。

Every coin has its two sides.

有利有弊。

Every man has his hobby-horse.

人各有所好。

Every man has his taste.

人各有所好。

Every one is born equal.

人人生而平等。

Every rose has its thorn.

每朵玫瑰都有刺。

Good things stay indoors while bad things will go far away.

好事不出門，壞事傳千里。

Gossip is a fearing thing.

人言可畏。

He who keeps company with the wolf will learn to howl.

近朱者赤，近墨者黑。

It is never too late to learn.

學習永遠不嫌晚。

Where there is a will, there is a way.

有志者事竟成。

Health is better than wealth.

健康勝於財富。

A contented mind is a perpetual feast.

知足常樂。

A friend in need is a friend indeed.

患難見眞情。

Every advantage has its disadvantage.

有利必有弊。

Every little makes a nickel.

積少成多。

Self-trust is the first secret of success.

自信是成功的第一祕訣。

Example is better than precept.

言傳不如身教。

No pains, no gains.

不勞無獲。

Throw the baby out with the bath water.

把洗澡水連同嬰兒一起倒掉。

One man's meat is another man's poison.

百人有百好。

If the old dog barks, he gives counsel.

不聽老人言,吃虧在眼前。

Parents are the first teachers of the children.

父母是孩子的第一任老師。

Different strokes for different folks.

各有所好。

An old man is treasure of a family.

家有一老如有一寶。

You live with a lame, you will learn to limp.

近朱者赤,近墨者黑。

He that lives with cripples learns to limp.

近朱者赤,近墨者黑。

It is good to learn at another man's cost.

前車之鑑。

The devil knows many things because he is old.

人老見識廣。

All bread is not baked in one oven.

人與人不同,花有幾樣紅 / 不能強求一致。

There is a good side and bad side to everything.

任何事情都有利有弊。

Forgetting history means betrayal.

忘記歷史意味着背叛。

Strictness helps, indulgence spoils.

嚴是愛;鬆是害。

Father is one hundred headmasters.

一個父親勝過百個老師。

All work without play makes Jack a dull boy.

只幹活不玩耍,聰明孩子會變傻。

Never put off until tomorrow what can be done today.

今日事今日畢。

If you want to understand today, you have to research yesterday.

要想懂得今天,就必須研究昨天。

Each man has his limitation.

人各有極限。

They that live longest see most.

人越老,越有智慧。

Think thrice before we leap.

三思而後行。

Too much liberty spoils all.

自由過了頭,一切亂了套。

A wise man and a fool together know more than a wise man.

三個臭皮匠勝過一個諸葛亮。

The older, the wiser.

智慧與時俱增。

The onlooker sees the game best.

旁觀者清。

The spectator sees most clearly.

旁觀者清。

Two heads are better than one.

三個臭皮匠勝過一個諸葛亮。

Years bring wisdom.

年歲增長智慧。

A friend is easier lost than found.

朋友易失不易得。

Time waits for no man.

歲月不待人。

Look before you leap.

三思而後行。

Every man has his liking.

人各有所好。

Variety is the spice of life.

多樣化是生活的調味品。

It is a two-edged sword.

它是雙刃劍。

Ill news travels fast.

壞事傳千里。

Knowledge is power.

知識就是力量。

Life is irreversible.

生命只有一次。

More gain for more pay.

一分耕耘，一分收穫。

No garden without weeds.

沒有花園無雜草。

No sweet without sweat.

苦盡甘來。

引用名人名言及諺語時，可使用如下的句型：

Just as the saying goes："No garden is without weeds"，computer games have also some disadvantages.

正如常言所說，"沒有無雜草的花園"，電腦遊戲也有一些不足之處。

As the proverb goes："Every coin has its two sides"，television has both advantages and disadvantages.

正如諺語所說，"任何硬幣都有兩面"，電視既有優點也有缺點。

❖ 十、如何寫出複雜的句子 ❖

1. 議論文中好句子的標準

在造句法結構正確的基礎上，好句子的標準只有一個，那就是：句型多樣化（sentence variety）。大家在寫文章時，應該交替使用各種句型，包括長句、短句以及簡單句、複合句、集合句。其中複合句又包括主詞子句、受詞子句、述詞子句、形容詞子句、副詞子句和同位語子句等。

很多同學在這個方面很欠缺。突出的表現是寫的句子都比較短，這表明作者的語言能力差。這樣的文章即使沒有文法錯誤，要想得 6 分也是很困難的。我們在前面講過，大部分支持句應該是複雜的句子。在議論文中，複雜的句子應該佔 60% 以上，簡單的句子佔 40% 以下。

複雜的句子簡單說就是長的句子。複合句和集合句通常都是複雜的句子，有的簡單句也很複雜（如使用動名詞片語、不定詞片語、分詞片語、介系詞片語等）。大家在文章中應多使用這樣的句子。

有的同學走到另一個極端，就是文章中全是長句，這樣也不好。我們在前面講過，主題句應該是簡單句，而且在兩三個長句中加入一個短句，可使句式富於變化。短句往往有強調的作用。

2. 句子成分

一個句子的句子成分包括：主詞、動詞、受詞、修飾語、副詞語、補語、述詞、同位語，相當於中文中的主、謂、賓、定、狀、補，再加上述語和同位語。

(1) 主詞

主詞是句子所敘說的主體，說明句子所說的是"誰"或是"什麼"，一般放在句首。主詞可以用下面這些內容表示：名詞、代名詞、數詞、動名詞、不定詞、子句。

Television can widen our sights.

電視能開闊我們的眼界。

（主詞是名詞 television。）

Playing games does not require students to use any of their creativity.

玩遊戲不要求學生們使用任何的創造力。

（主詞是動名詞片語 playing games。）

What the old need is spiritual consolation.

老年人需要的是精神安慰。

（主詞是句子 what the old need。）

（2）動詞

動詞表示主詞所發生的動作、主詞所具有的特徵或主詞所處的狀態，一般放在主詞之後，有時態、人稱、語態的變化。

Television plays an educational role in our daily life.

電視在我們的日常生活中起到教育的作用。

（這是簡單現在式。）

Nowadays, raising pets such as dogs and cats is becoming more and more popular in big cities.

現在，飼養寵物如貓和狗在大城市裏正變得越來越流行。

（這是現在進行式。）

Solving problems in the dorm will enrich their social experience.

解決宿舍裏的問題將豐富他們的社會經驗。

（這是簡單未來式。）

Some schools have tried using other forms of assessment.

一些學校已經嘗試使用其他形式的評估方法。

（這是現在完成式。）

After graduation from university, I left my family and entered the society.

從大學畢業後，我離開了家庭，走進了社會。

（這是簡單過去式。）

On the contrary, some people are attracted by the convenience of the city.

相反地，一些人被城市的便利所吸引。

（這是被動語態。）

(3) 受詞

受詞表示動作或行為的對象或承受者。在英文中,及物動詞或相當於及物動詞的動詞片語必須帶受詞。充當受詞的可以是名詞、代名詞、動名詞、受詞子句等。

Television can widen our sights.

電視能開闊我們的眼界。

(our sights 是受詞。)

Studies reveal that there is a definite link between smoking and some serious diseases such as lung cancer and heart disease.

研究顯示,在吸煙和一些嚴重的疾病如肺癌和心臟病之間有一個確定的關聯。

(that 至句尾是受詞子句。)

(4) 修飾語

修飾語用來說明人和物的狀態、品質、數量等,它修飾名詞或代名詞。用作修飾語的有形容詞、名詞、數詞、名詞所有格、分詞、形容詞子句等。單字作修飾語時通常放在被修飾的字的前面,片語或子句作修飾語時,放在被修飾的字的後面。

Television presents a vivid world in front of us.

電視在我們面前展現了一個生動形象的世界。

(形容詞 vivid 做 world 的修飾語。)

Nowadays there are more and more young people going abroad for study.

現在出國留學的年輕人越來越多。

(現在分詞片語 going abroad for study 做 young people 的修飾語。)

Another factor we must consider is that television plays an educational role in our daily life.

我們必須考慮的另一個因素是電視在我們的日常生活中起到教育的作用。

(形容詞子句 we must consider。)

(5) 副詞語

副詞語修飾動詞、形容詞、副詞或整個句子,用來說明動作或狀態。副詞語可分為時間副詞語、地點副詞語、原因副詞語、條件副詞語、方式副詞語、目的副詞語、結果副詞語、讓步副詞語等。通常用作副詞語的有副詞、介系詞片語、不定詞、分詞和副詞子句。用來修飾動詞的副詞語通常位於動詞之後,而用於修飾形容詞和副詞的副詞語通常位於它們之前,副詞子句的位置既可以在句首,也可以在句末或句子中間。

Television tells us the news instantly.

電視及時地告訴我們新聞。

(副詞 instantly 做副詞語。)

Telephone is very convenient especially when we have something urgent.

電話是非常方便的,尤其當我們有緊急的事情時。

(副詞子句 when we have something urgent。)

(6) 補語

某些及物動詞接受詞後,句意不完整,必須加一個名詞或形容詞去補充說明,這個所加的名詞或形容詞就是受詞補語。這樣的及物動詞包括: make、elect、consider、name、appoint、call 等。

Wearing uniforms makes life dull and monotonous.

穿校服使得生活無趣和單調。

(形容詞 dull and monotonous 就是受詞補語。)

I appointed him the president of the class.

我任命他爲班長。

(名詞片語 the president of the class 是受詞補語。)

(7) 述詞

述詞用來說明主詞的身份、性質和狀態,通常位於連綴動詞之後。可用作述詞的詞類有名詞、形容詞、代詞、數詞、不定詞、動名詞、分詞、副詞、介系詞片語和述詞子句。

It is hard to come to an absolute conclusion.

要得到一個絕對的結論是困難的。

(形容詞 hard 做述詞。)

The first reason is that raising pets is harmful to people's health.

第一個原因是飼養寵物對人的健康有害。

(述詞子句 raising pets is harmful to people's health。)

(8) 同位語

　　一個名詞或代名詞後面有時可跟一個名詞(或起類似作用的其他內容),對前者做進一步的解釋,說明指的是誰、是什麼等,稱爲同位語。名詞做同位語的情況最多,有時也可用句子做同位語,稱爲同位語子句。

Shopping, a necessary activity in everyday life is more convenient in the city.
購物,這個每天生活中必須的活動,在城市裏更方便。
Love can tear students away from learning, the students' main task.
愛情能將學生從學習,學生的主要任務中拉開。
From what I have mentioned above, it is not difficult to get the conclusion that students should go abroad to study.
從上面我所提到的,不難得到這樣的一個結論:中學生應該出國留學。

3. 英文句子的結構分類

　　按照結構,英文句子分爲三類:簡單句、複合句、集合句。
　　簡單句:句子只包含一個主謂結構, 句子各個成分都只由單字或片語表示。
　　複合句:複合句中包含有兩個或更多的主謂結構,其中,有一個(或更多的)主謂結構充當句子的某一(些)成分,如主詞、受詞、述語、修飾語、副詞語、同位語等。充當一個句子成分的主謂結構稱爲子句。由於子句在句子中的句子成分不同,可分爲主詞子句、受詞子句、述詞子句、形容詞子句、副詞子句和同位語子句等。
　　有時複合句的一個(或多個)子句可能包含有一個(或多個)子句,即子句裏套着子句,這種句子稱爲多重複合句。
　　如果句子包含有兩個或更多互不依從的主謂結構,就是集合句。集合句中的分句通常用一個對等連接詞來連接,最常見的是 and 和 but。
　　有時,一個集合句中的一個(或更多)分句可能包含有一個(或更多)子句,這種句子稱爲並列複合句。
　　簡單句、複合句、集合句,這種按照結構的分類方式是非常重要的,下面我們分別詳細講解。在講解句子結構時,我們會列出一些例句,這些例句都是與常考的題目有關的,所以它們不僅能幫助大家理解各種句子結構和語言現象,而且還能在思路上給大家一些啓發。大家將其中的句子背熟,可以直接運用到作文當中。

4. 簡單句

句子只包含一個主謂結構, 句子各個成分都只由單字或片語表示。

簡單句一般比較簡單, 比較短。但這不是簡單句的本質特徵, 有的簡單句很複雜, 有的比複合句還長。

(1) 簡單的簡單句

Television can widen our sights.

電視能開闊我們的眼界。

Television also plays an educational role in our daily life.

電視在我們的日常生活中還起到教育的作用。

Advertisements provide much useful information for us.

廣告提供給我們很多有用的訊息。

Outdoor activities can improve our health greatly.

戶外活動能大大促進我們的身體健康。

Students can get opportunities to experience a totally different culture.

學生們有機會體驗一種完全不同的文化。

Children will suffer from loneliness and homesickness.

孩子們將忍受孤獨和思鄉。

They enrich our cultural life.

它們豐富了我們的文化生活。

It brings us a lot of pleasure and amusement.

它為我們帶來了很多快樂。

Pets have some practical uses.

寵物有一些實際的用處。

It calls for the joint efforts of the government, the young and the old people themselves.

它需要政府、年輕人和老年人自己的共同努力。

It prevents children from being polluted by some negative influence.

它使兒童避免受到一些負面的影響。

Tobacco industry contributes a lot to the government's tax income.

煙草工業對政府的稅收做出很大的貢獻。

(2) 動名詞做主詞、受詞、述詞

動名詞是動詞的一種形式,它在句子中具名詞的作用,可單獨或引導片語做句子的主詞、受詞、述詞或介系詞的受詞。動名詞或動名詞片語做主詞時,述詞通常用單數。

動名詞是動詞的一種形式,因此也具有動詞的特點,它可以在後面帶一個名詞做自己的受詞,如 keeping pets(飼養寵物)、playing games(玩遊戲)。

Smoking is just a personal hobby and entertainment.
吸煙只是一種個人愛好和娛樂。
Nowadays raising pets such as dogs and cats is becoming more and more popular in big cities.
現在,飼養寵物如貓和狗在大城市裏正變得越來越流行。
Playing games does not require students to use any of their creativity.
玩遊戲不要求學生們使用任何的創造力。
Living on the campus brings us great benefits.
住在校園裏帶給我們很大的好處。
Living on the campus is beneficial to the students not only academically but also psychologically.
住在校園裏對學生有益處,不僅在學術上,而且在心理上。
Many students are not used to taking care of themselves.
很多學生不習慣於自己照顧自己。
Family plays an important role in shaping children's characters.
家庭在塑造孩子的性格方面起到重要的作用。

(3) 分詞做副詞語、修飾語

分詞是動詞的另一種形式,主要起形容詞和副詞的作用,可以做副詞語、修飾語,也可以做述詞。

分詞有兩種:現在分詞和過去分詞。這兩種分詞在句子中的作用大致相同,其區別主要是現在分詞表示主動,過去分詞表示被動。有時表示的時間不同,現在分詞表示正在進行,過去分詞表示已經完成。

和動名詞類似,分詞也可以有它自己的受詞或副詞語。
Living far away from home, one will suffer from loneliness and homesickness.
離家生活,人要忍受孤獨和思鄉。

Smoking costs a large sum of money, laying a huge economic burden on the smoker's family.

吸煙花費大量的錢,爲吸煙者的家庭帶來巨大的經濟負擔。

I stayed at home, sleeping, eating and making myself fatter and fatter.

我待在家裏,又睡又吃,使自己越來越胖。

You visited me in the hospital, bringing flowers.

你們帶着鮮花到醫院來看我。

They spend too much time in front of the television, ignoring their studies, outdoor activities and even their family.

他們在電視前花費了太多的時間,忽略了他們的學習、戶外活動,甚至他們的家庭。

Compared with the large family, the small family has a unique advantage.

和大家庭相比,小家庭有一個獨特的優點。

Nowadays, there are more and more young people going abroad for study.

現在出國留學的年輕人越來越多。

A country only depending on its tradition will never become a powerful nation.

一個只依靠自己傳統的國家將永遠不能成爲一個強大的國家。

You can always see young people and even adults addicted to the computer games.

你總能看到沉溺於電腦遊戲中的年輕人,甚至成年人。

The commodities and service provided by society have become more diversified.

由社會提供的商品和服務已經變得更多樣化。

Children are hurt by pets raised by their family.

孩子們被他們家飼養的寵物所傷害。

There are some disadvantages brought about by raising pets.

有些弊端由飼養寵物引起。

(4) 不定詞做主詞、受詞、述詞、副詞語、修飾語

不定詞是動詞的另一種形式,可以做主詞、受詞、述詞、副詞語、修飾語。不定詞也可以有它自己的受詞或副詞語。

It is hard to come to an absolute conclusion.

要得到一個絕對的結論是困難的。

(其中,it 是形式主詞,不定詞片語 to come to an absolute conclusion 做眞正主詞。)

The practice of censorship helps maintain a stable and orderly society.

審查的做法有助於維持一個穩定和有秩序的社會。

What we should do is to tell children how to solve these problems properly.
我們應該做的是告訴孩子們如何正確地解決這些問題。
To dispel loneliness and kill the time, they can cultivate some other hobbies such as growing flowers, collecting stamps and learning to paint.
為了趕走孤獨和消磨時光，他們可以培養其他的嗜好，比如養花、集郵和學習繪畫。
It brings us serious problems to solve.
它給我們帶來了需要解決的嚴重問題。

(5) 形容詞片語做後置修飾語

Television shows the news in pictures more powerful than words.
電視用比文字更有力的圖像來顯示新聞。
The government should organize various activities suitable for the old people's participation.
政府應該組織各種各樣適合老年人參與的活動。

(6) 介系詞片語做副詞語

With the limited budget, the government is unable to invest much money in education.
預算很有限，政府不能投資很多錢在教育上。
With the development of society and the improvement of people's living standard, a lot of changes have taken place in their daily life.
隨着社會的發展和人民生活水準的提高，他們的日常生活發生了很多變化。
Without formal examinations, it will be hard for universities to select qualified candidates.
若沒有考試，大學很難選擇合格的候選人。

(7) 並列述詞

有時兩個或更多的述詞可以共用一個主詞，這樣的句子仍然是簡單句，這些述詞稱為並列述詞。

Raising pets gives them great happiness and helps relieve their pressure and depression.
飼養寵物帶給他們很大的快樂而且幫助他們減輕壓力和抑鬱。
Nowadays, young people face fierce competition and suffer from great life pressure.
現在年輕人面臨激烈的競爭，承受很大的生活壓力。
Wearing uniforms, to some extent, discourages individuality and hinders the development of creativity.

在某種程度上,穿校服不鼓勵個性,阻礙創造力的發展。

They bring great pleasures to young people, train them to respond quickly and arouse their interest in computer science.

他們帶給年輕人很大的快樂,訓練他們反應迅速,激起他們對電腦科學的興趣。

5. 時 態

用動詞來表示動作發生時間的各種形式稱為時態。在中文中,不管動作是什麼時候發生的,動詞形式基本上沒有變化,例如,"我昨天學習"、"我今天學習"中,動詞"學習"沒有任何變化。英文則不同,不同時間發生的動作,要用不同形式的動詞來表示。

英文共有十六個時態,在寫作中,最常用的時態有五個,即簡單現在式、現在進行式、簡單未來式、現在完成式和簡單過去式。

(1) 簡單現在式

簡單現在式主要由動詞原形表示,但第三人稱單數後要加 s。簡單現在式主要表示經常性或習慣性的動作。

Communicating with other people by telephone is very convenient.
和別人用電話交流是非常方便的。
Children do not have enough experience.
孩子們沒有足夠的經驗。
Television plays an educational role in our daily life.
電視在我們的日常生活中起到教育的作用。

(2) 現在進行式

現在進行式由助動詞 be 的人稱形式加現在分詞構成,主要表示現在或現在這一階段正在進行的動作。

Nowadays raising pets such as dogs and cats is becoming more and more popular in big cities.
現在,飼養寵物如貓和狗在大城市裏正變得越來越流行。
They hold that people are forgetting their tradition, history and culture.

他們認為人們正在忘記他們的傳統、歷史和文化。

(3) 簡單未來式

簡單未來式由助動詞 will 加動詞原形構成，表示將要發生的動作或情況。

This will eventually undermine national culture by encouraging the spread and popularization of western customs and values.
經由鼓勵西方風俗和價值觀的流行，這將會損害本國的文化。
A country only depending on its tradition will never become a powerful nation.
一個只依靠自己傳統的國家永遠不能成為一個強大的國家。
Solving problems in the dorm will enrich their social experience.
解決宿舍裏的問題將豐富他們的社會經驗。

(4) 現在完成式

現在完成式由 have 的人稱形式加過去分詞構成。表示現在以前發生的動作或情況。

The parents have devoted all their energy to taking care of their children.
父母們已經把他們所有的精力都投入到照顧他們的孩子上。
Surplus advertisements have interfered in people's normal life.
過多的廣告已經干涉了人們的正常生活。
Some schools have tried using other forms of assessment.
一些學校已經嘗試使用其他形式的評估方法。

(5) 簡單過去式

簡單過去式由動詞的過去式表示，表示過去某時發生的動作或情況。在議論文的寫作中，採用例證法舉例時，一般用簡單過去式。在 A 類第一篇圖表作文中，也常用簡單過去式。

After graduation from university, I left my family and entered the society.
從大學畢業後，我離開了家庭，走進了社會。
The number of cars increased significantly from May to June.
汽車的數目從五月到六月快速增長。

6. 語態動詞

在議論文中,最常用的語態動詞是 can 和 should,有時也會用到 may、must 和 need。can 常用來表示能力,意思爲"會"、"能",常用在主題句中。should、may、must 和 need 的意思分別是"應該"、"可能"、"必須"和"需要"。

Outdoor activities can improve our health greatly.
戶外活動能大大促進我們的身體健康。
Using computers can make us work more efficiently.
使用電腦能使我們工作更有效率。
Forcing a person to retire can do harm to his physical and mental health.
強迫一個人退休會損害他的生理和心理健康。
They can also cultivate some other hobbies such as growing flowers, collecting stamps and learning to paint.
他們可以培養其他的嗜好,比如養花、集郵和學習繪畫。
We should compete for our survival.
我們應該爲生存而競爭。
What we should do is to tell children how to solve these problems properly.
我們應該做的是告訴孩子們如何正確地解決這些問題。
They may spread some fatal diseases.
它們可能會傳播一些致命的疾病。
Good intention may sometimes lead to the adverse result.
好的意圖有時可能會帶來相反的結果。
When a person writes, he must organize his ideas.
當一個人寫作的時候,他必須組織他的思路。
We need not rely on pets at all.
我們根本不需要依賴寵物。

7. 被動語態

當述詞表示一個動作時,主詞和它可以有兩種不同的關係:主動關係和被動關係。

在表示主動關係時（即主詞為動作的執行者時），述詞的形式稱為主動語態；在表示被動關係時（即主詞為動作的承受者時），述詞的形式稱為被動語態。

被動語態由助動詞 be 加過去分詞構成，時態藉由 be 表現出來。

(1) 簡單現在式

Important events are often broadcast live on television.
重要的事件經常在電視上現場直播。
On the contrary, some people are attracted by the convenience of the city.
相反地，一些人被城市的便利所吸引。
When a person reaches his old age, he is forced to retire from his position.
當一個人到老年的時候，他被迫從他的崗位上退休。

(2) 現在完成式

It has long been recognized as a beneficial practice to require students to wear school uni-forms.
要求學生們穿校服一直被認為是一個有益的做法。
University TV has been regarded as the most effective method of part-time education.
電視大學已經被認為是最有效的業餘教育的方法。

(3) 簡單未來式

We should compete for our survival, otherwise, we will be thrown out of the tide of the soci-ety.
我們應該為生存而競爭，否則，我們會被社會潮流所淘汰。

(4) 語態動詞

Young people should be encouraged to take part in more meaningful and valuable activities such as reading, studying and exercising.
年輕人應該被鼓勵做更有意義、有價值的事情，如閱讀、學習和運動。

8. 主詞子句

一個句子做主詞，稱為主詞子句。主詞子句有三類：

(1) **what 引導的主詞子句**

表示"……所……的(東西)",在結構上相當於一個名詞加一個形容詞子句。

What the old people need is spiritual consolation.
老年人需要的是精神安慰。
What they emphasize is that formal examinations are harmful to students' creativity.
他們強調的是考試對學生的創造力有害。
What we should do is to tell children how to solve these problems properly.
我們應該做的是,告訴孩子們如何正確地解決這些問題。

(2) **由連接詞 that 引導的主詞子句**

大多數情況下主詞子句都放到句子後部去,而用代名詞 it 做形式上的主詞。

It is sagacious that all relevant factors should be taken into account before taking any action.
在採取任何行動前,所有相關的因素都應該被考慮,這是明智的。
It is obvious that wearing the uniforms would make school life dull and monotonous.
穿校服會使學校生活乏味單調,這是顯然的。
It is well known that there is a clear link between smoking and some kinds of serious diseases.
眾所周知的是,在吸煙和一些嚴重的疾病之間有清楚的關聯。
It is said that mothers know what is most suitable for their children.
據說,母親們知道什麼最適合她們的孩子。

(3) **由疑問詞(如 how、whether 等)引導的主詞子句**

可以直接用在句首做主詞,也可以放在句子後部去,前面用 it 做形式上的主詞,這兩種結構基本上可以互換,意思上沒有什麼差別。

Whether young people should study abroad should be left to individuals to judge.
年輕人是否應該出國留學,這應該留給個人去判斷。
也可以說:
It should be left to individuals to judge whether young people should study abroad.
Whether students should wear uniforms is a controversial issue.

中學生是不是應該穿校服,這是一個有爭議的問題。

也可以說:

It is a controversial issue whether students should wear uniforms.

9. 受詞子句

和主詞子句一樣,受詞子句也分三類:

(1) what 引導的受詞子句

They want to imitate what they see.

他們想要模仿他們所看到的東西。

From friends, we can learn what we need.

從朋友那裏,我們能學到我們所需要的東西。

(2) 由連接詞 that 引導的受詞子句

用 that 引導的子句做受詞的情形最爲普遍,在這類子句前的連接詞 that 在有些情況下可以不用。但在大多數情況下還是不省略爲妙,特別是在書面語中。

Studies reveal that there is a definite link between smoking and some serious diseases such as lung cancer and heart disease.

研究顯示,在吸煙和一些嚴重的疾病如肺癌和心臟病之間,有明確的關聯。

Some people suggest that the old people's children have the obligation to look after their old parents.

有些人認爲,老年人的子女有義務照顧他們的父母。

They insist that the practice of censorship should be abolished.

他們認爲審查的做法應該被廢除。

Some think that the school should be more responsible for children's education compared with the parents.

有些人認爲,與父母相比,學校更應負責孩子的教育。

(3) 由疑問詞(如 how、whether 等)引導的受詞子句

We need to know where we can buy these products.

我們需要知道在哪裏能買到這些產品。

10. 述詞子句

述詞與受詞類似,所以述詞子句也與受詞子句類似。

The first reason is that raising pets is harmful to people's health.
第一個原因是飼養寵物對人的健康有害。
It seems that people who know little about the internet are out-dated.
不太懂互聯網的人好像已經落伍了。

11. 同位語子句

在某些單字(如:idea、fact、conclusion、suggestion 等)後,可以用 that 或連接副詞(如 whether)引導的子句做同位語,稱為同位語子句。

The issue whether internet has more advantages has aroused a heated debate.
互聯網是否有更多的優點已經引起了熱烈的爭論。
Some people even propose a suggestion that smoking should be totally banned in all public places.
一些人甚至提出了建議,在所有公共場所完全禁止吸煙。
From what I have mentioned above, it is not difficult to get the conclusion that students should go abroad to study.
從上面我所提到的,不難得到這樣一個結論:中學生應該出國留學。

12. 形容詞子句

形容詞子句是很活躍的語言現象,大家在作文中一定會用得很多。做形容詞用的子句一般都是由關係代名詞或關係副詞引導。

(1) 由關係代名詞引導的形容詞子句

關係代名詞包括：that 、which 、who。如果修飾物,一般用 which,如果修飾人,一般用 who,兩種情況都可以用 that。

關係代名詞 that 、which 、who 在形容詞子句中做主詞或受詞,當它們做受詞時,可以省略,做主詞時,不能省略。

The main reason that everyone can see is that television presents a vivid world in front of us.
每個人能都看到的主要原因是,電視在我們面前展現了一個生動形象的世界。
(前一個 that 在形容詞子句中做受詞,也可以省略。)
Another factor we must consider is that television plays an educational role in our daily life.
我們必須考慮的另一個因素是電視在我們的日常生活中起到教育的作用。
(factor 和 we 之間已經省略了 that 或 which ,因爲它們在形容詞子句中做受詞。)
They believe the violence they see is normal and acceptable.
他們相信他們所看到的暴力是正常的和可接受的。
In a short vacation, the only thing I can do is to stay at home, sleeping, eating and making myself fatter and fatter.
在短假期裏,我能做的唯一的事就是待在家裏,又睡又吃,使自己越來越胖。
There are many other factors that bring about the problem.
有很多其他因素導致這個問題。
(that 在形容詞子句中做主詞,不能省略。)
There are still some people who hold that we should travel with friends.
還有一些人認爲我們應該與朋友一起去旅行。
Those people who strongly oppose the practice claim that it violates people's basic rights of working.
強烈反對這種做法的人聲稱它侵犯了人們基本的工作權利。
Those who welcome the internet hold that it brings us great convenience and efficiency.
贊成互聯網的人認爲它帶給我們很大的方便和效率。

(2) 由關係副詞引導的形容詞子句

關係副詞包括：when、where、why、whose 等,在形容詞子句中分別作時間副詞語、地點副詞語、原因副詞語、修飾語。

We live in the country where people enjoy their legal rights.
我們生活在人們享有合法權利的國家。
There are numerous reasons why I hold this opinion.
我之所以持有這個觀點是有很多原因的。
I like to make friends with people whose characters, hobbies and social status are similar with me.
我喜歡和性格、愛好和社會地位與我相似的人交朋友。

(3) 介系詞前移的形容詞子句

形容詞子句的最後部分如果是一個介系詞,在書面語中應把它放在關係代名詞之前,而且這時只能用 which,不能用 that。

I hit upon an article in which some people hold that students should wear uniforms every day.
我看到一篇文章,其中寫道,一些人認為中學生應該每天都穿校服。
The critics argue that the practice does not coincide with the present-day civilized world in which liberty and individuality are highly worshiped.
批評家們認為這種做法與目前高度尊崇自由和個性的文明社會不一致。
In kindergartens, there are many educational facilities from which children can benefit.
幼稚園有很多教育設施,孩子們可以從中受益。

(4) 非限制性形容詞子句

形容詞子句可分為限制性形容詞子句和非限制性形容詞子句兩種。限制性形容詞子句與被修飾的單字關係密切,這類子句是不能拿掉的,若拿掉了,剩下的部分就會失去意義,或意思不清楚,甚至顯得荒謬。在譯成中文時,這類子句一般也譯成子句。比如:
A man who doesn't study constantly can't hope to achieve much.(一個沒有不斷學習的人是不能指望有很大成就的。)如果去掉形容詞子句,變成: A man can't hope to achieve much.(一個人不能指望有很大成就。)顯然這樣意思是很不清楚的。前面所列舉的形容詞子句都是限制性形容詞子句。

非限制性形容詞子句只對所修飾的字做進一步的說明,拿掉之後,其他部分仍然成立。這類子句通常和句子的其他部分用逗號分開,譯為中文時,子句常可譯為一個並列的句子。非限制性形容詞子句在修飾人時用 who、whom 或 whose,在修飾物時用 which,兩種情況都不能用 that。

　　修飾語子句一般修飾名詞或代名詞,但非限制性形容詞子句更常用於修飾前面的整個句子。

They want to imitate what they see, which is sometimes dangerous.
他們想要模仿他們所看到的東西,這有時是危險的。
(which 修飾的是 They want to imitate what they see。)
Mothers can concentrate on their work and advance their careers, which is also helpful to the social development.
母親們可以專注於她們的工作,發展她們的事業,這對社會發展也是有利的。
(which 修飾的是 Mothers can concentrate on their work and advance their careers。)
It is a controversial question, which has aroused heated discussion among people.
這是一個有爭議的問題,它引起了人們的熱烈討論。
(which 修飾的是名詞 question。)
As soon as a child becomes old enough to communicate with other children, he begins having friends, who sometimes influence him more rapidly than do families.
當一個孩子長到足以和其他孩子交流時,他開始交朋友,這些朋友有時比家庭影響他更快。
(who 修飾的是名詞 friends。)
Nowadays, more and more people agree that smoking is an unwholesome hobby, which is equivalent to committing suicide.
現在,越來越多的人同意吸煙是一個不健康的嗜好,它等同於自殺。
The old people can look after their grandchildren, which may to some degree release the pressure of the young.
老年人可以照顧他們的孫輩,這也會在一定程度上減輕年輕人的壓力。
Some students spend too much time playing computer games, which would be harmful to their health and have a negative influence on their studies.
一些學生在玩電腦遊戲上花費了太多的時間,這對他們的身體有害,也會影響他們的學習。

　　有時,限制性形容詞子句和非限制性形容詞子句的區別不是特別明顯,前面的一些限制性形容詞子句也可以改為非限制性形容詞子句。比如:
Those people who strongly oppose the practice claim that it violates people's basic rights of working.
強烈反對這種做法的人聲稱它侵犯了人們基本的工作權利。

這是一個限制性形容詞子句，也可以寫為：

Those people, who strongly oppose the practice, claim that it violates people's basic rights of working.

強烈反對這種做法的人聲稱它侵犯了人們基本的工作權利。

這就變成了一個非限制性形容詞子句。

13. 副詞子句

副詞子句是可以和形容詞子句比擬的另一個使用很廣泛的語言現象，大家在作文中一定會用得很多。做副詞語的子句通常由一個連接詞引導。

副詞子句的種類最多，可分為時間、地點、原因、目的、結果、條件、比較、讓步等。其中用得比較多的是原因、目的、條件、時間、讓步、比較，下面我們分別講解。

(1) 原因

常用的連接詞有：because、as、since、for。

掌握好表達原因的結構是十分重要的，幾乎所有的寫作試題都要求寫原因或可以寫原因。議論文的基本模式是擺事實、講道理，講道理就是說明原因。寫作測試的文體決定了表達原因結構的重要性。原因副詞子句就是使用最多的表示原因的結構。

I still like to travel with friends because I think the most important thing during travel is to get pleasure and relaxation.

我還是喜歡和朋友一起去旅行，因為我認為在旅行中最重要的是得到快樂和休息。

I think it is sagacious to raise pets because it is beneficial in many ways.

我認為飼養寵物是明智的，因為這在很多方面都有好處。

Some people suggest that we should not help the adventurers, because any kind of help would ruin their pleasure of exploring.

一些人認為我們不應該幫助探險者，因為任何形式的幫助都會破壞他們探險的樂趣。

(2) 結果

常用的連接詞有：so、so that。

Most people marry and have children, so they need a steady reliable income because of their family responsibilities.

大多數的人結婚並且有孩子,所以他們爲了家庭責任需要穩定而可靠的收入。

Nowadays, people face fierce competition and suffer from great life pressure, so they spend little time with their families.

現在,人們面臨激烈的競爭,承受巨大的壓力,所以幾乎沒有時間和家人在一起。

Important events are often broadcast live so that the audiences feel as if they were participating.

重要的事件經常在電視上現場直播,以至於觀眾就好像身臨其境。

(3) **時間**

常用的連接詞有:when、as、while、before、after、until、since、as soon as 。

Telephone is very convenient especially when we have something urgent.

電話是非常方便的,尤其當我們有緊急的事情時。

When one finishes his study abroad, he will have more opportunities for his future career.

當一個人完成留學時,他將會有更多的機會開拓未來的事業。

(4) **讓步**

常用的連接詞有:though、although、even if、no matter、while。

Although it is indispensable to human beings, it also brings a lot of inconvenience to us.

雖然它對人類而言不可缺少,它也給我們帶來了很多的不便。

While the small family has a unique advantage, it cannot compete with the large family.

雖然小家庭有獨特的優點,但它在很多方面不能和大家庭競爭。

Reasonable and attractive as the opinion seems, it cannot hold water.

這個觀點雖然看起來有道理和吸引人,但是它經不起推敲。

Nowadays, people face fierce competition and suffer from great life pressure, so they spend little time with their families, though they want to.

現在,人們面臨激烈的競爭,承受巨大的壓力,所以幾乎沒有時間和家人在一起,雖然他們想這麼做。

Most people marry and have children, so they need a steady reliable income because of their family responsibilities even if they are dissatisfied with their jobs.

大多數的人結婚並且有孩子,所以他們爲了他們的家庭責任需要穩定而可靠的收入,即使他們不滿意他們的工作。

Some people suggest that we should not help the adventurers even if they are in danger, because any kind of help would ruin their pleasure of exploring.

一些人認爲我們不應該幫助探險者,即使他們處於危險中,因爲任何形式的幫助都會破壞他們探險的樂趣。

One must learn to stick to one's own confidence and hope, no matter how little the hope may be.

一個人必須學會堅持自己的信心和希望,不管這個希望是多麼的微小。

(5) 條件

常用的連接詞有:if、unless、in case。

If smoking is banned totally, more serious problems will arise, such as unemployment.

如果吸煙被全面禁止,更嚴重的問題就會產生,例如失業。

If we tear down the old buildings, we are ruining the cultural heritage and the traditional value as well.

如果我們推倒老建築,我們就破壞了文化遺產和傳統價值。

If they continue to work in a way their health permits, old people can still make a great contribution to the society.

如果他們繼續以他們的健康允許的方式工作,老年人仍然會爲社會做很大的貢獻。

If you leave your present job, you have to start at a much lower rank.

如果你離開你現在的工作,你不得不從一個低得多的職位上重新開始。

An important aspect of traveling with friends is that in case emergency takes place, your friend will give you a hand immediately.

和朋友一起旅行的一個重要方面是,萬一緊急情況發生,你的朋友會立即給予你幫助。

14. 集 合 句

如果句子包含有兩個或更多互不依從的主謂結構,就是集合句。集合句中的分句通常用一個對等連接詞來連接,最常見的是 and 和 but。

有時一個集合句中的一個(或更多)分句可能包含有一個(或更多)子句,這種句子稱爲混合句。

Solving the problem of traffic jams is not an easy job and I don't think any individual or organization can easily handle it.

解決交通擁擠問題不是一件容易的工作,我不認爲任何個人或單位能很容易地解決它。

Some people are indulged in raising pets and they will feel uncomfortable and lonely if they are forbidden to do so.

一些人沉溺於飼養寵物,如果他們被禁止飼養寵物,他們會感到不舒服和孤獨。

With the steady growth in the country's economy as well as the people's living standard, the rhythm of people's living is speeding up and a lot of changes have taken place in their daily life.

隨着國家經濟的增長和人民生活水準的提高,人們生活的節奏加快了,他們的日常生活發生了很多變化。

In the countryside, the air is clean, the food is fresh and the houses are usually spacious with large yards around them.

在鄉村,空氣是乾淨的,食物是新鮮的,房子通常是寬敞的,四周環繞寬大的庭院。

15. 英文句子的用途分類

(1) 敍述句

無疑地作文中絕大部分應該是敍述句,有的文章中 100% 都是敍述句,這也不足爲奇。

(2) 疑問句

疑問句提出問題。

Is it a good phenomenon that pets enjoy better meals than some poor people?

寵物比一些窮人享用更好的飲食,這是好現象嗎?

How can we solve the problem of traffic jams?

我們能如何解決交通擁擠問題呢?

If the students are forced to wear uniforms every day, how can they develop their individuality and creativity?

如果學生們被迫每天都穿校服,他們怎麼能發展個性和創造力呢?

(3) 感歎句

感歎句表示說話時的驚訝、喜悅、氣憤等情緒。這類句子一般是由 what 或 how 引起的，what 用來修飾一個名詞，how 用來修飾一個形容詞、副詞。

大家在寫議論文時應注意要以理服人，不要以情動人，所以應慎用感歎句。有時使用感歎句時，可以將感歎號改為句號，以減輕它的感情色彩。

What a pleasure it is to have a friend with the same taste.
有同樣品味的朋友是多麼高興的事。
How wonderful it is to compete with your friend in a green field.
和朋友在綠茵場上競爭是多麼美妙。
How dull and monotonous it is that all the students are wearing the same uniforms.
所有學生穿同樣的校服是多麼的單調。

(4) 祈使句

祈使句表示勸告、請求、命令、叮囑、邀請等，動詞用原形。這種句子的否定式多以 do not 引起，也可用 never 引起。祈使句的主詞通常是不出現的。

Never bring your work home. Leave it in your office.
永遠不要將工作帶回家。把它留在你的辦公室。
Let good advertisements facilitate communication between business people and the public, and help keep the business world moving.
讓好的廣告促進商人和大眾之間的交流，並幫助商業界運行。

文章當然要絕對以敘述句為主，但在合適的時候，用上一句問句、感歎句、祈使句，也能使文章的句式多變。但要注意，一要合適，二不能太多。

16. 插入語

一個單字、片語或子句插入到句子的兩個句子成分之間，稱為插入語。使用插入語可以使句式富於變化。

Many people, however, argue that children should be looked after in the kindergarten.
然而,很多人認爲兒童應該在幼稚園被照顧。

Students who have part-time jobs can relieve, to some extent, the economic burdens of their parents.
有兼職工作的學生能在某種程度上減輕他們父母的經濟負擔。

Solving problems in the dorm will, in the long run, help students understand how to communicate with others.
解決宿舍中的問題從長遠看將幫助學生懂得如何與其他人打交道。

Artistic projects, which are symbols of the city, can boost local tourism.
藝術項目,作爲城市的象徵,能促進當地的旅遊業。

People who favor the practice of censorship insist that, among other reasons, it helps maintain a stable and orderly society.
另外的原因之一是,贊成新聞審查的人認爲,它有助於維持一個穩定而有秩序的社會。

17. 倒　裝

主詞和述詞有兩種順序:一是主詞在前,這和中文是一致的,稱爲自然語序。另一種是述詞在主詞之前,叫做倒裝語序。

敍述句絕大多數都是自然語序,但在某些情況下卻需要用倒裝語序。倒裝的情況有很多種,比較好用、比較常用的情況有以下三種:

(1) **Only** + 副詞語成分

Only in this way, can the problem be solved successfully.
只有用這種方式,這個問題才能成功地解決。

Only when we have a healthy body, can we work more efficiently.
只有當我們有個健康的身體時,我們才能更有效率地工作。

Only if one has enough self-control, can he benefit from playing games.
只有當一個人有足夠的自制能力時,他才能從玩遊戲中獲益。

(2) 比較子句

than 後面的句子可以倒裝,也可以不倒裝。例如下面兩個句子都是正確的:

Tom plays tennis better than John does. Tom plays tennis better than does John. 但有時 than

後面句子的述語常常省略,比如上面的句子常寫爲:Tom plays tennis better than John.

Old workers are more likely to be stable, skillful and experienced than are young workers.

老工人比年輕的工人更穩定、更有技術、更有經驗。

(than 後的正常語序是: young workers are。)

As soon as a child becomes old enough to communicate with other children, he begins having friends, who sometimes influence him more rapidly than do families.

當一個孩子長到足以和其他孩子交流時,他開始交朋友,這些朋友有時比家庭影響他更快。

(than 後的正常語序是:families do。)

(3) **Not only ... but also...**

以 not only 等字引起的句子,常用倒裝語序。

句子模式:Not only 句子 1, but (also)句子 2。

意思是:不僅句子 1,而且句子 2。其中句子 1 要倒裝,句子 2 不倒裝。but also 的 also 可以省略。

In a dispute, not only do the interests of one party not coincide with those of the other party, but they are in conflict.

在一個衝突中,一方的利益與另一方不僅不一致,而且它們是矛盾的。

18. 平行結構

　　平行結構是由兩個或兩個以上的對等對象構成。但一般來講,兩個有點少,四個或四個以上又有點多,一般三個比較合適。三個對象平行的形式是:X, Y and Z,也就是前兩個之間用逗號連接,後兩個之間用 and 連接。同時還要注意三個對象在形式上的一致性。

　　平行結構在英文寫作中算一種修辭方法。同學們如果做一些練習,還是不難掌握它的。在你的文章中,如果有一個使用得較好的平行結構,一定會在語言這一項增加分數的。

They spend too much time in front of the television, ignoring their studies, outdoor activities and even their family.

他們在電視前花費了太多的時間,忽略了他們的學習、戶外活動,甚至他們的家庭。

I stayed at home, sleeping, eating and making myself fatter and fatter.

我待在家裏,又睡又吃,使自己越來越胖。

They bring great pleasures to young people, train them to respond quickly and arouse their interest in computer science.

他們帶給年輕人很大的快樂,訓練他們反應迅速,激起他們對電腦科學的興趣。

Old workers are more likely to be stable, skillful and experienced than young workers are.

老工人比年輕的工人更穩定、更有技術、更有經驗。

Formal examinations put great stress on students, generate an unhealthy spirit of jealousy and competition, and even bring about psychological problems.

考試給學生帶來很大壓力,產生一種不健康的嫉妒和競爭的思想,甚至帶來心理問題。

Those people who are addicted to playing games tend to be isolated, unsociable and self-centered.

沉溺於玩遊戲的人傾向於孤立、不擅社交和以自我為中心。

In the countryside, the air is clean, the food is fresh and the houses are usually spacious with large yards around them.

在鄉村,空氣是乾淨的,食物是新鮮的,房子是寬敞的,四周環繞寬大的庭院。

19. 常用句型

　　下面我們列出一些常用的句型,這些句型的涵義比較好,也比較通用。在寫作時,只要你想用就能用上。

(1) **Not only... but also...** 不僅……而且……

Not only ... but also... 一般表示遞進關係,幾乎可以連接句子的任何兩個成分,包括動詞、受詞、述詞等,也可以連接兩個句子。

Television not only gives us the news in which we are interested but also shows it in pictures more powerful than words.

電視不僅告訴我們感興趣的新聞,而且還用比文字更有力的圖像來顯示它。

Advertising brings us not only benefits but also problems.

廣告帶給我們的不僅有益處還有問題。

(2) **No matter** 不管/無論……

In sports, one must learn to fight with no matter what is left in his body.

在運動中,一個人必須學會不管身體中還剩下什麼也要奮鬥。

One must learn to stick to one's own confidence and hope, no matter how little the hope may be.

一個人必須學會堅持自己的信心和希望,不管這個希望是多麼的微小。

No matter how similar they are, every two friends have differences, and no matter how different they are, as friends, they have at least one similarity: the sincerity towards friendship.

不管他們多麼相似,兩個朋友會有不同。不管他們多麼不同,作為朋友,他們至少有一樣相似:對友誼的忠誠。

(3) **It is well known that** 眾所周知的是……

一般用於表示很確定的說法。

It is well known that there is a clear link between smoking and some kinds of serious diseases.

眾所周知的是,在吸煙和一些嚴重的疾病之間有清楚的關聯。

(4) **It is said that** 據說……

一般用於表示不太確定的說法。

It is said that mothers know what is most suitable for their children.

據說母親們知道什麼最適合她們的孩子。

(5) **It is obvious/apparent/evident/self-evident/clear that** 顯而易見……

一般用於表示比較確定的說法。

It is obvious that wearing the uniforms would make school life dull and monotonous.

顯而易見,穿校服會使學校生活單調。

(6) **It can be imagined that** 可以想像的是……

一般用於表示比較確定的說法。

It can be imagined that there must be some inconvenience brought about by raising pets.

可以想像,飼養寵物肯定會帶來一些不便。

(7) **It goes without saying that** 不用說……

一般用於表示比較確定的說法。

It goes without saying that wearing the uniforms would make school life dull and monotonous.

不用說,穿校服會使學校生活單調。

(8) so... that.../ such... that... / so that 那麼的……以至於……

The vacation is so short that I cannot even complete one thing.

這個假期是那麼地短,以至於我甚至不能完成一件事。

The computer plays such an important role in education that someone even suggests we will no longer need schools anymore.

電腦在教育上起到如此重要的作用,以至於有人甚至提出我們不再需要學校了。

It brought up more than 20 great scientists and mathematicians so that there are so many formulas titled with the name：Bernoullis.

它培養了 20 多個大科學家和數學家,以至於有很多公式以貝努里命名。

(9) too... to 太……不能……

The vacation is too short for me to complete one thing.

這個假期對我來說太短,我一件事都不能完成。

(10) the more... the more 越……越……

Some students have become drop-outs because through part-time jobs they have found that the more education they have, the less money they earn.

一些學生退學了,因為,他們經由兼職工作發現,他們受的教育越多,賺的錢就越少。

Therefore, a fear has arisen among some people that the more machines will be used, the more workers will be unemployed and the lower our living standard will become.

因此,一些人當中存在一種恐懼,那就是,機器被用得越多,越多的工人會失業,而我們的生活水準會越低。

　　我們在上面詳細介紹了寫作時對句子的要求,同學們應儘量使用複雜的句式,並做到句式的多樣化。有的同學會問,寫複雜的句子容易出錯,怎麼辦? 這一方面需要在複雜和準確性之間做一個平衡,另一方面應加強練習,爭取寫出既正確又有一定複雜度的句子。練習寫複雜句子的最好方法是在理解的基礎上大量閱讀、背誦與考試題目相關的好句子。

　　另一方面大家要注意,IELTS 議論文屬於淺顯的學術性寫作,它不要求很多的描述和修飾,比如下面兩段話,雖然優美,但在文章中不宜過度出現。

When I take some outdoor activities, I feel refreshed. It is a feeling of a bird rushing out of the cage. When I am running in bright sunshine in the afternoon, I believe I become a hunting dog running in the wild, persuing a rabbit.

當我做戶外活動時,我感覺精神振奮。這是一種小鳥飛出籠子的感覺。當我在一個陽光明媚的下午跑步的時候,我相信我已經成爲一隻在野地裏奔跑的獵狗,在追逐一隻兔子。

In the beautiful seasons of spring and autumn, riding a bicycle to travel and appreciate the natural views is a wonderful experience. We can see buds on the tree branches, flowers in bloom, blue sky with white cloud and so on. With the breeze kissing our faces, it is a feeling beyond description.

在美麗的春季和秋季,騎腳踏車旅行並欣賞自然景色是一段美好的經歷。我們可以看到樹枝上的綠芽、盛開的鮮花以及藍天白雲等等。微風輕吻我們的臉頰,這是一種無法言喻的感覺。

❖ 十一、常見文法錯誤分析 ❖

在考試中,文法錯誤的普遍性和嚴重性十分驚人,主謂不一致、名詞單複數不分、動詞時態和語態的濫用、常用字拼寫錯誤比比皆是,這些嚴重地影響了思想的表達。考試經驗顯示,多數考生在寫作上欠缺的不是系統的寫作理論和方法,而是最基本的單句寫作能力。

文章無論長短,都是由句子組成的,句子是表達思想的最基本的單位。因此,句子是否能寫得正確、達意和清楚,將直接影響整篇文章的品質。考生寫作成績長期得不到明顯提高的主要原因是欠缺寫好單句的能力。下面我們將剖析考生作文中的一些典型病句。

1. 用字錯誤

Nowadays is the golden time for us to improve our English.

病句分析:Nowadays 是副詞,不能做主詞。

改爲:Nowadays, it is the golden time for us to improve our English.

With the society development, more and more young people go abroad to study.

病句分析：society 是名詞，應該用它的形容詞形式 social。

改爲：With the social development, more and more young people go abroad to study.（或：With the development of the society, more and more young people go abroad to study.）

Changes have been taken place.

病句分析：take place 應用主動語態。

改爲：Changes have taken place.

My English has made a great progress.

病句分析：取得進步的主詞應爲人，而且 progress 不可數。

改爲：I have made great progress in my English.

They dress uniforms.

病句分析：穿校服應爲 wear uniforms，或 be dressed in uniforms。

改爲：They wear uniforms.

Some people think we needn't to rely on pets.

病句分析：混淆了 need 作爲語態動詞和作爲普通動詞的用法。need 作爲語態動詞時，主要用於否定句，後面的動詞不帶 to，needn't rely 作 some people 的述詞。need 作爲實意動詞時，可用於肯定句、否定句和疑問句，don't need to rely 中的 to rely 作 don't need 的受詞。

改爲：Some people think we needn't rely on pets.（或：Some people think we don't need to rely on pets.）

Nowadays, many people don't like to read books, too.

病句分析：混淆了 too 和 either，這兩個字都表示"也"的意思，但是在英文中 too 和 also 只能用於肯定句，而 either 只能用於否定句。

改爲：Nowadays, many people don't like to read books, either.

2. 斷句錯誤

It is raining, I can not go out.

病句分析:集合句之間要用對等連接詞連接,主要子句與子句之間要用從屬連接詞連接。但有的同學在寫句子時,不管句子各部分之間的關係如何,一律用逗號連接。這就是斷句錯誤。

改爲:It is raining, so I can not go out.

I like sports, they can improve my health.

改爲:I like sports, because they can improve my health.

3. 句子中出現多個動詞

Raise pets is becoming more and more popular.

病句分析:動詞片語不能做主詞,應改成動名詞片語或不定詞片語。

改爲:Raising pets is becoming more and more popular.

I am a student lived Taipei.

病句分析:句子中有兩個動詞:am 和 lived。

改爲:I am a student living Taipei.（或:I am a student who lives in Taipei.）

Students spend too much time on television, ignore their studies.

病句分析:句子中有兩個動詞:spend 和 ignore,應該將後一個改爲分詞作副詞語,或加對等連接詞。

改爲:Students spend too much time on television, ignoring their studies.（或:Students spend too much time on television, and ignore their studies.）

4. 缺、多連接詞或使用錯誤

It is known to us, practice makes perfect.

病句分析:it 作形式主詞,後面的主詞子句必須由 that 引導,不能省略。

改爲:It is known to us that practice makes perfect.

We grasp the latest knowledge is a must.

病句分析:主詞子句前的連接詞 that 不能省略。

改為:That we grasp the latest knowledge is a must.

The first reason is television is entertaining.

病句分析:述詞子句前的連接詞 that 不能省略。

改為:The first reason is that television is entertaining.

Because China is developing country, so many people are living below the poverty line.

病句分析:because 和 so 只能用一個,否則這句話無主要子句。類似的還有 although 和 but。

改為:China is developing country, so many people are living below the poverty line.

(或:Because China is developing country, many people are living below the poverty line.)

The reason for this is because many people face fierce competition.

病句分析:because 這個字不能引導述詞子句,在本句中只能改用 that。

改為:The reason for this is that many people face fierce competition.

5. 主謂語不一致

I am a student who live in Taipei.

病句分析:形容詞子句的述語應與先行詞一致。

改為:I am a student who lives in Taipei.

How can we solve this problem are a controversial issue.

病句分析:句子做主詞(主詞子句),動詞用單數。

改為:How can we solve this problem is a controversial issue.

Raising pets are a great pleasure to many people.

病句分析:動名詞做主詞,動詞用單數。

改為:Raising pets is a great pleasure to many people.

The problems which are brought about by raising pets is hard to resolve.

病句分析：主詞 problems 與動詞 is 不一致。

改為：The problems which are brought about by raising pets are hard to resolve.

My arguments is presented below.

病句分析：主詞 arguments 與動詞 is 不一致。

改為：My arguments are presented below.

6. 並列成分不一致

Students should cultivate some meaningful hobbies such as reading, studying and to sing.

病句分析：平行結構中並列成分 reading, studying and to sing 不一致。

改為：Students should cultivate some meaningful hobbies such as reading, studying and singing.

When one reaches his old age, they have to retire.

病句分析：代名詞 one 和 they 不一致。

改為：When one reaches his old age, he has to retire.

7. 重複累贅

Sharing a room with others together has more advantages.

病句分析：Sharing 與 together 意思重複。

改為：Sharing a room with others has more advantages.

It is a true fact that pets have some practical uses.

病句分析：true 與 fact 意思重複。

改為：It is a fact that pets have some practical uses.

From what we have discussed above, we can draw a final conclusion that students should wear uniforms.

病句分析：final 與 conclusion 意思重複。

改為：From what we have discussed above，we can draw a conclusion that students should wear uniforms.

In my opinion，I think students should wear uniforms.

病句分析：In my opinion 與 I think 意思重複。

改為：In my opinion，students should wear uniforms.

But，however，I can not agree with them.

病句分析：But 與 however 意思重複。

改為：However，I can not agree with them.

8. 非完整句錯誤

With the limited budget. The government is unable to invest much money in education.

病句分析：介系詞片語 With the limited budget 不是一個完整的句子。

改為：With the limited budget，the government is unable to invest much money in education.

I know some children. Who are from one-child family.

病句分析：形容詞子句 Who are from one-child family 不是一個完整的句子。

改為：I know some children who are from one-child family.

9. There be 結構

考生病句：

1. There are many people go abroad to study.
2. There are some disadvantages bring about by raising pets.

　　這兩個例句的錯誤比較有普遍性，雖然同學們一開始學英文就接觸了 there be 這一最常用的句式,但還是不能正確地運用它。在這種結構中,there 是引導詞,沒有實際意義。be 在句中作動詞,有時態和數的變化,所以在句子中不能出現其他的動詞。上面兩句中,都出現了其他的動詞片語 go abroad to study 和 bring about by raising pets。改正辦法是將 there be 之後的動詞改為分詞片語做後置修飾語或形容詞子句。

上面兩句應改為:

1. There are many people who go abroad to study.（或 There are many people going abroad to study.）

2. There are some disadvantages which are brought about by raising pets.（或 There are some disadvantages brought about by raising pets.）

10. 比較結構

考生病句:

1. Comparing with the large family, the small family has a unique advantage.

2. The climate in Taichung is better than Taipei.

在作文中常用 compare 或 than 表示比較,比較結構是常用結構,正確地使用這一結構可以使文章的句式增加變化,有利於提高寫作成績。但許多考生受中文表達習慣的影響,有相當多的表達錯誤。

在例 1 中,對兩個事物進行比較的句式為 Compared with A, B...,只能用 compare 的過去分詞,不能用現在分詞,因為 B 是分詞的邏輯主詞,只能被比較。在例 2 中,考生誤將"天氣"與"城市"進行比較,而二者沒有可比性,只有將後者改為"台北的天氣"才符合邏輯。

上面兩句應改為:

1. Compared with the large family, the small family has a unique advantage.

2. The climate in Taichung is better than that of Taipei.

十二、範　文

下面我們按照"辯論式題目－五段論式寫法","辯論式題目－對稱式寫法","論說式題目"三類分別提供一些範文。這些範文在考試中大部分都能得 8 分。

筆者在準備範文時,沒有請 native speaker 寫範文。主要是因爲筆者深深感覺到一些由 native speaker 寫的範文好是好,但同學們只能歎爲觀止,很難學習和模仿。筆者也沒有將範文寫到"極精緻"的程度,很多"IELTS 範文選"中的文章達 400 字,語言盡善盡美,但決不是 40 分鐘寫出來的,給人一種望而生畏、失去信心的感覺。筆者選的這些範文都是比大家的層次稍高一些,大家經過努力也能達到。我想這對大家的幫助會更大。

大家要正確對待範文的作用,它們主要是使大家對文章的整體結構有更深的理解。筆者並不贊成大家背誦很多的整篇文章。背誦整篇文章有一個弊端:如果考試題目完全相同,很多同學寫的文章會完全相同,這些同學的分數肯定會很低。另一個弊端是:如果題目略有不同,這時將背好的文章原文抄上,極易牛頭不對馬嘴。

筆者建議的準備方法是:準備並背熟屬於自己的文章模板(詳見本章第六節),同時背誦大量的寫作素材,並注意按照題材分類,如電視、廣告、電腦等。這樣在考試中,同學們在結構、內容、語言等方面都會有不錯的表現。

1. 辯論式題目 – 五段論式寫法

Topic 1:*Who should be responsible for children's education, the school or the parents? Give your opinion and tell the reasons.*

Nowadays, as the competition in the whole world is much more intensive than ever before, lots of people pay more attention to their children's education for the purpose of success achieved by the educated children in the future. In other words, education is one of the most important stages in children's lifetime. Therefore, the realistic question in front of everyone is who should take the responsibility for children's education. In fact, it is very difficult to answer it. From my point of view, school should take the responsibility rather than children's parents. There are some reasons I would like to explain below.

In the first place, school is a place where students receive systematic education. In general speaking, students are taught knowledge and skills regularly by the teachers with professional training. In school, students are able to accumulate a lot of knowledge in their mind for their development in the future. School education, that is to say, is the prerequisite and cornerstone of their achievements.

In the second place, school plays a significant role in improvement and development of children's ability to cope with the society. They are educated and instructed how to deal with what they will come across in accordance with the requirements specified by their school, and then they will be equipped with the sufficient capacity to distinguish what is "right" and "wrong".

Furthermore, one of the original purposes of establishment of school is to relieve parents from educational responsibility for their children. In the case of liberation, parents have enough time to devote themselves to their jobs so as to contribute more to the society.

But, on the other hand, if possible, parents should furnish to their children educational activities in spare time in order to widen children's outlook and extend children's scope of knowledge. Nevertheless, parents never replace school in education.

As afore mentioned, I take it that children never receive perfect education without school and never succeed without school education. As an educational institution is supervised by the public and authorities, the school's unique commitment to the nation and society is to educate children.

Topic 2: Some people say that it is not right for the government to spend so much money on artistic projects, such as galleries and sculptures. Do you agree with them? Please explain your reasons.

For the purpose of beautification of cities, which develop quickly in construction, the governments offer lots of funds to the artistic projects. For instance, there are more and more paintings and sculptures at the public places. The behavior of the governments raises a sharp controversy as people stand on different positions. Some hold the opinion that the governments ought to invest in the artistic projects. Others, however, contradict it. At the option of mine, I vote for the latter one. My arguments for the point of view are presented as follows.

First of all, governments should give priority to the construction of infrastructure. As our country is a developing nation with limited funds, through the effective and perfect operation of the authorities, money collected from the taxpayers should be invested into the projects which are beneficial to majority of common people other than minority. Regardless of his position and opinion, everybody, especially the official with strong power, should comprehend clearly that the infrastructure, such as roads, transportation, communication, energy and housing, is the most essential framework of the development of our nation.

Next, it is important for the authorities to focus on education. According to the official statistics, nearly half of children in the rural regions are unable to finish their elementary education, and some of them fail to go to school because of lack of money. Therefore, the governments should provide a part of revenue to educational institutions so that a perfect educational system will be established for every child's opportunity of being educated.

Last but not least, it is necessary for the authorities to furnish the financial assistance to those who live below the poverty line. Perhaps, those people will lose the self-confidence of living, and even their lives without the government's aid and the care of the society. So, the authorities ought to spend money to set up social insurance system for the satisfaction of each person's essential demands for survival.

On the other hand, I take it for granted that the governments, without the expense of the above-mentioned aspects, put less money into the artistic projects that are beneficial to people's psychological health. Nevertheless since we have a very limited budget, we should make full use of the money to benefit the common people.

Generally, infrastructure, education and poverty, instead of artistic projects, are the principle problems which the authorities shall solve prior to the others by the effective utilization of the limited funds.

Topic 3: Should uniform be introduced into schools and should students be required to wear uniforms?

At present, more and more students are asked to wear the school uniform in accordance with the provision specified by school authorities. In the case of the popularity of the uniform, some think that it has many disadvantages. Everything in the world has two sides. Without exception, wearing school uniforms has both advantages and disadvantages. From my point of view, I believe that its advantages outweigh its disadvantages. Some of my opinions will be demonstrated below in front of you.

I agree with the statement without reservation since the students with the school uniform can pay attention to their study rather than fashionable cloth. One of the functions of the uniform is, that is to say, to make the students understand that their most essential task in school is not chasing fashion but learning knowledge. Only if they study hard, will they be qualified to create their own bright future.

It might also be noted that forcing students to wear school uniforms help cultivate their sense of team spirit and cooperation. They are well aware that each of them is one of a member of the school and also the society, and the teamwork is the basis for their success. Furthermore, all of them in the team will provide assistance for one another in order to accept the new challenges in front of them.

Moreover, wearing school uniforms will remind students that they should comply with the requirements and regulations. It helps them gradually realize that they really belong to a school and not just individuals. Being afraid of damaging the prestige of their schools, wearing uniforms also helps students restrain themselves because it is convenient for people, according to their school uniform, to distinguish which school they belong to.

But on the other hand, the students may have some opportunities to opt for their favorable clothes in spare time so as to strengthen their self-confidence to make some decisions by themselves. Flowers in different colors make a garden more beautiful. Nevertheless, the functions of any other clothes could not replace ones of the school uniform in many areas.

In conclusion, it is more beneficial for the students to wear the school uniform than not to do it. The uniform plays a significant role in their studying and living.

Topic 4: Some people believe formal examination has more disadvantages so we should not use it as a means of assessment. Do you agree or disagree with this statement?

Examination has long played an important role in education. Although a growing number of people have begun to challenge its reliability, I think examination has more advantages. There are numerous reasons why I hold this opinion, and I would explore a few of the most important ones here.

Certainly no other reason in my decision is more crucial that the one as follow. Examination is important because it is an effective means of assessment. How can teachers and parents know how well the students are learning? How can students themselves know? There is only one answer: examination. Some schools have tried using other forms of assessment alone, but the individual attention required makes it too time-consuming. Besides, the individualized evaluation is not dependable and it also makes regional and national assessment of students impossible.

There is another factor that deserves some words here. Examination is necessary because it requires students to learn facts which are important for the students. Unfortunately, learning facts is now often regarded as out-of-date. It is said that students should think for themselves. But storing facts is a prerequisite for independent thinking. No one can think with an empty mind.

Finally, examination is vital because they make students hard-working. Laziness is part of human nature. It is not helpful for students to learn. Examination can make students work hard and help them learn to make full use of their study time.

On the other hand, we must say that examination also has some disadvantages. First, it can't assess the whole qualities of the students. Secondly, it can generate an unhealthy spirit of jealousy and competition. We can't use examination as the sole evaluation of students. But without examination, it will be harder for educational institutions to select qualified candidates.

No matter what other means of assessment we add, examination must remain a vital part of schooling.

Topic 5: What are the advantages and disadvantages brought to your daily life by computers?

Modern technological devices such as computers have found their wide application in our daily life and industrial work. Although some people claim that they have some bad influence on students, I think the advantages outweigh the disadvantages. Among countless factors which influence my decision there are three conspicuous aspects.

One of the advantages of using computers is the convenience. We can store and take out files by using computers and no longer need to rewrite the same file again and again. It is especially convenient when we want to make a new file by slightly changing an original one.

Another reason for my propensity for computers is that they make us work more efficiently. Huge amounts of data processing can be done with the help of computers, which saves us a lot of time. If we use them properly, we can get the results we want directly from what we put in through computers.

Finally, using computers can minimize errors made by human subjectivity. We usually make mistakes because we can not take everything into account. By using computers choices can be made by computers more objectively.

On the other hand, there are some disadvantages induced by using computers. The most serious is that it makes students lazy, for they do not analyze the process step by step, which is sometimes necessary. Relying on computers, they do not calculate for themselves. It is harmful to the development of their intellectual ability. How can we solve the problem? Instead of restricting the use of computers and calculators, what we should do is to educate students how to use them properly.

On the whole, computers have both advantages and disadvantages. But fairly speaking, everyone should admit that the advantages outweigh the disadvantages. We should make use of them more and more in our work.

Topic 6: Some people believe television has more disadvantages. Others think it is more advantageous. What do you think?

Everything in the world has its own two sides. Without exception, there are both advantages and disadvantages brought about by television. In my opinion, everyone should admit that its advantages outweigh its disadvantages.

The main reason that can be seen by everyone is that television presents a vivid world in front of us. It tells us what is happening right now in the world. Television not only gives us the news in which we are interested but also shows it in pictures more powerful than words. In particular, important events are often broadcast live so that the audiences feel as if they were participating.

Another factor we must consider is that television also plays an educational role in our daily life. We are often attracted by the programs about life in foreign countries which we want to know about. We can also learn about history by watching related programs. English programs are popular among the people who are studying this language. What is more, university TV has been recognized as the most effective method of part-time education.

On the other hand, there are some complaints about the television. For example, some children spend hours before the little screen, ignoring their study, outdoor activities and even their family. Parents say that these kids are indifferent to nearly everything and premature somehow. Nevertheless, it is not the television's fault. We should tell our children how to handle these problems properly.

In short, given the factors I have just outlined, it is safely to draw the conclusion that television is more advantageous.

Topic 7: Some people argue that television affect family relationship. Family members are no longer as close as before. Do you agree or not?

Television is undoubtedly one of the most powerful means of communication in the history of humankind. Television, with its wide availability and rich media with image and sound, is difficult to ignore. Naturally, the more time one spends watching television, the less time he has with his family and friends. Thus, we can clearly see why some have claimed that television has been harmful for communication among family and friends. However, I do not think their arguments can bear much analysis.

No one could neglect/deny the fact that most people much prefer spending time with their families and friends to spend time watching television. Most educated people are aware of the deleterious effects of too much television and either avoid excessive time watching television, or actually do not enjoy it. I, for example, after a long day at work, would much rather spend time talking with my wife and playing with my children than I would watching some unrealistic life on television. For me and my family, our time together is precious and beautiful, and could never be replaced or hurt by television. Even if sometimes I watch television I would rather enjoy it with my family members.

A more essential factor is that it is the life pressures that destroy communication among family members. Communication among family and friends in industrialized countries has decreased in recent years, it might be tempting to blame this problem on television since its rise roughly coincided with the decrease in time we spend with our families. However, I believe this situation is more likely due to increased pressures from work, school, and the economy. In a word, people nowadays have very little time for anything, but television is not the cause —— it is increased desire to succeed.

In some situations, however, television has surely contributed to a decrease in communication among family members. It is self-evident that people who indulge themselves in television will not spare time for communication with others. Due to the television, families communicate less with each other and enjoy less family activities together. However, most people realize that television is merely a temporary diversion and do not use it to replace interpersonal communication.

In short, I do not believe that television has destroyed or even harmed interpersonal communication among most people. I believe that the damage attributed to television is greatly exaggerated and that such damage is most likely attributable to other more powerful social factors.

說明：有時在考試中遇到的題目與以前見過的題目特別類似，這當然是件好事。但也不要欣喜若狂，不要急於下筆。很多考試題目是重複使用的，但也有些題目會稍作變動，這時，要注意這些變動，否則容易文不對題。例如本題是問電視的利與弊，與 Topic 6 有關係，但差別也很大。

Topic 8: Some people believe that children should engage in educational pursuits in their spare time, otherwise they are wasting their time. Do you agree or disagree?

Many parents regretfully observe that their kids seem unable to come up with anything to do in their spare time besides turning on the TV or playing video games. I agree that children should make the best use of their spare time, and therefore educational programs should be their first choice when they are free.

The first reason is that educational activities, if properly planned and carried out, play a fundamental role in building children's characters. Children are in the process of forming their outlook of the outside world as of themselves. By engaging in educational pursuits in their spare time, they have the opportunity to develop themselves, to enlarge their horizons and to discover the pleasure of doing things in a creative way. Educational activities may also help children to learn and develop the skills of gaining fulfillment from doing things.

The second factor is that educational activities also help children to learn and develop the skills. What is the main task of children? It is not only playing but also learning. Almost all the parents do not wish their children can only watch TV after they grow up. Children themselves also hope they can contribute to the world and the people when they enter the society. Therefore, it is important for children to do meaningful and valuable things in their spare time such as reading and studying.

At the same time, the problem with pursuits such as watching TV and playing video games, although entertaining, is that they do not contribute to children's exploration of either themselves or the outside world in the process of their growing up. They do not require children to use any of their imagination or creativity. What is more, they are harmful to children's intellectual development. The children tend to be satisfied with being couch potatoes, happily watching the screen all the time.

To sum up, it is wise for children to discover the joy of doing educational things when they are not otherwise engaged. They will find that the experience of searching and understanding is both useful and thoroughly satisfying as well as being the basis of many skills applicable to both academic and non-academic tasks.

Topic 9: Nowadays, the trend of fashion changes very rapidly, and gradually people become the slaves of it. Some people think that a person should choose comfortable clothes, which he or she likes, regardless of fashion, do you agree? Write an essay to state your opinion.

One of the most fickle things in modern society is fashion. Fashion leaders are constantly inventing new trends in clothing and decoration, and consequently a great amount of time and money is spent on this endless pursuit. To correct this human failing, some people advocate that one should wear comfortable clothes which are in line with one's personal taste. To me, this is a very sensible idea.

We all admit that clothing should be able to illustrate a person's individual characteristics. Everyone has the right to seek his or her unique style, instead of surrendering to the latest fashion. If you want to be different from others, you should not follow the fashion; you should have your own style. Following the latest fashion trend only makes you a tiny drop in an ocean of people.

At the same time, we should be clear that the basic function of clothing is to keep us warm and comfortable, therefore, it is stupid to choose clothes which may be pleasant to our eyes, but are torture to wear. The impression we make on others is often important, but it can never be important enough to make us willingly undergo discomfort.

In a word, it is unwise to follow the trend of fashion aimlessly. To be relaxed, modern people, we should form our own style and wear clothes that make us comfortable and self-confident.

Topic 10: Some people argue that television affect family relationship. Family members are no longer as close as before. Do you agree or not?

Today, almost all of the families have got TV sets in the world. An increasing number of people are addicted to programs of TV instead of communication among the families. This is a serious social problem.

In the first place, watching TV occupy our precious time. As a kind of entertainment, TV are wasting much of our time. Generally, most people choose to sit before the screen after dinner. They are attracted deeply by those interesting programs. As a result, they forget to keep in touch with their families and friends.

Next, watching TV is also a sort of tiring work. It is necessary that people take enough rest after they complete a day's work. Their spirit will suffer continuously from X-ray if they are used to watching TV. For a long time, these people are more likely to become hot-tempered. It must bring an adverse influence on their relationship.

Moreover, it is especially harmful to children. If children spend hours before the little screen and ignore their study, outdoor activities and even their family, then the result will be more serious. Parents have to worry about their children and their study. Consequently there must be some frequent quarrels between them, which contribute to the generation gap.

On the other hand, however, an inevitable fact is that TV has played an important role in today's society. It widens our sight and offers more information. It will add more beautiful color to the world if it is used more reasonably. But unfortunately there are so many people addicted to it and therefore the relationship between families is seriously affected.

Based on the discussion, an excess of indulging in TV would affect the relationship among the families and friends. We must strengthen management for ourselves.

Topic 11: Which is more important for you in your life: knowledge from books you read, or personal experiences in reality? Please use details to explain your answer.

Books and experience are the main two channels for people to gain their knowledge. Each plays different roles for people. In my opinion, knowledge from experience is more important than that from books.

To begin with, experience can prove if the knowledge from books are true or false. Textbooks are very wonderful in teaching people essential principles. How does the world looks like? What is the basic law of change of people and things? We can learn a lot through primary school, secondary school until university. However, people can only understand the really meaning of those from books and justify them if they are right through practices. A few hundred years ago, people learnt from textbook that the earth was flat. However, scientists found that was wrong through observations and measurement.

Next, the knowledge from experience can improve and advance the world and our society. As books have limitation, they only teach us what people found in the past. The knowledge from the books are constrained to the certain conditions and environment. For example, mould and tools design for plastics industry, the university course only taught me very simple cases, most knowledge are obtained from various and complicated cases in my career.

Furthermore, there are a lot of new inventions and new products which could not be found from textbooks. Our society and world are developed through continuous practices, those knowledge, never found in books, such as internet, e-business etc. are all developed through new practices.

Just as the saying is "The truth comes from practices and experience", people are continually discovering new things and assessing the creditability of the knowledge written in books. The knowledge from experience helps us much more than those from books.

Topic 12: Do you support building a factory in your hometown?

Building a factory in my hometown will bring a lot of advantages and disadvantages, but I believe that my hometown will mostly benefit from the building of a new factory for all the reasons I will describe below.

First of all, the factory's construction will surely improve the local infrastructure. To run smoothly, the factory will has to have a steady, reliable supply of water and electricity. Some old pipes will be changed, and some facilities will be renovated. The residents' living standard get improved as a result of these widespread changes, an important benefit in Arroz of Feijao, where many people do not have access to clean water.

Secondly, to make the employee commute more conveniently, the local roads will have to be rebuilt and broadened, resulting in improved public transportation. The town's residents can take a public bus to go shopping or go to work. As a result, air pollution and fuel consumption might be reduced.

Most important, a factory's establishment will bring up a lot of employment opportunities for the community. A factory need experts from various fields. The residents can take just a few minutes to go to the factory to work. So, the local residents can get great benefits from this factory.

On the other hand, as you know, factories usually bring pollution. If this factory is not managed very effectively and efficiently according to specific rules, it's prone to polluting the local air and water. What's more, factories usually make noise. Beside clean drinkable water and fresh air, an ideal community should be quiet. If the factory cannot maintain this situation to the community, it will not last long. A factory that is too noisy or pollutes too much will eventually be relocated to a new area.

Generally speaking, I agree with the plan to build a factory near my community. If the factory can be managed successfully, the factory and local residents can have mutual benefit.

Topic 13: Most high level jobs are done by men. Should the government encourage a certain percentage of these jobs to be reserved for women?
You should spend no more than 40 minutes on this task. You should write a minimum of 250 words. You should use your own ideas, knowledge and experience to support your arguments with examples and relevant evidence.

Now, most of the jobs in society that are high-paying, powerful, and demand a lot of responsibility are held by men. I think the government should reserve a percentage of these jobs for females.

Firstly, the problem of unfair employment distribution comes from social convention. At a young age most girls are not encouraged to pursue political office, business success, or professional prestige. On the other hand, boys are told to do these things. As a result, men hold the high level jobs but this does not mean they are very good at what they do. If the government set a quota for hiring women to do high level work, such as working in the government itself, then perhaps women would be more inspired to be ambitious in their life plans.

Furthermore, to legislate a percentage of high level jobs for women would work to fight the unwritten sexist rules of the workplace. For instance, if a man and a woman both competed for a managerial position of a company, and both were equally qualified and had the same experience and background, there is little doubt who would get the job. Even more, if the man was less qualified and less experienced than the woman, the man would still probably get the job because of his sex. Therefore, the government should reserve a certain percentage of high level jobs to ensure that some highly trained women could be hired.

On the other hand, there are many arguments against the use of a quota system for women. It is true that the injustice and discrimination could be reversed. This is to say that some qualified men might be denied a job while some unqualified women would be given one. Nevertheless, a quota system would break down some barriers between the men and the women. With the help of this practice, the sexism in the workplace will disappear gradually.

To sum up, from what I have mentioned above, it is not difficult to get the conclusion that the government should reserve a percentage of these jobs for females.

Topic 14: "*When people succeed, it is because of hard work. Luck has nothing to do with success.*" *Do you agree or disagree with the quotation above? Use specific reasons and examples to explain your position.*

Success is always what human beings chase. Someone succeeds for his luck while someone succeeds for his hard work. As far as I am concerned, I fully agree with the claim that there is no correlation between success and luck.

First of all, an education is the key factor of success. One wishing to be admitted to the university will have to take several tests. It is doubtful that someone will be so lucky that knowing nothing, he could pass the test with a high score. Therefore, in order to be successful, one should prepare for the tests and work hard, because a good education will provide him with a good job and an opportunity to accomplish some of his goals and dreams. In my lifetime, I have never met a person who could graduate from a college without working hard.

Secondly, it is impossible to make a career if one is lacking knowledge. Luck plays no role in achieving this success. Even if someone was unbelievably lucky enough to become a manager not being qualified enough, he will be asked to resign in the near future because of his inability due to lack of knowledge and experience to make right decisions. For instance, I used to work for a very small company owned by a friend. Although he had no knowledge or experience in business, the company had been profitable for a short time, which he contributed to his luck. But this company was finally closed because of the wrong strategies and decisions made by him.

On the other hand, it can not be denied that many businessmen become successful only for their new ideas, not for their long time of hard work and many people having done a lot of work still can not be successful men. Sometimes luck may play an important role in success. But it is mainly acting through one's diligent work. It is the hard work that leads us to the front of luck.

In sum, success is every person's pursuit. We always dream that someday we will be successful businessmen, famous scientists, or distinguished politicians. All of these things are simply not possible without hard work. Luck has no place in such a scheme of events.

Topic 15: Should criminals be punished with lengthy jail terms or re-educated and rehabilitated using, for instance, community service programmes, before being re-introduced to society?

The ways in which a society deals with those who break the law has long been a contentious issue. Some people think criminals should be punished with lengthy jail terms. Others claim that we should seek to re-educate criminals before they are re-introduced to society. I vote for the latter one.

Firstly, it is helpful to re-integrate criminals into society. If they remain outside of society they not only are dangerous, but also cost society a lot of money. Punishing criminals with long jail terms will no doubt create a "them and us" society by establishing and reinforcing a criminal community within prisons, which results in more crime. Bringing criminals back to members of society is in everybody's best interests and the best way to do this is to re-educate them to help make these adjustments.

Secondly, it in fact saves money. Longer jail terms would entail even greater costs, but with rehabilitation programmes, prisoners can be put to work in community service projects, which not only provide the prisoners with valuable training, but also provide the public with much needed services. Although it seems to cost much money of the taxpayers, it will save more in the long run.

However, it cannot be denied that rehabilitation programmes are sometimes not effective. They also often bring great financial cost to the government and the public. But having a re-habilitation programme is more effective than not having one at all, and it also offers prison-ers more options when they are released. More importantly, long time prisoners often report that they repeat offend simply because they are unused to, and unprepared for civilian life.

On the whole, I think compared with punishing with lengthy jail terms, re-educating crimi-nals is more advantageous.

說明：此題在審題上有一定的難度。首先要抓住題目中的關鍵字：should、or、for instance 和 lengthy jail terms 、rehabilitated。前三個字是重要的,因為它們指出了問題的類型。should 和 or 結合,意味着這是一個在兩個相對立的事物或觀點之間的選擇。後兩個字 lengthy jail terms 和 rehabilitated 指出了這兩個相對立的事物或觀點。如果你不確定 re-habilitated 的意思,for instance 給出了一個例子,有助於你的理解。

Topic 16: Some people propose that smoking should be banned in all public places. What is your opinion? Give your reasons.

Smoking is a major killer in our society today. Should smoking be banned in all public places? I strongly approve of the ban.

At the risk of sounding too simplistic, it seems to me that the main propositions can be summarized in one saying. Smoking is harmful to the smoker's health. It is well known that there is a definite link between smoking and some kinds of serious diseases such as heart dis-ease and lung cancer. Everyday, there are many people dying from the effects of smoking in the world. According to a survey, the life expectancy of smokers is 10 – 15 years less than that of nonsmokers.

Another reason why I agree with the above statement is that I believe smokers have to spend a lot of money on cigarettes. It is not a small amount, especially for people in develo-ping countries. In order to smoke, some people spend the money which should be used for other more important things. This can sometimes bring quarrels among family members.

Finally, smoking is also harmful to the passive smokers. Even if you don't smoke, your health can be threatened by the smoking of your co-workers or family members. For example, if you are a pregnant woman and your husband doesn't give up smoking, you'll risk some big dangers such as premature birth. And even if your child is born, his health may be in bad condition.

Smoking has so many disadvantages. Why do so few governments take efficient measures to stop it? There is only one answer: money. The tobacco industry can provide billions of tax dollars to the government. But I think it is the most short-sighted policy. While the tax is collecting in a vast sum, countless valuable lives are lost, which is not worthwhile at all.

Smoking has brought us enormous harm. We should take more efficient efforts to stop it.

Topic 17: Advertisements are getting their way into people's lives. Discuss the effects of advertisements on people. Should all ads be banned?

Nowadays more and more advertisements are seen in all kinds of media such as newspaper and television. However, there are both advantages and disadvantages brought about by the advertisements. In my opinion, its advantages outweigh its disadvantages.

Firstly, it is important to the manufacturers. In our highly competitive market economy, it is necessary that the manufacturers make their products widely known. This increases the sales and the manufacturers can get the profits. Obviously, advertising in the media is the best way to do that. In this way, it helps keep business world moving.

Secondly, it is necessary for the media. Supporting a newspaper or a TV station needs a certain amount of money. With the limited budget, the government is not able to invest much money on the media. So all kinds of media must survive by themselves. For example, TV stations need the money brought by TV commercials to support other programs such as news programs, weather forecasts, TV shows and children's cartoons.

Finally, it is helpful to consumers. We consumers also need to learn what new products are available for us to choose from, in which stores discount goods are sold, what special functions a product has and if a product fits us. We are busy with working and studying, and therefore, the advertisements are the best way to provide us the useful information.

On the other hand, there are some disadvantages induced by the advertisements. First, consumers can be cheated by false advertising. Secondly, sometimes there are too many advertisements which ruin exciting television shows and waste our time. We should take efficient measures such as making laws to prevent these disadvantages.

On the whole, advertisements have both advantages and disadvantages. But fairly speaking, everyone should admit that its advantages outweigh its disadvantages.

2. 辯論式題目－對稱式寫法

Topic 1: *Who should be responsible for children's education, the school or the parents? Give your opinion and tell the reasons.*

Who are more responsible for children's education, the school or the parents? People rarely reach an absolute consensus on such a controversial issue.

It seems that parents should play a more important role in children's education. It is said that parents are the best teachers at the beginning of our lives. And of course, implicit learning occurs when children unconsciously copy some of their parents' habits and styles of behavior.

During the second stage of child development, adolescence, parents can still be in the best position to offer advice even though the children might not accept it. Parents may also give their children some guidance to help them to enter the society.

On the other hand, some people argue that it is the school's duty to educate children. Parents are not professional teachers and they tend to be very biased by their love of their children. In any case, parents usually can present only one viewpoint of the world, while good teaching should be based on different attitudes. Thus, when children go to school and have a great diversity of teachers, they learn much more than their parents could probably give them. Furthermore, once our parents get older, they become more conservative and cannot always be objective in regard to modern trends and fashions. Thus we need to take their advice with caution during that period.

In my opinion, while parents are not the ideal teachers, and well-rounded children will generally need a great diversity of teachers in their lives in order to have a more accurate view of the world. In schools, children can get professional and systematic education, and are given opportunities to learn to be independent and therefore are more likely to succeed in their future.

Topic 2: Who should be responsible for children's education, the school or the parents? Give your opinion and tell the reasons.

Who is responsible for the education of the students? Some people claim that it is the school's duty to educate children. Other people argue that parents should play a more important role. On such a controversial issue, people seldom reach an absolute consensus.

Some hold the opinion that school should take the main responsibility. In the school, there are many professionally trained teachers and therefore children can be taught knowledge and skills more systematically. There are also a lot of well-equipped educational facilities from which children can benefit. More importantly, children are given opportunities to communicate with peers. These people maintain that the original purpose of the establishment of schools is to release parents from educating their children.

On the other hand, other people hold the opinion that parents should be more responsible for children's education. Parents are the first teachers of their children. What they say and what they do will have deep influence on their children who usually imitate them. Because the family is children's most direct source of knowledge and other experience, those who are brought up by good parents tend to possess many pleasant characters. What is more, in school, there are so many children and relatively much fewer teachers so each child gets inadequate individual attention. At the same time, parents know their children more than teachers and they know what is the most effective way suitable for their children.

From my point of view, both teachers and parents should be responsible for the students' education. The school is a place where children can not only master knowledge and skills they need in their future but also learn how to adapt themselves to the society. Family education is also very important in addition to school education. They should cooperate with each other to achieve our common goal, which is to raise our children to be useful people in society.

說明:此題與前一個題目完全相同,也是採用對稱式寫法。此篇文章在最後一段說出自己觀點時,採用的是折衷方案,而不像前一篇文章傾向某個觀點。

Topic 3: The idea of having a single career is becoming an old fashioned one. The new fashion will be to have several careers or ways of earning money. Do you think having several careers throughout life is a new fashion?

With the development of society, nowadays more and more people change their jobs frequently. Whether having several careers throughout life is the new fashion is an interesting question.

There are several reasons which suggest it may be the new fashion. Firstly, in today's economy, job security is lowering and many companies are dismissing highly trained people who are therefore often forced to seek other careers. Secondly, many people often do not like their jobs, perhaps because they initially choose the wrong field of work and these people are likely to have many careers in their lives as they seek what they want. Finally, technology is changing quickly. Old jobs are becoming obsolete, thus making workers redundant and new opportunities are emerging. The result is many careers change.

However, there are several reasons why having multiple careers may not be the new fashion. Firstly, most people marry and have children, and so they need a steady reliable income because of their family responsibilities, even if they are dissatisfied with their jobs. Secondly, people are generally afraid of change, and like the security of doing what they know. Finally, most people are ambitious and want to advance their careers as quickly as possible, and usually the best way to do this is to stay at the same job.

In my opinion, I do not think having several careers is the new fashion. Almost everyone marries and needs reliable income to support his family. Everyone likes job security. Everyone has ambition to develop his career. If people leave their jobs, they usually have to start again at a much lower rank, and they usually do not like to do this. For these reasons, I believe having multiple careers throughout life will never be popular.

Topic 4: Some people are of the opinion that keeping pets such as cats and dogs is beneficial to city dwellers. What do you think?

Should the keeping of pets be banned? Answers to this question vary greatly.

Some people are of the opinion that keeping pets is beneficial to them physically as well as mentally. For one thing, giving pets, such as dogs, exercise is good for the owner's health too. With the development of society, pet keeping is no longer the luxury it used to be. Aged people, those in retirement in particular, walking dog every morning in parks is a common sight. They even run after their beloved pets. Obviously, their pets keep them young both mentally and physically. For another, keeping pets can help kill time and dispel the feeling of being lonely, the greatest threat encountered by the old. They say that having a pet to talk to is a better remedy for loneliness than any pills or potions.

From a certain point of view, these remarks may sound reasonable. But taking everything into consideration, one may consider the keeping of pets, especially in urban areas, inappropriate. First, pets are harmful to people's health. It is well known that pets can spread some serious diseases. Second, raising pets is a costly and time-consuming hobby, and therefore, we can not concentrate on our work and studies. The last advantage of keeping pets is that it has a negative influence on the relationship between neighbors. Some pets, such as dogs, are dangerous to children. If a dog bites a neighbor's child, this will disturb the harmony of the neighborhood.

In my opinion, there is some truth in both arguments, but public sanitation and safety are far more important than anything else. And it is a waste of time and energy to raise pets. Pets are also troublemakers to the neighbourhood. Therefore, keeping pets has more disadvantages.

Topic 5: Some people think children should be taken care of at home by their mothers. Others argue that it would be good for them if they are sent to kindergartens? What is your opinion?

Everything in the world has its own two sides. Without exception, the discussion about whether or not children should be taken care of at home by their mothers is a very controversial one. There are people on both sides of the argument who have very strong feeling.

Looking after children at home does seem to have a number of advantages. Firstly, mothers may be able to provide a more practical education for their children than kindergartens can. Secondly, a child's home is likely to provide a more relaxed atmosphere than what a kindergarten can offer. Mothers can also keep their children away from negative influences. The last advantage is that mothers are often said to know what is best for their children.

Many people, however, argue that children should be sent to the kindergarten. Firstly, children are isolated at home, while in the kindergarten, they are given opportunities to develop in the social context and become accustomed to communicating with peers independently. Next, kindergartens can provide professionally trained teachers and all kinds of educational facilities from which children can benefit. Finally, mothers can concentrate on their work and develop their career, which is also helpful to the social development.

In my opinion, I believe that children should be taken care of in kindergarten instead of being educated at home by their mothers. In this way, both children and their mothers can get benefits. Mothers are able to advance their careers and the family need not live on one income. At the same time, children can get better education. They can learn to be independent and to solve problems by themselves.

Topic 6: *Nowadays surveillance cameras are widely used in supermarkets, some think that this is a violation of human rights, while others insist that they are for the benefit of the supermarkets. Discuss both views and give your opinion.*

Nowadays supermarkets not only make a lot of money for their owners, but also bring them some trouble. How can they prevent theft without annoying their customers? The use of surveillance cameras seems a good solution. But more and more arguments arise with the increasing use of such cameras. Before giving my opinion, I think it is important to look at the arguments on both sides.

Those who support using surveillance cameras in supermarkets insist that it is the best way to protect the owners' profits. Firstly, a camera is more effective than security guards. One camera can easily cover an area for which 3 ~ 4 security guards. Secondly, a camera is much more objective, sometimes our eyes might deceive us, while a machine can record exactly what happens, it can prevent much unnecessary embarrassment.

On the other hand, some people voice doubts about the installation of surveillance cameras. The most important reason for their disapproval is that such instruments show distrust of customers. Customers should not be watched suspiciously as if they were prisoners. Cameras can become evidence of a serious violation of human rights.

From my point of view, the best solution is for both sides to respect each other's needs. The shopkeeper should place surveillance cameras in such a way that the customer does not feel that he or she is being spied upon. At the same time, the customer should respect the shopkeeper's concern about theft.

Topic 7: Some people would like to live in the city. Others prefer to live in the country. What is your choice?

Some people like to live in the city. Others prefer to live in the country. Both sides of the argument are supported by good reasons.

Many people argue that living in the city has more advantages. Many people appreciate the conveniences of the city. Living in large cities, people can participate in political activities and they have easier access to news. The cultural lives in the city are colorful. For example, people can often visit exhibitions and see the latest films. In the city, there are good schools and universities for the children where they can get a better education, there are good hospitals for the patients where they can get better medical treatment and there are big department stores for the housewives where they can buy a great variety of goods made in every part of the world.

While many people in the countryside are trying to come to the cities, the city dwellers have recognized the attractions of the country. The country is free from contaminated environment. In the countryside, the air is clean, the food is fresh and the houses are usually spacious with large yards around them. Air pollution, noise and overcrowding which are the biggest problems confronting townspeople seem strange for rural residents. If one enjoys fishing and gardening, the countryside is where he should live. Medical studies have proved that rural residents can live longer than urban residents.

However, living either in the city or in the country has its disadvantages. The city is always noisy and overcrowded, and its air is heavily polluted. But in the countryside, far away from numerous exciting activities, one may feel isolated and uninformed.

In my opinion, I prefer to live in the countryside, relaxing and appreciating the quiet and peaceful natural beauty. Besides the benefits I mentioned above, the crime rate is much lower in the countryside than in the city. So the safe, quiet and cheap life in the country appeals to me deeply.

Topic 8: Which do you think is preferable? Some people believe that the Earth is being harmed (damaged) by human activity. Others feel that human activity makes the Earth a better place to live.

Has human activity done more harm or good to the Earth? It's a question worthy of discussing.

Some people believe that human activity brings us more benefits. There is no doubt that the advancement of technology and science has improved the living standards of people. We don't need to shrink in a cave during the chilly winter any more. The electrical warmer enables us stay at home with only a shirt, no matter how cold it is outside. In a hot stuffy summer, we do not have to subject to the high temperature with the air conditioning. In addition, the skyscrapers are able to put up thousand times more people in a same size land than hundreds of years before. It seems very important considering the exploding population.

However, other people argue that human activity has done more harm to us. Human beings are concerned more and more about the pollution and the extinction of other creatures, which are the results of incautious actions of human beings. During the development of human culture, we plunder the resource from the planet without considering its ability to reproduce. Therefore, the area of desert has enlarged several times during the recent three hundred years; many underground rivers have disappeared; and the air pollution and water pollution have becoming more and more serious. The damage to the environment also brings on the extinction of many precious animals and plants. If we do nothing to stop the trends, the planet will only has human beings before long.

As far as I am concerned, the human beings on the one hand have been making the Earth more comfortable to live, on the other hand, damaging the perfect environment of the blue planet to some extend. we must see the advantage of technology advancement, but what is more important is that we should admit the bad results of human activity and take effective measures to refresh the blue planet.

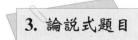

3. 論説式題目

Topic 1: Why do people attend university?

Nowadays, many people go to university after graduation from high school. Why do they attend university? Different people have different purposes. In my mind, the following factors need to be taken into consideration.

The most important reason is that students can learn new knowledge from the study in the university. There are many teachers, professors with abundant teaching experience who teach students lots of new knowledge and help them to solve the problems in their study. With their help, students can learn a lot of useful basic and professional knowledge which is very helpful for their future work. Without the necessary knowledge, students can not contribute to the society after they finish their study in the university.

Secondly, students are given opportunities to enrich their experience. Usually, people often have uncomfortable feeling to live with a stranger, because they do not know each other and perhaps their habit and personality are different. But for the long run, it is good for them. They have to cooperate with each other and solve a lot of problems they will face together. Gradually, they can learn how to care and understand other people. It is a preparation for students, who will definitely cooperate with other people after they enter the society.

Finally, studying in university is helpful to students' psychological development. Before their studying in college, their life is often arranged by their parents and their study is often arranged by their teachers. It is very different for them to live and study in college, because students studying in college have to arrange their life and study by themselves. They have to learn to be independent and solve the problems by themselves. Therefore, the experience of studying in the university does play an important role in shaping students' characters.

In conclusion, by studying in the university, students can learn lots of new knowledge, learn how to adapt themselves when they enter the society and learn to be a strong man in spirit.

Topic 2: When you are seeking for a job, what factors do you consider?

How can we choose a satisfactory job? In my experience, I think you will make the decision according to the following factors.

Firstly, salary is the most important factor. Most people marry and have children. Some people even need to provide financial support for their parents. So they need a steady reliable income because of their family responsibilities. To live more comfortably is a part of human nature. Everyone wants to live in a big house, often travel abroad and have his own car. All these things need enough money which you should consider at first when you choose your job.

Secondly, I must like the job. Most people are ambitious and want to advance their careers, and usually the best way to do this is that they like their jobs. Only if they are interested in what they do, can they put all of their energy into it, and therefore, they are likely to gain great achievements in their field of work.

Finally, the job should be promising as a stable career. In today's economy, technology is developing quickly. Some old jobs and skills are becoming out-dated, and many highly trained people doing these jobs are dismissed and therefore are forced to seek other careers. Some new emerging jobs are full of development potential. The skills and training gained from working in these jobs are in demand. Therefore, these jobs are often well-paid and have good future prospects. I will undoubtedly choose these jobs.

To sum up, when I choose my job, I consider if it is well-paid, if I like it and if it has a good future prospect.

Topic 3: Traffic is developing rapidly all round the world at present, what are the traffic problems in your country? What causes these problems? Make some recommendations.

Transportation has been developing rapidly in recent years, especially in large cities. However, it must be admitted that, along with the benefits of the rapid development of urban traffic, it causes some certain problems. One of the biggest problems, in my opinion, is traffic jams in some heavily-populated cities. It has become common to see passengers and drivers having to wait in long lines of buses and cars moving at a snail's pace on the streets during the rush hours.

There are several reasons for this problem. First, the number of vehicles is increasing much more rapidly than the building of roads. No sooner has a new road been completed and opened to public traffic than it is crowded with all kinds of vehicles. Second, there seem to be too many private cars and not enough public buses. In most cases, a car carries only one or two people, while it occupies almost half the space a bus does. Third, many people, including drivers, pedestrians and cyclists do not obey traffic rules properly, especially at busy intersections. And this undoubtedly worsens the already grave situation.

In view of the seriousness of this problem, effective measures must be taken before things get worse. On the one hand, the government should invest more money in the building of new roads and the repairing and maintenance of the old ones, particularly those in busy areas of the cities. On the other hand, the number of private cars in urban areas should be limited while the number of public buses should be increased. At the same time, it is essential that stricter traffic rules and regulations be issued to strengthen traffic control and facilitate the normal and efficient running of all means of transportation.

With such efforts made and persisted in, I am confident that it will not be long before city traffic flows in a smoother and more efficient manner.

Topic 4: Families are not as close as before. Give reasons for this change, and suggest some ways to bring families closer.

Nowadays, the relationship between family members is not as close as before. But as what factors contribute to this problem, different people have diverse opinions. As for as I am concerned, it results from the following reasons.

The first reason is that people spend more time on their study and work. Compared with the past, social competition is becoming more and more fierce and people have to face greater work pressure. Therefore, people have to devote almost themselves to their careers. What is more, many jobs require people to work in other cities and many children have to leave their parents at an early age to study or work elsewhere. As time passes, these people become emotionally estranged from their parents.

Another reason is that people enjoy more forms of entertainment and amusement. Nowadays there are various kinds of recreational facilities such as watching TV, surfing the Internet or playing video games which occupy people's spare time. As a result, they would be diverted from enjoying chats with their family members.

To bring families closer, urgent steps must be taken into effect. Firstly, people should keep frequent touch with family members especially those who live away from one another. A regular phone call can bring them the care they need. Secondly, never bring your work home and leave it in your office. It is a good idea to spend more time with family members. And most importantly, we should often convey the concept of family to our children.

In the final analysis, a close family relationship can surely be maintained as long as we realize the significant role it plays in our lives.

Topic 5: Many young people find their first day at high school or college difficult, because they feel very alone. What do you think are the other difficulties they face on their first day? What can schools and colleges do to make them feel more comfortable?

It is not uncommon these days for high school or college freshmen to feel lonely on their first day at school. They get lost on campus, fail to catch sight of any familiar face and have nobody to turn to for help. In my view, this increasingly common and serious phenomenon is an indication of the wide gap between these students' unrealistic vision of school life and disappointing reality.

Some of the difficulties students encounter concern logistics. For example, they are puzzled as to the location of the students' cafeterias, where to register, or how they can retrieve information from the school library. To tackle these problems, a well-organized "orientation session" starting from the very first day would seem helpful. Students feel more at home if they have a detailed campus map, with every place they need to go marked on it.

More often, students' sense of alienation arises from their own assumption of inadequacy as they face the new period of an independent life. This is natural enough after long years of childhood, when they were completely under their parents' control. On their first day in the new environment, they are frustrated to find that what they aspired for "a brave new world" turns out to be a strange and alien one, and they are afraid that they may become even more disillusioned in the days to come.

Yet, with efforts from both the school and the students, the prospect of their gap being bridged is far from dim. Students should be encouraged and motivated to recognize the fact that they are now beginning to be responsible for themselves. To make this transitional period go smoothly, students should be given the opportunity to prepare themselves. Schools and colleges can invite prospective students for a brief campus tour before the new semester starts. Junior or senior students can be organized to share their experiences of campus life with freshmen. As a result, instead of beginning to doubt their own abilities to adapt to their new school life, students will develop a confident feeling about themselves as capable people.

❖ 十三、寫作素材 ❖

1. 宿舍生活

Dormitory rooms are small and crowded.
宿舍空間狹小擁擠。
This lack of space can limit one's privacy and make it difficult for students to concentrate on studies and books.
缺乏足夠的空間會限制人的隱私，使學生很難集中精力學習。

2. 兼職工作

A part-time job offers you a chance to demonstrate your ability and to apply what you have learned in school. A part-time job helps you become more independent of your family. Thirdly, the experience that you gain through job can broaden you school life. You may lose time needed for sleep, rest, study, club activities, and recreation. Working several hours a day consumes a lot of time and energy and may affect study. You may find it hard to adjust to what the school expects from you as well as what your employer has the right to expect.

一分兼職工作給你一個機會展示你的才能,應用你在學校裏學到的知識。一分兼職工作幫助你從家庭中獨立。第三,你從工作中獲得的經驗可以拓展你的學校生活。你可能失去了睡覺、休息、學習、參加社團活動和娛樂的時間。每天工作幾小時消耗了許多時間和精力,可能會影響學習,你也許發現很難調整學校期望你做到的和僱主希望你付出的兩者之間的關係。

Because of the advantages and disadvantages of a part-time job, you have to strike a balance between school and the job. As a student, acquiring more knowledge, especially more learning , is your first important task.

由於兼職工作既有優點又有缺點,你必須在上學和工作之間找到一個平衡。作為一個學生,獲得更多的知識,特別是花更多的時間學習,是你的首要任務。

3. 實踐、旅行和讀書

As a matter of fact, real knowledge comes from practice and direct experience. Only outside the classroom can we apply what we have learned and get new knowledge. Although we can learn more outside, the study in class also plays an important role.

實際上,真正的知識來自於實踐和直接經驗。只有走出教室才能應用我們所學到的和獲得的新知識。雖然我們外出能學到許多知識,在教室裏學習仍扮演有很重要的角色。

Books are of various kinds and have different contents. We have history books recording past events, geography books dealing with the earth, mathematics books focusing on space and numbers. We have various books dealing with different things in the world. Reading books can enrich our knowledge. We can learn lots of things we did not previously know, and be aware of what has happened in the past as well as what is going to happen in the future. It's impossible for a man to learn everything through his own experience, while books can help him to achieve this purpose. It is by reading that we can learn many things without actually seeing or hearing them.

書有很多種,並且有不同的內容。歷史書記錄了發生過的事件,地理書定位在地球,數學書定位在空間和數字。不同的書籍處理世界上不同的事件。讀書能豐富我們的知識。我們能學到許多我們以前不知道的事情,知道過去發生了什麼,並可以預料到將來會發生什麼。對一個人來講,不可能經由自己的經歷知道所有的事,書籍可以幫助我們達到這個目的。正是借助讀書,我們能了解許多沒有看到和聽到的事情。

Life is limited, but knowledge is boundless. The more books we read, the more knowledge we get. To read books is necessary to one who wishes to get knowledge. Different books give different kinds of knowledge.

生命是有限的,但知識是無限的。讀的書越多,我們獲得的知識就越多。一個人若想獲得知識,必須讀書。不同的書提供不同種類的知識。

Now there're various kinds of books available and we learn lots of things from them. Books become the main source of knowledge we obtain.

現在,有各種各樣有益的書籍,我們從中學到很多東西。書成為我們獲得知識的主要來源。

Books provide us with various aspects of knowledge. By reading, we can travel to the North Pole, without having to endure the freezing cold. We can also go to the desert without having to fear the threat of thirst. We can also go back to the ancient times to have a look at the people's life without any difficulty.

書為我們提供不同方面的知識。透過閱讀,我們能到北極去旅行,而不用忍受嚴寒。我們也能到沙漠中去,而不用擔心口渴的威脅。我們能毫無困難地回到古代去看看人們的生活。

Traveling gives us direct experiences. It's much more exciting and active than reading. It's necessary for a person to expand his horizon. When you have a chance or enough money and time, you can travel around the world. It will make your life more pleasant and make you have a deep understanding of the people and the world.

旅行給我們直接的經驗。這比讀書更開心、更積極。人們需要開闊視野。當你有一個機會,或者有足夠的時間和金錢,你能周遊全世界。這會使你的生活更快樂,使你更深入地了解人和世界。

But as students, we don't have enough time and money to travel around, and studying is the most important thing for us to do.

但是作爲一個學生，我們沒有足夠的時間和金錢去旅遊，並且學習對我們來說是最重要的事。

4. 出國留學

By looking at our own country from the outside, we can best see the strong points and weak points of our nation and therefore widen our vision and broaden our minds. While studying in a foreign country, we can travel widely, visit famous scenic spots and make friends with the local people. We can use the foreign language in our daily life so that our ability in the second language may be improved quickly. But the most important thing in attending a foreign university is to get acquainted with the latest knowledge in science and technology and make use of the first-rate facilities available.

從外面看我們的國家，我們能很淸楚地看到我們民族的強項和弱點，因此，可以開闊我們的視野，拓展我們的思路。在外國學習時，我們在這個國家裏廣泛地旅行，參觀著名的風景點，和當地人交朋友。我們在日常生活中使用外語，所以我們使用第二種語言的能力能很快提高。但最重要的是，在外國大學學習可以接觸科學技術方面最先進的知識和利用最先進的設備。

However, as everything has two sides, there are also some disadvantages in attending a foreign university. The most serious problem is the language barrier. Most of the students who are ready to go abroad do not have adequate proficiency in the language spoken there. On arriving there, they will find it diffcult to understand what the instructors are saying. For lack of knowledge of the customs and way of life of the local people, they may run into trouble in dealing with various situations. The cost of living is much higher than that in our country, so most students have to find part-time jobs in order to help support themselves. Faced with these difficulties, many students find themselves unable to pay full attention to their studies and some students may even fail in their courses and learn little. One must consider both sides of the factors carefully before making up his mind. It is a good thing to go and study abroad particularly when the subject is very weak or not available in our country. But on the other hand, one must not lose sight of the disadvantages.

但任何事情都有它的兩個方面，在外國大學讀書也有它的缺點。最嚴重的問題是語言障礙。大多數準備出國的學生外語都不夠熟練。到達之後，他們發現很難理解老師課堂上在說什麼。由於缺乏當地人生活習慣方面的知識，他們會在處理各種情況時遇到困難。

生活花費比在我國要高得多，所以許多學生不得不尋找兼職工作來養活自己。面對這些困難，許多學生發現自己不能把精力全部放在學習上，一些學生甚至會不及格。在做出決定前，你必須仔細考慮各個方面的因素。出國留學是一件好事，特別是學習那些在我們國家是弱項或沒有的專業。但是另一方面，你必須看到它的缺點。

5. 考　試

There are many arguments about the advantages and disadvantages of examination. Some people think examination is the only way to test how examinees have mastered what they have studied, and it is the only measurement for examiners to select which persons they need. On the other hand, some object that examination can't measure how the students have really studied. They say it can do nothing but burden the students.

關於考試的優缺點有許多爭論。一些人認為考試是測試被考人所學的知識的唯一方式，而且它是測試人選擇他們需要的人的唯一標準。另一方面，一些人認為，考試不能衡量學生真正的學習狀況。他們認為考試只能增加學生的負擔。

As for me, I think for both examinees and examiners, the examination can show what and how much the examinees have mastered. The results of examinations are just like mirrors for both examiners and examinees. Through examination the examiners can check their work and become aware of which aspects they have not done well, so that they'll make much improvement in their work. As far as examinees are concerned, they can not only know how they have studied but also find out what they still don't know or what they haven't mastered well. Thus they will be inspired to greater efforts to improve their studying method so as to make greater progress. Of course too many examinations are burdens to both examiners and examinees.

對我來講，我認為對測試者和被測試者來說，考試能夠體現出被測人學到了什麼，考試結果對被測者和測試者都像一面鏡子。藉由考試，測試人能檢查他們的工作，知道他們哪些方面做得不夠好，以便他們改善工作。至於被測試者，他們不僅能了解自己的學習效果，而且能了解他們沒有學到什麼，還沒有掌握什麼。因此他們將付出更多的努力改變他們的學習方式，以便取得更大的進步。當然，太多的考試對考試者和被考者都是負擔。

In summary, the examination does more good than harm for both examiners and examinees. We must take a positive attitude towards examination. We should take full advantage of it and avoid its disadvantages.

總而言之,對測試者和被測試者而言,考試是利大於弊。我們必須以積極的態度對待考試。我們必須利用它的優點,避免它的缺點。

We might marvel at the progress made in every field of study, but the methods of testing a person's knowledge and ability remain as old as ever. Examinations may be a good way of testing memory and cleverness of work rapidly under pressure. They can, however, tell you little about a person's ability.

我們也許驚訝於學習在各個方面取得的進步,但測試一個人知識和能力的方式卻相對落後。考試也許是測試記憶力和在壓力下快速工作的好方式。但它們不能告訴你一個人的能力。

Because they are the marks of success and failure, examinations are nothing but anxiety-makers.

因爲它們是成功和失敗的標誌,所以考試只是焦慮的製造者。

Your whole future may be decided on one fateful day. It doesn't matter whether you were ill or not.

你的整個未來可能只由一天來決定,不管你那天生病了沒有。

What is more, teachers' judgements may sometimes be unfair, for they may get tired and make mistakes. We are looking forward to a simpler and more effective way of judging a person's true ability.

而且,老師的評判有時會有失公平,因爲他們可能會疲勞或犯錯誤。我們期待着一個更簡單有效的方式評判一個人眞實的能力。

In short, examinations motivate passive memorizing instead of creative thinking.

總之,考試激發被動的記憶而不是創造性的思維。

6. 堅持 / 自信

Perseverance means steadfastness in purpose. It is perseverance that keeps us continually doing something valuable and admirable in spite of difficulties and discouragement. Therefore, perseverance is momentous and fundamental to any one who undertakes great deeds.

堅定不移意味着目標堅定。堅定不移使我們在遇到困難和挫折的時候繼續做一件有價值的事,直到成功。因此,堅定不移對那些擔負重大任務的人極爲重要,是成功的基礎。

It admits of no doubt that in doing things whether great or small there are more or less difficulties, and the greater the thing is, the more numerous the difficulties that will come forth.

But it is much better for one to persevere than to despair. Mencius said, "when heaven is a-bout to confer a great office on any man, it first exercises his mind with suffering, and his sinews and bones with toil. It exposes his body to hunger, and subjects him to extreme pov-erty. It confounds all his undertakings. By all these methods, it stimulates his mind, consoli-dates his character, and increases his efficiency." So let us be patient. Indeed, if we do a thing without perseverance, nothing will be done in the end.

必須承認，做任何事情，不論大小，或多或少都會遇到困難，事情越大，困難越多。但堅定不移比絕望好，孟子說："天將降大任於斯人也，必先苦其心志，勞其筋骨，餓其體膚，空乏其身，行弗亂其所為，所以動心忍性，增益其所不能。"因此讓我們更耐心些。確實，如果我們做事沒有堅定不移的精神，什麼事情也不會做成。

Don't stop halfway.

不要半途而廢。

When a man does a piece of work, he hopes to derive some benefit from it. In order to get this benefit, he must hold the work to the end and completely finish it.

當一個人做一件工作，他希望從中得到一些益處。為了得到這個益處，他必須堅持工作到結束，徹底地完成它。

A piece of work, whether hard or not, requires patience and firmness for completion. There-fore, when you have some work to do, you must do it faithfully, not caring about the diffi-culty. Difficulties and obstacles are unavoidable. If you turn back on meeting them, you will succeed in nothing, but if you can overcome them, you will accomplish something.

一件工作，不論難易，都需要耐心和完成它的決心。因此，當你有一些工作要做時，你必須如實地做，不考慮困難。困難和障礙是不可避免的。如果你遇到它們就退縮，你永遠也不會成功，但是如果你能克服它們，你將取得收穫。

To stop halfway in doing something is very bad. Suppose that a precious stone is at a great distance from you and you want to obtain it, you must reach for it, you must not stop half-way.

做一件事情半途而廢是非常不好的。假設你想獲得離你很遠的一顆寶石，你必須去得到它，你不能半途而廢。

Whatever one does, one should do it with confidence. If one had no confidence, there is lit-tle possibility that one would ever achieve anything. This truth seems to be self-evident, es-pecially for those who are faced with drawbacks or hardships. For those people, confidence keeps their spirits up whenever times or things are hard for them.

不論你做什麼，你必須有信心。如果你沒有信心，你就不可能把事情做成功。這個事實非常明顯,特別是對那些遇到挫折和困難的人。對那些人,不論時代或事情多麼困難,信心都會使他們熱血沸騰。

However, in reality we do see a lot of people who complain that their difficulties are too great to overcome. For some, this might be true, but for many others, this only shows that they lack confidence. There are two main reasons why those people often feel frustrated even though they are capable of doing something. First, they do not have a correct estimate of themselves, and second, they overestimate the difficulties.

但事實上我們確實看到很多人抱怨他們的困難多麼難以克服。對一些人來講,這確實是真的,但對於另外許多人,只能顯示出他們缺乏信心。有兩個主要原因來解釋為什麼那些人經常有失敗感,儘管他們能夠做成一些事。第一,他們不能正確地評估自己,第二,他們高估了困難。

It is possible to build up confidence in oneself by having the right attitude toward one's own abilities. We should never underestimate our abilities but should believe in the proverb: "Where there is a will, there is a way." Confidence is the promise for fulfilling a task successfully.

通過正確對待自己的能力建立起信心是可能的。我們不能低估自己的能力,而應該相信諺語所說的:"有志者事竟成。"信心是順利完成任務的前提。

7. 不 滿 足

The advice given to young men or women by most people is : " Be content. " Doubtless there is truth and strength in this. But one man's meat may be poison for another. There are people who, progressive in spirit, are always discontent, yet they are happy and are highly revered. To this group belong discoverers, scientists, and people doing research work. It is this spirit, the spirit of being unsatisfied with the existing state of things, that is responsible for improvements. It is due to being discontent with gestures to express our thought and feeling that a language develops. Thus, discontent is really a progressive force. It is wrong to preach to everybody against discontent. Those who can only grumble at things, but cannot think of means of bettering them, should be censured as severely as possible. But those who are willing to labor hard for betterment ought to be encouraged in every way. Their discontent bears good fruit.

大多數人對年輕人的忠告是:知足。毋庸置疑,這句話是真的,有它的好處。但百人有百味。有一些精神進步的人卻常常不滿足，但他們也快樂，並且備受尊敬。這部分人包括發現者、科學家和做研究工作的人。這是一種精神，一種不滿足現狀的精神，進步歸功於它。由於不滿足於用手勢去表達我們的想法和情感，人類發展了語言。那些抱怨事情有問題，卻不想辦法解決問題的人必須受到嚴厲的責備。而那些願意付出辛勤勞動以求更好的人，無論如何都應受到鼓勵。他們的不滿足帶來了豐碩的果實。

8. 成功的關鍵因素

No doubt, everyone wishes to be successful in life. In discussing this, three fundamental principles should be borne in mind: diligence, devotion, and perseverance.
毫無疑問地每個人都希望成功。討論成功，三個基本規律必須要記住：勤奮、投入和持之以恆。

The first key factor to success is diligence, which simply means no waste of time. Diligence can help us remove ignorance, overcome difficulties, and enlighten our minds. Diligence can make a fool wise, and a poor man rich. If we idle away our time now, our future life will be a failure. If we are diligent now, we will surely be successful in the future.
成功的第一個決定因素是勤奮。它僅僅意味着不要浪費時間。勤奮能幫我們去除無知，克服困難和啓發我們的思維。勤奮可以使傻子變明智，使窮人變富裕。如果我們現在浪費時間，我們未來的生活將會失敗。如果我們現在很勤奮，我們將來肯定會成功。

Furthermore, perseverance, or a strong will, is also necessary in order to make success a certainty. If we study or work day after day, there is nothing that can not be achieved. Without a strong will, on the other hand, we are likely to give up when we meet some difficulties. In short, a strong will can urge a person to perform wonderful deeds.
此外，持之以恆或者很強的願望對保證成功來說也是非常需要的。如果我們日復一日地學習或工作，沒有一件事不會做成功。另一方面，如果沒有很強的願望，當我們遇到困難時，我們很可能放棄。簡言之，很強的願望推動個人獲得令人驚奇的成績。

To conclude, all great men achieve success through diligence, devotion and perseverance. Just as the famous English saying goes, "No pains, no gains."
總而言之，所有人的成功都離不開勤奮、投入和持之以恆。正如一句著名的英語諺語所說："沒有痛苦，就沒有收穫。"

Opportunities do not come often. They come every once in a while. Very often, they come quietly or go by without being noticed. Therefore, it is advisable that you shall value and treat them with care. When an opportunity comes, it brings promise but never realizes it on its own. If you mean to achieve something or intend to fulfill one of your ambitions, you must work hard, make efforts and get prepared. Otherwise, you will take no advantage of opportunities when they come to visit you.

機會不會經常光顧。它們每次只來一會兒。通常,它們沒有通知而靜悄悄地來。因此,認真地評估和對待它們是明智的。當機會到來時,它帶來允諾,連它自己也沒有意識到。如果你想完成某件事或想履行你的一個雄心,你必須勤奮工作、做出努力和做好準備。否則,當機會到來時,你就不會抓住它們。

The difference between a person who succeeds and one who does not lies only in the way each treats opportunities. The successful person always makes much preparation to meet opportunities as they arrive. The less successful person, on the other hand, works little and just waits to see them pass by.

一個人成功與否,僅僅在於對待機會的不同態度。成功的人在機會到來時總是做好許多準備。不成功的人很少做準備,只能看着機會擦肩而過。

9. 友誼／朋友

Friendship is important to us. Everyone needs friendship. In all our lives, we cannot live without friendship just as we cannot survive without air and water. True friendship must be sincere and unconditional. It is based on mutual understanding, not on mutual benefit. Some people try to get something from their friends, and their friends also try to make use of them. If such a relationship can be called friendship, we need no friends at all.

友誼對我們很重要。每個人都需要友誼。在我們的生活中,沒有友誼不能生存,就像我們不能離開空氣和水一樣。真正的友誼必須是真誠的和無條件的。它基於互相理解,而不是互相得利。一些人試着從他們的朋友那裏得到一些東西,他們的朋友也利用他們。如果這種關係也被叫作友誼,我們一點都不需要朋友。

The mutual understanding between two friends means both of them have similar ideas and trust each other. Otherwise, it is impossible for them to help each other and to make their friendship last long. So real friendship should be able to stand all sorts of tests. It is advisable to have as many good friends as we can. A good friend can always be a good teacher to us. By his advice, we are persuaded to go the right way; by his help, we can be free from many difficulties; by his warning, we are aware of the danger of doing wrongs. Therefore, the more friends we have, the more help we can expect from them; and the more pleasure we can share with them. And we will live a beautiful life, because we can find friends everywhere all our lives. Every one of us needs to have friends.

兩個朋友之間的相互理解意味着他們有相似的想法和相互信任。否則,他們不可能互相幫助,使得友誼更加長久。因此,眞正的友誼應經得起考驗。儘量多交好朋友是明智的。一個好的朋友也是我們的一個好老師。透過他的建議,我們被說服去走正確的路;透過他的幫助,我們能從困難中解脫出來;透過他的警告,我們能意識到做錯事的危險。因此,朋友越多,我們從他們那裏得到的幫助越多,我們和他們分享的快樂越多。我們生活美好,因爲我們能在一生中處處找到朋友。我們每一個人都需要朋友。

By associating with friends one can gradually get into the society and become sociable to some extent. Man is sociable creature so that children should understand the society, get used to it, and get pleasure out of it. Frankly speaking, I really get a lot of valuable things from my friends.

透過與朋友的交往,你可以逐漸進入社會並在某種程度上建立社會關係。人是社會性動物,因此孩子應該理解社會,適應社會,從中獲得樂趣。坦率地講,我確實從朋友那裏得到很多有價值的東西。

What a pleasure it is to have a friend with the same taste, maybe you are interested in playing tennis, then how wonderful it is to compete with your friend. Having friends whose characters, hobbies and social conditions are similar to you can bring you many advantages. They are easy to get along with, and between you and your friends, there are always something that all of you are familiar with.

有同樣品位的朋友使我們很快樂,也許你喜歡打網球,和你的朋友比賽是多麼快樂。如果有這樣的朋友,他的性格、愛好和社會條件和你相似,這會給你帶來很多好處。他們很好相處,在你和你的朋友之間,總有相似的地方。

They may have not what you give, but they have what you have not. A different friend is a mirror which can reflect your virtues and shortcomings. From him, you can find what you lack and you can learn what you need. When viewed from these perspectives, different friends may do more in shaping you than do the similar ones.

你給他們的一些東西他們也許沒有,但他們可能也擁有一些你沒有的東西。一位與你不同的朋友像一面鏡子,可以反射出你的優點和缺點。從他身上,你可以找到你的不足,可以學習你需要的東西。從這個觀點出發,與你不同的朋友比與你類似的朋友更能幫助你完善自己。

No matter how similar they are, every two friends have differences, and no matter how different they are, as friends, they have at least one similarity: the sincerity towards friendship. In the sincere friendship, you can find shelter from danger, courage in need, and hands willing to help.

不管他們多麼相似,任何兩個朋友都有不同之處;不管他們多麼不同,他們至少都有一個共同點:忠於友誼。在眞摯的友情中,你能找到躲避危險的港灣和所需要的鼓勵,朋友隨時願意幫助你。

10. 代 溝

Despite various improvements in all aspects of social life, the generation gap between the grown-up and the young remains unbridged. In order to narrow the gap, both groups should respect each other, listen to the words of each other and should discuss their problems patiently.

儘管社會生活的各個方面都有了各種各樣的進步,老年人和年輕人之間的代溝始終不能消除。爲了縮小代溝,兩代人要互相尊重,聽對方的觀點,並且耐心地討論問題。

There has always been an argument between the young and the old about what kind of life to live —— realistic or romantic. Young people tend to think that real life is as dramatic and fascinating as it is in the novels and movies while more experienced adults think this naive daydream is certain to be broken by later experiences and everyone should learn to get used to the dull routine of his everyday life. Life will be unimaginable if everything we do is only for realistic purposes, and the same is true if what we do every day is just to enjoy ourselves. So it's not difficult for us to see that neither way can ensure a happy life.

年輕人和老年人經常爲了過什麼樣的生活爭論 —— 現實的還是浪漫的。年輕人趨向於把現實生活想像成同小說和電影一樣的生動迷人,但有經驗的成年人認爲這些幼稚的白日夢會被以後的經驗打破,每個人都應該學會適應日常生活的單調。如果我們做每件事都只是爲了現實目的,生活會變得無法想像;同樣地如果我們每天都按我們喜歡的方式去生活,生活也同樣不可想像。因此不難看出,兩條路都不能確保我們快樂地生活。

11. 婦女解放

Women's problems exist all over the world mainly in two respects —— in work and life.
世界性的婦女問題主要存在於兩個方面 —— 工作和生活中。

It is rather difficult for women, even post graduates with honors, to get high-paying jobs. Some enterprises positively reject their applications, just to avoid the trouble of child-birth and child-care. Some bosses think women inferior in professional skill and initiative. They argue that before marriage, females' dependent nature largely chains their attention to fashionable dresses and various high-grade cosmetics, and after matrimony, especially with a child, their minds dwell on nothing but the comforts of life, baby-care and housework.

對婦女來說,甚至是獲得榮譽的研究生,都很難找到高薪工作。一些企業斷然拒絕僱用她們,只是避免生小孩和撫養小孩的問題。一些老闆認為婦女在職業技能和主動性上表現差。他們認為在結婚之前,女孩子們一心只想着時裝和各種高級化妝品,但在結婚之後,特別是有了孩子之後,她們的腦子裏只有舒適的生活、照顧小孩和家務勞動。

Even if some ambitious young ladies fight their way to get a position, promotion for them is out of the question. The number of top women executives in science, government, business, education etc. is so few as to be only tokens. Besides, a female's success may become a great obstacle to her love life, as most males prefer a good wife and wise mother.

儘管一些雄心勃勃的年輕女孩子為得到一個職位而奮鬥,然而升職是不可能的。在科學界、政府、商界、教育界做領導的婦女為數不多,甚至只是一種象徵。而且,女性的成功可能成為愛情生活的巨大障礙,因為大多數男人更欣賞好妻子和明智的母親。

As for housework, these gentlemen usually think it is the women's task; the wives' sacrifices are sure to set the husbands up for great success. So work for females involves the responsibility for household, baby and job as well.

說到家務勞動,紳士們通常認為那是女士的任務。妻子們犧牲自己確保丈夫的成功。因此婦女的工作包括了家庭責任、孩子和工作等多方面。

In a word, as long as men's traditional ways of thinking dominate, the above mentioned problems of sex discrimination may linger on.

總而言之,只要男人的傳統思維方式佔主導地位,上述性別歧視的問題還會存在很長的一段時間。

Should men and women be equal? This is a question much talked about by many people. Some hold the opinion that men are superior to women in many ways. For one thing, many a job men do can hardly be done by women, who are physically not strong enough; and for another, most of the world famous scientists or statesmen are found to be males. Moreover, the whole human society seems to have all along been dominated by men only. Isn't it evident enough to show that men are a lot stronger than women? Hence, the former should enjoy more rights than the latter.

男人和女人應當平等嗎？這個問題被許多人所談論。一些人持有這樣的觀點：男人比女人在許多方面優越。舉一個例子，許多男人能做的工作，那些在體能方面並不強壯的婦女做起來卻有困難。此外，大多數世界知名的科學家和政治家是男人。而且，整個人類社會似乎一直僅被男人主宰。這不明顯說明了男人比女人強很多嗎？因此，前者應比後者享有更多的權利。

Other people, however, think quite differently on this question. They fimly believe that men and women are born equal and women are certainly as talented as men if they are given equal opportunities of education. Isn't it a fact known to us all that women have been working side by side with men in Taiwan and elsewhere in the world? Like their menfolks, they have been distinguishing themselves not only in research institutions, but in government bodies and other organizations as well.

另外一些人卻不這樣認為。他們認為男女生來平等，如果婦女得到和男人平等的受教育的機會，她們一定與男人一樣能幹。不是嗎，在台灣和世界各地，我們已經看見婦女們和男人肩並肩地工作着。和她們的男同胞一樣，她們正從研究機構、政府和其他組織中脫穎而出。

Personally, I am firmly standing on the side of those women's rights defenders. Since men and women are playing an equally important role in all human activities, why should they not be on an equal footing? Furthermore, from time immemorial, there have been two sex groups, namely, men and women. Our human society could definitely not have existed or advanced without either of them. Is it any wonder that men and women ought to be equal and enjoy equal rights accordingly?

我個人是婦女權利的維護者。在人類的活動中，既然男人和女人起到同等重要的作用，為什麼他們不站在同等重要的位置呢？而且，從遠古時代，人類就按性別分成了兩組，男人和女人。人類社會失去了任何一方都不能生存和發展。男人和女人享受平等權利又有什麼好奇怪的呢？

In modern families, it is still commonly seen that women do all the housework. Keeping their full jobs, women routinely rise the earliest, take care of babies, serve three meals, and do washing , shopping and cleaning.

在現代家庭中，女人做家務的現象仍非常普遍，在全日上班的同時，她們每天很早起床，照顧小孩，準備三餐，洗衣服，買東西和打掃。

What is the exact cause of this social phenomenon? Despite the social development and women's liberation, women are still considered extensively less competitive and effective in the business world, thus are naturally left with housework as the main task. Inside the family, husbands, being self-important as the first breadwinners, seldom lift a finger to those boring and repetitive affairs.

是什麼引起了這種社會現象？雖然社會發展了,婦女解放了,婦女仍然被廣泛地認爲在商業社會中缺乏競爭力,所以很自然地把家務勞動變成了主要工作,在家裏,丈夫因爲是重要的經濟來源而自以爲是,很少插手這些令人乏味的、重複性很強的勞動。

Actually, if both partners work to earn money, they must share the household chores. They should realize marriage is partnership, and housework-sharing can lead to more harmonious relations. Consequently, it may help both enjoy their family life.

實際上,如果夫妻雙方都工作賺錢,他們必須分擔家務勞動,他們必須意識到婚姻是雙方的事,分擔家務勞動可以帶來更和諧的關係。它可以幫助他們享受家庭生活。

12. 金　錢

Money is considered by some people to be the most powerful and important thing in life. In their opinion, everything in the world such as luxurious cars, magnificent mansions, etc. can be bought with money, if you can afford them. In some capitalist countries, even a post as a senior official could be bought with money.

金錢被一些人看成是生活中最強大和重要的東西。以他們的觀點,世界上任何東西例如豪華轎車、金碧輝煌的宮殿等,都可以用金錢買到,如果能買得起。在一些資本主義國家中,甚至可以用錢買到很高的官方職位。

But there are certain things that cannot be bought with money. A millionaire who suffered from serious cancer was willing to buy his health by selling all his expensive property. But he failed and soon died in despair. An old rich merchant was willing to buy the true love of a beautiful young girl at cost, but his wicked dream never came true. Many other things such as devoted friendship and real honor are invaluable and cannot be bought with money, either. So money is far from omnipotent.

但有很多東西不能用錢買到。一個患有癌症的百萬富翁願意用他所有的財產買回健康,但他失敗了,並且很快在絕望中死去。一個富有的老商人願意用錢買到一個年輕美麗的女郎的眞愛,但他這個夢想永遠也不能實現。許多其他的事情,例如深厚的友誼和眞正的榮譽是無價的,不能用錢買到。金錢不是萬能的。

Money can bring us misery as well as happiness. Those who make money through their own mental or physical labor usually lead a frugal but happy life. But those who make 'dirty money' through illegal means such as stealing, smuggling, or corrupting, will never have true happiness. Everyday and every hour they will be worrying about being arrested and imprisoned by the authorities. And in the end this may well happen. They are doomed to a miserable future.

金錢可以給我們帶來快樂,同樣可以給我們帶來痛苦。那些藉自己的腦力和體力勞動賺錢的人通常過着簡樸而快樂的生活。但是那些藉不合法的手段,例如:偷竊、走私、貪污,賺取"髒錢"的人永遠不會得到真正的快樂。每天,每小時,他們都在擔心被捕,最後,這種情況很有可能發生。他們注定會有痛苦的未來。

Few people in the world today can survive without a certain amount of money. In ancient times people were, for the most part , self-sufficient, individuals farmed, bred animals and livestock, and supported themselves without having to depend on a market. With improvements in technology and transportation the world's economies changed to include a greater variety of goods, most of which came from distant sources. In order to exchange goods, money is needed. Today money has become the requirement of an improved life style.

在今日的世界,沒有一定數量的金錢,沒人能夠生存。在古代,大部分人過着自給自足的生活,單獨耕種,餵養動物和牲畜,不依靠市場就能養活自己。隨着技術和運輸條件的改善,世界經濟變得容納更多品種的貨物,大多數商品來自很遠的地方。爲了交換貨物,需要錢。今天,錢已經成爲改善生活方式的必要條件。

Though the system of monetary exchange has helped to improve the life of modern man, it has also created new social problems. It is a fact that money is the major cause of crime and violence in the world today. Robbery, theft, burglary, and murder are most commonly committed for the sake of money. Money often drives powerful people such as officials and distinguished businessmen to corruption and dishonesty. In addition to crime, money has been the cause of class differences in many countries throughout the world. These class differences have, in turn, created much political strife and discontent.

雖然金錢交易系統幫助現代人提高生活品質,但也產生了新的社會問題。金錢是當今世界上犯罪和暴力的主要起因。搶劫、偷盜、謀殺大多是爲了錢。金錢經常導致有權的人,例如官員和著名的商人,貪污和不誠實。除了犯罪之外,金錢是全世界許多國家階級差別形成的原因。這些階級差別又產生了更多的政治鬥爭和不滿。

Perhaps the problem at hand is not actually money itself but greed. If human beings could learn to be satisfied with living simply and moderately, if they could learn to share, to think about the good of the public rather than the good of the self, money might not be such a source of trouble in the world.

也許問題並不是出在金錢本身，而是貪婪。如果人類能學會滿足於簡單適度的生活，如果他們能夠學會分享，去思考對公眾的好處而不是對自己的好處，金錢也許不會成爲世界上麻煩的來源。

13. 健　康

Nothing is more valuable than health. It is the foundation of one's future success. If you become sick, it is nearly impossible to pursue your career effectively, and much less likely to make your dreams come true. On the other hand, if you are stout and strong, you can go all out to overcome the obstacles that lie ahead of you.

沒有什麼比健康更有價值。它是一個人未來事業成功的基礎。如果你病了，就不可能再去追求事業，你的夢想難以實現。另一方面，如果你結實而強壯，你能克服所有擺在自己面前的障礙。

Now that we know that health is the source of our energy, what should we do to maintain and enhance our health? First, we should exercise every day to strengthen our muscles. Second, we must keep good hours as well. If we get up early, we can breathe fresh air and see the sunrise. Third, there is a proverb that says, "Prevention is better than cure." If you pay close attention to your health, you can avoid getting sick, or at least cure yourself of a disease while it is still in its incipient stage.

既然現在我們知道，健康是精力的來源，我們怎樣做才能維護和提高我們的健康層次呢？首先，我們每天必須運動來增強我們的肌肉；第二，我們必須早睡早起，如果我們很早起床，我們能呼吸到新鮮的空氣和觀看日出。第三，有句諺語說得好："預防勝於治療。"如果你很注意自己的健康，你能避免生病，或者至少在初期治好疾病。

In conclusion, health is more important than wealth. Those who are rich but lose their health are no more fortunate than those who are poor, and if you want your wish to come true, health is the most important ingredient of your success.

總之，健康比財富更重要。那些富有但失去健康的人不比貧窮的人更幸運，如果你希望成功，健康是最重要的事。

Some think that wealth means everything. In their eyes, they can have anything done with enough money. Some of them take risky chances to make money only with the result that they get neither wealth nor health.

一些人認爲財富意味着任何事情，在他們的眼裏，他們能用足夠的錢做任何事情，有些人冒着風險去賺錢,卻既沒有得到健康也沒有得到金錢。

Actually, health is more important than wealth. Health is the foundation of one's success. If you become sick, it is nearly impossible for you to pursue your career successfully. On the other hand, a person suffering from illness can never enjoy his wealth.

實際上,健康比財富更重要,健康是一個人成功的基礎,如果你生病了,你就無法追求事業的成功,另一方面,一個被病痛折磨的人也無法享受他的財富。

Keep healthy first if you want to become wealthy. Maybe wealth can improve health. However, health is more valuable because it is the source of energy. Therefore, you should keep healthy by exercising every day with proper diet, forming good living habits and trying to avoid any minor diseases.

如果你想富有,首先要保持健康。也許財富可以改善健康,但是健康更有價值,因為它是精力的來源,因此,你應該通過每天鍛鍊身體和適當的飲食來維持健康,形成好的生活習慣,盡量避免任何小病。

First, good health is the prerequisite for career success. Only when we have healthy body can we work efficiently and energetically. A strong body built up in youth is a solid foundation for future career success, no matter what we do. Universities and colleges should not only be a place for students to expand their minds, but also be a place to build their body.

首先,健康是職業成功的先決條件。只有有了健康的身體,我們才能有效率地和精力旺盛地工作。不管我們做什麼,年輕時建立起來的強健體魄是未來事業成功的堅實基礎。大學不僅是學生發展智力的地方,也是他們強健體魄的地方。

Second, through sports activities, students can benefit both physically and mentally. Anyone who has played in a football game knows that, to win a game, one not only needs a robust body, but also needs to be cooperative and competitive. Cooperation and competition are two basic characters for those who want to succeed, and students who can combine these two characters harmoniously have better chance of success in the future.

第二,通過體育活動,學生能從身體和精神上都獲得好處。任何參加過足球比賽的人都知道,為了贏得比賽,不僅需要強健的體魄,而且需要合作和競爭。合作和競爭是一個想成功的人的基本特點,那些能夠將這兩點很好地結合的學生在未來有更多的成功機會。

Third, investment in sports facilities can save a lot of money in the long run. If students' health is improved, the money to be saved each year can be considerablely great, considering the large number of students in Taiwan. In the long run, a lot of money can be saved and the money can be used to build more classrooms or libraries. They are valuable assets both for teaching and researching faculty. A good library with its large collection of books is the pride and symbol of a prominent university. Both libraries and sports facilities are indispensable for universities.

第三,體育設備的投資從長遠角度看能節省很多錢。考慮到台灣學生的數量,如果學生身體健康了,每年能省下相當可觀的錢。從長遠看,大量的資金可以被省下來建造更多的教室和圖書館。這些設施對教學和研究都是有價值的資產。擁有大量藏書的圖書館是一個著名大學的象徵和驕傲。對大學來說,圖書館和體育設施都是不可缺少的。

14. 體育鍛鍊和智力活動

Physical activities and intellectual activities are the two basic ways on which we spend our leisure time. While most people have interests in both pastimes, we also have favorite ways to spend our time off.

體育鍛鍊和智力活動是我們度過休閒時光的兩個基本方式,雖然大多數人對這兩種娛樂方式都喜歡,我們還是有最喜歡的度過時光的方式。

Physical recreation affords us the opportunities to strengthen our bodies and to satisfy our competitive nature. The activities range from participation in sports such as ball games to running slowly.

體育鍛鍊為我們提供了增強體魄的機會,滿足我們競爭的本性,這些活動包括球類活動和慢跑等體育項目。

Besides physical recreation we have intellectual activities. Activities such as reading a good book, listening to a favorite record, and going to a play serve to restore mentality to our mental processes.

除了體育鍛鍊,我們還可以進行智力鍛鍊,讀書、聽自己喜歡的錄音帶、看戲能夠促進智力發展。

I prefer a balance of these activities to provide both the physical conditioning and mental relaxation. For me, physical recreation is necessary for good health, but intellectual activities, such as writing stories, provide the most pleasure.

我更喜歡體育鍛鍊和精神享受相結合。對我來說,體育活動對身體健康是非常必要的,但智力活動,例如寫故事,會為我提供更大的快樂。

The first reason can be seen by every person. Outdoor activities can improve our physical health greatly. Outdoor activities made our heart and muscles strong. They make us full of life and strength.

第一個原因每個人都能看到。戶外活動能大幅度地改善我們的身體健康狀況。戶外活動使我們的心臟和肌肉更強壯。它們使我們充滿活力。

The second reason for my propensity for outdoor activities is that they can build my mind greatly. In sports, one must learn to struggle for the victory, and learn to fight, no matter what is left in his body. And one must learn to stick to one's own confidence and hope, no matter how little the hope may be. And one must learn to accept failure, learn to start again after failure.

我傾向於戶外活動的第二個原因是它可以增強意志。在體育活動中,一個人必須學會爲勝利而奮戰,學會不管他的體力還剩多少也要戰鬥的精神。一個人必須學會堅持自信和希望,不管還有多少希望。一個人必須學會接受失敗,學會從失敗中重新開始。

However I still prefer outdoor activities, for they teach me how to be a strong man, both in health and in spirit.

但是,我仍然傾向於戶外活動,因爲它們教會我如何成爲一個強壯的人,不論是健康方面還是精神方面。

Sports, together with scientific diet and adequate sleep, help to keep people healthy and happy. Without necessary exercises, a person would not be able to keep up his enthusiasm and strength to associate and communicate, and as a result, he would be unable to enjoy his life as others do. Sporting people are usually more confident and successful than those who rarely take part in sports.

運動和科學的飲食、充足的睡眠一樣,使人們健康和快樂。沒有必需的鍛鍊,一個人不能保證溝通與交流的熱情和體力。結果,他將不能像其他人那樣享受生活。運動的人經常更有信心,而且比那些缺乏運動的人更成功。

Sports also play a positive role in social development. Team sports and games provide chances for people to come together, thus helping to promote understanding and enhance friendship. The sense of competition and the spirit of cooperation acquired in races, matches and games are valuable merits that can indirectly help to achieve social progress.

運動在社會發展中起到積極的作用。團隊運動和遊戲提供人們一起來的機會,這會幫助他們增進理解和加強友誼。在比賽、競賽和遊戲中獲得的競爭意識和合作精神是有價值的優點,能間接促進社會的進步。

15. 旅 遊 業

Tourism is now becoming a boom industry in many countries. It is obvious that it leads to the development of hotels and shopping facilities, and this creates jobs for local people, which would not otherwise exist. Since visitors are especially fond of examples of local crafts, a number of new industries tend to be developed to meet this demand.

旅遊業在許多國家成爲一個繁榮的產業。顯而易見的是它促使旅館業和購物設施發展，爲本地人提供了本不存在的工作機會，因爲旅遊者喜歡當地的手工藝品，爲了滿足這個需求，一些新工業發展起來。

Still, the arrival of visitors always leads to improvements in docks, airports and roads. Local people then benefit from these improvements themselves. Meanwhile, the amusement parks, zoos and other amenities gradually develop to attract more and more tourists.

旅遊者的到來導致了碼頭、飛機場和道路的改變，使得本地人從這些改變中獲利。同時，娛樂場所、動物園和其他令人愉快的事物逐漸發展起來，吸引越來越多的旅遊者。

With the frequent contact between people from different places and different nations, the exchange of culture and science is bound to be promoted, possibly leading to the better understanding of people all over the world.

隨着不同國家和地區的人經常性的交流，文化和科學技術的交流也得到了促進，這加强了全世界各民族的相互理解。

16. 旅 遊

Travelling is a very good activity. When you are fed up with your work and study, and when you can get a holiday, you can go to the beautiful spots to enjoy the beauty of nature and the special character of other cities. You can breathe fresh air, meet different people and make friends with them. In so doing, you will forget your tiredness and troubles and build up your health. As a result, you will feel fully relaxed and you will have the energy to undertake the new tasks waiting for you.

當你厭倦了工作和學習時，旅遊是一項非常好的活動，當你得到了一個假期，你可以去美麗的景點享受自然和其他城市的特殊風情，你可以呼吸新鮮空氣，遇見不同的人，並與他們交朋友。這樣一來，你可以忘掉疲勞和麻煩，增加健康。結果，你可以完全放鬆，你將有精力去承擔等待你的新任務。

But sometimes, travelling is not an enjoyable thing. For example, when the bus or car you ride in has an accident, you just sit in it and waste your precious time. Furthermore, the weather can be changeable. If you are climbing a mountain, it may rain suddenly, and you may be caught in the rain and may catch a cold, and the worst thing is that you may have your money stolen and you may have an injury. All these are terrible things which can happen to a tourist.

但有時旅遊也會是一件不愉快的事,例如當你坐的車出現交通事故時,你只能坐在裏面浪費你寶貴的時間,而且天氣可能有變化,如果你正在登山,可能會突然下雨,你也許會淋雨並且感冒,最糟糕的是,你可能被偷去金錢,你可能受到傷害,所有這些都是一個旅行者可能遇到的麻煩事。

Therefore, when you are going on a trip, you must prepare yourself carefully. Firstly, you must have clear information about the weather. Secondly, you should choose a good companion so that you can help each other. Thirdly, you must be careful everywhere and try to avoid accidents. If you do this, you will surely enjoy your travels and avoid any unnecessary troubles.

因此,當你旅行時,你必須仔細準備。首先,你必須清楚地了解天氣訊息。第二,你必須找一個同伴以便可以互相幫助。第三,你必須在每個地方都小心翼翼,避免發生事故。如果你做到這些,你將確保旅行快樂,並且避免不必要的麻煩。

17. 汽 車

Automobiles have been playing a vital part in the daily activities of our society; trucks are the most convenient for carrying goods directly from one place to another; in most cities, the majority of people get around either by car or by bus. Also, the automobile industry provides jobs for countless workers and strong support for other industries. In our world, automobiles are indispensable.

汽車在我們日常的活動中起關鍵的作用,卡車把貨物很方便地從一個地方直接運到另一個地方,在大多數城市裏,多數人藉由汽車和公共汽車走動。同時,汽車工業提供無數工作給工人,並且強力支持其他工業。在我們的世界中,汽車是不可缺少的。

But automobiles have given rise to a series of problems. They are responsible for a very large proportion of air pollution, causing a lot of diseases to men, animals and plants, and traffic accidents kill hundreds of thousands each year and disable many more. Slow movement and jams on busy roads delay us painfully; automobiles drink up precious gasoline and new roads eat up precious land. The consequences of all these are becoming even more serious.

但是汽車也帶來了很多問題。它們必須對大面積的空氣污染負責,它們導致人、動物和植物的各種疾病,交通事故每年使成百上千的人喪失了生命,使更多的人成爲殘廢。在路口的緩慢行駛和擁塞耽誤了我們的時間,汽車消耗了寶貴的汽油,新的道路佔用了寶貴的土地資源。所有這些結果正在變得越來越嚴重。

Obviously, automobiles, like anything else, have more than one face. Engineers are working hard to give fuller swing to their merits and overcome their shortcomings. Improvements are being made, we believe future automobiles will be better.

顯然,汽車像其他任何事物一樣,都有多面性。工程師們正在努力工作,以更充分地發揚它的優點,克服它的缺點。改變正在進行,我們相信汽車的未來會更好。

Compared with cars, bicycles have many advantages. Firstly, they are not very expensive and almost every family can afford to buy and repair them. Secondly, though they are more slowly than cars, bicycles are very handy and convenient. With a bicycle, you can go wherever you like and needn't look for a large parking place in a crowded downtown area. Thirdly, bicycles don't cause air pollution. On the contrary, they do good to your health. In addition, it is much easier to learn to ride a bicycle than to drive a car.

和汽車比較,腳踏車有很多的優點。首先,它們不貴,任何一個家庭都能買得起,修得起;第二,雖然它們比汽車的速度慢,但卻很方便,使用腳踏車,我們可以到想去的任何地方,並且不需要在鬧市中尋找停車場地或在家裏準備車庫;第三,腳踏車不會導致空氣污染,另一方面,它有助於我們的身體健康。而且,學騎腳踏車比學開汽車更容易。

However, bicycles have also brought about many problems. For example, they make the streets more crowded and cause many traffic accidents every year. But as long as these problems can be properly solved, bicycles will still be widely used by people.

但是,腳踏車也帶來很多問題。例如,它們使道路更擁擠,每年引起很多的交通事故。但是只要這些問題能得到妥善解決,腳踏車還將廣泛地被人們使用。

Problems brought about by automobiles

汽車帶來的問題

Although the automobile has brought convenience to us, many people have begun to realize that it is the source of trouble as well. Because of too many automobiles, traffic accidents happen again and again all over the world. Worst of all, gases sent out by the automobiles give rise to air pollution and do great harm to people.

雖然汽車帶給我們很多方便，許多人開始意識到它也是問題的來源。因爲有太多的汽車，全世界的交通事故發生了一次又一次，最糟糕的是，汽車排出的廢氣增加了空氣的污染，爲人們帶來很多危害。

In order to solve the problem of air pollution, some automobile manufacturers are trying to build a car that does not pollute and some inventors are working on cars powered by steam and electricity, but now this is only a dream of people.

爲了解決空氣污染的問題，一些汽車製造商試着製造沒有污染的汽車，發明家正在研製以水蒸氣和電爲動力的汽車，但現在這只是人們的一個夢想。

The governments in some countries, for example, in the United States, are trying to reduce the number of privately owned cars and ask the people to use public buses. But this also causes a lot of problems, so now it is very difficult to make these changes.

一些國家的政府，例如美國，正在減少私人擁有汽車的數量，並且要求人們使用公共汽車，但是這也帶來了很多問題，所以現在很難實行這種變革。

18. 城市生活

Hundreds of people rush into cities, especially big cities. They come for better education and better jobs, for information about the latest developments in science and technology, and for better medical care.

成百上千的人湧入城市，特別是大城市。他們爲了更好的教育和更好的工作，爲了最先進的科學技術訊息，爲了更好的醫療保障而來到城市。

I enjoy living in a big city where life is convenient. Advanced public transport may widen variety of goods to choose from, all the latest modern conveniences, plenty of public places for enjoyment, and, above all, the perfect health care system allow you to live in great comfort.

我喜歡生活在大城市，因爲生活方便。先進的公共運輸使我們可以選擇更多種類的貨物，所有最先進的設施、足夠的公共娛樂場所，以及好的醫療系統使你生活得更舒適。

However, big cities are confronted with many problems, and the biggest is that ever-increasing population flow toward the city, which results in crowded stinking buses, traffic jams, traffic accidents, poor housing conditions, etc. Noise and pollution, mostly from factories and cars, are two more serious problems which damage people's health.

但是大城市也有很多問題，最大的問題是城市人口的增長，這會導致公共汽車的擁擠、交通阻塞、交通事故、住房條件差等問題。主要由工廠和汽車排放的噪音和污染,是兩個嚴重的問題,危害着人們的健康。

With the development of modern industry, more and more people are flowing into big cities. Accordingly, the housing problem in big cities is becoming more and more serious.

隨着現代工業的發展,越來越多的人湧入了大城市。因此,大城市的住房問題變得越來越嚴重。

People have offered many solutions to this problem. I think building satellite cities in the suburbs is more practical. The fresh air and beautiful scenery in the suburbs will be appealing to the city citizens, who suffer from air pollution, noises, etc. In the overcrowded city, with more people leaving the city, more space will be available for those remaining. The housing problem in big cities will thus be solved.

人們爲這個問題提供了很多解決方案。我認爲在郊區建立衛星城市是非常可行的。郊區新鮮的空氣和美麗的風景將會吸引那些飽受空氣噪音和污染等問題困擾的城市人。在過分擁擠的城市,隨着更多的人離開城市,會爲留下的人提供更多的空間。大城市的住房問題就會得到解決。

In the meantime, I'm against the idea of utilizing the underground space to solve the problem. We can imagine how uncomfortable it will be to live under the ground, having to probe in the dark. The air there will be very stuffy, and the cost of building underground houses will be tremendous.

同時,我反對利用地下空間去解決問題。我能想像住在地下是多麼不舒服,不得不在黑暗中摸索,空氣很悶,建地下房子的花費也會很大。

In brief, building satellite cities can not only improve the housing condition in big cities, but also provide a much better living environment. But the housing problem is very complicated. Perhaps people can hardly rely on only one way to solve the problem completely.

總之,建衛星城市不僅改善了大城市的住房情況,而且提供更好的居住環境。但是住房問題很複雜,也許人們很難只依靠一種方法就能徹底解決住房問題。

19. 城市生活與鄉村生活

Country people are in close contact with nature. Living in peace and quiet, they can breathe fresh air and listen to the songs of birds. They need not worry about any pollution problems that always bother city-dwellers. The people living in the country can enjoy many out-door activities. They can go fishing in rivers and hunting in forests. Another advantage that country people enjoy is that they can easily get fresh vegetables, fruits and milk at a lower price.

鄉下人和自然聯繫得很緊密。住在和平和寧靜的環境裏,他們能呼吸到新鮮空氣,聽小鳥唱歌。他們不需要擔心任何煩擾城市居民的污染問題。住在鄉下的人能享受許多戶外活動。他們能在河裏垂釣,在森林裏打獵。鄉下居民的另一個優勢是他們能很容易地以低價吃到新鮮蔬菜、水果和牛奶。

Country life, however, has some inconveniences. The people living in the country cannot enjoy all the miracles of the latest scientific achievements. Sometimes they have transportation or communication problems. Their daily life is not as easy as that of city people. For example, they cannot go shopping in big supermarkets. As for cultural recreations, as there are few cinemas or concerts halls in the country, people there cannot often see movies or plays.

但鄉村生活也有許多不方便的地方。住在鄉下的人們不能享受最新科學成就的奇跡。有時候,他們會有運輸和通訊方面的困難。他們每天的生活不會像城市人那樣方便。例如,他們不能在大的超級市場裏購物;談到娛樂活動,因為在鄉下很少有電影院和音樂廳,人們不能常看電影和戲劇。

People may have different opinions about country life. Some would think that country life is too hard and tedious, whereas others might enjoy it. It all depends on one's personal point of view and experiences.

人們對鄉村生活持有不同的意見。一些人可能會認為鄉村生活太艱苦和乏味,而另一些人可能會喜歡它。這全取決於每個人看問題的出發點和經歷。

Many people appreciate the convenience of the city. Cars, buses and underground trains here can take you wherever you want to go. A great number of restaurants provide you with delicious and time-saving food. For leisure time entertainment, people have a great choice of going to a cinema, a theatre, watching sports games and visiting museums. Shopping is always a pleasure, too. The fact that famous universities and modern factories are concentrated in big cities means that people have more education and employment opportunities.

許多人欣賞城市的方便。汽車、公共汽車和地鐵可以把你帶到你想去的任何地方。大量的飯館為你提供了美味省時的食物。至於休閒時光的娛樂活動,人們可以選擇電影院、劇院,觀看體育比賽和參觀博物館。購物也是一種娛樂。著名大學和現代化工廠集中在大城市,這意味着人們有更多的教育和從業的機會。

The countryside is attractive with its rural scenes. Here you will find little pollution or noise and no crowded streets. Nothing can be compared with the pleasant songs of birds, the fragrance of flowers and the beautiful sight of the rising sun. Working in the field, eating fresh vegetables and fruits and being close to nature will keep you healthy and energetic.

鄉村由於田園風光而吸引人。這裏很少發現污染和噪音,沒有擁擠的街道。沒有什麼能比鳥鳴、花香和太陽初升的美麗景色更令人愉快了。在這種地方工作,吃着新鮮的蔬菜和水果,更接近大自然,可以使你健康而且精力充沛。

However both the city and the country have their own disadvantages. In big cities fumes of cars and industrial wastes pollute the atmosphere. Moreover, overpopulation makes accommodation more and more difficult to find and the cost of living is very high. Similarly, the country has its own problems. Lack of modern housing facilities and advanced effective transport system creates many difficulties. In a word, both the city and the country have their virtues and shortcomings. Everyone can judge them in a particular way and make his choice accordingly.

但是城市和鄉村都有自己的不足之處。在大城市裏,汽車廢氣和工廠的廢棄物污染着空氣,而且人口的過度增長使住處很難找到,生活的花費非常大。同樣地鄉村也有它的問題。缺少現代化的住房條件和先進有效的運輸系統會產生很多困難。總而言之,城市和鄉村都有各自的優點和不足。人們可以根據自己的情況判斷和選擇。

Urban citizens can appreciate a more colorful life than rural citizens. Townspeople are well-informed because they have easier access to news, while country people are uninformed because these districts are hard to get to. Urban traffic is so well-developed that the residents there often visit exhibitions and parks which are only a short bus ride away. Shopping, a necessary activity in everyday life is more convenient in the city than in the country.

城市人比鄉下人有更豐富多彩的生活。城鎮人見多識廣是因爲他們更容易獲得新聞,鄉下人訊息不靈是因爲他們很難直接獲得訊息。城市交通發展很快,居民可以經常看展覽,去短途公共汽車經過的公園。每天必需的購物活動在城市比鄉村更方便。

Air pollution, noise and overcrowding which are the biggest problems confronting towns-people seem strange for rural residents. Medical studies have proved that rural residents can live longer than urban residents, because the former are free from a contaminated environment. In addition, the crime rate in the city is several times higher than that in the country-side. So the safe, quiet and cheap life in the country appeals to many citydwellers.

城市人面臨的最大問題:空氣污染、噪音和過度擁擠對於鄉下人卻顯得陌生。醫學報告證明鄉下人比城市人活的時間長,因爲前者生活在沒有污染的環境中。而且,城市的犯罪率比鄉村高幾倍。因此,安全、寧靜和便宜的鄉村生活吸引了很多城市居民。

20. 科學技術

Human life can not continue without science and technology. For many years, human society has developed with the advance of science and technology, while the development of science and technology has in turn brought the process to mankind. Because of this, the life we are living now is more civilized than that of our forefather's.

離開了科學技術,人類生活不能繼續。許多年來,人類社會隨着科學技術的進步而發展,同時,科學技術的發展也帶動人類發展。正因爲這樣,我們現在過的生活比我們的祖先更文明。

The development of science and technology has brought about many changes in people's lives.

科學技術的發展爲人們的生活帶來很多改變。

Owing to the invention of spaceship and rocket, the dream of man's landing on the moon, which was impossible several decades ago, has now come true.

由於火箭和太空船的發明,在許多年之前不可能實現的人類登上月球的夢想現在已經實現了。

21. 電 腦

It is believed that the computer can do almost everything. It was gradually used not only in mathematics, physics, chemistry and astronomy, but in places like the library, hospital and military army to replace the works of man. Although a computer works much faster and accurately than man, a fact is undeniable: It is designed, manufactured and programmed by man, and therefore controlled by human beings. A horse helps man a lot and runs much faster than we, but it is only a slave.

電腦被認爲幾乎能做任何事。它不僅被用在數學、物理、化學和天文上,在圖書館、醫院和軍隊,它也取代了人的工作。雖然電腦的工作比人更快更精確,一個事實是不可否認的,它是由人設計、製造和設計程式的,因此由人來控制。馬幫人做很多事,比人跑得快,但它只是人類的奴隸。

The future for the computer is very promising. With the help of it, we can do things that could not be done before. Conquering the universe, discovering new things, explaining mysterious phenomena puzzling us at present are all made possible by computer.

電腦非常有前途。有了它的幫助,我們能做許多以前不能做的事,征服宇宙、發現新事物、揭開困擾我們的神祕現象,電腦使這些成爲可能。

With the wide use of computer technology, more and more automated machines replace man's labour. Our banks are managed by computers and the tickets at the airport are issued by computers, too. In addition, the instruments and devices controlled by computers have entered offices, departments and houses to help people to work shorter and shorter hours and to enjoy longer and longer leisure hours in their own homes. The computerization, certainly, relieving men of heavy labour, makes many workers be out of work.

隨着電腦技術的廣泛使用,越來越多的自動化機器代替了人的勞動。銀行由電腦來管理,飛機場也由電腦來出票。而且,由電腦控制的機器和設備進入了辦公室、部門和住宅,幫助人們用更短的時間工作,在家裏享受更長的休息時間。電腦化確實把人從繁重的勞動中解脫出來,卻使許多工人失業。

Therefore, a fear has arisen among some people that the more machines will be used, the more workers will be unemployed and the lower our living standard will become. The fear, I think, is a groundless one, like the fear that the sky might fall. It is well-known that newly-invented machines need to be produced. What's more important is that automation increases production of public wealth and the people will gain a happier life.

因此一些人開始擔心機器使用得越多,失業的工人越多,我們的生活水準會下降。這種擔心我認爲是沒有根據的,是杞人憂天。眾所周知,新發明的機器需要靠人生產。而且,更重要的是自動化增加了公共財富的生產,人們將享受更快樂的生活。

If primary students are permitted to use calculators whenever they do their homework, they may calculate everything with the aid of the calculators. This can be harmful to their mathematics abilities. The students should be banned from using calculators when they do their homework or take part in examinations.

如果小學生在做作業時被允許隨時使用計算器,他們可以在計算器的幫助下計算任何東西。這對他們的數學能力有害。當學生做家庭作業和參加考試時,必須禁止他們使用計算器。

Besides the harmful rays from computers, the screen is inclined to lead to near-eye sight in users.

除了電腦放出的有害射線,電腦的螢光幕還會使使用者近視。

In the first place, children will acquire more knowledge by using computers and calculators.

第一,孩子將藉使用電腦和計算器來獲得更多的知識。

Secondly, by using computers, children will have more interests in their studies. This clearly demonstrates that children are more enthusiastic about their studies when they use computers.

第二,透過使用電腦,孩子將對學習更感興趣。當他們使用電腦時,確實對學習有更高的熱忱。

First of all, with a computer, the only thing we need to do is to press a button when we want to find out something. If you are good at making friends, you can communicate with people who have different customs and traditions in the net world.

首先,有了電腦,當我們想找什麼時,我們只需要按一下按鈕。如果你擅長交朋友,在網路世界中你能聯絡到很多有不同習俗和傳統的人。

Secondly, computers are becoming our teachers at home.

第二,電腦正成為我們家中的老師。

Last but not least, a computer is essential for improving the quality of our life. Computers make it possible to buy everything we want all over the world.

最後但並非不重要,電腦對於改善我們的生活品質是必需的。電腦使我們可能在全世界購買任何想要的東西。

It is very clear that computers have already brought children enormous benefits in many aspects of their lives —— studying with the aid of multi-media computers is easy and interesting; surging on the Internet provides children with chances to know more about the world, and so, helps them to widen their horizons; sending e-mails saves them a lot of money and time and seems to be the most convenient and efficient way of communicating; and playing computer games is really fun.

確實,電腦在生活的很多方面帶給孩子巨大的好處——在多媒體電腦的幫助下學習會很容易而且有趣;在網路上馳騁為孩子提供了了解世界更多的機會,幫助他們開闊視野;發送電子郵件會省很多錢和時間,並且是最方便有效的溝通方式;玩電腦遊戲確實也很有趣。

However, it cannot be denied that some side-effects have unavoidably occurred along with wider computer use.

但是不能否認的是隨著電腦的廣泛使用,一些負面的影響不可避免地產生了。

Children who sit for long hours before computer screens are more likely to suffer from short sight and backache. Since some of them are obsessed with electronic games and Internet surfing, they don't have enough time to review what they learned in classes and read books. Consequently, they fail to pass exams and learn valuable knowledge and skills. As children stay longer and longer in the fancy and perfected world in computers, they tend to form misconception and have incorrect expectation of the realistic world. They lose contact with their friends, relatives and more importantly the nature. Internet offers unhealthy information, which also has impact on children in forming healthy mentality.

孩子在電腦螢幕前坐的時間長了,很容易近視和背痛。由於一些孩子被電子遊戲和上網迷住了,他們沒有時間讀書和複習上課所學的知識。結果他們考試不及格,不能學到有用的知識和技能。當孩子在電腦世界中花費的時間越來越長,他們將形成一些誤解,對現實世界產生不正確的期待。他們將失去和朋友、親戚的聯絡,更嚴重的是,他們喪失兒童天性。網路也提供不健康的訊息,這也有礙孩子形成健康的心理。

Although lots of negative side effects occur, and are difficult to accept, the benefits outweigh the side-effects in any sense. What we should do is to educate our children to be able to distinguish the good from the bad, to form appropriate view of the world and to manage time. We should take more effective measures to avoid and minimize these side-effects.

雖然發生了很多負面的影響,並且很難讓人接受,但從任何意義上說,優點多於不足。我們必須做的是教育我們的孩子區分好與壞,形成正確的世界觀並管理好時間。我們必須使用更有效的方法去避免負面影響,將其降至最少。

22. 電子遊戲

Games give ue ample teaching and inspiration on life.
遊戲提供我們豐富的教導和生活上的靈感。

At the same time, games teach us strategy and intelligence about life. By playing chess, our brains are trained to think quickly and analysis precisely. Through playing electronic games, we learn to react promptly and imagine wildly. What's more, games build up our characters —— carefulness, courage, confidence, etc, with which we know how to cope with those difficulties in the life.

同時,遊戲教會我們生活的策略和智慧。下棋訓練我們的大腦快速思考和分析。藉由玩電子遊戲,我們學會了迅速反應並且豐富了想像力,而且遊戲可以塑造好的性格——細心、信心、勇氣等等,有了它們我們就會懂得如何處理生活中的困難。

And to the last point, no teacher in the world can be compared to games.
最後一點,世界上沒有老師能和遊戲相比。

They are nothing but a waste of time, money and energy. Teenagers should be doing valuable things like reading, studying , and going to concerts and museums.

做這些事情需要花費時間、金錢和精力。年輕人應該做一些有價值的事情,例如讀書、學習和去音樂會和博物館。

Young people could spend their time in far healthier places than inside video arcades. The lights are often dim and the games are noisy, which damage people's eyes and ears. A lot of money is spent by teenagers on these games. Playing video games does not allow people to use any of their creativity. There is also no opportunity for physical exercise, something young people are sadly lacking these days. Video arcades should be banned from cities and towns.

年輕人可以把他們的時間花在比電子遊戲場更健康的地方。那裏光線昏暗,遊戲的噪音很大,這些都會損害人們的眼睛和耳朵。年輕人把大量的金錢花在遊戲上。玩電子遊戲不會讓人有任何的創造力,也沒有機會去鍛鍊身體,今天,令人悲哀的是,年輕人正在喪失創造力和健康。電子遊戲場必須在城鎮中被禁止。

23. 各種媒體

Newspapers and magazines can give much information about a particular event. They usually provide some history of the event and some of its causes and effects. Sometimes they also give an opinion or point of view on a particular development. Many people may enjoy reading a newspaper or magazine while waiting for a bus or before going to sleep. Thus they can become informed without spending much time.

報紙和雜誌能帶給我們有關事件的很多訊息。它們通常提供一些事件的歷史、起因和影響。有時它們也提出對一項特別發展的觀點和意見。許多人在等公共汽車和睡覺前喜歡看報紙和雜誌。因此他們不必花多少時間就能得到大量訊息。

Radio and television can help a person to be well informed about what is happening each day. They always keep people widely and promptly informed. It is also possible to listen to the radio or watch TV and do something else at the same time. Many people can even listen to the news on their car radio while driving. That's one of the reasons why radio and television are becoming more and more popular with the people who want to be informed about the news.

收音機和電視能幫助人們了解當天發生了什麼事。它們使人們廣泛快速地得到訊息。收聽廣播和觀看電視可以和別的事一起進行。許多人甚至在開車時收聽新聞。這是為什麼收音機和電視在需要了解新聞的人中變得越來越普及的原因之一。

Thoughtful parents will definitely not allow their children to view the bad programs. A child's viewing time should be limited to watch educationally beneficial programs.

有思想的父母會堅決不讓他們的孩子去看壞節目。孩子必須被限制只能觀看有教育意義的節目。

24. 廣 告

Advertisements appear everywhere in modern society. For example, when you walk along the streets, you can see large advertisement boards with pretty girls smiling at you. In newspapers, for another example, you often see half of the pages covered with advertisements. As still another example, you turn on the TV set and you see advertisements again. Whether you like it or not, they are pouring into your life.

現代社會到處有廣告。例如,當我們在街上走時,你能看到巨大的廣告招牌,上面的美女正向你微笑。在報紙上,你經常看到一半的版面被廣告覆蓋。你打開電視機,同樣能看到廣告。不管你是否喜歡它,廣告正侵入了你的生活。

Although advertisements enable you to make decisions quickly, sometimes they can cause trouble. The most unbearable thing is to watch the advertisements before and during the films on TV. There are always so many of them that they make you forget what you are sitting there for. The ironical thing is that the advertisements of the same type of things are often shown one after another so that you are confused that to which product you should choose.

雖然廣告使你能夠快速地做出決定,有時它們也會帶來麻煩。最難以忍受的是在電視節目前或中間插播廣告。在一個節目中廣告出現過多會使你忘了自己正坐在那裏做什麼。最諷刺的是同類事物的廣告一個接一個重複出現,使你無法打定主意選擇哪一個。

First of all, they convey business information. Another use of advertisements is to make the public interested in what manufacturers want to sell.

首先,它們傳達商業訊息。廣告的另一個用處是使大眾對製造廠商要賣的東西產生興趣。

Surplus advertisements have interfered in people's normal life. Every ten minutes a television program will be interrupted by commercials for a couple of minutes, which ruin good movies and exciting television shows.

廣告過多會妨礙人們的正常生活。每十分鐘電視節目插播幾分鐘的商業廣告,會破壞一部好電影和電視劇的正常放映。

According to the laws, advertisements must be completely truthful and healthy. Let good advertisements facilitate communication between business people and the public, and help keep the business world moving.

依據法律,廣告必須是完全眞實的和健康的。讓好的廣告把商人和大眾聯繫起來,並且幫助商業界向前發展吧。

25. 污 染

Pollution is becoming more and more serious all over the world. The poisonous gas sent off by factories and automobiles has made the air unhealthy for people to breathe. Waste water keeps pouring into rivers and lakes; as a result, many water species are dying out. Scientists have warned that unless effective solutions are worked out, the problem of pollution will eventually get out of hand.

污染在全世界變得越來越嚴重。工廠和汽車排出有毒的氣體,使人們吸入的空氣不利於身體健康。廢水湧入江河,結果導致許多水中生物的死亡。科學家警告,除非有效地解決問題,否則污染問題將會變得無法控制。

Fortunately, measures are being taken to cope with the situation. First, many new laws have been passed to place strict control over industrial pollution. Secondly, a large-scale program is now underway to educate people to be responsible citizens in fighting pollution. Finally, the government has started building various facilities such as sewage treatment plants and has encouraged scientists to work out more and better ways to reduce pollution. It is hoped that all these measures will be effective and bring back a healthful world.

幸運的是,人們正在採取措施處理這種情況。首先,許多地方已經通過了許多新的法律來控制過度工業污染。第二,實行了大量的規畫,教育人們做個為防制污染而負責任的公民。最後,政府正在建立各種設施,例如:污水處理廠,鼓勵科學家們找到更多更好的方法去減少污染。人們希望所有這些措施都有效並且恢復健康的社會。

Everyone agrees that water pollution is a serious problem today. Factories contribute to the problem because they rely on rivers for disposing of wastes. Recently, certain counter measures have been taken. Above all, many governments both in developed countries and in developing countries have laid down rules and regulations in respect to the pollution problem. Factories in towns and cities are forbidden to drain waste liquids into rivers, lakes and seas before they are totally treated and purified. With the progress of science and technology, a series of advanced methods have been developed to treat contaminated water. And certain re-markable results have been achieved in this respect.

任何人都同意，在今天水污染是一個嚴重的問題。工廠是問題的來源，因爲它們依靠河水來除去廢物。近來，應對措施正在被採用。首先，已開發國家和發展中國家的政府已經制定了法律法規來解決污染問題。城市和鄉鎮的工廠被禁止在廢水未經處理和淨化的情況下向河裏、湖裏和海裏排放廢水。隨着科學和技術的發展，一系列處理污水的先進方式已經發展起來，並且已經有了顯著的效果。

26. 環境問題

There are two basic sources of these problems. One is man-made. Someone does such a thing as cutting down trees to receive benefits or to get necessities, so that natural environ-ment is damaged. The other is natural catastrophies. How should we protect the natural envi-ronment? One method is by creating laws although this method has worked, laws alone in poor places, where people damage the environment out of necessity, are not enough. Or per-haps imposing a fine is a better way to stop the man-made destruction. In addition, new en-vironmentally constructive means must be found through scientific and technical work.

這些問題有兩個基本來源。一種是人爲的。一些人爲了獲利或者獲得他們需要的東西而砍伐樹木，所以自然環境被毀壞了。另一種是自然災難。我們怎樣保護自然環境？一種方式是制定法律。雖然這種方式已經有作用，但在貧窮地方，人們破壞環境滿足需求，只靠法律是不夠的。也許罰款是阻止人爲破壞的更好的方法。而且新的環境建設方式必須藉由科學和技術方式來建立。

With the rapid growth of modern cities, urban vegetation has been greatly reduced.

隨着現代化城市的快速增加，城市植被大量減少。

27. 動　物

Animals in their natural state are part of the wonder of creation and the beauty of our world. However, as a result of the steady growth of the world population, there is less room on our planet for wild animals. Unless something is done, some species of animals will cease to ex-ist in their wild state, which also means a disaster to human beings.

生活在自然環境中的動物是造物者的一個奇跡，是我們世界的美麗之處。但是隨着世界人口的穩定增加,越來越少的空間留給了我們這個星球上的野生動物。除非採取措施,否則一些物種將不會在野生環境中生存,這也意味着人類的災難。

One of the effective measures to avoid the extinction of wild animals is for all countries to create nature reserves where all the native species of animals can wander free and be protected from man. Certain rare species that are going to be extinct should be collected, fed and reproduced artificially.

一個避免野生動物滅絕的有效方式是讓所有國家都建立自然保護區,在那裏自然界的動物可以自由地活動,並且被人類保護。那些瀕臨滅絕的動物被集中起來,受到餵養和人工繁殖。

From what we see happening in many parts of the world, the main danger to animal existence comes from man's activities. I should like to see an international law forbidding the use and sale of meat, skins, horns and tusks from wild animals. We do great wrong if we allow any of their species to die out.

就我們在許多地區看到的正在發生的事而言,動物生存主要的危險來自人類的活動。我希望能有一個國際法律禁止使用和銷售野生動物的肉、皮、角和牙齒。如果我們聽任任何野生動物滅絕,我們就犯了大錯。

Animals can protect us.

動物能保護我們。

Second, animals can provide us with many useful things. Wherever we live, we gain profits from animals. Imagine what our life would be like if we were dispossessed of meat, egg and milk.

第二,動物提供我們很多有用的東西。不管我們住在哪裏,我們都能從動物身上獲得好處。想像一下,如果我們沒有肉、蛋、奶,我們的生活將變成什麼樣子。

Finally, animals are our friends.

最後,動物是我們的朋友。

God created animals before man. So we must try our best to make sure that animals, one of the most valuable natural resources, can live long.

上帝在創造人之前創造了動物。所以,我們必須竭盡全力使動物,一種最有價值的自然資源,能生活得長久。

28. 大學生談戀愛

Some college teachers argue that students should give up love for the sake of learning. They maintain that love is time-consuming and tears students away from learning, students' main task. If a student falls in love, he will certainly neglect his studies and cannot catch up with his class.

一些大學教師認爲,學生爲了學習應該放棄愛情。他們認爲愛情很浪費時間,並且把學生從學習的主要任務中拖走。如果學生陷入愛河,他必然忽略學習,並且不能跟上學習進度。

Some of their friends who are falling in love, study harder and make greater progress in order to please their girl (or boy) friend. Someone else, on the contrary, who has not fallen in love, cannot concentrate on learning.

一些正在戀愛的朋友努力學習和進步,以取得他們女(男)朋友的歡心。另一些人卻相反,他們沒有陷入愛河,因此不能專心學習。

In my opinion, as a coin has two sides, love can be positive and negative. If you do not give yourself away in love but take it as a drive, you will make more progress in your learning and achieve much. But if you forget everything else except love, then you will become a "perfect" lover and a definite loser in your studies.

我的觀點是,問題都有兩個方面,愛情也有正面和反面。如果你不沉湎在愛情裡,而是把它作爲動力,你會在學習方面取得很大的進步和成功。但是,如果你心裏只有愛情,那麼你將成爲一個好的愛人和學習上的徹底失敗者。

29. 吸　煙

It is well known that there's a definite link between smoking and bronchial troubles, heart diseases and lung cancer. But, ignoring the danger, the governments of most countries haven't stood for complete prohibition of cigarette smoking.

眾所周知,吸煙和支氣管疾病、心臟病和肺癌之間有直接的關聯。但是,大多數國家的政府卻無視這個危險,沒有徹底地禁止吸煙。

Surely, this is the most short-sighted policy. While the tax is collected in vast sum, much larger amounts are spent on cancer research and on effort to cure patient. Not to mention, countless valuable lives lost as victims of smoking.

這只是短視策略。在聚攏大量稅收的同時,許多錢被用來做癌症研究和治療病人。不用說,無數有價值的生命成為了抽煙的犧牲品。

30. 古典音樂和流行音樂

Most people like something very close to them, because they want to be relaxed. Classical music is a little far away and requires some special knowledge for people to appreciate it. When one listens to pop music, he can easily understand what the singer sings.

大多數人喜歡離他們近的東西,因為他們希望得到放鬆。古典音樂離我們有點遠,需要一些特殊的知識去欣賞。當一個人傾聽流行音樂,他很快就能懂得歌手在唱什麼。

At the same time, I can't deny there are also many merits in the classical music.

同時,我不能否認古典音樂有很多優點。

I can't appreciate it very much because I can't really comprehend it.

我不太能欣賞它,因為我不能真正理解它。

31. 家庭對孩子的影響

After one is born, the first and nearest surroundings is the family in which he will grow up. So family does play a significant role in shaping children's inclination and character. Almost as soon as a child becomes old enough to communicate with other children, he begins having friends, who sometimes influence him more rapidly than do families. Then as far as I am concerned both of their influences are indispensable for children's growth.

當人出生後,最先接觸的和最近的環境是他生長的家庭。因此,家庭確實在形成兒童的愛好和性格方面起到了關鍵的作用。孩子一長到能和別的孩子交流的年齡就有了朋友,朋友有時會比家庭更快地影響他。因此我認為,家庭和朋友的影響對孩子的成長來說都是不可缺少的。

There is a forceful example to demonstrate the importance of the family. Because the family is children's most direct source of knowledge and other experiences, those who are brought up in good family tend to possess many pleasant characters, and vise versa.

有一個強有力的例子來證明家庭的重要性。因為家庭是孩子獲得知識和其他經驗的直接來源,那些在良好家庭中成長的孩子會有更好的性格,反之亦然。

Nowadays, when someone praises me for my academic excellence, I thank my parents, since it is they who taught me a good study habit in my unawareness. When I succeeded in an experiment after many failures, I owe it to my parents who have been encouraging me "try, and try again" since the time I could remember. Not until today do I really understand their patience, their consideration and their deep love to me. What they gave me is not only the life of my body, but the life of my mind as well.

現在,當一些人讚美我的學業優秀時,我要感謝我的父母,因爲他們在我無意識時教會我好的學習習慣。當我經過很多次失敗後取得一個實驗的成功,我把它歸功於我的父母,他們從我有記憶時便鼓勵我"努力,再努力"。直到今天,我才眞正理解他們的耐性、他們的用心和他們對我深深的愛。他們不僅給我身體,而且給我思想。

Little children are like young trees. In order to grow well, they need to be carefully irrigated, fertilized and trimmed. Some parents control their children tightly but poorly. They don't understand them, and always exact the standards of adults to the young. Some parents indulge their child too much. They prepare everything for the child except the most important character, independence.

小孩子像小樹。爲了長得好,他們需要被仔細地灌漑、施肥、修剪。一些家長把他們的孩子控制得太緊,卻太拙劣。他們不了解孩子,總是把成人的標準施加給他們。一些家長太縱容他們的孩子。他們爲孩子準備好了所有的事,除了最重要的獨立精神。

32. 電 話

Communication is very important both in the past and at present and tends to be more essential in modern society. With the development of transportation, letters can be sent much more quickly than ever before, but when the telephone appeared, most people have turned to it.

交流在過去和現在都非常重要,並且在現代社會中更爲重要。隨着運輸的發展,信可以比以前更快地送到,但是當電話出現後,大多數人已改用電話。

Communicating with other people by telephone is very convenient indeed, especially when you have something urgent. Today, with the quick rhythm of life people usually don't have as much time to write letters as before. It seems that telephone shortens the distance between people, and men can keep in touch with each other more easily. From this point of view, telephone is one of the most wonderful inventions in the 20th century.

透過電話與其他人交流確實非常方便,特別是當你有什麼急事時。今天,隨着人們生活節奏的加快,通常沒有像以前那麼多的時間寫信。電話似乎縮短了人們之間的距離,人們可以很容易地互相聯絡。從這一點看,電話是二十世紀最好的發明之一。

People are becoming too dependent on telephone. Even when they have time to write a letter, they prefer the telephone. With the little magical implement at hand, it isn't difficult for a man to find excuse for not writing letters and feel at ease. Telephone is making people lazy. When a person writes, he must organize his mind to express his ideas and feelings more logically. People can not only greet each other but also exchange their thoughts by letters.

人們太依賴電話了,雖然他們有時間寫信,他們更願意打電話。用手中這個不可思議的小工具,人們不難找到不寫信的藉口,並且感到心安理得。電話使人們懶惰。當人寫作時,他必須組織自己的思想並表達出來,並且使它們更有邏輯性。透過寫信,人們不僅能互相祝福而且能交流思想。

33. 保護森林

We see and hear from newspaper, radio and TV programs that forests have been disappearing at an alarming speed in many places in the world. We know that forests are essential for many aspects of human life. They provide wood, food, mild climate and balanced environments, without forests, our lands will be covered by deserts. We will suffer with hunger, hot climate and lack of life materials. Life will be extremely difficult if we have no forests.

我們從報紙、廣播和電視節目中了解到,在世界上的很多地方,森林正在以驚人的速度消失。我們知道森林在人類社會的很多方面起關鍵作用。它提供人們木材、食物、溫和的氣候和平衡的環境,沒有森林,我們的陸地將被沙漠覆蓋。我們將遭受飢餓、炎熱的氣候,缺乏生活原料。如果我們沒有森林,生活將非常困難。

Let's save the forests. Don't cut down them any more. We should plant and protect them instead. In order to make the world better and life easier for ourselves and our children and our children's children, let's be the gardeners instead of the destroyers.

讓我們保護森林,不要亂砍亂伐。我們必須種樹並且保護它們。為了使世界更好,使我們自己、我們的孩子、我們的孫子生活得更輕鬆,讓我們成為園丁而不是破壞者。

34. 穿 校 服

In the first place, demanding students wearing uniform in school is not good to their psychological health development. What to wear everyday is a person's own business, and for children, it's the same. So school authorities have no right to deprive their right for choosing clothes. If they do so, they are forcing students to do what they don't like and interfere in students' business.

首先,要求學生在學校穿校服不利於他們心理發育。每天穿什麼是每個人自己的事,對孩子而言也一樣。因此校方沒有權利剝奪學生選擇衣服的權利。如果他們這樣做,他們就是在迫使學生做他們不願意做的事和干預學生自己的事。

The second reason is that wearing school uniforms is not good for students' physical health development.

第二個原因是穿校服不利於學生的身體發育。

Another consideration is that demanding students wear school uniform increases parents' burden, especially comparatively low income parents. If students are permitted to wear other clothes, parents have more choice to choose less expensive clothes for their children.

另一個需要考慮的原因是,要求學生穿校服增加了家長的負擔,特別是相對來說收入較低的學生家長。如果學生被允許穿其他服裝,家長們可能會選擇花費更低的服裝給孩子穿。

To sum up, nothing looks nicer than to see all the children in a school neatly and tidily dressed in uniform. Uniform encourages frugality.

總而言之,沒有什麼比看到所有孩子在學校裏穿乾淨整潔的校服更美的事了。校服鼓勵學生樸素。

Uniform, in a way, can also prevent students from being diverted from study to fashion. Students will focus more on their study instead of what they look like and how to and what to dress.

校服在某種程度上可以防止學生把注意力從學習轉向時尚。學生將把心思更集中在學習上而不是外表上,講究衣服怎麼穿和穿什麼。

Dressing uniform helps students realize that they really belong to a school and are not just individuals.

穿校服幫助學生意識到他們真正屬於學校而不只是個人。

Wearing school uniforms can encourage pupils to compete among themselves. Pupils who study in good schools can be proud of their uniforms.

穿校服可以鼓勵學生競爭,在好學校學習的學生能因他們的校服而自豪。

Maybe it is true that pupils in school uniforms lose their individual style.

穿校服的學生會失去他們的個人風格,也許確實如此。

However, it is useful to cultivate their abilities of obeying regulations and team spirit which are not possessed by some pupils. School uniforms make pupils understand that they are not alone but belong to a collective, so they need help and cooperate with others.

但是,它在培養學生的遵守紀律的能力和團隊精神方面是有用的,一些學生缺乏這種精神。校服使學生懂得他們不孤獨,他們屬於集體,因此他們需要幫助和與其他人合作。

35. 速 食

Traditional food is more nutritious than fast food.

傳統食物比快餐食品更有營養。

Comparatively speaking, fast food, always contains more meat and butter and much less vegetables. In the long term, always eating fast food will result in some diseases, because of a lack of vitamins and high cholesterol levels, especially for children. A traditional diet provides us more opportunities of cooperation and communication with family and friends. Traditional food is a kind of culture that should be protected and improved. Besides being delicious and nourishing, many kinds of traditional food are made as art. Eating fast food can save time, when you are so busy that you have no time to prepare food, fast food may be a good choice.

相對而言,快餐食品總是包含很多肉和奶油,而缺乏蔬菜。從長遠講,特別是對孩子,總吃快餐食品會導致很多疾病,因為快餐食品缺乏維他命並且含有高膽固醇。傳統飲食為我們提供了很多和家庭與朋友合作和交流的機會。傳統食物是一種必須受到保護和發揚的文化。除了美味和營養,許多傳統食物被做得像藝術品。吃快餐食品可以節省時間,當你很忙時,你沒有時間做飯,快餐食品也許是很好的選擇。

國際IELTS應考叢書

寫 作

CHAPTER III

信

WRITING

❖ 一、總體介紹 ❖

1. 字數和時間要求

G 類同學的 Task 1 是要求寫一封信,150 字左右,建議用 20 分鐘。

2. 寫作格式

與議論文相同,中間部分段落有兩種分段方式:

(1) 傳統式(或稱經典式)

這種格式,每段的第一行向右縮進去一點,與寫中文文章類似。這時,段與段之間可以加空一行,也可以不空行。由於每段的第一行向右縮進去一點,也可以依外觀稱爲縮進式。

(2) 現代式(或稱流行式)

這種格式,每段的第一行不向右縮進,但段與段之間空一行分開。由於每段的第一行不向右縮進,從左邊看是齊頭的,也可以依外觀稱爲齊頭式。

與議論文不同的是,寫信還要有稱呼和落款。稱呼和落款有以下三種形式:

(1) 正式信件,不知道收信人的姓名。

Dear Sir/Madam,

…

Yours sincerely,
Danny

（2）知道收信人的姓名，但並不熟悉此人。

Dear Mr. Wang,

…

Yours sincerely,
Danny

（3）收信人是你的朋友或親戚。

Dear Michael,

…

Best wishes,
Danny

　　另外要注意，稱呼都不向右縮進，都是齊頭的，但如果中間段落採用縮進式，落款應寫在右下角，如果採用齊頭式，則落款也應是齊頭的。例如下面兩種格式都是正確的。

例 1　*Topic：You bought a walkman in a store recently. But a week later, you found that there was something wrong with it. Write to the manager of store. Ask him to replace the walkman or refund your money.*

Dear Sir/Madam,

I'm sorry to trouble you, but I'm afraid that I have to make a serious complaint.

I bought a SONY walkman from your shop a week ago. Your sales assistant told me that I needn't question about it because SONY is an international brand name. Since I was busy then, I took it without testing. After I came back to my dormitory and tried to enjoy my favorite music from the looking-good walkman, I couldn't hear anything from its earphones. I borrowed earphones from my classmate and this time I heard the sound very clearly. So I think there must be something wrong with the earphones. As a foreign student, I must improve my English as quickly as possible. That's the main reason why I bought the walkman. But unable to use it, now I can not study according to the schedule.

Please exchange my earphones for new ones. Otherwise, I would ask you to give me a refund, or I would complain to the Consumers' Association.

Yours sincerely,
Danny

例 2 Topic: *You bought a walkman in a store recently. But a week later, you found that there was something wrong with it. Write to the manager of store. Ask him to replace the walkman or refund your money.*

Dear Sir/Madam,

I'm sorry to trouble you, but I'm afraid that I have to make a serious complaint.

I bought a SONY walkman from your shop a week ago. Your sales assistant told me that I needn't question about it because SONY is an international brand name. Since I was busy then, I took it without testing. After I came back to my dormitory and tried to enjoy my favorite music from the looking-good walkman, I couldn't hear anything from its earphones. I borrowed earphones from my classmate and this time I heard the sound very clearly. So I think there must be something wrong with the earphones. As a foreign student, I must improve my English as quickly as possible. That's the main reason why I bought the walkman. But unable to use it, now I can not study according to the schedule.

Please exchange my earphones for new ones. Otherwise, I would ask you to give me a refund, or I would complain to the Consumers' Association.

Yours sincerely,
Danny

下面的格式是錯誤的:

例 Topic: *You bought a walkman in a store recently. But a week later, you found that there was something wrong with it. Write to the manager of store. Ask him to replace the walkman or refund your money.*

Dear Sir/Madam,

I'm sorry to trouble you, but I'm afraid that I have to make a serious complaint.

I bought a SONY walkman from your shop a week ago. Your sales assistant told me that I needn't question about it because SONY is an international brand name. Since I was busy then, I took it without testing. After I came back to my dormitory and tried to enjoy my favorite music from the looking-good walkman, I couldn't hear anything from its earphones. I borrowed earphones from my classmate and this time I heard the sound very clearly. So I think there must be something wrong with the earphones. As a foreign student, I must improve my English as quickly as possible. That's the main reason why I bought the walkman. But unable to use it, now I can not study according to the schedule.

Please exchange my earphones for new ones. Otherwise, I would ask you to give me a refund, or I would complain to the Consumers' Association.

Yours sincerely,
Danny

由於採用縮進式,落款應在信的右下角。

3. 寫作步驟

(1) 審題
確定信的類型,明瞭寫作要求。一般用時 1~2 分鐘。

(2) 列題綱
確定寫作結構,構思寫作的重點內容。一般用時 1~2 分鐘。

(3) 正式寫作
一般用時 10~15 分鐘。

（4）檢查錯誤

主要檢查文法錯誤，一般用時 1～2 分鐘。

4. 信的類型

從要求上，分爲具體和籠統兩種。

（1）題目中提出的具體的事實、內容和要求，不要漏掉，或多或少都要在信中寫出來，應該有所側重。在題目中的要求都滿足的前提下，可以編造細節。

例 *Topic：Write a letter to a roommate to apologize for not saying good-bye to him/her when you left school the last day of a semester. Explain the reasons why you were not able to say good-bye to him/her and invite him/her to visit you.*

（2）如果題目要求很籠統，則需要自己編造合理的細節，以滿足字數的要求。

例 *Topic：Write a letter to apply for a job in a company.*

從內容上，分爲抱怨信、諮詢信、感謝信、道歉信、說明信和混合信等。

✦❖ **二、各種信的結構** ❖✦

信的正文部分一般分為三段。第一段和第三段比較簡單,主要內容在中間一段。下面我們分別介紹各種信的寫法,每種信給出了一篇範文。更多的範文請參見本章的第五節。

1. 抱 怨 信

抱怨信是考得最多的一種信,大概佔30%左右。

第一段:寫信的目的(purpose)

第二段:

(1) 介紹背景(background)

(2) 出現的問題、抱怨的原因(problem)

(3) 給自己帶來的不便和麻煩(inconvenience or trouble)

第三段:提出公平的解決方案(fair settlement)

Topic:You bought a walkman in a store recently. But a week later, you found that there was something wrong with it. Write to the manager of store. Ask him to replace the walkman or refund your money.

Dear Sir/Madam,

I'm sorry to trouble you, but I'm afraid that I have to make a serious complaint.

I bought a SONY walkman from your shop a week ago. Your sales assistant told me that I needn't question about it because SONY is an international brand name. Since I was busy then, I took it without testing. After I came back to my dormitory and tried to enjoy my favorite music from the looking-good walkman, I couldn't hear anything from its earphones. I borrowed earphones from my classmate and this time I heard the sound very clearly. So I think there must be something wrong with the earphones. As a foreign student, I must improve my English as quickly as possible. That's the main reason why I bought the walkman.

But unable to use it, now I can not study according to the schedule.

Please exchange my earphones for new ones. Otherwise, I would ask you to give me a refund, or I would complain to the Consumers' Association.

Yours sincerely,
Danny

2. 諮詢信

諮詢信是考得最多的另一種信,比例大概也在30%左右。
第一段:寫信的目的(purpose)
第二段:
(1) 介紹背景(background)
(2) 詢問詳情
第三段:表示感謝,期待回信,詢問進一步的訊息。

Topic: Write a letter to apply for a job in a company.

Dear Sir/Madam,

From your advertisement in the New York Times, May 5, I have learned that you need a programmer in your application department. I would be interested in exploring the possibility of obtaining such a position within your firm.

I received Bachelor of Science degree in computer science from Taiwan University in June 1997. Since then I have been working in the Great IT Company as a programmer for 2 years and I have participated in several important projects. I am confident that I am an excellent C/C++ programmer whom you need. And I also have some experience in database administration. Details of my educational background and working experience are contained in the enclosed resume.

May I schedule an appointment for an interview with you to discuss my qualifications in detail?

I'm looking forward to your reply.

Your kind help would be greatly appreciated.

Yours sincerely,
Danny

3. 感 謝 信

第一段：感謝（thanks）
第二段：原因（reasons）
第三段：再次感謝（thanks again）

Topic: *Write a letter to your friends to thank for caring you when you were in hospital after an accident.*

My dear friends,

I'm writing to thank you for your visiting me in the hospital.

I was injured in an accident and was sent to the hospital a month ago. After the treatment, I still had to stay at the hospital for a month. Being alone, I felt so depressed that I even considered committing suicide. It was you, my dear friends who gave me encouragement and consolation. You came to see me the next day of the treatment, bringing me colorful flowers sending out fragrance which put me in a better mood. You also chatted with me about many interesting things which made me feel happy. And you told me not to worry about the work because you would do it for me. Now I have recovered completely. But I believe that without your care, I couldn't have recovered so quickly.

Thank you again, my dear friends. I'll appreciate our friendship forever.

Best wishes,
Danny

4. 道歉信

第一段：道歉（apologize）
第二段：原因（reasons）
第三段：彌補措施

Topic: Write a letter to apologize to your friend for not being able to meet him/her on time as promised.

Dear David,

I'm writing to say sorry that I can't meet you at the airport on time.

I was glad to hear that you would come to see me and I thought I must go to the airport to meet you. But yesterday I was informed that I must attend an important business meeting on the day when you arrive. The meeting, at which I'll give a speech, is on a project of which I am the leader. My manager will also attend the meeting. The meeting is supposed to be over at 11:00 am, which will be an hour later than your arrival time.

Being unfamiliar with the city, please wait for me at the gate of the airport. You can sit in a chair and read newspapers while waiting. I'll go there as quickly as possible after the meeting.

I'm sorry again for the inconvenience.

Best wishes,
Danny

5. 說 明 信

第一段：寫信的目的（purpose）
第二段：說明情況
第三段：其他

Topic：You are studying at a university in England. Your passport was stolen two days ago. Write to your embassy in London, giving details of what happened and asking what you should do next.

Dear Sir/Madam,

I'm writing to report the loss of my passport and to request a new one.

I lost my passport two days ago at about 8:30 in the evening when I bought three dictionaries at MBC bookstore. By accident, I left my passport at the shop. When I realized what I had done, I telephoned the shop, but the shop assistants there could not find it.

I would be grateful if you could tell me what documents I need to send you in order to be issued with a new passport. Do you require any passport photographs, and if so how many? How much will a new passport cost and in which currency would you like me to pay?

I must apologize for any inconvenience caused and look forward to hearing from you. I'm looking forward to your reply.

Yours sincerely,
Danny

6. 混合信

一般題目要求比較多,比較具體。注意不要漏掉任何要求,或多或少都要在信中寫出來,而且應該有所側重。在題目中的要求都滿足的前提下,可以編造細節。

混合信也是考得比較多的一種信,比例大概在25%左右。

Topic : Write a letter to a roommate to apologize for not saying good-bye to him/her when you left school the last day of a semester. Explain the reasons why you were not able to say good-bye to him/her and invite him/her to visit you.

Dear David,

How are you doing? I was very busy on my last day of staying on campus before summer vacation. I am sorry that I didn't have time to say good-bye to you.

That day, I spent the whole morning with my professor in his office. We were discussing a project which we will conduct next semester. I also have to collect some materials for it during the vacation. How poor I am! That afternoon, I went to the library to return some books I had borrowed. Then I went downtown to buy some gifts for my parents and I took the evening train to go home.

What do you want to do during the vacation? How about coming here? I know you haven't visited my hometown before. It is a beautiful city and I'll show you around when you are here.

When you make the decision, let me know and I'll meet you at the train station.

Best wishes,
Yours Danny

三、各種信的常用句式

1. 抱 怨 信

（1）I'm writing to complain that

（2）I must complain about

（3）I am not satisfied with

（4）I feel something should be done about

（5）I'm writing to place a complaint against your service.

（6）I'm writing to place a complaint against sb. about sth.

（7）I'm writing to complain about the poor service at your restaurant.

（8）I'm sorry to trouble you but I'm afraid I have to make a serious complaint against one of your assistant about his bad service.

（9）In the instruction booklet you have not mentioned this defect and neither have you told the user how to solve the problem.

（10）It didn't work properly but I couldn't find the problem.

（11）Please change a new one for me. Otherwise, I would ask you to give my money back, or I would complain to the Consumer's Association.

（12）I wish you would look into the matter for me and talk to the person responsible for this mistake.

（13）I expect to hear from you very soon.

（14）Please give this matter your immediate attention.

2. 諮 詢 信

（1）I'm writing to ask if

（2）Could you please

（3）Could you possibly

（4）Would it be possible to

(5) I would be grateful if you would

(6) Would you mind doing sth.

(7) I wonder if you could

(8) I'm writing to explore the possibility of obtaining the position in your firm.

(9) I'm writing to seek accomodation in your hotel.

(10) I'm writing because I wish to pursue my master's degree in your university.

(11) Please send me all the relevant information concerning the courses you offer.

(12) I would appreciate it very much if you could consider my suggestions.

(13) I should be most obliged to you if you could

(14) I would be most grateful to you if

(15) I wonder if you could

(16) Would you be kind enough to

(17) May I

(18) I'm looking forward to hearing from you.

(19) Your prompt response would be appreciated.

(20) Thank you for your time and attention.

(21) Thank you for your consideration.

(22) Thank you for your attention to this matter.

(23) I look forward to your prompt response.

3. 感 谢 信

(1) Thanks for

(2) It was very nice/kind of you to do sth.

(3) Thank you for

(4) I must thank you for

(5) I am most grateful for

4. 道 歉 信

(1) I'm writing to say sorry for

(2) I'm terribly sorry, but

(3) I must apologize about (not) doing sth.

(4) I am afraid I

(5) Once again, I am sorry for any inconvenience caused.

(6) Please accept my apologies once more.

5. 說 明 信

(1) I'm writing to report

(2) I'm writing to advise you of the loss of my credit card.

6. 邀 請

(1) Why don't you come to

(2) How about coming to

(3) I think it would be a good idea if

(4) I'd really like you to

(5) Is there any chance of your coming?

(6) I wonder if you could come

(7) I'd like to ask you to come

7. 安 排 信

(1) I'm planning

(2) I'm thinking of

(3) I'd like to

(4) I've arranged to do sth.

8. 建 議

（1）I'd like to suggest that

（2）May I suggest that

（3）Perhaps we could

（4）Could you please

❖ 四、寫信的注意事項 ❖

1. 題目中若提出了具體的事實、內容和要求，不要漏掉，或多或少都要在信中寫出來，而且應該有所側重。在題目要求都滿足的前提下，可以編造細節。

2. 如果題目要求很籠統，則需要自己編造合理的細節，以滿足字數的要求。

3. 150 字左右，不能太多，也不能太少。有的同學寫得很多，用了很多時間，結果影響了議論文的寫作。由於與議論文相比，信相對簡單，實際上只要將 150 字寫得比較好就可以了，完全可以得 7 分。

4. 20 分鐘之內一定要完成。筆者建議大家儘可能在 17 分鐘左右完成，為議論文空出更多的時間。

五、範　文

Topic 1：You plan to pursue your master's degree in UK. Write to the university to state your background and ask for necessary information.

Dear Sir/Madam,

I am a graduate from Taiwan University, Taiwan. I am planing to study in your university this summer. So I am writing to ask for some necessary information.

I received a Bachelor of Science degree in computer science from Taiwan University in June 1999. After graduation, I began working in the Bank of Taiwan as a computer engineer. During working, I deeply felt that my computer knowledge was limited and I couldn't solve crucial problems sometimes. So I am thinking of studying in the computer science department in your university to gain a Master degree. Could you please tell me something about your university? For example, how many professors are there in the computer science department? How much should I pay for the tuition fee? Do you provide scholarship to international students? Do you provide dormitory to students?

Would you please send me an application form and other materials necessary for my application so that I can begin the application procedure?

I am looking forward to your reply.

Your kind help would be greatly appreciated.

Yours sincerely,
Danny

Topic 2：Write a letter to your brother in America to introduce the club in which you work. Invite him to visit you and the club.

Dear Bob,

How are you doing recently? I'm glad to hear that you'll come to see me next month. We haven't seen each other for a long time. I miss you very much.

As you know, I am working in the Great Tennis Club, one of the biggest tennis clubs in the city. There are about 100 members in our club. We have close relationships with some professional tennis teams. And we often invite professional players to instruct our members. After a period of time, the members' levels improve significantly and they are very satisfied with our service.

Next month, we'll organize a contest between members and non-members. How lucky you are! I know you are good at playing tennis and have kept up playing for many years. You can participate in the contest. I bet you must be interested in it.

When you decide your arrival time, let me know. I'll meet you at the airport.

Best wishes,
Yours Danny

Topic 3：You live in the dormitory in the university. Some accident happened and it damaged some of your property. Write to the housing office to describe the damage and the reasons for the damage. What do you intend to do?

Dear Sir/Madam,

I'm writing to report an accident which happened in my dorm two days ago.

I am a student in the Computer Science Department and live in Room 340, building No. 14. Two days ago, my roommate Liu Jian smoked in our dorm and it caused a fire which damaged some property of mine. They are a tape recorder, some clothes and one pair of shoes. Among them, the most valuable thing is the tape recorder which was used for English-studying. My total loss amounts to $200.

There is no doubt that Liu Jian should be responsible for the accident. So I think I have the right to ask him to compensate me for my loss. The most important thing is that I must have a new tape recorder as quickly as possible.

Feel free to ask me for the more information about the accident.

Yours sincerely,
Danny

Topic 4: There is a tree near your house. It causes some problems for you. Write to the authority, describe the problem, ask them to look into it, suggest a solution and inquire the related cost.

Dear Sir/Madam,

I'm writing to complain about the problem of a tree near my house.

I live in No. 220 Canel Street. It's clean and quiet. But there is a tree near my house which has caused me a lot of trouble. First, it blocks the sunlight because it is south of my house. I have a 70-year-old mother and a 5-year-old son. Getting sunlight is helpful to their health. Second, there are many birds gathering on the tree, especially in summer time, which is very noisy. My mother and my son both need to take a nap during the daytime, but they can't.

I look forward to your investigation into the facts. I have a suggestion. Could you move the tree to the north of my house? This way, it won't block the sunlight. And the bedrooms of my house are all on the south, so it won't affect our rest either. I would like to pay for the moving. If you want to do that, please let me know the cost.

Yours sincerely,
Danny

Topic 5: Write a letter to ask for some advice on choosing a suitable major: history, in which you are very interested, or computer science, which offers better job prospects.

Dear Sir/Madam,

I am a student from Taichung No. 1 High School. I am planing to study in your university this summer. But which major should I choose, history or computer science? I hope to get some advice from you.

I have shown great interest in history since childhood. When I was a child, I was attracted to heroes of historical novels and dreamed of becoming such of person. When I grew up, I felt deeply that history can make people wise and we can know the future from history. When I encountered a problem in my daily life and studying, I could always find its answer from the history books. But it is said that computer science graduates find jobs easier and are usually wellpaid. Some young computer engineers who own their house and private cars are proof of this.

Do you think it is worthwhile for me to give up my interest to study a discipline which I don't like at all?

I'm looking forward to your reply.

Your kind help would be greatly appreciated.

Yours sincerely,
Danny

Topic 6: Assume that you wish to study in England. Write a letter to the university and ask if there is any sport club.

Dear Sir/Madam,

I'm writing to ask if there is a tennis club in your university.

I'm planning to study in your university for 2 years. I have a special interest in playing tennis. I started training and playing tennis when I was 10 years old. The most rewarding thing that happened as a result of my dedication to the sport is winning the championship in Taiwan University in 1998. When I go to your university, I hope there is a tennis club where I can improve my tennis skills, learn more from coaches, have partners who can play with me and participate in all kinds of related activities. In this way, my college life would be interesting. I was wondering if there is such a tennis club in your university and how I could join it.

I'm looking forward to your reply.

Your kind help would be greatly appreciated.

Yours sincerely,
Danny

Topic 7: You are organizing a group of high school students to visit Cambridge University. Write to the university and ask if you can rent a room in their library.

Dear Sir/Madam,

I'm writing to ask if I could rent a meeting room in the library of your university on June 5th.

Cambridge is one of the most famous universities in Britain, which attracts many high school graduates. Our school is planning to organize some students to visit your university on June 5th so that they can become more familiar with it. In the morning, they will visit your beautiful campus. In the afternoon, I'll invite two professors to introduce the history of your university, teaching methods and teaching facilities to the students. There are about 40 students in total so I hope to rent a room in your library to hold the introduction meeting. I was wondering if I could rent it, how much I should pay for it and how I could rent it.

I'm looking forward to your reply.

Your kind help would be greatly appreciated.

Yours sincerely,
Danny

Topic 8: Complain to the agency, and ask to be transferred to another apartment.

Dear Sir/Madam,

I'm sorry to trouble you but I'm afraid I have to make a serious complaint about the poor quality of my apartment.

I rented the apartment from your agency two months ago. In the beginning, everything was OK. Only after ten days, there seemed to be something wrong with the air conditioner. It was very noisy, especially in the quiet night. I have told the matter to one of your assistants. But he said that there was nothing he could do about it. The noise disturbs my sleep so that I can't concentrate on my work during the work time, and as a result, I have made several mistakes these days. I'm afraid to be dismissed by my boss if the situation is not changed.

Please find another apartment for me. Otherwise, I would change to another apartment agency.

Yours sincerely,
Danny

Topic 9: *There is a mistake in the bill mailed by a bank*, *ask to have the mistake corrected*.

Dear Sir/Madam,

I'm sorry to trouble you but I'm afraid I have to make a serious complaint about a bill mailed to me by your bank.

When I got the bill, I was surprised that it was much higher than usual. Usually, I spent about $500 per month. But the bill showed that I spent $5000 last month. I can promise that I did nothing special last month. How could I spend so much money?

After examining the bill, I realized that there must be something wrong with your billing system. I've never been to France, but a round trip airline ticket to France was charged on my account. I can promise that I've never lent my credit card to anyone.

Please check the bill and refund my money. Otherwise, I would change to another bank.

Yours sincerely,
Danny

Topic 10: *You plan to go sightseeing with your brother but he can't go with you*. *Write to your friend and invite him to go*.

Dear David,

How are you doing recently? I'm writing to invite you to go sightseeing with me this weekend.

My brother planed to go with me but he must attend an important business meeting on Saturday. Would you like to go with me? A bus from the Taipei Main Station will take us to the Ali Mountain on Saturday morning. It's a beautiful mountain and we'll spend the whole day there. At night we'll live in a 4-star hotel. On Sunday we'll go to Sun-moon Lake to enjoy its natural beauty. In the afternoon we'll return. All these plans will be arranged by my company. I really hope you can go with me.

I am wondering if you can let me know before Friday.

I am looking forward to your reply.

Best wishes,
Danny

Topic 11: You have an interview for a course in college next week, but you have an appointment with the hospital. Ask to change the interview time.

Dear Sir,

I'm sorry to inform you that I can't make it next Monday for the English course interview with you.

I had a bad toothache and went to the hospital three days ago. Mr. Lee, the most famous dentist in the hospital gave me a careful examination and told me he would pull out one of my teeth for me next Tuesday. But yesterday one of the hospital's receptionists informed me that my treatment must be changed to Monday because Mr. Lee will go to another city on Tuesday for an emergency. Otherwise my treatment will be postponed for 10 days. Recently my tooth is aching so much that I can't concentrate on anything. So I think I must have my tooth treatment first.

I have been seeking the position of English teacher for some years. And I am confident that with my educational background and work experience, I am competent for the position. Would you mind if I change the appointment time? I am free the entire week next week except Monday. You can arrange it.

I am really sorry for the trouble.

Yours sincerely,

Danny

Topic 12: *You'll attend an international conference. You'll give a speech in the conference. Write to your friend and introduce the title and the contents of your speech.*

Dear David,

How are you doing recently? I miss you very much.

I'll attend an international computer conference in London next week. The conference is on database performance. You know, with the development of computers, more and more data is stored on computers and needs to be processed quickly. But we find that we often can not be satisfied with the processing speed. How do we solve the problem? Our group has been studying this issue for 2 years and has made some progress. As the group leader, I'll give a speech entitled "How to improve the database performance" at the conference. I'll give our advice. They are: How to configure your computer to get the best performance? How can index improve database performance? If you want to get better performance, how can the data be stored in your computer? What else can we do to improve database performance?

I'll come back next Friday. If you want me to bring something for you, please let me know.

Yours sincerely,
Danny

國際IELTS應考叢書
寫 作

CHAPTER IV

圖表作文

WRITING

一、總體介紹

1. 字數和時間要求

　　A 類同學的 Task 1 是要求寫一篇短文,說明一個或幾個圖表中描述的數據。我們稱之爲"圖表作文"。寫 150 字左右,建議用 20 分鐘。

　　雖然比寫議論文要簡單,但與 G 類同學的 Task 1 所要求的寫信相比,圖表作文還是有一定難度的。也有些同學不怕寫議論文,但總覺得圖表作文不好寫。這樣的同學在考試時,圖表作文可以多花些時間,如 20 ~ 25 分鐘,尤其是遇到比較難寫的題目。

2. 寫作格式

　　與議論文相同,不用寫標題,段落間分段有兩種方式:

(1) 傳統式(或稱經典式)

　　這種格式,每段的第一行向右縮進去一點,與寫中文文章類似。這時,段與段之間可以加空一行,也可以不空行。由於每段的第一行向右縮進去一點,也可以依外觀稱爲縮進式。

(2) 現代式(或稱流行式)

　　這種格式,每段的第一行不向右縮進,但段與段之間空一行分開。

3. 題目樣式

Topic: *The table below summaries some data collected by a college bookshop for the month of February 1998.*

Write a report to describe the sales figures based on the information shown in the table.

	Non-Book Club Members			Book Club Members	Total
	College Staff	College Students	Members of Public		
Fiction	44	31		76	151
Non-Fiction	29	194	122	942	1287
Magazines	332	1249	82	33	1696
Total	405	1474	204	1051	3134

圖表作文的題目一般分為三部分:

（1）解　釋

一般為一句話。如上題中的:

The table below summaries some data collected by a college bookshop for the month of February 1998.

這句話扼要介紹了圖表的內容,對理解圖表很有幫助,要仔細看這句話。

（2）寫作要求

即上題中的:

Write a report to describe the sales figures based on the information shown in the table.

一般每個題目都一樣,稍微看一下是否有不同之處就可以了。

（3）圖　表

可能是一個圖表,也可能是多個圖表。

無疑地,這是題目中最重要的部分,你需要描述的就是這個（或這些）圖表,一定要仔細明瞭其含意。

4. 圖表類型

現在的考試一般考以下四種圖表：

（1）line graph（曲線圖）

例 *Topic：The graph shows the demand for energy and the energy available from fossil fuels in Freedonia from 1985 to 2005.*

Write a report to describe the information shown in the graph. You should write a minimum of 150 words.

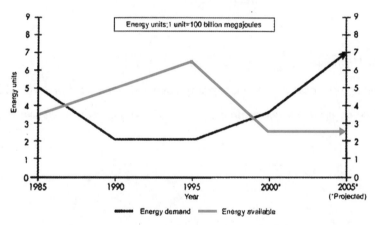

（2）bar chart（柱狀圖）

例 *Topic：The bar chart shows the different modes of transport used to travel to and from work in one city, in 1950, 1970, 1990.*

Write a report to describe the information shown below. You should write a minimum of 150 words.

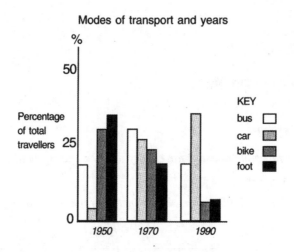

Modes of transport and years

(3) pie chart(餅圖)

例 *Topic：The two pie charts show the types of communication used in 1962 and in 1982. Write a report to describe the information shown in the graph. You should write a minimum of 150 words.*

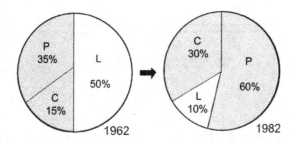

- *P：phone*
- *C：computer*
- *L：letter*

（4）table（表格）

Topic：The table below summaries some data collected by a college bookshop for the month of February 1998.

Write a report to describe the sales figures based on the information shown in the table.

	Non-Book Club Members			Book Club Members	Total
	College Staff	College Students	Members of Public		
Fiction	44	31		76	151
Non-Fiction	29	194	122	942	1287
Magazines	332	1249	82	33	1696
Total	405	1474	204	1051	3134

　　有時，是兩個或多個圖表，這些圖表的種類還可以不同。

例 *Topic：The two pie charts show the types of communication used in 1962 and in 1982.*

Write a report to describe the information shown in the graph. You should write a minimum of 150 words.

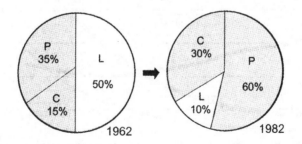

- *P：phone*
- *C：computer*
- *L：letter*

這個題目是兩個餅圖。

Topic：*The chart below shows the amount of money per week spent on fast foods in Britain. The graph shows the trends in consumption of fast foods.*

Write a report for a university lecturer describing the information shown.

Expenditure on fast foods by income groups

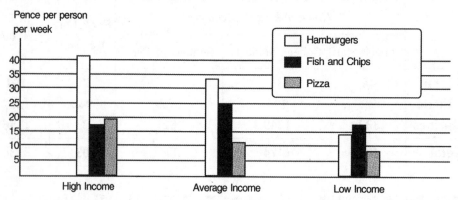

Consumption of fast foods 1970－1990

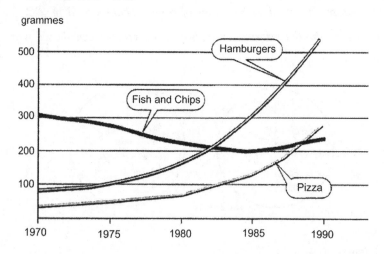

這個題目中有兩個圖表，一個是 bar chat，一個是 line graph。

以前還考過一種描述物體的構造及其工作原理或做一件事情的過程的圖表，有些比較簡單，但大部分比較難。考生普遍寫得不好，得分較低。這種圖表在近一兩年的考試中幾乎沒有出現過，再次出現的可能性也很小，本書中不做介紹。

❖ **二、寫作步驟** ❖

寫圖表作文時,一般採用以下的步驟:

(1) 審題,看懂圖表

一般用時 3 分鐘。尤其是對一些訊息多、與一般的圖表略有不同的圖表,一定要仔細看清楚。

例

Topic:The graph shows the changes in the popularity of cinema and television from 1957 to 1974.

Write a report to describe the information shown in the graph. You should write a minimum of 150 words.

The changes in the popularity of cinema and television 1957 – 1974.

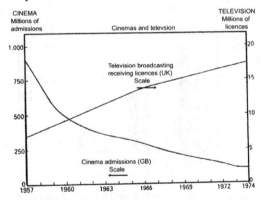

請同學們看完圖表後,回答下面兩個問題:

1957 年電視的許可數(television licence)是多少?

1974 年電視的許可數(television licence)是多少?

答案:1957 年電視的許可數(television licence)大約是 7 million。

1974 年電視的許可數(television licence)超過 17.5 million。

這是考過的最難看懂的一個圖表。本國學生很少使用這樣的有兩個縱座標的曲線圖,但在國外經常使用。

(2) 列題綱,進行材料的組織和取捨

一般用時 2~3 分鐘。這一步也很重要,尤其是對一些訊息多的圖表,先要搞清楚有多少個變量、各變量之間的關係、數值的單位等。然後對材料進行組織和取捨,列出寫作題綱和寫作重點。如何列題綱,請參見本章第三節"結構"。

例 Topic: *The bar chart shows the different modes of transport used to travel to and from work in one city, in 1950, 1970, 1990.*

Write a report to describe the information shown below. You should write a minimum of 150 words.

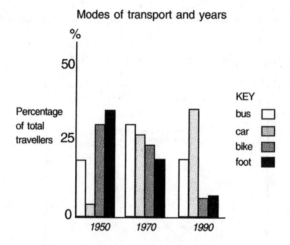

這個題目的訊息屬於一般性。題目包含兩個變量:年分和交通工具類型。年分有三個:1950、1970、1990。交通工具類型有四種:bus、car、bike、foot。數值(縱座標)是百分比。

(3) 開始寫作

一般用時 12~15 分鐘。請參見本章的以下各節。

(4) 檢查

主要檢查文法錯誤,一般用時 1~2 分鐘。

不像議論文要求那麼嚴格,但最少應分爲三段。

第一段:引言(Introduction)

第二段:描述圖表

最後一段:歸納出一個結論

1. 第一段:引言

一般是一句話,簡單而概括地告訴讀者圖表顯示了什麼。這句話的用處是作爲一個介紹(Introduction)。它一般是題目中解釋的改寫,注意不要將題目中的解釋照抄過來。

引言可以有一些常用的句型,大家應該熟記。

(1) The table / chart / diagram / graph shows / describes / illustrates / indicates / outlines / compares / summarizes that _____.

(2) According to / As shown in / As can be seen from the table / chart / diagram / graph, _____.

(3) It can be seen from / We can see from / It is clear from / It is apparent from the table / chart / diagram / graph that _____.

2. 第二段:描述圖表

這無疑應是文章的精髓所在。可以寫成一段,但最好根據不同的對象分爲多段,這樣結構更清晰。但應注意,這部分分段也不宜過多,一般 2 ~ 3 段爲宜,畢竟這只是一篇 150 字左右的短文章。

例1 *Topic*:*The table below summaries some data collected by a college bookshop for the month of February 1998.*

Write a report to describe the sales figures based on the information shown in the table.

	Non-Book Club Members			Book Club Members	Total
	College Staff	College Students	Members of Public		
Fiction	44	31		76	151
Non-Fiction	29	194	122	942	1287
Magazines	332	1249	82	33	1696
Total	405	1474	204	1051	3134

可以根據橫行寫三段(非圖書俱樂部成員、圖書俱樂部成員和總計),也可以根據直行寫四段(小說、非小說、雜誌和總計)。

例2 Topic: *The bar chart shows the different modes of transport used to travel to and from work in one city, in 1950, 1970, 1990.*

Write a report to describe the information shown below. You should write a minimum of 150 words.

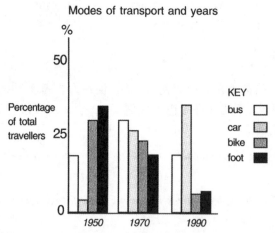

Modes of transport and years

可以按時間寫三段(1950、1970、1990),但一般最好對象分段,而不是按時間分段。對象有四類:bus、car、bike、foot,其中 bike 和 foot 在三年中的變化趨勢相同,可以將它們寫為一段。所以,分為三段比較合適(car、bike and foot、bus)。

一般而言,如果題目中有多個圖表,一個圖表寫一段比較合適。

例 3 *Topic：The chart below shows the amount of money per week spent on fast foods in Britain. The graph shows the trends in consumption of fast foods.*

Write a report for a university lecturer describing the information shown.

Expenditure on fast foods by income groups

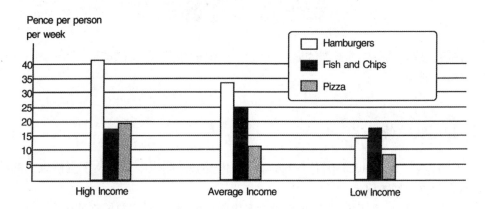

Consumption of fast foods 1970 – 1990

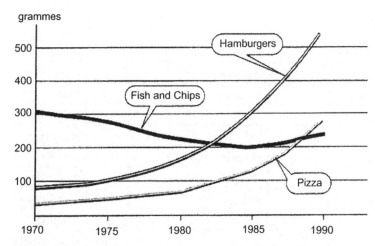

中間部分寫兩段,第一段描述 bar chart,第二段描述 line graph。

描述數據是寫作的重點,字數應在 100 字以上。請詳見本章第四節。

3. 第三段:歸納出一個結論

是全文的最後一段,用一兩句話再次說明從圖表中能看到什麼。應注意:

（1）不要寫得太多,一兩句話就可以了。寫作重點應在第二部分:描述數據。

（2）不要加入主觀想像的東西,如分析原因或展望未來等。

❖ 四、描述數據 ❖

描述數據重要的是描述數據的變化、比較不同的數據、突出特徵數據,千萬不能只是羅列一些具體數據。

1. 描述數據的變化

一般曲線圖(line graph)中肯定有數據的變化,另外,圖表中若涉及了兩個以上的時間,也肯定要寫數據的變化。

數據的變化是最重要的,如果圖表中能看出數據的變化,一定要把它寫出來。

變化的種類一般有:增加、減少、波動、不變四種。通常用動詞和副詞,或者形容詞和名詞來表示。

常用的單字如下:

verbs to show increase	verbs to show decrease	adverbs
increase	decrease	slightly
go up（went up）	go down（went down）	slowly
rise（rose）	decline	gradually
grow（grew）	fall（fell）	steadily
jump（up）	is（was）reduced	rapidly
surge	drop	moderately
shoot up（shot up）	sink（sank）	significantly
	dip	sharply
		dramatically
		drastically

並非所有的副詞皆適合所有的動詞。

adjectives	nouns to show increase	nouns to show decrease
slow	increase	decrease
gradual	rise	decline
steady	growth	fall
rapid	jump	reduction
slight	surge	drop
moderate	fluctuation	
significant		
sharp		
dramatic		
drastic		

並非所有的形容詞皆適合所有的名詞。

其他一些有用的單字：

adjectives	nouns	verbs	adverbs
downward	change	change	downward
upward	fluctuation	fluctuate	upward
	(reach a) peak	peak	
		remain the same	
		reach a plateau	
		stabilize	
		remain stable	
		remain constant	

描述數據變化的句式有三種：

(1) 變化的主體 + 動詞(+ 副詞)

The number of television licences increased significantly from 1957 to 1974.

The number of cinema admission dropped slightly from 1957 to 1974.

The number of television licences remained stable from 1957 to 1974.

The number of television licences fluctuated between 100 and 200 from 1957 to 1974.

(2) There be + 形容詞 + 名詞 + in + 變化的主體

There was a sharp decrease in the number of television licences from 1957 to 1974.

There was a significant increase in the number of television licences from 1957 to 1974.

There was little change in the number of television licences from 1957 to 1974.

There was a fluctuation between 100 and 200 in the number of television licences from 1957 to 1974.

（3）時間＋saw＋形容詞＋名詞＋in ＋變化的主體

The last 17 years saw the sharp decline in cinema admissions.

　　大家對這些句式應熟練運用，並應注意儘量都使用上，而不是只使用一種。

2. 比較不同的數據

　　描述數據的變化是非常重要的，同時也要注意比較圖表中不同的數據，通常用到比較級。常用的句式有：

（1）In managerial positions, there are more males than females.

（2）A greater percentage of men than women are found in managerial positions.

（3）A smaller percentage of women than men are employed in managerial positions.

（4）The percentage of men employed in managerial positions is much larger than that of women in these occupations.

（5）College students bought more fiction books than others.

（6）More urban dwellers have a water supply than rural dwellers.

（7）Fewer rural dwellers have a water supply than urban dwellers.

（8）In 1980, 30% of rural dwellers had drinking water compared with 50% in 1990.

（9）In 1980, 30% of rural dwellers had drinking water, whereas in 1990 50% had it.

（10）The students in class A are three times as many as those in class B.

（11）The profit doubled from May to June.

（12）The profit increased three-fold from May to June.

（13）They made twice the profit in June than in March.

（14）They made three times the profit in June than in March.

　　大家對這些句式應熟練並靈活運用。

3. 抓住特徵數據

常常是指最大值、最小值、最高點、最低點。

常用的句式有：

(1) England had the largest percentage of the students.

(2) Tailand accounted for the smallest number of the students.

(3) In 1998, the number reached its peak/top/highest point.

(4) In 1998, the number increased to its peak/top/highest point.

(5) In 1998, the number reached its bottom/lowest point.

(6) In 1998, the number dropped to / reached its bottom/lowest point.

(7) The profit peaked at 2000.

4. 描述靜態數據

並非從所有圖表中都能看出數據的變化，但是任何圖表中都包含靜態數據。描述靜態數據不是特別重要。尤其當圖表中訊息很多時，只選擇有代表性的靜態數據寫一兩句就可以了。重要的是描述數據的變化和比較不同的數據。如果圖表中數據比較少，可以適當地多描述一些靜態數據，以滿足字數的要求。

常用的句式有：

(1) The number was 2000.

(2) The number reached 2000.

(3) The number increased to 2000.

(4) The number decreased to 2000.

(5) The number increased by 100 from 200 to 300.

(6) Tailand had 15%.

(7) Tailand represented one third.

(8) Tailand accounted for two thirds.

(9) Tailand occupied one quarter.

(10) Tailand made up three quarters.

(11) College students bought 200 fiction books.

圖表中訊息很多時，不要在描述靜態數據上着墨太多，可以在描述數據變化及比較

不同數據時,順便將靜態數據寫出來。如:

(1) In managerial positions, there are more males than females(10% and 5% respective-ly).

(2) College students bought more fiction books(224) than others.

(3) Tailand accounted for the smallest number(234) of the students.

5. 使用的時態

第一段(引言)和最後一段(歸納出結論)一般用簡單現在式(注意第三人稱單數形式)。第二部分描述數據,如果題目中指出了具體的時間,一般用簡單過去式(注意不規則動詞的過去式),否則用簡單現在式。當然,兩種情況都會用到完成式及進行式。如:

(1) 題目中指出了具體的時間,一般用簡單過去式,例如:

① The number of television licences increased significantly from 1957 to 1974.

② The number of cinema admission dropped slightly from 1957 to 1974.

(2) 題目中沒有涉及具體的時間,一般用簡單現在式,例如:

① In managerial positions, there are more males than females.

② A greater percentage of men than women are found in managerial positions.

(3) 兩種情況都會用到完成式及進行式,例如:

① By 1974, the number has reached 2500.

② In 1995, 30% of the people were cycling to work.

6. 涉及的時間

常用的表示時間的片語如下:

(1) in 1997

(2) before 1957

(3) after 1957

(4) since 1997

(5) between 1957 and 1974

(6) from 1957 to 1974

(7) by 1974

(8) until 1974

7. 描述數據不必太精確

除非圖表中很確定,否則描述數據不必太精確,適合使用下列單字。

(1) 大約:approximately、about、almost、nearly

(2) 超過:more than、over

(3) 不到:less than、under

五、多個圖表的寫作

有時題目中有兩個或兩個以上的圖表讓你描述,這實際上比一個圖表更簡單。你有足夠的訊息可以寫,可供選擇的內容更多。

結構上一般維持三個部分不變。

第一段:引言(Introduction)

第二部分:描述圖表

最後一段:歸納出一個結論

其中第二部分:描述圖表,一般按照圖表來分段,一個圖表寫一段。如果兩個圖表之間有關係,應該再寫一段說明它們之間的關係。當然也可以按照對象來分段,大家應該結合具體的題目靈活運用。

例 *Topic*:*The chart below shows the amount of money per week spent on fast foods in Britain. The graph shows the trends in consumption of fast foods.*

Write a report for a university lecturer describing the information shown.

Expenditure on fast foods by income groups

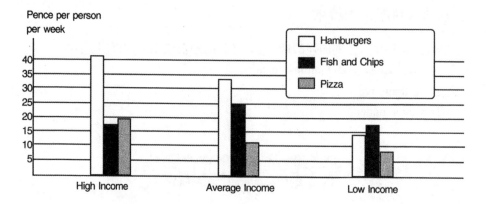

Consumption of fast foods 1970 – 1990

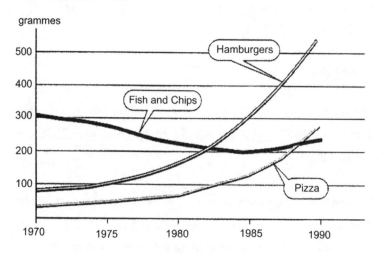

The bar chart and line graph show how popular three types of fast food are in Britain.

Firstly, the bar chart shows the amount of money expended on fast food according to three different income groups. Hamburgers are the most popular fast food in the high and average income groups. Although fish and chips are the most popular food for those with low income who spend almost 20 pence per person per week, they are the least popular with those in the high income.

Secondly, the line graph outlines the general pattern of fast food comsumption between 1970 and 1990. Obviously, there was a greatest increase in the consumption of Hamburgers during this time period. In 1970, people in Britain ate less than 100 grammes per person per week. By 1990, this number increased to over 500 grammes. Pizza also increased but it is not so dramatic. Fish and chips, however, dropped slightly.

To sum up, we can see from the two charts that the more the people eat, the more the fast food they consume and hamburgers are more and more popular among British people.

六、範文

Topic 1: The graph shows the changes in the popularity of cinema and television from 1957 to 1974.

Write a report to describe the information shown in the graph. You should write a minimum of 150 words.

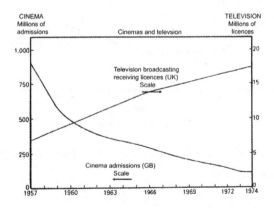

The graph illustrates the dramatic changes in the popularity of cinema and the television from 1957 to 1974.

In 1957, according to the graph, cinema admission was nearly 870 million. But after that the gradual changes happened. The last 17 years saw the sharp decline of cinema admissions. By

1974, the number of cinema admissions has dropped to less than 100 million.

On the other hand, during the same period, the number of television licences increased significantly. In 1957, the number was only about 7 million. But by 1974, this number has jumped to over 17.5 million.

We can see from this that more and more people would like to stay at home watching TV rather than going out to see films.

Topic 2: *The graph shows the demand for energy and the energy available from fossil fuels in Freedonia from 1985 to 2005.*
Write a report to describe the information shown in the graph. You should write a minimum of 150 words.

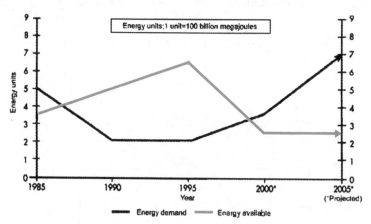

The line graph indicates the changes of demand for energy and the energy available from fossil fuels in Freedonia since 1985.

The amount of energy available from fossil fuels increased significantly from approximately 3.5 units(each unit is quivalent to 100 billion megajoules) in 1985 to 6.5 in 1995, which was its peak. But after that it dropped sharply until 2000 when it begins keeping the same at about 2.5 units.

On the contrary, between 1985 and 1990, the demand for energy decreased gradually from 5 units to nearly 2 units. There was little change in this number from 1990 to 1995. Since 1990, it jumped suddenly. In 2000, this number increased to less than 4 units but after then it will go up more rapidly and is predicted to reach 7 units in 2005.

The graph tells us that along with the time, the energy available can not catch up with the energy demand.

Topic 3: The bar chart shows the different modes of transport used to travel to and from work in one city, in 1950, 1970, 1990.
Write a report to describe the information shown below. You should write a minimum of 150 words.

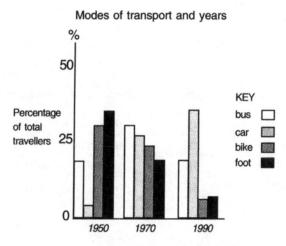

According to the bar chart, there are many dramatic changes in the use of transport from 1950 to 1990.

The use of cars increased significantly from 1950 to 1990. In 1950, only a few people drove to work. But, in 1970, about one quarter of the people owned a car. By 1990, the number of people who went to work by car jumped to over 30%.

During the same period, there were gradual decline in the use of bicycle and on foot. In 1950, more than half of the people were cycling or walking to work. In 1970, the use of bicycle and on foot still occupied over 40%. But in 1990, the number of these people decreased to less than 20%.

The use of bus went up from 1950 to 1970(approximately 20% and 30% respectively) and went down from 1970 to 1990(under 20%).

The bar chart shows that automobiles have become the most popular means of transportation by 1990.

Topic 4: The tables below are the results of research, which examined the average percentage marks scored by boys and girls of different ages in several school subjects.
Write report for a university lecturer describing the information below. You should write a minimum of 150 words.

Boys:

Age \ Subject	Maths	Science	Geography	Languages	Sport
7	63%	70%	63%	62%	71%
10	65%	72%	68%	60%	74%
13	69%	74%	70%	60%	75%
15	67%	73%	64%	58%	78%

Girls:

Age \ Subject	Maths	Science	Geography	Languages	Sport
7	64%	69%	62%	62%	65%
10	65%	73%	64%	67%	64%
13	64%	70%	62%	65%	62%
15	68%	72%	64%	75%	60%

The tables show averaged percentage scores achieved in the school subjects of Maths, Science, Geography, Languages and Sport by children aged 7, 10, 13, and 15 according to sex.

For boys, between the ages of 7 and 15, improvement can be observed in these ranges of scores: Maths (63 – 67%), Science (70 – 73%), Geography (63 – 64%), and Sport (71 – 78%). In general, for boys, children tended to improve as they got older. But they recorded a drop between particular ages. For boys, the ages at which this occurred were 13 to 15, when Maths and Languages both fell by 2%, Science 1% and Geography by 6%. Boys' scores for sport actually increased by 3% during this period.

For girls, it can be observed in these score ranges: Maths (64 – 68%), Science (69 – 72%), Geography (62 – 64%), and Languages (62 – 75%). The increase in scores for girls for this last subject, Languages, was the greatest overall improvement across the different age groups, and its rise from 65% to 75% also constituted the greatest margin between scores for any two particular age groups.

The subjects for which the highest average scores were recorded were Sport, at 78% (boys), and Languages, at 75% (girls). The strongest subject for each sex was revealed to be the weakest for the opposite sex, with these two subjects also comprising the lowest recorded scores, at 60% and 70% respectively. Apart from these two subjects the performance of boys and girls was comparatively similar.

Topic 5: The two pie charts show the types of communication used in 1962 and in 1982. Write a report to describe the information shown in the graph. You should write a minimum of 150 words.

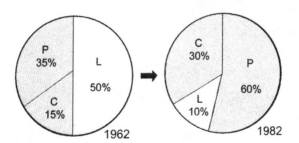

- *P: phone*
- *C: computer*
- *L: letter*

The two pie charts compare different methods of communication used in 1962 and 1982. We can see that for the three mediums surveyed, there are significant changes for each.

In 1962, letter writing was the most popular form of communication, taking up 50% of the total. However, its use decreased dramatically after that. By 1982, this figure dropped to only 10%, the smallest of that year's figures.

On the other hand, during this same period, we can see that the use of the phone and computers both increased significantly. In 1962, the use of telephone just occupied 35% and computer was the least used form of the three methods (15%). In 1982, the telephone, at 60%, has become the most used form of communication. Similarily, the use of computers doubled to 30%.

Overall, we can see some important changes in the forms of communication used during the two decades. More and more people appreciate the convenience brought about by the phone and the computer.

國際IELTS應考叢書
寫 作

CHAPTER V

IELTS 作文
考前培训

WRITING

一、考前兩週

這時,一定要達到時間要求,甚至應該比實際考試更加嚴格。具體而言,寫信應該在 18 分鐘之內完成,圖表作文在 20 分鐘之內,議論文在 38 分鐘之內。在這一階段,應至少做兩次模擬練習,體驗實際考試的感覺,尤其是要測試時間的分配。

二、考前一週

寫作模板一定要準備好,並將它們背熟。同學們應該至少準備五個寫作模板(五段論式三個、對稱式一個、論說式一個),以適應不同類型的題目。寫作模板應該從開始複習時就準備,這一週的工作是將它們最後確定,並將它們背得滾瓜爛熟。

三、考試時携帶的東西

膠擦
鉛筆(自動鉛筆或 B 型鉛筆)
寫作模板(當然是在記憶中)

❖ 四、考試時應注意事項 ❖

1. 合理安排時間，不要前鬆後緊，也不要前緊後鬆。

如果心理不是太脆弱，可以先將兩個題目都看一下。哪一個題目更熟悉、更有準備就先寫哪一個。一般 Task 1 比 Task 2 要簡單，可以考慮先寫 Task 1，再寫 Task 2。

在時間安排上，應該把握一切時間。不要前鬆後緊，以至於寫不完或者後面部分寫得不好。但也不要過於緊張，筆者有個學生，基礎還是不錯的，但在考試時過於圖快，寫完兩篇文章後，還剩下 15 分鐘，這就有些前緊後鬆了。畢竟檢查和修改只能修改些文法錯誤，不可能對文章再做大的改動。

2. 沒有時間打草稿，但應在寫作之前列一個題綱。

絕對沒有時間打草稿，但應在實際寫作之前，想一下用哪種寫法，要寫幾段，每段寫些什麼內容等。

3. 一定要滿足字數的要求。

字數太少肯定會被扣分。不管寫得怎麼樣，先要滿足字數的要求。

在考試中，也沒有必要一個一個地數字數。一般而言，每行大約 10 個字。所以數一下行數，就可以知道大致的字數了。實際上，評卷官也不會一個字一個字地數，只是根據他自己的感覺。

字體不要太大（這樣顯得沒氣質），也不要太小（這樣讓人看不清，而且寫了很多，但看起來字數不多，很吃虧），保持每行大約 10 個字比較合適。

4. 字跡要工整。

不管寫得怎麼樣，首先要讓人看得懂。英文書寫體不僅快，而且能顯示作者良好的文化修養。但很可惜，絕大多數同學都不會，但也沒有必要花時間去學它。在考試時，只要工整地書寫就可以了。一篇潦草不清、整片塗改的文章，即使語言及內容再好，也不可能得高分。很可能評卷官只草草看幾眼，就給一個 5 分而已。

5. 要留出一定時間檢查。

重點檢查：
(1) 結構是否完整,例如有沒有結尾段。
(2) 冠詞、定冠詞
(3) 名詞的單複數
(4) 主謂一致
(5) 時態問題
(6) 第三人稱動詞形式
(7) 標點符號
(8) 單字的拼寫

6. 嚴格遵守考場紀律。

監考老師還未宣佈打開考卷時,不要打開;宣佈停止答題時,一定要停止。否則很可能會被記錄下來,影響成績,甚至被取消考試資格。